Do You Want What I Want?

DENISE DEEGAN

PENGUIN BOOKS

PENGUIN BOOKS

Published by the Penguin Group
Penguin Books Ltd, 80 Strand, London WC2R ORL, England
Penguin Group (USA) Inc., 375 Hudson Street, New York, New York 10014, USA
Penguin Group (Canada), 90 Eglinton Avenue East, Suite 700, Toronto, Ontario, Canada M4P 2Y3
(a division of Pearson Penguin Canada Inc.)
Penguin Ireland, 25 St Stephen's Green, Dublin 2, Ireland (a division of Penguin Books Ltd)
Penguin Group (Australia), 250 Camberwell Road, Camberwell, Victoria 3124, Australia
(a division of Pearson Australia Group Pty Ltd)
Penguin Books India Pvt Ltd, 11 Community Centre, Panchsheel Park, New Delhi – 110 017, India
Penguin Group (NZ), 67 Apollo Drive, Rosedale, North Shore 0632, New Zealand
(a division of Pearson New Zealand Ltd)
Penguin Books (South Africa) (Pty) Ltd, 24 Sturdee Avenue, Rosebank, Johannesburg 2196, South Africa

Penguin Books Ltd, Registered Offices: 80 Strand, London WC2R ORL, England

www.penguin.com

First published by Penguin Ireland 2007
Published in Penguin Books 2008

2

Typeset by Palimpsest Book Production Limited, Grangemouth, Stirlingshire
Printed in England by Clays Ltd, St Ives plc

ISBN: 978-1-844-88171-0

www.greenpenguin.co.uk

Penguin Books is committed to a sustainable future
for our business, our readers and our planet.
The book in your hands is made from paper
certified by the Forest Stewardship Council.

To Joe, at last

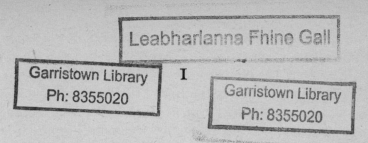
I

Rory skids his Alfa Romeo to a halt outside the church.

'Will you park it, Lou?' he asks his girlfriend. 'It'll have started.'

'Yeah, go,' she says, sliding into the driver seat.

He runs towards the church, coat flapping. He checks his watch again. Twenty minutes late. He could slip in at the back. If he weren't godfather, part of the ceremony, *noticeable*. His sister has surprised him with this responsibility and already he's letting her down. Reaching the door, he tells himself it's Ireland – everything starts late. It'll be fine.

Inside, he realizes it's not.

The congregation has settled and the priest is at the altar. Rory does a quick scan. There seems to be more than one christening. Where is his sister? Where's Siofra? The back of the church is empty. He starts to walk up the aisle, eyes skimming the crowd ahead. At last he sees the back of a familiar head, its white hair thick and wiry, cut short as though to tame it. Rory tenses – as he always does in the presence of his father. He *would* be on time, Rory thinks. Twenty minutes early, probably.

He spots Siofra in the row in front. Beside her is her husband, Tony. Did they *have to* sit right at the top of the church?

Head down, in an effort to make himself less conspicuous (impossible given his height), Rory goes to join them.

Heads turn.

Not soon enough, he gets to the top.

Siofra, visibly relieved to see him, hooches in.

'Sorry,' he whispers. Looking to her right, he raises a hand to greet Tony. His brother-in-law is holding Daisy, the baby. Rory leans in to see her. She may be his godchild but she is a stranger to him. Last time he saw her was three months ago when he'd made the obligatory trip to the hospital after her birth. She's cute – as babies go. Rory smiles at his nephew, Alex, who seems to have grown a lot since he last saw him. He must be what, two, three? Three. Definitely. Blond curls, blue eyes, navy round-necked pullover, white shirt and striped scarf, he is a cross between a Harvard preppie and an angel. Beside him is Rory's sister-in-law, Orla. Given her location in the front row, Rory assumes that she must be godmother. He is surprised. Siofra and Orla have always been close, but won't this be awkward? It certainly is for him. Since Orla and his brother Owen separated, a year and a half ago, Rory has made no effort to keep in touch with her. They used to be close.

Orla looks in his direction, catching him by surprise. His reaction is to raise an apologetic hand. Her smile is warm, as though nothing has changed between them. Guilty, Rory turns to face the altar. The priest is baby-faced with long hair and Jesus sandals. A knitted scarf in Rastafarian colours hangs brightly down on either side of his neck, a refreshing adaptation of priestly attire. Rory knows what his conservative father must think of *that*. And develops an instant fondness for the cleric. His thoughts turn to Louise, who he hopes has found a parking space and by now a seat. He'd like to turn around and check, but is conscious of his father behind him, already fuming, no doubt, about his late arrival – disturbing the congregation, disrespecting God. To look back now would drive him over the edge. To hell with him, Rory decides – at thirty-six, he is too old to care what his father thinks. And yet, he doesn't turn around.

The priest asks parents and godparents to make their way to the back of the church. Rory's 'old man' thinks there are too many gimmicks in modern religious ceremonies, and, for once, Rory finds himself in agreement. Why the need to jump through hoops? Can't they just get on with it? The spotlight has never held any attraction for Rory. At school plays, group photographs, he has always found room at the back. Halfway down the aisle, he spots Louise and brightens. He winks at her. And she returns it. She's looking great. At thirty-eight, she could be twenty-five, in that fitted black shirt he loves, and matching trousers she bought in LA that grip her ass and legs. As for the knee-high boots? Rory has always had a soft spot for them.

In the last pew, he catches sight of his brother, Owen. He is alone. Which is both unusual and a relief. Rory wonders why he came at all. A good excuse would have made it easier for everyone. That's what Rory would have done.

They take their seats again. And the ceremony continues. Rory has to hand it to the priest. His laid-back approach has him listening. When he mentions *The Exorcist* though, Rory thinks he may have gone too far. He imagines his father, apoplectic behind him, and wonders if you can tip men of the cloth.

The ceremony, as far as Rory can tell, goes well. No crying or dropped babies. No catastrophes generally. There is the startling issue of his godfatherly duties as outlined by Father Groovy – to make sure that Daisy is brought up in the Christian faith – but Rory doubts that anyone will hold him to it. Modern Ireland being what it is, godparenting, he gathers, is mostly about presents. Siofra and Tony are great parents. There's no place for Rory to become as involved in Daisy's life as his own godfather was in his. If she'd been a boy, maybe there would have been other ways to play a role – the odd game of rugby, a pint at eighteen – but the fact is Daisy is a girl. And Rory wouldn't know what to do with a girl.

Then the christening is over. Done. Painless enough, after all.

In unfortunate familial co-ordination, Rory and his father, Declan, step out onto the aisle at the same time. Their eyes meet. Rory raises his chin in greeting. Eye contact seems the best Declan can do. Rory stands back to let everyone out ahead of him, creating a welcome distance between himself and his old man. His mother, when she sees him, gives a little wave. She is loving all this, the fuss, the glamour, meeting her family, revelling in the day out. A rare stab of guilt hits Rory. He should put more effort in, go further than just showing up at family celebrations – births, fortieth birthday parties, christenings. But then he looks at the back of his father's head and is reminded of why he doesn't.

Outside the church, he scans the crowd for Louise. And finds her talking to Orla's teenage daughter, Jenna. When the hell did she get so grown up? She looks eighteen. But couldn't be. Last time he saw her, a year and a half ago, she was still a kid. With her is a boy of about eight whom Rory doesn't recognize. He remembers hearing something about Orla taking in a foster kid. Must be him. Lean and wiry, with alert eyes and cropped hair, he is a stark contrast to Rory's dimpled nephew. He looks like he might dart away at a second's notice.

'Hey, Jenna,' Rory says to his niece. 'Who's this?'

'Jason,' she says.

'The foster kid,' the boy says, as though to cut short further discussion on the subject.

4

'Hi,' Rory says to him. And makes a point of adding, 'Nice to meet you.'

The boy just looks at him. Expressionless.

Rory runs a finger inside his shirt collar. 'Have you got the present?' he asks Louise.

'In the car. I thought we'd give it to Siofra at the party.'

He nods. 'Good idea.'

Orla and Siofra join them. Unfortunately for Rory, his parents also seem to be on their way over, not that he has a problem with his mother.

Louise slips an arm around him.

June, his mum, comments on how well-behaved the children were in the church.

'What did you think of the priest?' Orla asks, smiling.

Declan's face is thunderous when he addresses Siofra. 'That wasn't the only bad choice you made.' He turns to Rory. 'Couldn't you have got here on time? Was that too much to expect?'

Louise tightens her arm around Rory in support. But he doesn't feel it. What he feels is sick. He'd been chuffed at this godfather thing. Had wanted to do it right. He'd got up early, been in plenty of time, even checked out where the church was in advance. Had it all sorted. Then he'd received an urgent call from the hospital and had to go in. One of his patients, an elderly man with a condition called Myasthenia Gravis, had gone into crisis. It was a medical emergency. Couldn't be helped. But he's not about to excuse himself to his father. Fuck him.

'I apologized to Siofra. I think you'll find that's the relevant person.' Taking Louise's hand, he turns and walks away from his family, making for the gates of the church. 'Let's get out of here,' he says.

'What about the christening party?'

'What about it?'

'We have to go. For Siofra.' She looks back at his father. 'Ignore him.'

'I spend my life ignoring him.'

'So you've plenty of practice,' she smiles, linking his arm. 'Come on.' She bumps his hip with the side of hers. 'We'll slag his hair – Cauliflower Head.'

'We're not staying long,' he says, still moody.

'We don't have to. Just make an appearance.'

That is something he has perfected.

The Dublin property market is responsible for many things – making multi-millionaires; changing post offices, petrol stations, garden centres into apartment blocks; parents remortgaging their homes so their grown-up children can afford to buy. It is also responsible for more subtle developments, such as the October barbecue. Siofra and Tony's house is too small to entertain everyone indoors, so the reception is outside under two giant heaters. Lanterns and fairy lights decorate an area estate agents would optimistically describe as a 'courtyard'.

Rory goes inside to get drinks. He's at the fridge when Siofra, holding Daisy, comes over to him.

'How're you doing?' she asks.

He closes the door. 'I'm OK.'

'Don't mind him,' she says. 'You'll be a great godfather.'

'Yeah.' It's not that that bothers him as much as the feeling that no matter what he does he will always be a disappointment to his father.

'Would you like to hold her?' Siofra asks.

Rory feels he should – to prove something. But she seems so small. Vulnerable. What if he drops her? He moves closer but instead of taking her, bends over her, bringing his face up to hers and raising his eyebrows, smiling and waving three fingers.

'Hello, Daisy,' he says. 'Hello. This is your uncle Rory.'

'Daisy, meet the man who's going to bring you up in the Christian faith,' Siofra jokes. She looks at her brother. 'Go on, take her.' She holds the baby out to him.

'Eh, maybe later.' As in, five years.

'What are you afraid of?' she asks.

'I'm not *afraid*.'

'You're a doctor.'

'*So?* Why does everyone assume doctors are good with kids? Why do they assume doctors are good, full stop?

She shakes her head as if to say, 'You're hopeless.' He *hates* it when she does that. Wants to tell her that they're not kids any more. They're equal now. The pecking order no longer exists. But to do that would mean confrontation, something Rory has always avoided. So, he quietly fumes. Why did she ask him to be godfather if she thinks he's such a goddamn idiot?

'Louise is waiting on a drink,' he says, to get away. 'Back in a sec.'

'Yeah, right,' she says, smirking.

That she knows him so well annoys him even more.

He heads back out to Louise. Passing his parents, he overhears his father.

'Sit down, June, we're old.'

'Speak for yourself,' she replies. But with a smile.

Rory smiles himself. She always was the one person who could handle him.

He finds Louise where he left her, standing directly under a heater, smoking, and listening to a well-dressed man in his fifties Rory has never met.

'I bought at four hundred thou in '94,' he's saying. 'Worth at least two point five mill now.' Another property market success story Rory does not want to hear. He hands Louise her drink and is about to make a quick exit, when she takes his arm and introduces him. The man is an uncle of Tony's. 'Of course, all the sensible money's going offshore now,' he continues, as though there is no doubt that Rory will be interested in the conversation. 'The bargains you can get in Croatia and Turkey . . .'

This is not the first person Rory has met who thinks he is a financial wizard because he had the good fortune to buy property at the right time.

'Have you bought anything over there yourself?' Louise asks.

'Me? No. I zig when the market's zagging. Berlin's the place to buy.' He taps the side of his nose. 'Market's in the doldrums. As I always say – buy when there's blood on the streets.'

Jesus, Rory thinks.

'You can snap up a block of apartments for a mill. Sure, you wouldn't get a decent three-bed semi in Dalkey for that.'

Rory looks at Louise. She crosses her eyes at him. And he relaxes a little. Property market conversations always stress him out. He looks at Tony's uncle, waiting for The Question.

Inevitably, it comes: 'So, where have you bought your-selves?'

Rory lets Louise handle it.

'We're renting,' she says. 'I've just started a business . . .'

'Oh, really, what?' asks the uncle.

There was a time when Irish people didn't demand the details of your life, Rory thinks.

8

'A florist shop,' Louise says.

'Riiight,' he nods. When he starts to offer his expertise on the subject, Rory excuses himself. It's always the same with these property hotshots. Once they discover that he hasn't bought in, they look at him like he's a loser, too tight or too skint to pony up the exorbitant prices demanded in this town. He wonders how *they* would handle his predicament, how they would approach buying property if they were living with someone they weren't committed to for life? Whichever way you look at it, sharing a mortgage is making a statement, a statement neither he nor Louise wants to make. Yes, he could buy a place independently (somewhere tiny on the outskirts of the city), but that would be making a statement too. He might not want to promise himself to Louise for life, but he can't imagine living without her either. In any case, who'd have guessed prices would have gone this crazy? Buying now would be a risk. What if it all came crashing down? Mind you, he has thought that for years.

He catches sight of the foster kid – Jake? Jason? – pocketing something from the table. Surprised and curious, he goes over, hands in his own pockets. Casual.

'Hi!' he says.

The boy eyes him warily. Says nothing.

'So, Jake, how's it going?'

'Jason.'

'Sorry, of course, Jason. What are you up to?'

'Nothing.'

'Good food, eh?'

Jason shrugs and looks back at the table, as if expecting Rory to go about his business.

'You play soccer?' Rory asks.

The boy seems surprised that he's still there. 'No.'

9

'Rugby?'

He looks Rory up and down. 'Rugby's for ponces.'

Rory tries not to laugh. 'Is that so?'

'Yeah.'

'So what *do* you play?' Rory asks.

'Nothing.'

'Just eat, right?'

'What do you want?'

'To talk to you.'

'Why?' Suspicious.

'Because, for one thing, you're not going to talk about property.'

The boy cocks his head. 'Who says? I know lots about property.'

'Oh?' Rory can't help smiling. 'What?'

'Lots.'

'Give me an example.'

'OK.' He sniffs, puts down the burger he has just picked up. 'If you're selling your house, right, and if you've two double bedrooms . . .'

'Double bedrooms?' Rory wonders where the kid learned that term.

'Yeah, you know, big bedrooms.'

'Oh, right.'

'If you put a double bed in both o' them, it'll make it look like you've more double rooms and you'll get more money.'

'That's pretty impressive. How do you know that?'

He shrugs. 'Just do.'

'You sound better than any estate agent I've ever met.'

Jason becomes more enthusiastic. 'I'm helping Orla sell her house. Giving her tips, like.'

'Orla's selling?'

'Yup,' he answers, his stance reminding Rory of rural boys

– men before their time. 'Owen, you know, Owen, who was her husband, he wants half o' the house. Slimy fecker.'

'Orla told you that?'

'Yeah,' he glances towards the house cautiously, 'but she didn't call him a slimy fecker,' he says, as if realizing that his comment might lead to trouble.

Rory smiles. 'Listen, I'll see you later, right?'

The boy shrugs as if he doesn't care either way. Rory remembers what brought him over in the first place and decides not to tackle him on whatever he has in his pocket. Rory might say something to Orla. Or not. He'll play it by ear.

He finds Orla at the kitchen sink, cleaning beer glasses. Always one to roll up her sleeves, Rory thinks.

'They never told me godparenting duties extended to washing glasses,' he says.

'Well, you're looking at the fairy variety of godparent.' She picks up a dishcloth and hands it to him. 'Here. Wouldn't want to show you up.'

He eyes the slightly damp cloth and can almost hear Jason say, 'Drying is for ponces.' He hands it back. 'I'll wash. You dry.' They swap places. And work in silence for a while. 'Can I ask you a question?'

'Shoot.'

'Are you really selling the house?'

She stops drying, stares out the window. 'Yep.'

'So Owen can get his half?'

She traps her lips between her teeth. Nods.

'But can he do that, force you to sell?'

She puts down the glass she has been drying. In a tight, controlled voice she asks, 'Can we talk about something else?'

He looks at her.

'Owen's your brother, Rory,' she says.

'I haven't taken sides,' he wants to say. But doesn't. Outside, Jason reaches for another burger. 'Some kid, eh?'

She smiles. 'He's a good little fellow.'

'A bit rough around the edges.'

'He's been through a lot.'

Rory looks curious. But she doesn't elaborate. Instead, she apologizes. 'I'm not supposed to talk about his background. It's confidential.'

'Oh, right.' He feels out of his depth, uncomfortable.

They wash and dry in silence until the repetitive action of handing her glasses returns things to normal between them. 'How long will he be with you? Can I ask?'

'Sure. But I don't know the answer. Weeks. Months, maybe. Whenever the health board decides his mother is ready to take him back.'

Rory nods, not understanding why he will be going back, if he had to leave in the first place. 'What if he doesn't want to?'

She looks out at Jason, and speaks with warmth. 'He does. Despite everything, he loves his mum. When he's not watching telly, he's sitting on the stairs, rocking back and forward, humming *Mad World*, her favourite song. When it's cold outside, he worries that she won't have her coat. First time I washed his clothes, he was so upset – I'd taken her smell away. More than anything he wants to go home. Most foster kids do. They want to go home but to a better home, where everything is fixed, perfect.'

Rory doesn't realize he has stopped washing. 'Won't it be hard for you, letting him go?'

Her jaw tightens. 'From day one, you have to remind yourself it's temporary; it's your job to get him ready to go back. And he knows that. You talk to him about going home. You tell him his mum is getting better.'

Rory wonders what's wrong with Jason's mother. He also wonders what Orla gets out of the deal.

'I saw you talking to him,' she says.

He smiles. 'For a kid, he sure knows a lot about property.'

She laughs. 'He loves his property programmes, anything to do with making money, though he'll watch anything, soaps, cookery, fashion. He *loves* Trinny and Susannah. First time he met Jenna, he told her black wasn't her colour.'

Rory laughs.

'In some ways he seems so young. And in others, old beyond his years. And I know it's not just from watching the box.'

'You've taken on a lot.'

'I'm getting a lot.' She puts down the dishcloth. 'After Owen left and Jenna went off to boarding school, the worst thing was the silence. I wasn't aware how much noise one person can generate. Music. The phone – always for her. Even the hairdryer. Then nothing. A neighbour who's a social worker told me about fostering. She knew of so many kids needing homes. I could hear the frustration in her voice. I did it to help out. But the fact is, I'm getting as much as I'm giving. Jason's brought life back into the house. The fridge is full. I've someone to cook for. Someone to collect from school.' She stops, laughs. 'Sound desperate, don't I?'

'No.'

They're quiet.

'You know, Orla, if you ever want anything . . .'

Rory tracks Siofra down in the children's bedroom, changing the baby.

'What is Owen up to?' he asks.

She looks up. 'What?'

'He's kicking Orla out on the street.'

She puts a used babywipe in an orange plastic bag.

'Can he do it?' he asks. 'Demand half?'

'Apparently so.'

'But I thought the law protected mothers. It's still the family home.'

'By law, he's entitled to half.'

'Isn't there any other option? Can't she buy him out or something?'

'Where's she going to come up with half a mill? She's an agony aunt, not an investment banker.' Siofra tapes the fresh nappy down, makes a face at Daisy, and starts popping fasteners on the white towelling babygro.

'Where'll she go?'

'She's looking for an apartment.'

'What about the dog?'

'She'll have to find a home for Lieutenant Dan.'

'For fuck's sake.'

'That about sums it up.'

'You know, I looked up to him. All my life.'

'I know. It was pathetic.' She rolls her eyes.

There was a time Rory would have defended Owen – as he often had to with Siofra. Growing up, his older brother by five years was his hero, the only one of them who didn't care what their father thought of him, the only one who stood up to him. Siofra was the dutiful one, always helping, always good. To her, Owen was a troublemaker, disturbing the status quo she so carefully tried to maintain. Rory tried to act as peacemaker between his siblings, but secretly longed to be like Owen. Sharing a room with him meant witnessing close up his efforts to break away – summer jobs from the age of fifteen meant money, good clothes, girls and music. Rory's abiding memory of Owen is combing his hair in front of the mirror to the sound of *Freebird* as he got ready to go out. Rory always felt left behind, though never as much as when Owen moved out of the house as soon as he'd done his Leaving Cert. No college for him. No more depending on his parents. A job in the bank meant money, freedom.

'Where is he now?' Rory asks.

'Gone. Didn't come back here at all after the church.'

2

Rory is coming back downstairs, in search of Louise, when his mobile rings. He breaks into a smile at the sound of his friend Barry's voice.

'Barry, what's up?'

'I'm supposed to be doing Doctor on Call tonight . . .'

Rory doesn't like the sound of 'supposed to be'.

'Dee's gone into labour. She's dilating at a rate of knots.'

Too much information, Rory manages not to say.

'I'm bringing her in. You couldn't bail me out, could you? Sorry to ask, but you're on their books from way back. All they'd need is your medical indemnity insurance and up-to-date registration. That's if you're free. If you can do it.' All this has been said in one breath.

Rory takes pity on the man at whose wedding he was Best Man. 'Sure,' he says, sounding more willing than he feels. The thought of a night of non-stop house calls followed by a Monday morning on the wards makes him want to lie down.

'Oh God, thanks.' Barry's relief is audible. 'I owe you one. I was due on at eight. I'll drop my bag off on my way past,' he says, knowing that as a hospital doctor Rory won't have one.

'I'm not home. I'll collect it from you.'

'We're leaving now.'

They arrange for Rory to pick it up from a neighbour.

Rory and Louise do a quick round of goodbyes.

In the car, she jokes, 'I know you wanted to leave, but isn't this a bit extreme?'

He smiles. 'What are you going to do for the rest of the evening?'

'Don't know. Work on my website, maybe.'

He was afraid she might say that. The christening was supposed to be an opportunity for Louise to take a break. She's been flat out since setting up the business.

'Will you be OK, working all night and tomorrow?' she asks.

'Won't be the first time.' However he managed as a junior hospital doctor he will never know. He pities Barry still having to do doctor on call at this stage of his career. 'Remind me never to have kids.'

'Never have kids.' She smiles.

'I mean, look what they've done to Barry. There he and Dee are, out in Vancouver, *Vancouver*, having the time of their lives and they have to go and start a family. Suddenly they're coming home, and he's starting over, setting up in practice from scratch. It's madness. His GMS list is *tiny*.'

'What?'

'He's hardly any public patients, any income. So, by night, he has to do Doctor on Duty; by day, try to stay awake in case the few private patients he has happen to become ill. And now they're having a second. Why do people put themselves through that?'

'Beats me,' Louise says, taking out the Blackberry Rory bought her so she could pick up emails on the move. A mistake, he now sees, as it only means she brings the business everywhere with her. Still, it could be worse. She might have wanted to start a family. The thought of all that responsibility, that pressure. It's enough to have a man consider vasectomy. Almost.

Rory eyes the logo on the side of the silver Seat Ibiza owned by the Doctor on Duty operation – a stethoscope and doctor's bag – and frowns. Talk about drawing attention to yourself. He ducks his head, climbing into the front passenger seat and is joined by his driver – a heavyset man, fortyish and Slavic.

Rory introduces himself, extending a hand.

'Renatis' shakes it.

'Many calls?' Rory asks.

'Three. We go first to Blackrock.'

They set off. Renatis seems to be the shy silent type.

'So, where're you from?' Rory asks eventually.

'Lithuania.'

Rory nods. He knows nothing about Lithuania. And doesn't want a geography lesson. On the dashboard, a Blackberry vibrates, its red light flashing. Rory watches Renatis check it when they next stop at lights.

'OK. So,' he says. 'A fever in Rathmines.'

'Are they *emailing* the calls from the office now?'

Renatis nods.

'The amazing world of technology.'

'Costs less,' Renatis says.

By the time they get to Blackrock, Rory has learned that Renatis is also a doctor, working as a driver while waiting for the Medical Council to recognize his qualification. While Rory will be in making his calls, Renatis will be reading the map, working out his route to the next call. Then he will listen to English language tapes.

'OK. So, is a good job. I learn English and the city also.'

'Your English is already good.'

'I learn too from my son. He is fast learner. At school. You know?'

Rory nods, hoping that's the end of the child talk. They've a long night ahead.

The Blackrock call and those that follow prove to be straightforward enough – anxious parents overly concerned. As the night wears on, Rory becomes aware that Renatis is repeating back to him a lot of his own expressions. Rory wasn't aware he said things like, 'Fair dues, man', 'Get off the stage' or 'Deadly'. And he'd prefer not to know. Their sixth call, heading for midnight, is at a block of flats not far from Dun Laoghaire.

'This is not so good area,' says Renatis, eyeing the poorly lit building.

Rory makes a face. 'Ah, it's not so bad. It's the inner city you'd be worried about.'

Renatis doesn't look convinced.

Rory, reaching for the door, reassures him. 'Don't worry, you'll soon get used to the city.'

Renatis nods as if he's taking that on board, but locks the doors anyway. Rory strides towards the flats, his footfall loud, confident. Catching sight of his shadow against the streetlights, he jokes to himself. Caped hero enters enemy territory. He reaches the stairs that go up into the flats. Passing a hooded youngster, he says a quick, 'How's it going?' and takes the steps two at a time.

On the first floor, he finds the flat he's after. A middle-aged man looks relieved to see him. Rory apologizes for the delay, as he does at every call. The average wait is two hours. He is ushered into a bedroom where the man's wife is lying curled up on her side, her face contorted by pain. Rory takes a history, gently palpating her abdomen. When he qualified,

Rory trained as a GP before returning to the world of hospital medicine and specialization. Had he not, he would not be qualified to do Doctor on Call. It's been a while, and though he's a little rusty on general medicine, it doesn't take a genius to work out that this patient needs to be admitted for urgent investigation, possibly surgery. He gives her a shot of pethidine to ease the pain and calls an ambulance. Ideally, Rory would like to stay with her until the paramedics arrive, but there's that long list of calls waiting. He offers reassurance that the ambulance will be along shortly.

Heading out of the flats and hurrying down the stairs, Rory is still debating whether or not he should have stayed, when out of the shadows steps the hooded figure from earlier, blocking his path. Rory stops. When he sees the syringe, he takes a hesitant step back. The guy moves forward into the weak light thrown from the window of a nearby flat. His face, still half-shaded by the hood, is long and thin, ghostly pale. He glances around quickly.

He says two words. 'The bag.'

Rory raises a palm. 'Look, it's not mine. There isn't much . . . Just penicillin . . .'

'Gimme the *fucking* bag, you *fucking asshole*.'

Rory's knees buckle. 'OK, here,' he says, trying to keep his voice steady. 'Take it.' He holds it out. But instead of snatching it from him, Rory's attacker grabs his arm and yanks him forward in a sudden violent movement so that they are face to face. A pair of constricted pupils. A reek of cigarette smoke. Rory lets go of the bag, about to back away when it happens, a sudden movement, a sharp downward jab into his right cheek.

'Next time, speed the fuck up.'

He is shoved backwards. He stumbles trying to regain his balance, watching wide-eyed as his attacker disappears around a corner, quickly and quietly into a night he seems to belong to, leaving Rory holding his bloodied cheek in total and absolute silence.

His survival instinct kicks in. He has to wash the cut out. And fast. He turns back towards the stairs, taking the steps two, three at a time, up, back to the flat he has just come from.

Covering his cheek with a hand, he tells the man he needs to use the bathroom.

In the mirror of a plastic bathroom cabinet, his black hair contrasts with the pallor of his face, making him even more ghostly. His eyes look haunted, darker than usual. Black almost. He feels for the tap, while examining the cut. He's seen worse. But it's not what it looks like that matters. It's what might be in there. HIV? Hepatitis B? C? Rates among Dublin's heroin addicts are high, very high. His attacker didn't look like the type to get involved in needle exchange programmes. When did he last use that needle? And why didn't Rory just throw the goddamn bag at him and run? He scrubs at the cut with soapy water, trying to make it bleed. He hears the paramedics arrive outside, and checks the cabinet for an antiseptic. Brylcream, toothpaste, shampoo, conditioner, razors and deodorant. He lifts the can of Sure Activresponse and directs it at his face.

Back out in the hall, he briefs the paramedics on the woman's condition, covering the cut with his hand. He stands aside as they help her onto a stretcher, then accompanies them down to the waiting ambulance, blue light flashing quietly in the night. If only he had waited with her in the first place. This would never have happened.

Renatis does not hesitate. He starts the engine and chases after the ambulance. Their destination is the same now. The remaining calls will have to be passed to another doctor. Outside the car, life goes on. Light traffic of mainly taxis in no hurry. On the pavements, people wander home after nights out. At empty intersections, traffic lights go through their usual routine. Rory sees none of this. Inside his head, there is a debate raging. If he does what Renatis insists he should, and what he himself would advise anyone else to do (go straight to casualty to get tested and vaccinated), he is putting his career on the line – if he tests positive for AIDS or hepatitis B or C, he becomes an infection risk; his career is over. But if he does nothing, ignores it, hopes for the best, he is gambling with his life.

Next time a Lithuanian tells him about his city, he'll bloody well listen.

3

Rory is waiting in a narrow corridor outside the casualty treatment area with an ever-growing line of Dublin's ill and wounded, some like him, well enough to sit, others lying on back-to-back trolleys. It is the standard A&E experience in one of the world's most successful economies. Rory's friend, Sinead, the casualty registrar, has knocked hours off his wait by having him bypass the actual waiting room. The people who are with him now have already spent hours there. And while part of him feels guilty about that, another part wishes he could have gone straight through with no wait at all. Infected blood is coursing through his veins. Time is everything. He'd do the tests, vaccines himself, if they'd let him and if he knew the protocol. But he is not a casualty doctor. And this doesn't happen too often.

So while Sinead and most of the casualty staff are busy with a man who has had a cardiac arrest, Rory sits, staring at his hands, rather than at the teenager in his direct line of vision with the blood-soaked bandage around his head. Or the grey-haired man behind him who has removed his shirt and is having electrodes applied to his chest by a nurse. Or the elderly woman whose daughter is trying to explain to her that they will be home soon and she can have her regular medication then. They have been in casualty eight hours and have yet to see a doctor. She has already missed a dose.

Two pairs of clean black shoes appear at Rory's feet. He looks up to see a duo of policemen. (When the Lithuanian told him to call 999, he had listened.) He wonders if they are going to question him right here in front of everyone, then reminds himself that privacy is something everyone else has sacrificed. One of the guards suggests going somewhere quiet. Rory opts to stay put. Better to sacrifice his privacy than his place in line.

He goes through everything, thinks he's doing a good enough job of remembering, until they ask for details: brand names on any of the clothes or runners, flashes of colour on the hoodie, any distinguishing features. They are patient. They tell him not to worry. He is probably in shock. He'll remember more tomorrow. Shock or no shock, Rory knows he won't. He doesn't have the level of detail they need. The 'youth' he has just described could be one of a thousand skinny, run-down, drug addicts. One of the guards, the older of the two, pulls out a business card and writes on it, telling him that he will be the investigating officer. However, as it's Sunday night, he will be going off duty at six and won't be back until Wednesday afternoon. Rory should call to the station in the morning to make a full statement. Rory, more concerned with his medical treatment, thanks the guard, takes the card and pockets it. He needs those vaccines.

At last, he is called to the treatment area. He squints in the glare of the light, notes how serious everyone looks, how fast the pace is, things that have never occurred to him before. How different it is when you're on the other side, how out-of-control you feel as a patient, powerless, afraid. He sits on the side of a trolley in a cubicle and waits. Again.

Sinead comes to him. Apologizes for the delay. Gets ready to take blood.

Looking down at his bare, pale, extended arm to which a tourniquet has been applied, Rory watches the needle go in and dark blood ooze into a rubber-topped tube. He has never found that sickening to look at – until now. He watches Sinead work with silent, calm efficiency. She is a good doctor, he decides, then realizes he has never once stopped to consider what that might be, or whether he himself qualifies.

He trusts Sinead. She is taking this seriously. Thanks be to Christ.

Having filled a variety of tubes, she slips the needle out, covers the injection site with cotton wool and releases the tourniquet. Rory holds the padding and bends his arm while Sinead collects the tubes and starts filling forms. That's when he notices that she is wearing gloves. He tries to shake off the hurt he feels, telling himself it doesn't matter – she has to protect herself, he'd do the same.

'Hep B and C and HIV, right?' he asks.

'Yeah. Listen, Rory . . .' She puts the bloods down on the bench, folds her arms. 'I was on to the Viral Reference Lab . . .' She pauses. 'It's not great. We can vaccinate you against Hep B. It'll provide good, but not full, protection and we can start anti-retrovirals to help prevent HIV, but there's nothing we can do to stop Hepatitis C if you've been infected.'

Of the three diseases, it is by far the most prevalent among the city's heroin addicts, as high as sixty per cent. Rory had seen a headline in the *Irish Medical Times* a week earlier. He'd have read the article if he'd thought it would be relevant. Already, he feels ill.

'How soon will you know if I've been infected?' he asks, trying to keep his voice calm.

'If you had the needle and syringe, we could test them and have results quickly. But without them . . .'

He curses himself for not thinking to collect the syringe, but then doubts that it was dropped. After all, it's a useful tool – weapon and instrument.

'We'll get an early result on Hep B from the bloods we've taken. Hep C and HIV will take longer. In six weeks, we can send bloods to UCD for molecular testing. They'll give us results of ninety per cent certainty within forty-eight hours.'

'Only ninety per cent?'

'It will take four to six months to get results that are one hundred per cent certain. I'm sorry, Rory.'

He closes his eyes and lets his head fall back. If someone were to select a torture for him, this would be as good as any.

All Rory wants is to get home to Louise, to hold her, say nothing, just hold her. He takes a taxi to collect his car from the Doctor on Duty office. By the time he gets home, it's four am. She is asleep. Of course she is. What did he expect? Still, he's disappointed. He'd put her down as his next of kin when asked at the hospital, but had declined the offer to call her. He didn't want to wake her, worry her, especially as she'd been working so hard. But now he wants her to be awake, though he knows it's unfair. He sits on the edge of the bed, gently smoothing back hair that has fallen across her face in waves. He loves its thickness, its colour, a rich red that she calls auburn, a colour he has always associated with sassy women. Louise is sassy, but also vulnerable, a combination that has him hooked. She is wearing his navy pullover, the tips of her fingers peeping out from sleeves that are too long for her. He smiles, imagining the spongy sports socks she will be wearing under the duvet. How is she always so cold? And how has he allowed himself to get to know her so intimately and feel so strongly? It wasn't the plan. But here they are, after four years, still together. Weird, considering how commitment-phobic they both are. But

26

maybe that's the explanation – neither puts pressure on the other with talk of marriage, kids. No. It's more than that. He loves her. Her funny laugh. Her ability to make him laugh. Her gutsiness in setting up the business despite inner self-doubt. Her determination to make her life her own. Hell, the way she brushes her hair. He stops himself. Suddenly, he is tired. All he wants to do is get in beside her, snuggle up to her. Maybe then he'll feel safe.

He undresses, dropping his clothes in a weary heap on the floor. He slips in beside her, relieved to be home, away from all that's happened. He inches closer, careful not to wake her, closes his eyes, listens to her breathing and begins for the first time to relax. He's done what he can. All that remains is to take precautions with other people. Louise, especially. If he has caught something, he'll sure as hell keep it to himself. He'll take his medication, forget what happened, get on with his life. He feels himself slipping into sleep. And welcomes the oblivion it will bring.

Then it is happening again. He is back. At the flats. Confronted by that face, those eyes. The syringe. Oh God. He wakes, sitting up, breath irregular, heart pounding. It's OK, he tells himself. It was a dream. A very real dream. But a dream. It's over. He's home. He lies back down. Half an hour later, he is still awake, afraid to close his eyes.

He gets up. In the kitchen, he roots out Paracetamol for the headache that is gripping his head like a vice. He zaps a glass of milk in the microwave. Throwing on a coat, he wanders out onto the balcony and looks down onto Dun Laoghaire's deserted and poorly lit west pier. Bizarrely, he thinks about Orla having to give her dog away. It is cold and he goes back inside. He burns his tongue on the milk and curses. Checks his watch. Almost five. He has to sleep.

Back in bed, he tries not to worry, but knows too much. Will his future include long-term liver disease, cancer, cirrhosis, liver transplantation? AIDS?

Louise turns in the bed. 'What time is it?' she asks, groggily.

'About five,' he whispers, expecting her to turn over and go back to sleep.

She does turn over, but then turns back again. 'What are you doing back so early?'

'Finished early. Go back to sleep.'

There is something in his voice. She reaches for the bedside lamp. 'Jesus, Rory. What happened to your face?'

His hand goes automatically to the cut. 'Nothing.'

'Rory. *That* is not nothing.' She is sitting up now.

'Some kid. Wanted the bag.'

'The *doctor's* bag?' Her eyes widen. 'Drugs? You were attacked for drugs? You were attacked by a junkie?'

Rory sits up beside her. 'He was a kid.'

But she's not listening. 'AIDS.'

'Louise, stop panicking. I've been to the hospital. I've had blood tests. I've been vaccinated . . .' But he is glad of her reaction, glad of her concern.

'Why didn't you call me?'

'I just wanted to get it done, get home.'

They're silent for a moment.

'Hang on,' she says. 'You can't get a vaccine against AIDS. If you could, everyone'd be getting it, wouldn't they? And there wouldn't be the problem there is. What are you talking about, a vaccine?'

'Sorry. Against hepatitis.' Rory was hoping he wouldn't have to bring that up.

'But what about AIDS?'

'I'm going to take medication, just in case.'

'And that'll protect you? Fully?'

'Yes.'

'Definitely?'

'Definitely.' He wishes he'd been given that assurance. Still, he is glad that Louise has skimmed over hepatitis, the real problem. Why worry her? Why have her inhabit the same limbo he will be in for the next four to six months?

4

Rory calls the ward to say he'll be late. He doesn't say why, just that Rounds will be delayed by an hour. For five months, he has been acting consultant, ever since the neurologist he worked under suffered a massive stroke, a condition he had been treating all his life. Professor Henry will not be returning. Applications have been sought for his post and though Rory has submitted his, he felt guilty doing so. Disloyal. Especially as he would like the job so much. Becoming consultant and staying on the ward he has become attached to would be the realization of a dream.

Dreams are far from his mind now, though. Arriving on the AIDS unit, he has never been more awake. The consultant examines him, takes a full medical history and prescribes a course of medication. He knows the drill. Then she offers him an appointment with a counsellor. He'll think about it, he says, planning to do the opposite. He'll take his medication, and get on with life.

At work at last, he strides into the nurses' station, anxious to get things going. News of his arrival spreads and members of the neurology team, at various locations around the ward, gather. As do three medical students who have been hanging around, going through patient charts, waiting as though for a performance to start. Together with a staff nurse, the group of white coats converge on the bed of the first patient.

The first few examinations run smoothly. Then they come to a man admitted three days previously with a cerebrovascular accident—in layman's terms, a stroke. He is unconscious, lying on his side, his pale face gaunt. Two women sit with him, one holding his hand, the other close to sleep. Rory knows them as his daughters. They have been here all night. When they see the team, they perk up, as though the presence of the doctors will improve their father's condition. Sadly, that is not the case. Rory listens to their questions (one of them has made a list). He patiently takes them through the answers, few of them positive. Finally, he asks if they would mind allowing the team to examine their father. He suggests they go for coffee. They want to wait in the corridor.

Team members take their place around the bed. Someone pulls the curtains for privacy. Rory commences the examination, explaining to the med students what he is doing at each stage, sometimes asking them questions so they feel included. At one point, he removes his pencil torch from his top pocket and explains that he is about to check the patient's pupils to see if they are equal and reacting to light. Gently, he lifts an eyelid and flashes the torch across one eye. The pupil constricts to a point. Rory freezes. He is looking into the eyes of his attacker, seeing his face, smelling the bitter reek of cigarette smoke.

He tries to shut down his senses and carry on. He tells himself it's mind over matter and proceeds to check the other eye. It too reacts. As does Rory's body, heart thumping, sweat breaking out on his forehead. He can't seem to get enough air. Needs to get out from behind the curtain. Everything is closing in on him. Palms wet, he hands the torch to the nearest med student.

'Patrick, isn't it?' He is breathless.

'Yes.'

'Why don't you get in a little practice?' His voice is choking.

Bemused, Patrick takes the torch.

And Rory is gone.

Over at the open window, he holds on to the sill with both hands, leaning forward, trying to control his breathing – slower, deeper. He tells himself to 'cop on', 'get a life'. He's at work. In charge. He has to be professional. He can't let this get to him. After a few minutes, still shaken, he rejoins the team.

He manages to get through Rounds without further incident, but as the day progresses, every so often, he is ambushed. Something triggers a flashback. A needle and syringe lying on a tray in the nurses' station. Laboratory forms. Tourniquets. The AIDS medication he has to take. He washes his hands more than he needs to. Avoids physical contact with patients. Finds more and more reasons to delegate. When he meets the eyes of other medical staff, he thinks *they know*, which they probably do – in hospitals, news spreads faster than a virus.

Sergeant O'Neill is a bear of a man with steady, unwavering eyes, the kind of man who when confronted by a junkie wouldn't stand rooted like a fool. They sit across a Formica table in a small, sparse 'interview room' at Dun Laoghaire Garda station. Rory has given his statement, gone over everything again. He wants them to get the bastard, make him pay, but given his inability to identify anything that would single him out, he is not optimistic.

O'Neill opens a file. 'From the description you gave last night, we have some photos for you to look at. A certain number of these youths would be known to us, others the computer selected, matching your description.' He pushes a small pile of ordinary colour photos across the table to Rory.

Rory is suddenly hopeful — maybe they already have a suspect. He pulls his chair forward, or tries to. It is nailed to the ground.

He goes through shot after shot. With each one, his enthusiasm fades. He turns over the last, more despondent than if there had been no photos in the first place. He shakes his head at the guard.

'Take your time,' O'Neill says. 'We're in no rush.'

Rory goes through them again, more slowly this time. He hopes he missed one, knows he didn't. He pushes them back across the table with a 'No.'

O'Neill starts to clear things away, giving the impression that the interview is over.

Rory's not ready to stop. If they talk some more, maybe they'll stumble on something. 'What happens next?' he asks, stalling.

'Well, as there are no CCTV cameras at the flats, we'll check cameras in Dun Laoghaire for anyone matching your description. We'll talk to intelligence sources in the community, check for eyewitnesses. If there are any developments, we'll keep you abreast.'

Rory can't let it go. 'What would the charge be, if you caught him?'

'Possession of a syringe, assault, theft. If we make someone amenable for the crime —'

'Sorry?'

'If we arrest someone, it will be Under Section Six of the Non Fatal Offences Against The Person's Act. He could get five years in prison.'

Non fatal? For all Rory knows, it *will* be fatal. Just might take a while. 'What about attempted murder?' he asks. 'He jabbed me deliberately with an infected syringe.'

O'Neill eyeballs Rory for an uncomfortably long moment,

until he begins to regret opening his mouth. Over the guard's head is a camera, pointing directly at Rory. He presumes it's not on. For the first time, he is relieved to be the injured party, not the accused under scrutiny.

'We don't know that the needle was infected,' O'Neill points out. 'Sometimes they use ketchup.'

'His pupils were constricted. He was high.'

'Even if it was his blood, we don't know that it was infected.'

Rory thinks about that. 'If you caught him, could you access his medical records?'

The guard is pumping the top of his pen with his thumb. 'No. Legally, no.'

'Could you have him tested for AIDS or hepatitis?'

'No. But we're getting ahead of ourselves, here. We have to apprehend him before we can charge him.' O'Neill is standing, replacing his pen in his pocket. 'If there are any developments, we'll be in touch. In the meantime, if you remember anything, please call me.' He hands Rory his card.

Rory follows him from the room. At the door to the waiting area, they shake hands. Rory doesn't want to go. If he could, he'd supervise the entire operation personally.

Outside, it is dark. He's nervous. Walks quickly to the car, and locks it as soon as he's inside. He sits for a moment, going over their conversation. How different it would be if the weapon had been a knife and he had died on the spot. Murder, it would be then, requiring a full-blown murder hunt, house-to-house enquiries, extra police drafted in, maybe. Rory grips the wheel, his jaw tight. The flats are only ten minutes away. He could go there, find him, beat him to a pulp, syringe or no syringe. What could he contract now that he hasn't already? But the thought of the flats, cloaked in darkness, the sound of his echoing footsteps, the syringe coming down on him, makes him feel like vomiting. Disgusted with himself, he turns the engine and pulls out, forgetting to signal, forgetting to check his rear-view mirror. He drives through the streets of Dun Laoghaire oblivious to the fact that the news on the car radio is in Irish, a language he no longer understands. This time yesterday, he'd have switched channels. This time yesterday, his life was normal.

Barry sounds on a high, tired and drunk all at the same time. '. . . Proud father of a baby boy.'

'Congratulations, Bar. That's great. Dee OK?'

'Dee's great.'

'And the baby?'

'Robert. A sturdy nine-pounder. Future prop forward.'

'Signed him up for Rock yet?' Blackrock College is an elite school they used to compete against in schools rugby – and invariably lose. 'Listen, Bar. Sorry to bring this up now, but your bag was nicked last night.'

'Nicked? How? Where did you leave it?'

He wasn't planning on going into detail. 'I was mugged.'

'Jesus. Are you OK?'

'Bar a needlestick injury.'

'I don't believe it. What happened?'

As he talks it through, anger grips him, anger at his attacker, but mostly at himself. 'He was a kid, Barry. A kid. I was bigger. Stronger. Could have taken him. Easily.'

'He had a syringe. No point being a hero in these situations. You were unlucky.'

'I could have flattened him – if I hadn't been so busy shitting myself.'

'Rory. I feel awful about this. If I hadn't . . .'

'Dee was having a baby. You had to be there. I was unlucky. Like you said.'

'You've been to casualty, right?'

'Yeah.'

'What prophylaxis did they give?'

As Rory takes him through it, he starts to suspect that he's making an interesting case history for his doctor friend. He tells himself to stop being paranoid.

'How are you now?' Barry asks.

'Fine. Though I've as good as lost that consultancy post. They're bound to count me out of the running now.'

'Jesus, Rory. This is all my fault.'

Rory's sorry he brought it up. 'Look, I probably wouldn't have got it anyway.'

'Come on. You're the perfect man for the job. You're there on the ground. You're in with all the right people. The job's yours, Rory.'

'Maybe,' he says, to make Barry feel better. He is less optimistic. If the panel finds out what's happened, how can they give him the job knowing they might have to sack him again in a few months should he turn out to be an infection risk?

'Anyway,' Barry says, 'they won't know about the attack unless you tell them.'

'Yeah,' he says, while thinking: at St Paul's? Are you kidding?

Rory considers another option. He could come clean, ask them to postpone the interview process until he has the results. He almost laughs. He's not that goddamn important. There are people coming back from the States for interviews. And anyway, what's the point in even thinking about it? If he tests positive, the consultancy post will be the least of his worries.

5

Rory gets in from work at six. He swallows the two sleeping pills he bummed from one of the nurses that afternoon and takes to his bed. He doesn't hear Louise come in, doesn't hear anything at all until morning, when he wakes, groggy, to the sound of the alarm on his phone, an upbeat reggae tune that is supposed to make getting up easier. It doesn't. He drags himself out of bed and into the shower. Towel wrapped around his waist, he clears the bathroom mirror of condensation and looks for his razor. He finds it on the edge of the bath. *Shit*, he thinks. He picks it up and heads for the bedroom.

'Louise. Did you use my razor last night?'

A pillow over her head, Louise doesn't answer.

He repeats the question.

She groans. 'Rory! Just change the blade.'

'Tell me you didn't nick yourself,' he says slowly.

The pillow moves back. A head emerges. They look at each other. Louise sits up, suddenly awake.

'No. I don't think so. No, I didn't.' She pulls back the duvet, and carefully checks her legs. She looks up. 'I'm OK.'

He breathes out. 'Thank God.' He sits on the bed beside her. 'Please, Lou, don't use my razor, my toothbrush, my anything, until I get the all-clear, OK?'

'Rory, you said everything was fine.'

'It is.' He puts his hand over hers. 'But we should take precautions, just till we're a *hundred* per cent sure. I'm sorry,

37

Lou. I meant to talk about this last night. Didn't think I'd sleep. Are you OK?'

She rakes her hair back from her face. A corner of her mouth lifts. 'One way to stop me using your razor, I suppose,' she jokes.

'I don't think we should have sex for a while either, just to be on the safe side, just till I get the results.'

Her face falls.

'It's just a precaution. The chances I've caught anything are tiny. *Minuscule*. I'm just being extra careful. Until I know.'

'When will you?'

'Four to six months.'

She speaks slowly. 'Rory, you *are* telling me everything, aren't you?'

'Yes.'

She looks into his eyes. 'Four to six months is a long time.'

'It will fly.'

She hesitates. 'We could use a condom?'

Even if he was infected for sure, a condom should provide enough protection. Should, though, isn't enough. He squeezes her hand, appreciating her gesture. 'Let's not take any chances.'

She nods slowly. 'Whatever you think.'

Is it his imagination or does she look relieved?

Hours later, Rory finishes examining a patient with advanced Parkinson's Disease. He helps her settle into a comfortable position and draws back the curtains. At the end of her bed, he lifts her chart and checks her drug sheet. He needs to alter her medication in light of the deterioration in her condition. But it is a challenge. As always with Parkinson's, a balance has to be struck between increasing the dosage and keeping side effects to a minimum. It is while considering the limited options available that suddenly he remembers: his own future is no longer certain. He could die. The thought stills him. He looks up from the chart at the frail elderly woman. He has been surrounded by death all his working life, but he has never thought about the possibility of his own. He frowns at the chart, forcing concentration. He doesn't want to increase the Sinemet. He'll have to up the Requip. He crosses out the current prescription and writes up a new dosage regime. He looks up at the woman and makes his smile say, 'I'm going to improve things for you.' Hanging the chart back, he can't help thinking that there's nothing he can do for himself, except wait.

When Rory goes to his locker to take his pills, he pulls out his phone. The call is to a mate, a fellow rugby coach. Along with medicine, rugby is Rory's great passion. He'd have made a career out of it if he'd been good enough. Next best thing is coaching. Missing a training session is something that does not happen. Normally. Now, he asks his friend, a New Zealander, to cover for him that evening.

'Unlike you, mate, to not turn out,' says the friend. 'Must be on your last legs.'

'Certainly feels that way. Food poisoning.'

'Crikey ... No worries. I'll do it. What about Thursday?'

'Should be OK. It's probably a twenty-four hour thing.'

By Wednesday, Rory has learnt to keep his face blank when he has a flashback, to clear sweat from his forehead by sweeping his hair back, to smile widely at people who are beginning to look concerned. Why can't he just forget? What

39

kind of wuss is he? When Louise suggests cancelling her yoga to be with him, he has to stop himself from agreeing. He is not letting this get to him. He's fine on his own. He'll watch the box. Chill. Or die trying.

Alone in the apartment, he fights an urge to call his parents. Scrap that, he thinks. Last time he called home was to say he couldn't make Christmas. He and Louise were going skiing.

By the time Louise gets home – singing one of her favourites, 'Everybody Hurts' by REM – Rory has never been so glad to see her. She pulls the white earphones of his borrowed iPod from her ears, appearing flushed and healthy, as she always does after yoga. He is up from the couch and over to her, taking her in his arms, closing his eyes and inhaling . . . *cigarette smoke*? Abruptly, he pulls back. But it is too late. There is a third person in the room, Rory's attacker, closing in on him. Louise is saying something but Rory doesn't hear it. He steps back, on his face a look of disgust.

'I thought you said you were going to quit,' he says, venom in his voice.

Her eyes widen. He sees the hurt in them and knows immediately that he is out of line. He tries to pretend he hasn't spoken so accusingly, his voice contrite when he says, 'You said you'd quit.'

But she is angry now, as well as hurt. 'Yeah, and if it were that easy, I would have. D'you think I felt good lighting up straight after yoga? Or that it helps for you to have a go at me as soon as I get in the door? Well, it doesn't. All it does is make me want to light up again.'

He is rubbing an eyebrow, regretting that he has directed his anger at the wrong person. 'I'm sorry,' he says. 'I'm not myself.' A pause. 'Sometimes I worry.'

'But you said there was nothing to worry about.' Now *she* sounds worried.

'There isn't.' His voice is weary. 'I'm just tired. Come here.'

She goes to him and he, breathing through his mouth, puts his arms around her, relieved to be finally holding her, taking comfort in the warmth and softness of her body.

'I love you.' He doesn't say it often. And never has to anyone else.

Friday morning, having missed a second coaching session the night before, Rory wakes with palpitations, chest pain and dizziness. He thinks he's having a heart attack. Where's Louise? Gone? Already? He reminds himself she leaves early on Fridays. Damn. He puts his hand to his chest, feels a racing, bucking heart. He should ring the hospital.

No . . . Wait. Stop . . . Calm down.

Take a deep breath.

Another.

A third.

'OK, let's be sensible here,' he says, aloud. 'You're young. Fit. No family history of cardiac problems.'

He checks his pulse. Rapid, but regular. Scrap the heart attack. What's happening here is simple – he's allowed himself to get so worked up that he's on the verge of a panic attack. There's nothing medically wrong with him. And he sure as hell isn't going to start taking anti-anxiety medication. He can control this. All he has to do is avoid situations that trigger flashbacks. That means work. For a while. Until this passes. If he doesn't go in today, that gives him three days. He hopes it will be enough.

He dials the ward, claiming to have a strep throat (something infectious) then asks to talk to his SHO whom he briefs on a few key issues he'd planned to deal with that day. She should call him at any time if she needs to. When he hangs up, he considers going back to sleep, but knows he will be haunted there too. He gets up, takes it slow. Swallows his numerous pills. And a mango smoothie that Louise has bought for him. He scans the apartment. It's a mess – thanks to a week of moping in front of the TV, finding comfort in Homer Simpson and distraction in Premier League Football. Even the intricacies of make-up application have proved preferable to the thoughts that have started to ambush him, thoughts about his life and what he's done with it, or, rather, what he hasn't. Being faced with your own mortality has a way of focusing the mind. Rory is a man with no footprints, a man who has taken no risks, has nothing to show for over three and a half decades on the planet. Will he ever get a chance to put that right?

He'll start by getting the apartment back in order. While he's at it, he'll change the sheets – seeing as he has mangled the ones on the bed. He should work on himself too. Enough slobbing around. He showers, shaves, does a few press-ups. He should really go for a run. The thought of that, though, makes him draw back. Out there, on his own, in the wide-open, no defences . . . Aw, fuck.

This is not Rory's usual supermarket. It's the one in the massive shopping centre where Louise's flower shop is based, though it's not called a shopping centre but a 'shopping experience'. Rory surprised Louise earlier by dropping in and taking her out to lunch. It wasn't simply that he wanted to see her, which he did; he needed to remind her that he could still make her laugh, that he was the same guy who had sex once with his gumshield in. He wanted to say sorry without words. Lunch was a success. Louise returned to work, looking at him the way she did a week ago.

Rory, with nothing else to do, wandered around the shops, or at least, the computer games shops, sports shops and Tommy Hilfiger. Passing a window featuring baby clothes, he was reminded to get a present for Barry's baby. He wondered where Louise had got that silver bracelet for Daisy. In a nearby jeweller, he finally settled on a no-frills, silver picture frame. One thing about babies – people photograph them. Not in a hurry to get back to the apartment, Rory decided to kill time by getting food in. He could cook Louise a meal, the one and only dish he knows, a chicken casserole he used to help his mother make – a long time ago.

He is reaching for a red pepper when he hears his name. He turns.

'Well, if it isn't the fairy godmother,' he says, smiling.

'What are you doing in this neck of the woods?' Orla asks. Then works it out herself. 'Louise's shop. Of course.' She moves the shopping basket to her other hand. 'I should go in there, give her a bit of business. Now that I think of it, that's exactly what I should be doing – buying myself flowers.'

'How are you?' he asks. 'I've been meaning to call.' Truth is, in the one week since the christening he had forgotten her existence.

'Yeah, right,' she says, laughing.

'OK, let me rephrase that. How're you fixed this afternoon?'

'I have to dash to the school to collect Jason. But after that I'm around if you want to drop by.' It sounds like a dare.

'Sure,' he says, shelving the frozen-food excuse that had popped into his head. He's a better person than she thinks.

43

Yes, he may have lost contact with her but, contrary to what she believes, it's not because he has taken sides. He just let things slip. More than that, he felt awkward, embarrassed on behalf of his brother. 'What time will you be home?'

'About three.'

'Right. See you then.'

6

Last time Rory was at Orla's house, she and Owen were still a couple, a family. Arriving now, he is reminded of the friendship she showed him over the years, welcoming him in time and again, including him in meals, and taking his side when Owen began his lectures on Rory's single, carefree life. Of course, the irony is, Owen has discarded his family in favour of the very life he had so frowned upon. Rory doesn't understand it. They were such an easy-going couple. He loved them both. They used to make him laugh. They used to make each other laugh.

Now he eyes with disdain the 'Auction' sign posted in the front garden. Nothing is 'For Sale' in Dublin any more. Not that it must matter to Orla how the place is sold. It's her home. And it's going. How must it feel to have to pack up and leave because your husband has left you?

'Lilies!' she says when she opens the door. Then her face changes. 'God. I hope you didn't think I was hinting . . .'

''Course I did. You're just so pushy, Dennehy.'

She smiles. And they go in.

'Wow, the place looks great,' he says, glancing around.

'If you want your home at its best, put it on view.'

'I can't get over how big it seems.'

'We're open to offers,' she jokes.

'I'd better buy a Lotto ticket then.'

They go into the kitchen. Jason is perched up at the counter on a high stool, a book open in front of him. He is leaning on an elbow and his ears are red from concentration.

Stretched out at his feet is Lieutenant Dan, Jenna's black Labrador. He lifts his head at the sight of Rory and wags his tail lazily. Slowly he gets up and comes to an old friend. Rory slaps his side.

'Hey, bud, how've you been?' he asks the dog, then looks up at Jason. 'How's the homework going?'

'Shite.'

Rory laughs. 'Would a glass of Coke help?' He puts a supermarket carrier bag on the table, then remembers Orla. 'Is Coke OK?'

She nods.

'Real Coke?' Jason asks.

'Real Coke,' Rory confirms, lifting it out.

'Then you were robbed. You can get a two-litre bottle at Tesco for thirty cent.'

'Is that right?' Rory suppresses a smile. 'And how did you know that?'

'Don't you *ever* watch the ads?'

'Not enough, obviously.' He's surprised he missed it, all the TV he's been watching.

Orla pours Jason a glass. He takes it and starts to climb down from the bar stool.

'Hey, hey, hey.' Orla says. 'One last page.'

'Aw.'

She underlines the words with a finger and he reads in a hesitant monotone, interrupting himself once to call a character in the story a 'dummy'. Last sentence barely finished, he slams the book closed and hops down. They watch him disappear into the TV room, Lieutenant Dan taking up the rear. A sudden realization hits Rory: if he tests positive, he can never be a father – trying for a baby would risk infecting Louise.

'Tea, coffee or extortionate Coke?' Orla offers.

'Sorry?'

She repeats herself.

He opts for the first, not caring. For a man who has never wanted kids, he can't believe the extent of the loss he suddenly feels. He tells himself he is being ridiculous. He doesn't want kids. They tie you down. Make demands.

'I shouldn't let him watch so much TV,' Orla is saying, filling the kettle. 'But it seems to be all he did at home, and, well, he'll have to go back. If I interest him in too many other things, he'll find the transition more difficult.'

Rory starts to listen.

'I've cut out all the adult viewing, though. When he first came, he thought I was a lesbian.'

Rory laughs. *What?*

'Jenna was away at school. My friend Sal's often around. She's separated too, and has been really good to me . . . Anyway, Jason put two and two together and got drama. Sal thought it was the funniest thing ever.' She pours biscuits onto a plate and tea into mugs.

'Orla?'

She looks up.

'I should have rung more often.' He hasn't rung at all, and they both know it. 'I didn't know what to say.' After a brief pause, he adds, 'I don't see Owen.' It's Rory's way of saying he hasn't taken sides.

'You should. He's your brother.'

But not the same brother, Rory thinks. Owen has changed. It's not just the new image – tight haircut, black polo necks, designer stubble – it's the way he fawns over this woman, feeling her up in public as if to prove his love for her. He never had to do that with Orla. With Orla, he could just be himself. It doesn't help that he brings her everywhere. Rory has nothing to say to her, can't look her in the eye without

47

feeling he is betraying Orla. And so he avoids the happy couple. Not that Kate is too interested in hanging out with Owen's family anyway. They are always off to some opening, some 'gig'. Rory wonders if Owen stayed still for five minutes would he realize what he has given up.

'How are you?' Rory asks Orla now.

'OK. Good. Better. You know.'

He doesn't. But he'd like to. He takes a biscuit, breaks it, but forgets to eat it. 'Must have been tough.'

'I loved him, Rory.' She gazes into her cup, silent then, as if that says it all. Rory is about to speak, when she continues. 'My life was our life, my dreams our dreams. When he left, telling me to get on with my life – as if it were that simple – it was like losing everything – my husband, my soulmate, my future, my identity. Everything. Except Jenna. Then she opted for boarding school.' Orla smiles. 'You know, we used to threaten her with boarding school when she was small. "Do that again and it's boarding school."' She shakes her head. 'I tried to get Owen to talk her out of it, but he wanted to keep her happy, so he coughed up the fees.'

Rory wants to shake the man who seems to believe that being with a younger woman makes him a younger man able to delete his past as though it's a computer file.

'I'm too young for empty nest syndrome,' Orla is saying. 'Sorry, *no* nest syndrome.' She is silent for a moment. 'I believed him when he said there was no one else.' She laughs. 'What a fool! No man leaves the comfort of family life unless there is another woman.'

To Rory's embarrassment, this makes sense to him.

'That Christmas, I tried to send cards, but I'd been writing our names side by side for twenty years. Half my life. It was easier to not send any.'

Rory doesn't know what to say, touched by the poignancy

of what Orla has said, but also stunned to realize that she has been married so long. She is only four years older than him.

'As soon as he left, every appliance in the house broke.' She glances at the dishwasher. 'In a weird way, though, I suppose it's been good for me. I've learnt to be more independent.'

Doesn't seem like much of a bargain to Rory. 'How's Jenna doing?'

'I'd love to be able to tell you,' she says. 'But it's a long time since we've had a proper conversation.'

'Because she's at boarding school?'

She snorts. 'Jenna's at boarding school to get away from me.'

Rory is confused. 'But you're so close.'

'*Were* so close. Now, with me, she's either silent or exploding. With Owen she's sweetness and light.'

'I don't get it.'

'I don't either. It's my fault he left. Something like that.'

Hearing all this reassures Rory he's right about not wanting to settle down. He sees the estate agent's brochure for the house, lying half-covered at the edge of the table. He pulls it out. 'Auction's next week?' he says, surprised that it's happening so fast.

She looks out the window.

'Will you go?' he asks.

She pushes her cup away. 'No.'

He replaces the brochure. 'Have you found a place?'

She shakes her head. 'I know I should be looking. But each Saturday passes without me doing anything.' She hides the brochure under a bill. 'When the hammer comes down, I'll have to move on.' She raises her eyebrows. 'I'd always hoped . . .' She stops. 'Anyway . . .'

49

'I could look at places with you. If you want.' Rory doesn't know where this has come from, but now that it's out, he's, surprisingly, fine with it.

'Would you?' Her face shows relief. 'I mean, if you've time?'

'Louise works Saturdays. I just pop into the hospital for an hour or two, early in the morning. After that, I've nothing specific on. We could start tomorrow if you like?'

'Could we?' Orla sounds like she's been offered anaesthesia.

'Sure.'

'Would you like to stay for dinner?' she asks, and for a moment it feels like old times.

'Thanks, but no. Louise and I have plans.' He is sorry then, for sounding so smugly coupled. He is anything but smug. The chicken casserole he is planning is simply another attempt to prove to Louise that he loves her, that he is happy, not worried. That everything is still OK.

Orla starts to prepare dinner for Jason who is 'usually starving by five'.

'I might go in to him, see if I can distract him from the box for a while,' Rory suggests.

'Good luck,' she says, as though he'll need it.

Rory finds Jason lying on the floor in front of the TV, using Lieutenant Dan as a pillow. He is sucking his thumb.

'Hey! Thought you might like to kick a ball around outside?'

Jason's thumb flies out of his mouth. Otherwise, he doesn't move. 'Huh?'

Rory repeats the offer.

The boy lifts his head and turns around. '*Why?*'

'Might be fun. Fresh air, exercise.'

'Doesn't sound like fun to me,' he says, turning back to the TV.

'All right, suit yourself.'

Rory is turning to leave when Jason sits up suddenly. 'If I play, how much'll you give me?'

Rory laughs. 'Nothing.'

'Forget it, then.' Jason turns back to the TV, but doesn't lie down.

'OK. Tell you what . . .'

The boy's head slowly turns.

'If you're enthusiastic out there, concentrate hard and get stuck in, I'll give you two euro.'

Jason squints. 'Two-fifty.'

'Done.' Rory offers his hand.

Jason jumps up and they shake.

'I'll just get the ball.' Rory keeps a rugby ball in the car.

Once Jason gets over the fact that it 'doesn't fucking bounce' and they have to pass 'backwards', they get into a rhythm, running up and down the garden, throwing the ball to each other. Rory, in front, passes back to Jason. Jason catches. Rory drops back, then Jason passes back to him. They speed up, everything working smoothly. The kid is good. Fast. Nimble. Still, Rory is waiting for the question – 'Are we finished yet?' But he underestimated the kid. The question never comes.

They've been outside for over forty minutes when Orla sticks her head through the patio doors and announces that dinner's ready. Jason throws the ball to Rory and runs ahead. Face flushed, he looks alive, like Pinocchio after he'd turned into a real boy. At the door, Rory wipes his shoes, noticing that Jason is walking mud into the floor, Orla too busy asking him how it went to notice. She gets monosyllables in response. Everything changes, though, when Rory produces the money. The boy's face breaks into a gappy smile, one new bumpy tooth coming up between two tiny milk ones. He pockets the coins, making sure they're deep down and safe. Walking to the table, he pats his trousers. Orla places his dinner in front of him.

'Chicken. Yum.' He starts to eat. Mouth full, he adds, 'Even if I was stinkin' rich, I still couldn't eat a full chicken.'

Leaving the house, Rory realizes he hasn't felt this good in a week.

7

Louise doesn't hear him come in. She has one of his favourite albums playing and is singing, off key, to *Sweet Home Alabama*, while setting down a vase filled with tiger lilies too open to sell, but perfect to display. Rory eases the shopping to the ground, sneaks up on her, slipping his arms around her waist. She jumps.

'Jesus, Rory. My heart!'

'You're home early,' he says, kissing her neck.

'You've the day off. Thought we'd spend some time together.'

It's the first time she has taken off work since setting up the business. And he appreciates it.

She spots the shopping. 'Let me guess — seventy per cent more than you'd planned?'

'No. I was firm today. About sixty-eight.'

She helps him bring the shopping into the kitchen. 'Let's go out tonight,' she says, with such enthusiasm that Rory begins to see the week from her perspective. She has stayed in every night, bar a few hours of yoga, to be with him in all his gloom. It didn't help — the last thing he wanted was to talk and her attempts to get him to do so had interfered with his need to vegetate in front of the wide-screen — but at least she'd tried. He can do the chicken thing another time. It's Friday night. And they're going out. Like a normal couple who have nothing to worry about, nothing to fear.

*

One quick stop on the way to the restaurant – Barry and Dee's. Present delivery. Barry answers the door, stifling a yawn with the back of a hand that holds a baby's bottle. His face brightens when he sees who it is and he hugs them both, Rory first, then Louise, banging each on the back with his free hand. He shoos them down the hall in front of him like sheep. Into chaos. Dee's parents and a woman who is later introduced as Dee's aunt are visiting, everyone congregated in the tiny, outmoded kitchen. The women are fussing over the baby, while Dee's father is trying to get his grandson out of the baby's Moses basket, saying he's too big and will break it. Dee is telling her father to leave him be, her hand on her forehead as if it's been a very long day. When she sees the surprise guests, she looks like she's going to burst into tears.

'Congratulations, Dee, we're not staying,' Rory says in one breath.

Louise leaves the gift on the table, pats it once, then backs away. 'It's a bad time,' she says. 'I'm sorry. We should have rung.'

'No, no,' says Dee, though not forcefully, pulling her baggy jumper down further over her hips and producing a smile that appears to have taken great effort.

'You're not leaving without champagne,' insists a jovial Barry, who hands the baby's bottle to his mother-in-law, with a 'should be all right now'.

She tests the milk on the back of her hand. 'I'll give it another minute.'

The baby bawls. And she sticks it in his mouth.

The proud father whips out three fat cigars from a half-empty box, while Dee makes her way to the fridge as if it's not the first time her husband has offered champagne.

'Dee. We're going. Honestly,' says Louise. 'We'll call again.

And phone first. Barry, we'll take a rain check on the champagne. Thanks, anyway.'

Dee, looking as if all she wants to do is lie down, doesn't argue. But Barry is already handing a cigar to Rory and another to his father-in-law.

Rory takes it with grace, sick at the thought of having to smoke it, hoping that it doesn't trigger a flashback.

Dee's mother frowns. 'If you're going to smoke those things, you'd better do it in the garden. There are babies in here.'

Standing outside the back door in the October chill, pretending to inhale, Rory listens to the intimate details of Robert's birth. Normally, this would bore him. Tonight, he is absorbed, not so much by the detail, as the change in Barry. His normally salt-of-the-earth mate is behaving as though he has witnessed a miracle, his voice awed, at times shaky, his eyes filling. And this is his *second* child. Surely, he should have got used to the experience – an experience, Rory remembers, he may never have. He stares out into the darkness. 'Back in a sec,' he says, his voice croaky, already making for the door.

Inside, he hurries past the women, failing to see Louise trying to catch his eye or Dee's mother frowning at the cigar still in his hand. In the downstairs loo, he lowers the toilet seat and sits on it. Remembering the cigar, he gets up again and goes to the sink, where he douses it under the tap, wraps it in toilet paper and stuffs it in his pocket. He sits back on the loo. Looks at the plastic step that has been placed in front of the sink for Jamie to reach the taps. He imagines hairless arms with dimpled elbows reaching for the frog-shaped soap dispenser and pressing down on its green and purple head to get the liquid soap flowing. He imagines the generous amount that will be taken. He imagines the smile on the boy's face when he sees the bubbles. What's wrong with him? He has no interest in children. And he's not going to start now, just because he knows he might never be able to have any. That would make him something his father was always fond of calling him, a spoiled brat.

'Fuck,' he says aloud.

He spots a book of Garry Larson cartoons lying on the top of a reading pile. That's more like it. He flicks through it and starts to smile. It takes a good five minutes before he's sufficiently distracted. Then he's ready to face the world. On his way back through the kitchen, he catches Louise's eye. It says, 'let's go'. He nods quickly. Outside, he waits until the men have finished their smokes before making his excuses.

Louise fastens her seat belt while Rory turns the ignition. Her voice is flat when she asks, 'What kept you?'

'A big smelly turd,' he jokes, sensing tension.

She doesn't laugh. 'I meant, what kept you outside?'

He indicates and takes a right turn, ignoring the question.

'Why did you leave me in there with the women and children? We're in the twenty-first century, not the bloody Titanic. Just because I'm a woman doesn't mean I want to hold the baby. Jesus.'

This is not what he needs. 'What did you expect me to do?' he asks, irritated.

'I don't know. Insist we go, straight away.'

'I did.'

'Not strongly enough.'

'Come on, Louise. I was letting Barry have his moment. Didn't you see him? He was over the moon. He just wanted to share it.'

'You could have asked me to come outside.'

His face says, 'You can't be serious.'

She pulls a piece of nicotine gum from her bag, unwraps it quickly, and stuffs it in her mouth. She chews as if her life depends on it. Then parks the gum. 'I just don't want it, that *life*.'

Rory looks at her. So this isn't about him after all.

'Not every woman does,' she says. She rummages in her bag and in seconds has a cigarette between her fingers and is snapping her lighter. She leans her cigarette into it and inhales deeply. Her head tilts back. After a moment, she removes the gum from her mouth.

Why not? he wants to ask. For the first time in their relationship he wants to say, 'What's wrong with that life?' Instead, he rolls down the window and breathes in the night air.

Rory chose the restaurant on the basis that they've always had good times here, fun times. Considering the week they've had, he thought they might need a little help on the atmosphere front. As soon as he enters, though, he is overcome by panic. What has always seemed a happy, buzzing vibe is now noisy, overcrowded, claustrophobic – a market in downtown Tokyo, too many people, too little space. His eyes dart to Louise. What excuse can he come up with to leave? She is chatting politely to the Asian waitress who is now walking ahead, leading them to their table. For a moment, he hesitates, letting them go. Then he tells himself to be a man. Be Sergeant O'Neill. And, for God's sake, breathe.

When Louise moves towards the seat with the view, Rory is tempted to make a dive for it. With a wall behind him, security at his back, no one could jump him, catch him unawares. But Louise is sliding in, leaving him the seat with its back to the aisle. Rory pulls the chair right in. His body is rigid. He tells himself that if he focuses on Louise, he will be all right. If he just concentrates on that face – those dark, dark eyes, those long thick lashes, the mole on her cheekbone – everything will be fine. She has curled her hair. Is that new lipstick? Fuck.

'So, how did it go with Orla?' she asks. 'Did she like the flowers?'

'She loved them,' he says, knowing how important Louise's business is to her. 'Said she'd have to give you some business herself.' He checks behind him, looking up and down the aisle.

'Did she? That's sweet.'

When another waitress, a blonde wearing a black T-shirt, arrives quietly and suddenly at his side, Rory jumps. Then apologizes. She asks if they're ready to order, her accent Australian. They select their usual, Malaysian Chicken. Rory plans to eat fast, get the hell home.

'So how's Orla doing?' Louise asks.

'Lou, would you mind if we swapped seats?'

She looks surprised. 'No.'

'The view,' he says. 'For a change.' He always lets her have the good seat. 'You don't mind, do you?'

'Nope.'

They swap over. 'So,' she says. 'Orla.'

He relates an abridged version of his conversation with his sister-in-law. Then the Australian is back, placing their meals in various bowls in front of them and asking if they know what to do with the dishes. They do. So she leaves them to it. Louise picks up her chopsticks, Rory his knife and fork. He starts to relax. They eat in silence for a few minutes, then Louise asks about 'the foster kid'.

'Jason,' he says.

'What's the story there?'

Rory is irked at how casually she has asked about him, as if his life is public property, just because it's a mess. This is how he must have sounded to Orla when he first asked about Jason. 'I don't know his situation. It's confidential.'

'Really?'

'To protect him.'

'So you know nothing at all about him?'

'Apart from the fact that it just seems to be him and his mother. Orla never mentions a father.'

'Well, why am I not surprised?' Louise's voice is bitter.

And Rory guesses what's coming.

'Another mess created by a man walking out on his family.'

He wants to ask how can she be so sure that's what happened, but leaves it. The subject is a sensitive one. Louise's father left when her mother became pregnant with her. Louise never knew him. All she knew was a mother whose best friend was a bottle of whiskey. Growing up in that environment has left its mark.

'All men, sooner or later, walk,' she says.

'Not all, in fairness.'

'All men, in one way or another, leave – if not physically, mentally.'

He wants to say 'not me' but doesn't want to personalize it. 'I can't imagine Barry ever leaving his family,' he says. Then again, he thinks, Owen was equally smitten when Jenna was born. 'Not all men are the same, Louise. I know lots of good fathers.'

'And I know lots of crap ones. Non-ones.'

If she asks him to 'name one', she's going to find that his own father isn't on his list. Neither is it a very long list.

He wonders, now, how the conversation ended up here. And decides to take control. 'I told Orla I'd help her look for an apartment,' he says, trying to move the conversation on and strike a blow for men at the same time.

Louise stops chewing. '*Oh?*'

'Their house is up for auction on Wednesday and she hasn't started looking.'

'How come?'

'I don't know. End of an era, I guess. She's leaving everything behind, once and for all.'

She stops eating. 'Poor thing.'

'I feel bad that I haven't kept in touch.'

'You were busy.'

'Not too busy to pick up the phone.' He puts down his fork. 'I've always used that excuse, and, yeah, work's busy, but, the fact is, I give no time to my family. Owen left her out in the cold and I did nothing to make her feel she was still included.'

'You can't be expected to make up for your brother's actions.'

'No. But I'd like her to know that just because *he* ditched her doesn't mean we all have.'

'Siofra has kept in touch.'

'Good for her. Well, now it's time for this man to do his bit. We're not *all* the same, you know.' It is something he'd like to prove, not only to Louise, but to himself.

Louise raises a doubtful eyebrow.

And that hurts. After all these years, couldn't she at least have a little faith in him?

8

There is nothing appealing about the first apartment building on their view list. It's a redbrick, featureless block on a busy main road. The only thing going for it is that it may be in Orla's price range. Jason, eager for his first experience of the property market, is out of the car before anyone. Orla hurries to catch up. Jenna, home for the weekend, stays where she is in the back seat, finishing a text to someone she gives the impression she'd much rather be with. Rory opens her door and finally she moves.

The show apartments are teeming with people, most of whom seem unfamiliar with the concept of standing back and letting a person through a door. And would an occasional smile be out of the question? But it is not the loss of social etiquette fuelled by a booming economy that is making Rory's stress levels rise, rather the feverish interest in the properties. With competition like this, Orla's chances of affording a place are seriously diminished. Such is his concern, that he almost loses sight of the fact that these apartments are nothing spectacular. Just around the corner is an area not unlike the one where Rory was attacked. Security is an issue.

A familiar face, coming towards Rory through the busy hallway interrupts his thoughts. He hasn't seen 'Rhino' Hynes since their school days. He tries to remember his real name and can't. Rhino has a baby on his chest in one of those slingy things and two blonde identical girls at his feet. Beside him is a beautiful woman, presumably his wife. All of a sudden, Rory does not want one of those 'So what are you doing with yourself?' conversations. He ducks into the bathroom, moving so quickly that Orla and the others carry on, Jason suggesting they turn the lights off to see how dark the hallway really is.

Rory is examining bathroom fittings when he hears the voice of Rhino Hynes behind him.

'Rory? Rory Fenton?'

Rory turns. Feigns surprise.

'I thought it was you,' says Rhino.

'Rhino Hynes,' says Rory.

Rhino clears his throat. 'I've dropped the nickname.'

Rory's memory is letting him down.

'Liam,' Rhino helps.

'That's right. Of course. Liam, how are you?'

Rhino's family has gathered in the hallway, looking in.

'Good, great. In Floxams Stockbrokers now. And you, you did medicine, didn't you?'

'Yup.'

'So,' Rhino says, eyes scanning the bathroom, 'you looking at investment properties?'

'Eh, yeah.'

'Me too. My third.'

'Good for you.' Rory is reminding himself of the Rhino he knew in school – weedy, always cogging, no friends. Looks like he has left that life far behind. As if on cue, his cherubic daughters dash in and hug his legs.

Rhino gives Rory a look that says *Kids!* 'You here on your own?' he asks.

'No. No. The wife's around here somewhere.' Rory has the decency to colour, especially when it occurs to him that the property tycoon might want an introduction.

'Liam,' the beautiful woman calls from the hallway, 'I'll be in the car.'

'Listen, I'd better go. Great to see you, Rory. Are you bidding on this, by the way?'

'Eh. Don't know yet. Just got here. We'll have to see.'

'Right. Right.'

Rhino, Rory notices, is keeping his own cards close to his chest. Like he always did. Rory watches him leave, baffled at himself. How had he allowed himself to be intimidated by a guy who earned his nickname by picking his nose?

He finds Orla, Jason and Jenna in 'the master bedroom'. Tastefully done, dark wood, white walls. Standing at the door, he watches his supposed family – Jenna looking bored, Orla checking cupboard space and Jason turning off the light – and thinks what a different man he would be if he had a family. A doer, risk-taker, a man unafraid to live life. Or is that a load of rubbish? Maybe he'd have ended up like his brother, and running from it all.

Orla turns, smiles and joins him. 'Where did you disappear to?'

'Checking the bathroom.'

'Again?'

'Again.'

She runs her eyes over the room. 'Not bad value, considering the market,' she says, voice low.

Jason moves closer to hear.

'I don't know, Orla,' says Rory. 'It's not a great area.'

'I know, but won't these new apartments bring it up?'

'I'd be very careful. The last thing you want is *junkies* on your doorstep.'

Orla's eyes widen. She glances quickly at Jason who, Rory

notices, is now glaring at him, chin jutting out. Rory looks at Orla for clarification.

Jason shoves clenched fists into his pockets and pounds from the room.

'What did I say?' Rory asks.

Orla shakes her head. 'Don't worry about it.'

But he does.

They find Jason in the sitting room, hands still in pockets, but standing tall, questioning a young woman in a suit, the estate agent presumably. 'How far is the nearest bus stop?'

'Just up the road,' she says, indulging him as though he is a genuine contender. When she sees Rory and Orla, she smiles as if to say, 'cute kid'.

Orla goes to him. Rory hangs back.

'So, what do you think, Jase?' she asks.

'It's *OK*,' he says, in a tone that implies that he's not interested, but is too polite to say so in front of the woman. Then he adds, 'Better go and see those *other ones* now.' In the lift on the way down, he ignores Rory, talking only to Orla, 'You can't let them see if you're interested.'

'Are we?'

'I think it's good.'

Rory doesn't want to imagine what Jason's own home must be like.

The more apartments they see, the quieter Orla becomes. Finally, she decides she's seen enough and they return to the house she has four more days of calling 'home'. Jenna disappears to her room, Jason to the TV. Orla heads for the kitchen, where she slumps at the table, head in her hands.

'You OK?' Rory asks, still standing, edgy, wanting to be somewhere else.

She looks up. 'Yeah, fine.'

'It'll be OK,' he says, making himself join her at the table.

'How? How will it be OK? Anywhere decent, I can't afford. Anywhere I can, I hate.'

It seems like tears mightn't be far off. He has sat down too soon. Now he is stuck. 'It was our first day. There'll be plenty of other options.'

She gives him a look. 'I've worked it out, Rory. The auctioneer said to expect about 1.2 million for our house.'

'Wow.'

'Wow nothing. Split it in two. Subtract our mortgage, and all the fees. Then to the places we've been looking at, add stamp duty.'

He recalls the extortionate prices – two bedroomed apartments for over seven hundred thousand.

'And what kind of mortgage will I get on my one income at my age? They only give thirty-year mortgages to kids. I'm in trouble, Rory. This is why I didn't want to look.'

'It'll be OK,' he says, not at all sure that it will.

To his embarrassment, he sees that she has started to cry. Elbows on the table, forehead in her hands, she says, aloud but to herself, 'Why do I have to be the one to make all the compromises, always?'

Fuck, Rory thinks. He injects confidence into his voice. 'We *will* find a place.'

'A place maybe, but not the right place, not a place I can bring Lieutenant Dan. Why should I have to find him "a good home"? He has a good home. He's part of the family.' Her voice wobbles. 'What's left of it.'

Rory's eyes scan for tissues. Hoping kitchen paper will do, he hands her two sheets from a roll decorated with snow-flakes.

She blows. 'I'm sorry. I'm an idiot.' She scrapes her fingers

65

through dark shoulder-length hair. 'I just don't know what to do, Rory. I'll have to move out of the area. I've lived here for so long. I don't want to go. And what about Jason's school?'

Rory decides against pointing out that Jason may have gone by the time she has to move. 'Look,' he says, 'maybe it was a mistake to view places until after the auction. We don't know what you'll have to spend. You might be surprised. The market's flying.'

She blows her nose again, but this time as if to mark the end of the tears.

Rory is encouraged. 'And I'm not sure that there's a whole lot of difference in price between a townhouse and an apartment. You might be able to afford a place with a garden. Let me check it out.' He'll talk to Siofra, who has been looking for a bigger house since Daisy was born. She'll know the name of that property website he's heard about on the radio.

Orla forces a smile. 'Thank you.'

Two mugs of coffee later, Rory has moved the conversation well away from property. He has even managed to make her laugh, which is what they're doing when Jason comes in to get a drink. He makes a point of ignoring Rory.

'God. I've really pissed him off, haven't I?' Rory says when he has gone again.

'He'll be all right.'

Rory hesitates. 'You don't have to tell me and I'm not fishing. I just don't want to keep putting my foot in it . . . His mother's a drug addict, isn't she? I can't come up with any other reason why he reacted like he did to what I said.'

She gets up to close the door. Back at the table, she lowers her voice. 'Yes. She's an addict.' Orla pauses. 'She overdosed. Jason found her, thought she was dead. Had to call 999.'

'Jesus.'

'He was taken into care. The health boards are his legal guardians for the moment.'

'Where's the mother now?'

'Out of rehab, trying to cope with life without drugs. According to the social worker it's the hardest time, back in your old environment, trying to change your ways.'

'D'you think she'll make it?'

'I don't know. I hope so. For Jason's sake. But then . . .' she sighs. 'You should have seen him when he arrived here, Rory, so thin, so neglected. He still hoards food, you know, hiding it in his room as if he still can't trust when he'll eat again.'

Rory remembers him pocketing food at the barbecue and tries to imagine what it must be like to have to depend on someone like the guy who attacked him – for everything, including love.

'She's coming on an access visit on Wednesday. Same day as the auction. Thought it'd take my mind off it.' She laughs without mirth.

'She's coming to your *home*?'

'With a social worker.'

Social worker or no social worker, Rory's not sure it's a good idea.

'I'm *so* nervous.'

Rory can imagine.

But he has misinterpreted. 'I want to like her, welcome her, but how can I forget how she's treated Jason? I keep telling myself that it was the drugs and it's a good sign she wants to meet him so soon after getting out of rehab.'

Rory isn't so trusting.

'Jason is dying to see her. He's been saving for weeks for a present . . .'

Rory understands now the bribe to play rugby, and his

heart warms to the boy. He won't be so quick to judge in future. 'What's he getting her?'

Orla's face drops. 'Cigarettes. He says she wouldn't want anything else.'

Rory tells himself it doesn't matter what the kid thinks of him, but for some reason it does. He is genuinely sorry to have upset him. Would like to start over. Jason ignores him when he enters the TV room. So he sits down and gives the television his full attention. It's *The Simpsons*. The boy has taste. They watch it together. Rory laughs out loud. Jason is quiet. Finally, when the programme ends, Rory says, as though it has just occurred to him, 'Hey. Thanks for all your help on the property hunt.'

Jason turns, looks him straight in the eye and says, 'I wasn't doing it for you.'

Rory considers apologizing. But what for? Saying the word 'junkie'? Surely that would make a bigger deal of the whole thing? He gets up. 'See you soon, OK?' He ruffles Jason's hair.

The boy reaches up and flattens it back down.

That night, there is a change in Rory's recurring nightmare. Jason is in it. Rory is trying to protect him. But he's out of reach. In danger. *The syringe!* Rory jolts awake, his own scream reverberating in his head. He looks at Louise, still asleep. He mustn't have screamed after all. He eases into a sitting position so as not to wake her. His body is still reeling, chest constricted by panic. It had been so real. He'd been there, felt everything, the fear, the panic, the horror when he couldn't save the child.

He is not slipping back into *that* nightmare. He reaches for his sweatshirt. Finds a pair of socks. Wanders through the apartment lit only by the orange glow of the streetlights outside. He opens the balcony door. Outside, a dense fog hangs and the air smells salty. A lone foghorn booms eerily in the distance. Rory goes back inside, switches on the TV. As the problems of Tony Soprano suck him in, he begins to forget his own.

He wakes to brightness and the smell of bacon. There is a duvet over him. The TV is off. His watch says eleven. He hasn't the energy to get up. Louise appears, looking wide-awake and fresh, in denims and black polo, her hair swept up. Her energy makes him want to go back to sleep. She sits beside him, kisses him good morning.

'Couldn't you sleep?'

'I was a bit restless.'

'This thing is worrying you, isn't it?'

'No,' he lies. 'I just keep getting these nightmares. The attack, over and over again.'

'Then you must be worried.'

'I'm *not* worried,' he barks, and is instantly sorry. He apologizes. 'I'm edgy, OK? I thought I'd have moved on by now. It's ridiculous.'

She's quiet, as if afraid that anything she says is going to be the wrong thing.

'What d'you want to do today?' he asks, cheerily.

It takes a moment for her to adjust. 'I don't mind. Nip in to Grafton Street?'

The thought of crowds makes his insides tighten. 'I'd like to go see Daisy.'

She looks surprised. '*Daisy?*'

He remembers the scene at Barry's. 'Don't feel you have to come. I won't stay long.'

'It's not that I don't want to come. It's just not like you, that's all.'

'What's not like me?'

'I don't know, visiting your family, I guess.'

'She's my godchild.'

'I know, yeah. And I think it's *good* you want to see her.'

'You don't have to come, if there's something else you want to do . . .'

'No, I'd like to come.'

'OK. Thanks.'

Why are they being so polite?

Siofra and family are just in from Mass. It's news to Rory that his sister goes. Mass was a habit they broke in their early teens, behind their father's back. Tony must be into it. Or maybe it's something you return to when you've kids. He looks around Siofra's busy kitchen. Of all the rooms in a home, he thinks, this is the one where families congregate. At the apartment, he and Louise always chill in the sitting room. Kitchens are cosier, he decides. But he can see that Siofra and Tony need more space. The worktop is cramped, with Siofra making coffee, and Tony sterilizing baby bottles, a job he cheerfully claims to hate. Daisy, asleep in her portable car seat, is occupying the only clutter-free corner of the kitchen, while Alex has giant pieces of Lego all over the floor.

'How's the property hunt going?' Rory asks.

'Disastrous,' Tony says. 'We may have to move out of the city.'

'How far out?'

Siofra sighs. 'Kildare, Meath, maybe.'

Kildare and Meath might be in what's optimistically described as the commuter belt, but they are separate counties. Rory thinks how far Siofra would be from their mum and the impact that would have. Siofra is the one person who makes sure June gets out of the house, bringing her shopping, doing girly things with her. 'Maybe there's a way round it,' he suggests.

Tony looks doubtful.

Alex gets aggressive with a remote control red mini, driving it into Louise's legs. Tony tells him to take it out to the hall, then relates how his son created havoc in church, breaking out of his seat and tearing up the aisle to get his hands on Holy Communion. By the time Tony had managed to pass the baby to Siofra and go after him, Alex was already on his way back down, in tears, shouting, 'I didn't get one of those fucking white things.'

Rory laughs. 'Imagine Dad's reaction if one of us had done that,' he says to Siofra. His father would have used the belt – once they'd got home. Their mother might have intervened. But you could never be a hundred per cent sure. His parents were a united front. Still, on a day-to-day basis, his mother was a buffer to his father's almost Presbyterian sternness. She was Good Cop to his Bad Cop. Rory remembers a game she used to play with him when he was the only one still too young to receive Communion. After Mass, she would buy Silvermints. Later, when they were alone, she would pretend to be a priest, holding out one cool white disc to Rory, and placing it on his tongue, saying, 'Dominus Vobiscum', Latin for Body of Christ, which is what was said to her in church when she was young. If his father had stumbled upon them, there would have been trouble. Which, of course, made the game better.

Alex follows his car into the kitchen. Rory winks at him.

'What would you say to a trip to the shop?' he asks.

Alex's eyes light up.

The two men walk to the corner shop. And Rory buys Silvermints for the nephew he is beginning to feel he should know better.

9

Back at work, Rory hears an elderly female patient tell a younger woman (who has just been diagnosed with multiple sclerosis), about miracles. They are possible, she says, and tells her of a church on the quays where every Tuesday a special novena is held. Rory doesn't know what a novena is. He's heard of them but they seem to belong to a different world, a world of old people and prayer. He listens. If you attend nine Masses in a row, the woman says, you get your miracle. Rory thinks that if it were that simple, the whole world would be down by the river every Tuesday night. He is about to return the chart he has been reviewing, when the woman mentions St Anthony, the saint behind the miracles. When he was a kid, his mother would have him pray to St Anthony whenever he'd lost something. It had always worked. Always. But that was for losing things. This is different. Though he has lost something – the certainty of his future.

The following night, he finds himself on the quays searching for the church. If he doesn't find it in the next five minutes, he's giving up. Up ahead, a steady stream of people is disappearing into a building. Closer inspection reveals a church. He hopes no one recognizes him. But then, who does he know that would turn up somewhere like this?

He sits at the back. And looks around him. He was wrong. It is not just old people. It is all types. Young, old, male, female, well dressed, not so well dressed, Irish, non-nationals.

The one thing that unites them is the way they pray – as if they really mean it. Heads bent, eyes closed. There is desperation here. It is a Mass, but different. There is a lot of talk about St Anthony. The priest reads out requests. People needing miracles. A woman whose son has leukaemia. A man who has lost his job. A woman whose daughter is in a difficult marriage. An alcoholic. So many people, so many problems. It is humbling. When the Mass is over and people queue in front of a statue of St Anthony, Rory, not knowing why, joins them. He feels part of something here – humanity, maybe.

When he leaves the church, he decides to do something he has avoided on the basis that it was none of his business.

The headlights of his car fall on Orla's home. It looks cosy and inviting, curtains open and pools of yellow light around the lamps within. He wonders what type of people will be bidding for it in the morning. That it's a family home won't exclude investors. They're everywhere, bumping up prices, making it harder for everyone else. He hopes it goes to a family, a family that likes it just as it is, with no plans to change or extend it.

Orla is surprised to see him. 'What's this, doctor on call?'

'Just here to wish you luck,' he lies. There is more to it than that.

They go through to the kitchen, a room that is growing on Rory as a place to hang out.

'This is your lucky day,' she says. 'Tonight, I can offer you some seriously fancy coffee.' She taps an espresso machine. 'Went out today and blew a fortune on this thing.'

'Nerves, eh?' he says, then instantly regrets the bluntness of his comment. He dives into a monologue about Daisy,

Alex, Holy Communion and Silvermints. At some point, he becomes aware of what he is doing and clams up completely.

'You sure you need caffeine?'

'Sorry. I'm waffling.'

'Waffling's good. I've run out of things to distract myself with. Thanks for coming.'

'No big deal. Louise is at yoga.' That didn't sound right. 'I didn't mean . . . How's Jason?'

Orla smiles. 'Took ages to fall asleep. Can't believe he's finally getting to see his mum.'

This is his cue. 'Listen. I was thinking.' A pause. 'Maybe you could hold the access visit somewhere else.'

She looks surprised. 'Why?'

'I don't know – I was just – D'you think it's *safe* allowing an addict into your home?' Over the last few days, in between flashbacks and nightmares, Rory has grown more and more convinced that Orla is making a mistake. 'I was just thinking, I mean, where does she get the money to support a drug habit?'

'She's been in rehab. I'm hoping she doesn't *have* a drug habit.'

'What if she went into rehab just to get her son back?'

Orla seems appalled. 'It's not a holiday camp. She's trying. We should give her a break. I mean addicts *are* people, people who happen to have an addiction.'

Something flips inside Rory. 'And that gives them the right to go around breaking the law, hurting other people? Oh, poor them, they've a drug habit. To hell with those whose lives they ruin.' He stops, face flushed.

Orla is staring at him.

'Sorry,' he says, standing. 'This is none of my business. I don't know why I'm here. I'm going.'

'Rory, sit down.'

He doesn't. But neither does he go.

'What is it?' she asks, standing herself now, her voice soft, encouraging.

He'd like to tell her ... He peers out at his car, parked under a streetlight. 'Look, I'm just a bit touchy about drug addicts – in case you haven't noticed.' His smile is lopsided.

'*No*. Never,' she says in mock surprise.

She sits. And that encourages him to. He looks at her. She is an agony aunt. Everyday, she advises people. And she's good at it. He listens to her on the radio and her advice always seems spot on to him. He doesn't buy the newspaper where she has a regular weekly page, but he assumes that the same wisdom is administered there. Of everyone Rory knows, over the years he has probably been most open with Orla, telling her things he'd never have told Owen or whatever woman he happened to be with at the time. Maybe, if he began with the basics, told her just what Louise knows ...

Once he starts, though, he finds it hard to stop. It's such a relief to let it out, free it from inside his head, that he keeps going until he has shared with her things he couldn't with Louise – his fears, his anger at his attacker, but mostly at himself for letting this hijack his life. Orla lets him speak. Doesn't react, only to nod, or encourage him on. And so, he is able to talk, for the first time, of how disillusioned he feels that he has done nothing significant with his life. She doesn't argue, doesn't tell him how wonderful he is being a doctor. And for that he is glad. He went into medicine for the wrong reasons. And he is tired of being canonized for it. He would like to do some good. He would like to make a difference.

*

From where she is sitting at the computer, Louise is watching him. He has come home a different man, his body lighter, not so weighed down, his smile a genuinely happy one, his kiss no longer needy. He did not make straight for the TV. Did not reach for a drink. Just selected some sounds and picked up Sunday's newspapers, finally settling down to read them. Louise has been trying for over a week to produce this effect.

She gets up, bringing her mug of green tea with her and sits on the couch beside him, cross-legged. 'How did it go with Orla?' she asks.

He puts the paper aside. 'Good.'

'What did ye talk about?' Her voice is casual.

He hesitates. 'Oh, not much, houses, Jason.' He feels a bit of a shit, telling her the boy's story to divert attention from his own, but knows that if he admits how much he told Orla, she will be hurt that he was able to tell his sister-in-law so much.

Louise is engrossed in Jason's story and genuinely sympathetic, knowing what it's like to be abandoned by a father and left with a mother who couldn't cope. Still, 'Wasn't all this supposed to be confidential?'

He explains how he came to know.

She seems to relax. Looking down at her green tea, she frowns. 'I can't drink any more of this.'

He peers into the mug and wrinkles his nose. 'I don't know why you started.'

'Drinking coffee makes me want to smoke. Thought this might break the cycle. But, you know what, give me cravings any day.'

He laughs.

Later, Rory needs a leak. Louise is in the bath. He wanders in. Candle flames flicker in his wake. An incense stick, its base plunged into a satsuma for balance, wafts a thin line of smoke that reminds Rory of old Westerns and smoke signals. He pisses against the porcelain to reduce the sound, then takes his time washing his hands, not in a hurry to leave the peaceful atmosphere. He lowers the lid on the toilet and sits, watching her.

She is resting against the back of the bath, hair tucked up out of the way, cheeks flushed, body wet. Gorgeous. She picks up a smooth wet bar of white soap, rests it on her chest, then nudges it forward so that it slides down between her breasts. It picks up speed as it skims over her, its final journey over the tiny bump of her almost flat belly. Then she starts over.

He laughs. 'What are you doing?'

'Playing.'

As he watches the soap travel again, he imagines the route it would take if Louise were pregnant. Its journey would shorten earlier, the larger her tummy became, eventually coming to a halt just below her breasts – which would be bigger by then. Rory experiences a renegade erection, his first since the attack. His libido is back. Which is both good. And bad.

Two things happen the following day to ensure that Rory isn't in a talkative mood. One: he receives a courtesy call from the detective in charge of his case, wondering if he has received the test results and admitting that they have no news at their end. Two: Rory goes in front of the interview panel for the post of consultant neurologist. And knows within minutes that the job will not be his. He can't tell if they've found out about the syringe attack or if they've simply decided on another candidate, but their questions are short and perfunctory, as if they are going through the motions. Not one of them shows any personal interest in him. The most depressing thing about the interview, though, is that Rory cannot motivate himself to fight for a job he may not be around to perform.

Back at the apartment, he vegetates in front of *Malcolm in the Middle*. Louise has given up on conversation and is flicking through a flower catalogue when the phone rings. It's Orla, looking for Rory. To Louise's amazement, he hops up. She hands him the phone and picks up the catalogue again, but her concentration is on the call.

'How did it go?' he asks. There is a long pause, while he listens. It is interspersed with, 'Really?', 'No', a laugh, and 'Go away.' Finally, 'Fantastic! You'll *easily* get a three-bed townhouse in your area with that. I'm delighted.' He's quiet for a moment, listening. Then he laughs.

Louise snaps her catalogue closed.

'How did the meeting with Jason's mum go?' He silently nods a few times. 'And how was Jason?'

Louise thinks he sounds like a man talking to his wife about their child. She gets up, walks to the window, folding her arms. He's known Orla a lot longer than her. They've always got on. Orla is alone now. What if she has begun to see him as someone who can rescue her from all her problems? And what if he likes this role . . . ?

'How long did she stay?' he asks.

Louise stares at him. If he nods his head one more time, she thinks she might have to kill him.

'How did you get on with her?' Pause. 'Yeah, I can imagine. You're right, plenty of time.' Silence again. 'What happens next?' Another pause. 'So a great day, all in all. I'm delighted. Really delighted for you.'

You said that already, Louise thinks, and is deciding she can't take any more, when she hears, 'Still want a hand finding a new home?'

He hangs up, smiling.

'You've certainly cheered up,' Louise says, her tone accusatory.

'Orla and Owen got one point six mill for their house. There was a bidding war. Three people wanted it. A retired businessman who'd just traded down and got millions for his place wanted it for his daughter. Money no object. Orla can easily afford a three bed with half of that.'

'Yeah, I heard.'

'What's wrong?'

'Nothing.'

He goes to her. 'What is it?'

'I don't know. It's just that nothing I do cheers you up, and the minute Orla rings you're bouncing out of your chair like a bunny at Easter.'

'I'm happy for her,' he says, afraid to admit that he's also glad to have a distraction from his own thoughts, and keen to help.

'Why?'

'Why? Because she's had a tough time and something's finally worked out for her,' he says, sounding irritated. 'God, Louise.'

'I'm going to bed.'

10

Sunday. Louise is laughing too loudly at something Mark has said. Rory notices how much wine she's been drinking. They're finishing lunch at a trendy restaurant in town with their friend and his new girlfriend, Lesley, the latest in a long line of non-national babes. To date, Mark has broadened his geographical horizons by dating women from Germany, Holland, Japan, France, Italy and Wales. Rory imagines a world map with a Mark flag stuck in each of the countries he has conquered. Lesley, his first English girlfriend, seems different. She doesn't laugh at all his jokes but when she does, it's loud and hearty. She is a speech therapist who works at the hospital. Rory likes her Birmingham accent.

They split the bill. Pulling his credit card from his wallet, Rory dislodges the prayer to St Anthony they were giving out at the church. He stuffs it back in before anyone can see it. He's not sure why he can't get rid of it. He's not normally superstitious. As they leave the restaurant, Mark wonders aloud how they might get their hands on next-season rugby international tickets.

Outside, they pile into Lesley's seen-better-days Opel Corsa, Louise joining her, up front. Two separate conversations begin. In the back, Mark picks up a folder that's lying on the seat. From it, he produces a series of cards featuring simple cartoon-like illustrations and accompanying words. He shows them to Rory.

'Lesley's speech therapy cards,' he explains.

When Rory sees the images, he is reminded of his godfather, who used to work as an illustrator and cartoonist before he died. Rory still has all the cartoon characters Tom created for him. And his own weak attempts at copying them.

'Hey, Louise!' Mark calls.

Louise turns.

'OK. Now, I want you to close your eyes. When I ask you to open them, I want you to look at the card I'm holding up, and tell me what you see.'

She raises a dubious eyebrow.

'Humour me.'

She closes her eyes.

He holds up a card. 'OK. Tell me. What do you see?'

'That would be a sheep, Mark.'

'A what? Could you repeat that word, *slowly*.'

'A sheeeeep.' She looks at Rory, laughing.

He is in a different zone, remembering how Tom used to bring him off on his own (no Owen, no Siofra), to the movies, the pool, the park. He was not like his older brother, Rory's father. He knew the meaning of fun. Even facing death, he joked. Which made Rory, aged fourteen, want to shout at him, tell him to shut up, there was nothing to laugh about.

Mark is glancing into the car that has pulled up on their right at the traffic lights. A Mercedes. Top of the range. Living room on wheels. In front is a blonde woman, in her fifties, wearing oversized black shades. Mark sits up. 'Hey, let's try it out on her.' He rifles through the cards, then holds up a picture of a cow and shows it around. 'What d'you think?'

'She'll think you're calling her a cow,' Louise warns.

'Nah,' he says, looking mischievous.

'Mark, don't,' says Lesley.

The woman glances across. Mark slowly raises the card. Then he moves it up and down. The woman lowers her shades, takes a closer look. Her appalled expression makes everyone laugh – everyone except Rory who is thinking about death. The woman turns to the driver next to her. Within seconds, he is leaning forward, glaring into their car.

'Shit,' says Mark, ducking his head back. 'It's Mulcahy.' A consultant oncologist at St Paul's, known for his lack of humour. And love of his wife. 'Drive, Lesley. Drive.'

'God, he's for the birds,' Louise laughs, as she and Rory watch the other couple drive off.

'Mmm.' Rory starts to walk towards the apartment.

'What's wrong with you?' she asks. 'Don't tell me you didn't think that was funny?'

'Yeah, it was funny.'

'You don't sound like it was.'

He wishes she'd leave it. 'OK, so, no. I didn't think it was particularly funny. I don't know why everything has to be a joke with him.'

'Come on, Rory. That's just the kind of thing you'd do.'

'No, I wouldn't.'

'Not any more,' she says.

He looks at her. And silence falls between them. He wants to say that maybe life's too short to waste on practical jokes, but that would only prove her point. Clearly, he has lost his sense of humour.

Last time Owen asked to meet Rory for a drink was well over a year ago, when he scrounged a pair of rugby tickets from him for someone influential at work. Rory, wondering what he wants now, suggests his local. Let Owen come to him.

He's already there and halfway through a pint when Rory arrives. Owen stops a passing bar-boy and looks at Rory. 'What are you having?'

'Coke,' Rory says, followed quickly by, 'Can't stay long.'

When they're alone again, Owen says, 'So, you heard what we got for the house?'

Rory nods. 'You did well.'

Owen seems pleased with himself, as though the result is down to him. 'The auction was a real blood bath.'

'I didn't know you'd gone to it.'

'Had to keep an eye on those estate agents.' He takes a long drink. Puts his glass down. 'So,' he says, his voice light, chatty, 'Jenna tells me you've been helping Orla look for a place.'

Something tells Rory to be wary. 'That's right.' The previous day, they'd gone viewing again, a different experience when you know you've enough money, when you can look at places and really imagine yourself living there. Even Jason forgot to be angry with Rory, chatting about his mother and the fact that he'd be seeing her twice a week. Only Jenna was glum. Nowhere they saw was right for her. And Rory guessed why – she simply does not want to move.

'Mind if I ask why?' Owen says.

'Nope.' Rory's not going to tell him it's none of his business, which it clearly isn't, but he's going to at least let him work for the info.

'Then, why?' Owen sounds annoyed at having to ask.

'Why not?' is delivered with a shrug.

'I'm not sure it's a good idea.'

'Why's that?'

'It looks like you're taking sides.'

'Is *that* what you think?'

'Not me. Jenna.'

'She *said* that?'

'No, but I know she's thinking it.'

'You're that in tune with her.'

Owen ignores the sarcasm. 'Look, can I ask you brother-to-brother to not get involved?'

'In what?'

'My family.'

Rory is tempted to laugh. His *family*? 'Can I ask you something – because I really want to understand here – did you just forget the good times or did you want better times?'

There is an edge to Owen's voice when he says, 'Is that a question or an accusation?'

Rory acts innocent. 'I just want to understand. I mean, if Orla was a wagon, or boring, or unfaithful, or you didn't get on, I might get it. But . . .'

'You've no *idea* what marriage is like.' Owen makes it sound like mild torture. 'Waking every day to the same thing, no surprises, asking yourself, *is this it?*, for the rest of your life.'

Rory says nothing.

'Then you meet someone who *notices* you, *gets* you. *Fancies* you. And she's gorgeous. Makes you laugh. She doesn't ask you to empty the goddamn dishwasher. She doesn't care if you haven't put the bin out. She wants you, for you . . . Let me tell you something, Rory. Marriage kills passion. After twenty years, we were dead in the water.'

'But you still had so much. Couldn't you have revived the passion, worked at it, gone out more, gone away together? I don't know.'

'Rory. It's over. Forget it.'

Rory can't believe it. Owen is dismissing everything he had, as if it's the easiest thing to do. The quick solution. How long does he think the passion will last? Rory eyes his brother, taking in the new clothes, new hair, new attitude and sees that it's not just passion he's chasing, but youth. Rory wants to shout at him. This woman won't make you younger. You'll age at the same rate, die at the same time. And in the meantime, you've blown your family apart. 'Have you forgotten how happy you were when Jenna was born?'

'What's Jenna got to do with this?' Owen snaps. 'I've left my marriage, not my daughter.'

'Jenna sees you every second weekend, at your girlfriend's place. Her home has been sold.'

'She's OK about that.'

'D'you think? Does she seem happy to you, Owen, *honestly*?'

'Don't lecture me.'

'Not everyone gets the chance at what you had.'

Owen slams down his glass. 'And you're Mr Fucking Wonderful, right?'

'I don't think I'd have sold their home from under them.'

Owen speaks very quickly now. 'I've been very fair about that. Most men would've sold up straight away. Most men would've done everything they could to pay out as little as possible, and, God knows, if Kate got her way . . .' He stops. 'Look, Rory, I know you think I'm a shit . . .' he pauses. 'But I'm entitled by law to sell the house.'

Trust the trade union man to know his entitlements. 'And you're *entitled* to walk out on your marriage, too. Doesn't make it right.'

Owen looks like he's going to hit him. 'You sanctimonious .. .' He stands.

'Oh, sit down.' The dismissive tone Rory uses with his older brother is a first. It takes them both by surprise.

Owen sits. But recovers quickly, leaning across the table, face tight, finger pointing in warning. 'I've asked you nicely. Now I'm telling you. Stay away from my family.'

Rory is incredulous. 'If you really cared about them, you'd be glad I was helping.'

'Are you or are you not going to butt out?'

It would be the easiest thing. Rory knows it. 'Owen, you left. Don't you think it's *you* who should butt out?' Now it's his turn to stand. 'Thanks for the drink.' He doesn't look back.

What kind of person leaves the woman he loved all his life and then tries to sabotage what little help she's getting to carry on with hers? Maybe Siofra was right – maybe their brother has always suited himself. Rory was just too busy hero-worshipping him to notice. If he's ever lucky enough to have a family, he won't throw it away.

The following Friday Orla rings to cancel their plans to view property, even though one of the houses they were supposed to visit for a second time has potential.

'Jason's mum has OD'd again.'

'Is she OK?' As in, alive.

'In hospital. He's devastated, Rory. Not talking. Not crying. Just staring at the telly sucking his thumb. I feel so guilty. There I was, all along, telling him she was getting better and he'd be going home soon.'

'They told you to say that, to prepare him. How were you to know?'

Silence.

'How much does Jason know about what happened?'

'The social worker said we should be honest.'

'Do you think that's wise?'

'Right now, no. I've never seen him like this. Even the dog knows something's up. He won't leave his side.'

'Want me to come over?' Rory asks, not exactly sure how he could help, but feeling he should offer.

'I don't know. I don't know what to do.'

Driving over, Rory tries to remember how close he was to his mother at the age of eight. He has a memory of coming home from *Bambi* with Tom, and clinging to her, aware for the first time in his life, of the possibility that he might some day lose her. She was the most important person in his world then and he loved her. As the youngest, it'd often been just the two of them, especially when Siofra started school. He always remembers her voice as soft, but her laugh loud. It seemed to him that she was the easiest person in the world to make laugh. She had laughed when he told her so. Their love was physical back then; she was the source of all his hugs. She would sit him on her lap and read about Setanta, Cu Chulainn, The Children of Lir. *The Selfish Giant* made her cry. Which is why he asked her to read it over and over. When had their relationship changed?

'Hey,' is all he says to Jason when he sits beside him on the floor. He doesn't expect an answer. And doesn't get one. He makes no attempt at conversation, just keeps him company. Programmes start and end, start and end. At last, it is Jason who turns to him.

'Did you bring the ball?'

Days later, Orla asks a favour of Rory.

He laughs. 'You've got the wrong man.'

'Your relationship with Jason means a lot to him.'

Relationship seems too strong a word. Rory has a lot of time for the kid, but doubts that the feeling is mutual.

'You're the first person to show an interest in him without being paid to.'

That stalls him.

'He's lost his mum – *again*.'

'I know, but what do *I* know about kids?'

'You don't have to be a parent to know about kids. You're good with him. Great with him. The one person who got him out of himself.'

'But –'

'In my line of work, I talk to psychologists all the time, read the literature. All the experts agree, boys over six need a male influence.'

'I know, but a *mentor*? It sounds so formal.' Mentors set a good example.

'All you'd have to do is show up every so often and kick a ball around with him.'

'I do that anyway.'

'Maybe take him to the odd movie.'

Rory's best times with Tom were at the movies, the one place he could go and pretend to be someone else – brave, adventurous, always victorious. To his father, movies were frivolous. To Rory, they were an alternative reality. He thinks of Tom and realizes, for the first time, that he grew up with a 'mentor'. Words like that weren't used then. Nothing was official. But that didn't mean people like Tom went unappreciated. Rory loved him more than his own father. He may well have saved Rory's sanity.

'So, it wouldn't be an *official* thing?'

'No, no.'

Rory hesitates. 'But what about when he has to eventually go home?'

Orla smiles. 'So, you're considering it. Great.' What Rory doesn't know is that she is doing this for him as much as the boy.

'You're taking him out *every* Saturday?' is Louise's reaction.

'I thought I would, yeah. You'll be at work, won't you?'

'Yes,' she says, quietly.

'Well, then. I'll pop into the hospital a bit earlier than usual so the morning's not gone, then I'll bring him out for a while, catch a movie or something, throw a ball around. Spend a bit of time with him.'

'How much time?'

Rory wonders what her problem is. 'I don't know. A few hours. You'll be at work. I thought I'd do something useful.'

'You're a doctor. You do something useful every day.'

His voice is flat. 'I get paid.'

'So does Orla, to mind Jason. I don't understand why *you* have to get involved.'

And *he* can't understand what's wrong with her. She never interferes with his plans. He is about to point that out, but given the tension between them lately, he tries, instead, to be patient. He explains about mentoring, about what the psychologists say.

'So you mean Orla won't be with you?'

'No. It's *man* time.' He puffs out his chest to make her laugh.

'But you won't be able to meet me for lunch?'

'Of course I will.' He thinks for a moment, then adds, 'I'll just have to bring him sometimes, if that's OK. Not always. I just don't want him to feel I'm rushing him back. I'd like him to think I'm enjoying my time with him, not doing him a favour. He's a bit sensitive at the moment. His mum —'

'I know,' she says, as though she does understand but would prefer not to.

I I

Four months later

The consultant's office is like countless others Rory has been in over the years. Spacious. Bright. Comfortable. Antique furniture. Reference books. The kind of place where he'd normally feel at home. But not now. Sitting on the other side of a large mahogany desk, he is concentrating on the expression of the AIDS consultant, a blonde woman in her forties, and trying to pre-empt the result. He tries to imagine how *he* looks when breaking bad news to patients. Does he put on a poker face, or does his expression give a hint of what is to come? He can't think. Can't concentrate. She is leaning forward. Handing him the test results. And he is no longer looking at her. Rather, he is staring down at the paper that will dictate his future. She starts to talk, but he shuts out her voice, concentrating only on the written words, underlining them with a finger as he reads. He does so twice.

'This is one hundred per cent accurate?'

She nods. 'I wish the news were as good for all my patients.'

Rory tries to adjust. He had walked in there, expecting the worst. Can he really trust that after four months of limbo, this is really over? Could the horizon that had shifted so abruptly, simply have slipped back into place? And suddenly, it's as if something that has been constricting his chest has snapped free, like an elastic band. He must ring Louise. Yes, Louise, that's how he moves forward from here.

She hadn't wanted him to get the results today, Friday the thirteenth, but he couldn't wait a whole weekend knowing they were back.

Outside, he takes his wallet from his back pocket, pulls out the prayer to St Anthony, kisses it, then throws it into the nearest bin. When the nine-week novena ended, he hadn't gone back. But neither had he been able to discard the prayer. Now he is free. He has been given his miracle. The deal is done.

Louise's line is busy. So he drives to her.

When she sees his face, she drops the rose stem she has been cutting and rushes to him. 'You're OK. Thank God. You're OK. It's over.'

He pulls her to him and kisses her full on the mouth. She is crying.

Lolita, Louise's Filipino assistant, clears her throat.

Rory ignores her.

Louise pulls back. 'Lolita. You can finish up here, right?'

'Sure.'

'Great, thanks.' To Rory, she says, 'Come on. Let's celebrate.'

For the first time in four months, Rory wakes up hungry. He stretches and turns in the gargantuan bed to face Louise, savouring the feel of crisp Egyptian cotton sheets against his naked skin. Some night! They hadn't planned to stay in the hotel, just dine and down champagne. But when, mid-way through his monkfish with white asparagus and smoked bacon, red wine sauce and pomme mousseline, Louise had slid her stockinged foot up the inside of his thigh, the apartment might as well have been on another planet. After four months of press-ups, cold showers and furious jerking-off, getting to the bedroom was a test of restraint so great that had it not been for that elderly American couple in the lift, he would have (happily) failed.

Louise opens her eyes. Smiles lazily. 'Worth the wait.'

He hooches towards her until their noses meet. They lie, eye-to-eye.

'Let's get married,' he says. He has no idea where this has come from, but is shocked to realize he means it.

Louise is very still.

'Let's get married and make babies, lots and lots of babies.'

The smile that creeps across her face is deliberate. If it makes him laugh, he is joking.

He laughs.

She hits him on the arm and moves back from him in mock horror. 'You messer!'

He loses his smile. 'I'm not messing.' He raises himself onto an elbow. 'We should do it, Lou. Just do it.'

She sits up, slowly, carefully, as if sudden movement might damage something, the status quo. She reaches for her top and puts it on. She frowns at him. 'What's brought this on?'

'You make it sound like a disease.' And he is hurt. He might be as surprised as she is, but he did just ask her to marry him.

'You've practically ignored me for the past four months and now you want to *marry* me?'

'I haven't ignored you.' Has he?

She raises her eyebrows. 'The only person you seemed to have any time for was Orla.'

'That's not true.' Is it?

'So why did you only seem to perk up when she called or when you'd been over there?'

94

'Come on, Louise. That's not fair.' But he wonders if maybe it is.

'I've tried to understand,' she says. 'I've told myself that it's all down to this thing that's been hanging over us. I've been patient. I've waited. And it's over now. And that's great. But we need to get back to the way we were. Not rush into something neither of us really wants.'

Who says he doesn't want it?

'You're relieved. I am too. It's so, so great. But let's not get carried away. Last night was amazing, better than amazing, but *marriage*; you don't want that life any more than I do. This is just a reaction.'

The way she says 'that life', so dismissively, depresses him. Does it mean she will never want it?

'We've spoken about this,' she says. 'We've agreed.'

They have spoken about it. But not a lot.

'Things have been tricky between us since this started. Let's just try to forget everything, have a bit of crack, let our hair down.' She smiles. 'Fuck each other's brains out.' She kisses him full on the mouth. 'Let's just be ourselves.' When her hand snakes under the covers, the easiest thing to do is stop thinking.

Not long after, Louise leaves for work. And Rory reaches for the remote.

He leaves it until the last minute to check out. Back at the apartment, he salutes his AIDS medication as he watches it disappear down the toilet. To his reflection in the bathroom mirror, he says, 'We can rebuild you.' He throws on his training gear and roots out the iPod he has ignored for four months. From the moment he closes the apartment door, he is running. To push himself, he opts for Monkstown instead of the pier, taking the first hill with determination. Out of breath at the top, he is glad to stop for traffic. Too soon, the road clears and he runs across. He takes the second hill with a little less determination. Halfway up, he stops and doubles over, hands on thighs, stomach contracting with every breath. His mouth is parched. He pulls off his rugby shirt and ties it around his waist. He'll walk the rest of the hill.

He looks up at the weak sun of early February and notices that the trees are in bud. A blackbird flies by, twigs in its beak. Has spring been happening without him? Has a whole winter passed without his knowledge? What else has he failed to notice? Well, Louise, obviously. Her accusation caught him off guard. He'd been trying hard to hold it together, keep his worries under wraps, be the same person he always was. Clearly, he fucked up there. He starts to run again, passing a boy and girl in tennis gear, hopping out of a car and racing each other into a local club. Is she right? Is this just a reaction? They'd always wanted the same thing before, an easy, pressure-free life. Maybe if he tries, he can go back to that. A car passes, an SUV, with yummy mummy and young daughter sitting up front, laughing. His eyes follow them as they drive by. He'd like that for Louise. He wouldn't want her to miss out.

When she gets home, he has his special chicken dish ready, the table set and his laptop out.

'Something smells nice,' she says, kicking off her shoes and going to him. She snuggles up beside him on the couch and peers at the computer screen.

He looks up from an airline website. 'Let's go away for a weekend,' he says. 'My treat. Lady's choice.' He waits, half-expecting her to bring up work.

Instead, she seems pleased. 'It'd do us good to get away.'

He meets her eyes. 'I'm sorry, Lou,' he says. 'I wasn't ignoring you . . . I was just so worried.'

'I know.' She kisses him.

'About Orla –' he starts.

'Forget it.'

'It felt good, helping. I needed to be useful.'

She puts a finger to his mouth. 'It's over. Let's put it behind us.'

He nods.

Her eyes return to the website. 'How about Berlin?' she says.

'Berlin?' He was thinking of Rome. Or Paris. Somewhere romantic. 'Why Berlin?'

'I don't know. It's supposed to be beautiful. And there's the history. And the nightlife.'

He shrugs. 'OK. Sure. Whatever.'

'Hey, why don't we go as a group, for the crack? Invite Mark and Lesley, Johnny, maybe a few more. Hang out. Have a laugh.'

It's not what he had in mind, but, 'OK'. He really wants to make it up to her. He kisses her. 'I love you, you know.'

She smiles. 'Love you.'

He hopes that that isn't conditional on them both wanting the same things in life.

12

Though Saturday mornings have become *man-time*, this weekend is different. There is an inter-schools rugby friendly on Sunday, to which Rory has promised to take Jason. Given Louise's comments about Orla, Rory wonders if he should cancel, avoid seeing his sister-in-law altogether. But he has taken on this responsibility and it's working out better than he had expected. Jason has come on so well. What would Rory have done if Tom had stopped showing up? He'd have blamed himself, somehow worked out that it was his fault. He wasn't good enough. Didn't deserve it. Rory says all this to Louise.

'Rory you don't need to explain. It's fine. I'd planned to go clothes shopping with Lesley anyway. Get some things for Berlin.'

'So, you don't mind?'

'Why should I mind?'

He shrugs, not about to bring up Orla.

'Rory. Do what you like. We're not joined at the hip.' She says it lightly.

But, coming so soon after his marriage proposal, it sounds more like a statement.

Before collecting Jason, Rory drops in to the hospital to review those of his patients that needed to be seen over the weekend by the medical team on call. There is one patient he avoids, though, because he shares a room with Tadgh O'Driscoll. O'Driscoll is a retired rugby international and

TV commentator, a favourite with rugby fans nationwide, Rory included. Rory has, until now, spent more time than necessary in O'Driscoll's company, dissecting games, making predictions, discussing the competency of various teams and players. Conversation has never been a problem. Now, though, Rory is getting uncomfortably close to making a diagnosis. A diagnosis he doesn't want to make. He hopes that he is wrong. Knows that he is not. Will run more tests. Tests he doesn't need to run. And, in the meantime, he will avoid looking O'Driscoll in the eye.

Rory stands at the sideline with Jason, wondering why, all of a sudden, he can't stomach breaking bad news. It's part of his job. He's never had a problem before. Why now? Mini-rugby players run onto the pitch. Mums and dads fuss over their little heroes. Laces tied? Gum shields secure? Rory looks down at Jason. Maybe this wasn't such a good idea. His mother might be out of rehab for a second time, and, by all accounts, doing well, but Jason is still only seeing her twice a week at access visits. How must he feel witnessing all the TLC that is missing from his life?

'Rory Fenton?'

Rory turns to see one of the coaches on his way over to him. Rory played rugby with Garry Cooke in college.

After a brief chat, Garry asks, 'So. Who've you got here?'

Rory puts his hand on Jason's shoulder. 'Future international out half. Jason O'Neill.'

'Is that right? Who does he play with?'

'No one yet.'

'He wouldn't be interested in turning out with us today, would he? We're down two players. That tummy bug thing that's doing the rounds.'

Rory looks at Jason. 'What do you think? Want to give it a go? You don't have to.'

Jason eyes the pitch longingly. 'I've no uniform.'

Rory appreciates the change in him. There was a time he'd have to be bribed to do anything.

Garry takes this as a 'yes' and goes off to check his car for one.

'I got no boots,' Jason says to Rory.

'Your runners will do.'

'Gum shield?'

'Ah, you don't need one. This is a friendly.'

The whistle blows. And it's total chaos, boys of various sizes milling around on top of each other. Rory starts laughing, but then sees that he is the only one. Parents are roaring at the boys; one woman, at the referee. Rory has never witnessed such aggression. No one in rugby gives the ref a hard time. He feels like telling that to the woman with the ruddy, hamster-like cheeks who is now shouting, 'He's handling it on the ground, ref!' Rory is so engrossed with this spectator that he almost misses Jason breaking away, taking off with the ball, skinny legs pumping, face determined. Rory starts to shout. 'Come on, Jason. Go. Go, go, go. *Yes!*' Jason crosses the line and dives for the ground, though he has left the field behind, and needn't be so dramatic.

'Wahoo!' Rory shouts. Jason looks for him in the crowd. And grins.

When the game-over whistle finally blows, Jason runs to Rory.

'Ai carumba,' Rory says, grabbing him and throwing him up on his shoulders. 'You certainly ate *their* shorts.'

Jason looks thrilled with himself.

Garry runs over. 'So when's he joining?'

Jason shouts down, 'Yeah, when?'

'We'll see.' He'll have to check with Orla.

They arrive back at Orla's modest but wonderfully located three-bedroomed semi, of which she is the proud sole owner. Purchased less than a month after the family home was sold, she has been living here for almost five weeks. And loves it. A room for everyone. A garden for Lieutenant Dan. And total control.

After a gulped-down Coke, loud burp and physical re-enactment of his try, Jason charges upstairs to change.

'He's a natural, Orla. Honest to God, you should have seen him.' Rory's eyes are still alight.

Orla smiles, handing him a mug of hot chocolate. 'This should thaw you out.'

He reminds himself he's not staying. 'They want him to sign up. I think it'd be great for him to have a passion like rugby, great for his confidence.'

'I'd have to check with his mum.'

Rory didn't expect this. 'Surely she wouldn't have a problem. For God's sake, she ignores him most of the time.'

'She's still his mum. She'd have to agree to anything like that.' Orla hesitates. 'I'm just wondering, though. The access visits are twice a week now. Won't be long before Jason's going home. I can't see Naomi bringing him to rugby training every week.'

Maybe Rory could. He doesn't know, though. Sunday is his only free day with Louise. 'Maybe if he took it up now and she saw how happy he is out there, how alive, she'd make the commitment?'

Orla grimaces. 'Maybe.'

'It's not going to happen, is it?'

'Doubt it.'

Rory feels like punching something. He tells himself to relax. He can't get emotionally involved. Funny that he has to remind himself of this – he thought it'd be a problem for Orla.

'So,' she says, in a tone that closes off that line of conversation, 'how does it feel to be a free man?'

He shakes his head. 'I still can't believe it.'

'Louise must be over the moon.'

A pause. 'Yeah.'

'So, any startling revelations? Have your eyes been opened?'

'What?'

'Brushes with death have a habit of changing your life, the way you look at things.'

This is the kind of conversation he can no longer have with Orla. He looks away. 'Nah.'

'No?'

'No.' He picks up Jason's orange coat that has fallen on the floor and puts it on the back of a chair. 'He'll be disappointed about the rugby.'

'I'll talk to her, Rory. I will try.'

'Thanks.' He pushes his chair back to go.

'Never thought I'd say it, but you'll make a great dad, some day.'

He snorts. 'Not me.'

'Give me one good reason.'

'Too easy a job to mess up.' This, he decided on the sideline, remembering how his father had never come to see him play, but how Barry's dad couldn't keep away, popping up at every game like a grinning jack-in-the-box, embarrassing everyone, especially his son. Still, at least he was interested . . .

'You won't be like him,' Orla says.

'What?'

'You won't be like your father.'

'What are you, some kind of mind reader?'

'I was married to Owen for twenty years, remember? I know the impact he can have.'

'He didn't have any impact on Owen.'

She looks doubtful, but lets it go. 'You mightn't think you have it in you, Rory, but let me tell you, I've learned a lot from watching you with Jason. You're so relaxed with him, never expecting anything, never crowding him. If only I'd been like that with Jenna. Instead of suffocating her.'

He is surprised. 'You didn't suffocate Jenna.'

'So why did she run off to boarding school?'

'To study?' he tries.

'To get away from me.' She smiles at his shocked expression. 'And I don't blame her. When Owen left, she was all I had. I didn't want to lose her. Every time she went out, I'd check she had her phone. I'd expect her back on time, not five minutes late, no minutes late. Three full meals a day, no less. I tried to get her to discuss her feelings about Owen. No wonder she had to get away.'

Rory scratches his head. He was right, parenting is way too easy to mess up. Still, he'll miss the little dude.

At Rounds, next day, Rory finds himself in a bind. Tadgh O'Driscoll's various test results are there for everyone to see. Rory's senior house officer, a nurse-turned-doctor, is more on the ball than most. If Rory doesn't make the diagnosis, she will, or at least she'll ask so many questions, he'll be forced to.

So he calls it. And it's official. There's no way out. Tadgh O'Driscoll will have to be told. But what words can you use to tell a person whose muscles have delivered him a glittering career, that they are going to kill him, wasting slowly away, to a point that in no more than five years, he will be dead? How can Rory, who got off with nothing more than a scratch, be the one to tell him that? O'Driscoll has a wife, a family. Why him? Why not someone like Rory, someone whose death would leave no mark? As soon as he tells O'Driscoll, his life will be as good as over. Rory curses the newly appointed consultant neurologist who is off getting close to nature on the Galapagos Islands before assuming his post. He should be doing this.

After Rounds, Rory finds plenty of jobs to keep him busy. As the day comes to an end, he reluctantly makes his way to the bedside, reminding himself that Tadgh O'Driscoll doesn't have much time. He needs what he has – to prepare.

'Is it that bad?' O'Driscoll jokes, when he sees Rory's face.

Rory's mouth opens. And closes again.

O'Driscoll's face falls.

They're both silent.

'What did you think of the game?' O'Driscoll asks suddenly, giving them both an out.

Rory mumbles something vaguely appropriate, wishing that that was all they had to talk about.

'I'm ready,' O'Driscoll says eventually.

Motor neurone disease. Three words. One death sentence. Rory does his best to explain, soften the blow. Does his best to be hopeful, where there is no hope. Does his best not to vomit. He escapes at the first opportunity, trying not to think about the future full of possibilities that stretches out ahead of him.

13

It's the end of February and although Berlin is freezing, Mark – self-appointed tour guide – insists that the best way to see the city is by bike. They wrap up in the caps, scarves and gloves they were advised to bring, rent bicycles and take off, Mark leading the way. The pace is slow and easy as they cycle through the Tiergarten, Berlin's Central Park. Rory and Louise are side by side, chatting together like they used to. It seems easier now that they are away. Rory hangs back a little. Louise slows to keep pace. They laugh at some private joke, handlebars almost touching. No room on this weekend for heavy conversations. This is about giving Louise what she wants: to forget everything, have a bit of crack, let their hair down and fuck each other's brains out. That's what she said. And that's what he plans to deliver.

Passing a bright yellow flower shop, lit up outside, Rory slows. They should check it out, he says, to see if they could pick up ideas for Louise's shop. They stop. Their comrades cycle on, unaware they have deserters. Rory smiles as he watches their backs disappear around a corner. In a few minutes, when they are well on their way, he will text Mark and suggest they meet up later.

Without him, though, they are lost. But happy to be. After the flower shop, they cycle directionless, choosing streets only by the way they look. Slowly, the face of the city changes, the apartment blocks becoming less modern, windows smaller, architecture more basic and sombre. They guess that they have crossed over into the East. Cold now, they stop for coffee and to buy a map if they can find one. They lock their bikes together and wander towards a cobble-stoned area with prettier buildings. They rub gloved hands together and blow into them. Louise puts Vaseline on her chapped lips then kisses Rory to share.

They find both map and coffee shop, pocket one and hurry into the other. It is tiny and narrow, with high, stuc-coed ceilings and gilt-covered walls. They order pastries and hot chocolate and wrap chilled fingers around mugs. Berliners come and go – families, lovers, friends – taking it easy on a Saturday afternoon. Hats and scarves are taken off. Glasses fog up. Conversation. Laughter. Not like a city in recession. Maybe that's what Dublin needs, Rory thinks, a recession to slow people down, remind them to take their time, remember each other.

Finally, they check their map and discover that they are in Prenzlauer Berg, on the East. They are miles from their hotel, but not bothered about it. Leaving the coffee shop, they decide to stay in this quaint neighbourhood. They wander in and out of tiny art galleries and boutiques. The sun sets early. And, suddenly, they are in a fairy tale place, with soft street lighting, cobblestones and pretty, brightly lit shop windows. The restaurant they stumble upon is authentic Italian – in the middle of Germany. A culture shock. Not for the locals, though. Everyone seems to know each other, staff and customers.

When Rory takes out his phone to invite the others to join them, Louise stops him.

'Let's just text. Tell them we'll see them in the morning.'

They lock eyes, smile. And the text is sent.

'Some day,' Louise says over coffee.

Mellow and happy, Rory smiles in agreement.

'We wouldn't be able to do this if we had kids,' she adds, breaking the spell.

To Rory, it's as if she's punctuating their perfect day with a closing statement, resting a case she has been building all afternoon. Well, she's wrong, he thinks. They *could* do this if they had children. They could have cycled around Berlin pulling one of those wheeled tent-like contraptions for kids, like the families he saw in the Tiergarten. Here in the restaurant, all they'd need is a portable car seat like Daisy's. The baby could sleep at his feet. He's seen it done plenty of times. A baby wouldn't have to curtail their life. But he says none of this. Instead, he goes quiet.

They taxi back to the hotel, deciding to collect the bikes in the morning.

'You're not saying much,' Louise says, back in their room.

'Tired,' he lies.

He had planned on sex, had been thinking about it all day. Now it's the last thing he feels like. He spends a long time in the bathroom. When he finally makes it to bed, she is reading. He kisses her goodnight, turns out his light and puts a pillow over his head. But he doesn't sleep. What if she never wants a baby, what then? He needs to know where he stands. Long term. He removes the pillow, turns to look at her. Her cheeks are rosy after their day in the cold. She would have a beautiful baby.

He tries to sound casual when he asks, 'Where do you see yourself in five years, Lou?'

She laughs, lowers the book and smiles. 'What's this, a job interview?'

'Do you see yourself with me?'

'Do you?'

'I'd like to,' he answers, putting it mildly.

'Me, too.' She snuggles down in the bed so that they are lying facing each other. She wraps a leg around him, like she used to. He wonders how to make the next step. Maybe if he talks about Daisy, how cute she is, how big she's getting, how amazingly quickly babies develop . . .

Louise's eyes narrow. She takes her leg back. 'Where is this going, Rory?'

'What? Nowhere.'

'I'm not stupid.' She sits up.

He joins her. 'I know that. And I know you don't want kids right now. And I understand that *completely*, but I'd like to know about the future. Do you see yourself having kids *sometime*?'

She sounds tired when she says, 'Rory, I've just set up the business.'

'I know. I'm talking about the future.'

'The *shop* is my baby. I need to prove I can do this, OK? It's important.'

'I understand that. I'm talking about some woolly time in the future. I know we've always thought, why bother? But I don't want us to make a mistake, find out too late that we should have had a family. Neither of us is getting any younger. I just think it's something we should discuss.'

'I don't want kids. I'm not ready.'

'I thought I wasn't either. Until it looked like I mightn't be able to have them.'

'*What?*'

'If I'd contracted AIDS or something, I wouldn't have been able to, not without the risk of infecting you.'

'Oh.'

'It made me think, Lou. We're not going to live for ever. Don't you want to leave something behind?'

'That's no reason to have a child,' she snaps. 'They're little

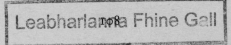

people. They can be hurt – so easily.' She looks away. When she looks back, her voice is firm. 'They change your life. Tie you down. You've seen Barry and Dee. Do you want that life?'

Yes, yes he does.

'This is a reaction,' she says. 'You know that's what this is.'

'But what if it's the right one?'

'We're happy together as we are. We've our freedom, our independence. We've each other. We can do what we want when we want – together. Go to the movies, eat out, travel.'

'We could still do that.'

'I have my career, things I have to achieve, for myself.'

'A baby needn't affect that.'

Her voice becomes emotional when she says, 'I'm not going to have a child then spend all my time giving out about it and how it ruined my life. I'm not going to be a hypocrite. I know what that does to a child.'

He speaks slowly. 'Are you saying you never want kids?' Everything around him fades.

'Don't push me into a corner, Rory.'

'I'm not trying to. I just think I should know what the story is. I think that's only fair.'

She sighs heavily. 'All I know is I don't want kids *now*. OK? And I'm not going to have them until I do.'

'What if that's too late?'

'Then it's too late.'

'You'll miss out.'

'Then I'll miss out.'

He is silent. He'll miss out.

'Not every woman has to be a mother.'

'I'm not talking about every woman, I'm talking about *us*.'

For a brief moment, Rory wishes Louise had gone through what he has – just the fright – not the injury – just so she could *see*. 'Our lives are empty, selfish . . .'

'I don't think my life is empty or selfish just because I don't want kids.' She flings back the duvet and is out of bed, walking to the window, pacing the room as though the space is confining her.

And he knows he has pushed too far.

She slows. Stops. Looks at him, her eyes wide, glassy. She speaks very slowly. 'I don't want you to stay with me, wanting something that might never happen. I don't want that pressure.' She puts her hand over her mouth, as though shocked by what she has said.

He is over to her in a flash, taking her in his arms, full of remorse.

'Forget what I said. I don't want anything. I love you. OK? I love you. That's enough. That's all I want.' He lifts her chin with his index finger, peers into her eyes. 'You're right. It's a reaction. That's all it is, a reaction.' He hugs her tightly, as though to rid his mind of any more thoughts of children. But no matter how tightly he holds her, he cannot quell the feeling that he is being forced into sacrificing something he passionately wants.

14

It's Thursday evening. Louise is working late. Rory doesn't tell her he's bringing Jason out to make up for the man-time missed when they were in Berlin. The whole subject of children has become a sensitive one. And so he avoids it.

He and Jason are queuing for popcorn at the local cinema.

'Who do you like the most, Jenna or me?' Jason asks.

Rory ruffles his hair. 'I like you both the same.'

'But you don't bring *her* to the movies.'

'No, that's true.' He lets the boy have that. He does wonder, though, why Jason cares. He's supposed to be going home. Maybe he doesn't want to get his hopes up after last time. Poor kid. It is happening, though. In two weeks, he will be gone. Rory looks down at him. He is going to miss the little guy.

'Hey! She's in my class,' Jason says, pointing to a tiny black girl with braided hair, rushing ahead of an exotic looking woman. 'I have to do Irish dancing with her.'

Rory notices the 'have to' and hopes it's not racist.

'Black people have big lips, haven't they?' Jason says, loudly.

Fuck. 'Eh, yeah.'

'Why?'

'I don't know,' Rory says, rather than getting into a discussion.

The woman in front turns around. She looks both of them up and down and then turns back.

'It's genes,' Rory explains, his voice low. 'Everyone gets their looks from their parents. Your friend's mum and dad have big lips, and their mum and dad have big lips and so on.'

Jason is quiet for a moment. Then, 'So that means that Adam must've been black and Eve must've been white or else there wouldn't be black people and white people in the world.'

'There's a thought,' Rory says, part amazed, part relieved to be reaching the counter.

They sit in the back row, waiting for the movie to start. Jason is sucking loudly on his straw. Rory never knew Slush-Puppies could be so noisy. The sound saddens him. It is a reminder of what he may miss out on. He blew it in Berlin. Why hadn't he just said he wanted to be a dad to some unique little person, yet to be created, to share the wonder of that with Louise, the woman he loves? Why did he have to bring up about leaving something behind? That's only part of it. How easy it had been when they'd both wanted the same thing. But in a way, Rory admires Louise. Would he be so totally confident in holding off on children if he had a biological clock? Then again, he does have a biological clock – as long as he is in love with a woman who has one. The lights lower and Jason lifts his face from the SlushPuppy and his eyes widen in anticipation. Rory smiles, under-standing what the hardened TV addict sees in the movies – the big screen, the treats, the escape and the feeling of being in a room full of strangers united in their love of film. Hard to believe that Jason had never been to a movie until Rory brought him. He is glad to have been able to do that for him.

*

Mid-March, Rory is throwing his rugby kit into the boot of his car after coaching when his mobile rings. He doesn't recognize the number but answers it.

'Rory?'

He stops. It couldn't be. 'Liz?'

She laughs.

They haven't spoken in over five years. The last conversation they had was to end their relationship. Rory hasn't worked out what to say, when she solves the problem for him.

'How're you doing?'

'Eh, good. *Great.*' He wonders what she wants. 'And you?'

'Good, yeah ... I was hoping you might have a free moment to meet up?'

He hesitates. 'Anything up?'

'I was just hoping you might be able to help me with something.'

'Yeah?' As in, what exactly?

'Are you free for coffee in the next day or two?'

He thinks it through. Might not be a good idea to tell Louise about this until he knows what it's about. 'I can meet you briefly, Saturday morning. Around ten-thirty?'

'Great.'

They arrange a time and place.

After he has hung up, Rory stays looking at the phone. Weird! What could she want after all this time? And why didn't she just ask him over the phone? He slams the boot shut and gets into the car. Driving home, he thinks about Liz, imagines her married with kids now. She had wanted that five years ago. Which had caught him off guard. He'd never seen her as the marrying kind. If he had, he'd never have gone out with her when she'd asked him to, at that party thrown by a mutual friend. She was the first and only techie he ever dated, a computer programmer with a grasp of maths that frightened him. Their year together was a good one. He was a model boyfriend, decent, thoughtful. Funny. Until it became clear that she had plans beyond sex and fun. That's when he'd panicked. And began to work out how he might disentangle himself. He feels guilty now, realizing what it's like to be that person who wants more. If Liz knew of his situation now, she'd probably think it sweet revenge. Then again, he has no idea what she'd think. Especially if she has, as he suspects, become a wife and mother with a full life. In which case, why would she want to see Rory again?

On Saturday, he arrives at the coffee shop ten minutes late and throws his umbrella into a stand. A quick scan reveals her sitting with her back to the door a few tables in. Dark hair, thick and wavy, posture erect. Has to be her. Liz never slumped. Well, not until their relationship began to sour.

She is reading.

'Hey,' he says when he reaches the table.

She looks up from the book. Smiles. 'Hey, yourself.'

He becomes aware that he is smiling and that it feels good to see her. 'Want anything up there?' He nods to the counter.

'I'm good, thanks.'

Rory does a double take. She sounds American. Looks the same, though. Which also surprises him – he'd imagined her different. More mumsy? Softer, maybe. But what does he know? He hangs his coat on the back of the chair and makes for the counter. He hasn't eaten but a latte will do. He's not staying long.

'So. How've you been?' he asks, pulling out the seat opposite her.

She tucks the book away in a canvas bag that suits her
sophisticated yet semi-bohemian image. Whoever said that
all techies are geeks?

'Good,' she says, 'and you? How're things with you?'

'Grand.' He stirs his coffee. 'The usual. Still in neurology.
Back at St Paul's again.'

'With anyone?'

Her directness throws him and he laughs. 'Yes, I'm with
someone. You?'

'No, no one.' She takes a sip of her espresso. 'Not that
it matters.'

Then why did she ask? he wonders. But says nothing.

'So. How serious is this relationship of yours?' she asks.

He feels like telling her to ask Louise. 'Four years,' he says,
instead.

'Wow! That's great. Congratulations. What's her name, this
lucky woman?'

He's not sure Louise would consider herself in that
category. 'Eh, Louise.'

'And what age is *Louise*?'

He shifts in his chair. Doesn't remember Liz being this
aggressive. 'Thirty-eight.'

'Kids?'

'Eh, no.' He is surprised that to validate his relationship
with Louise he feels the need to add, 'Not yet.'

She raises already arched eyebrows. 'You'd want to get
moving, then.'

It's like that moment in chess where you give up trying
to work out your opponent's strategy. He laughs – what else
can he do?

'You'd make a great father.'

The second woman in under a week who has said this to him. Pity one of them wasn't Louise. 'So you've called me up after five years to tell me to get moving on kids?'

She holds his gaze. 'In a way, yes.'

'Liz. You've lost me.'

'Sorry.' For the first time, she falters. She picks up her yellow napkin and puts it back down, running her fingers along it as though to remove invisible creases. 'I should just say it.' She folds the napkin over. 'I've been in the States, for a while now. Silicon Valley. Since we split, actually.' She looks up. 'Life's been great. A lot of laughs. A few relationships. Nothing serious. You know yourself.'

He tries to adjust to this. Maybe she changed her mind. If she'd wanted marriage, she'd have got it, wouldn't she? She's an attractive woman, with no shortage of interest ...

'But I'm tired of that life,' she continues. 'I've outgrown it, I guess. I've come home. And that's been good for me. It's made me see how pointless my life would be – without children.'

For the first time, he knows exactly what she means. She is speaking his language. She could be describing his own experience. But why is she is telling *him*?

'I'm heading for forty. I'm tired of waiting for the right guy to show up. And I'm not going to settle for someone who isn't right, just to have a baby.' Her voice becomes firm. 'I've a good setup at work. Good family support. Plenty of money.'

Rory's lips are dry. His palms damp. What is this? An offer of some sort?

'I don't need a man.'

He lets out a breath. For a moment there ...

'I've thought about sperm banks.'

That's it, sperm banks. She's come to ask his professional

opinion. Not that he's going to be much help. He hasn't a
clue about sperm banks.

'But you don't know what you're getting, do you?'

Oh.

'I've thought about a casual fling.'

Whatever rocks your boat.

'Same problem.' She is looking directly at Rory. 'You are
the smartest, funniest, loveliest guy I know.'

Oh oh.

'You're physically gorgeous.'

No *way*.

'I know you. I like you. I trust you.'

Rory thinks of Louise.

'Our energies are compatible.'

'I'm in a relationship, Liz.' For one thing.

'I don't expect anything.'

'Just sperm,' he says. It seems so clinical.

'You wouldn't ever have to see the baby.'

Baby.

'I'd never hit you for maintenance.'

It hadn't crossed his mind.

'We could sign a legal agreement . . .'

'Hang on. Slow down. Whoa!'

'Sorry.'

'I need another coffee,' he says. 'Want one?'

'Double espresso.'

At the counter, he tries to think. He glances back at her
but she is looking at him and he quickly faces forward again.
As he watches the teenager who reminds him of Jenna fill
two fresh cups, it occurs to him that he is living in the wrong
generation. Whatever happened to asking the girl you loved
to marry you, her saying yes, and off you went and had a
family? Simple. None of this *complication*.

When he gets back, he has his answer.

'You don't need me, Liz. You've millions of options. Sperm banks . . .'

'Why shouldn't I try to create the perfect baby?'

Perfect? How can *he* guarantee perfection? 'I'm flattered, who wouldn't be, but . . .'

'I want nothing from you, Rory, just that chance. No strings.'

'It's not that simple, Liz. If I was responsible for a baby coming into this world, I'd want strings.'

'You could see the baby any time you wanted.'

The baby. It sounds so real. So tangible. So possible. Outside, crowds mill past. He can't believe that of all the men in the world – or at least all the men in Liz's – she has chosen him. Given Louise's rejection, it helps. He imagines a stallion, a bucking, full-blooded stallion with a shiny black coat. A breeding stallion. Which reminds him – the logistics. He's not having sex with her if that's what she thinks. He'd never be unfaithful to Louise. But doesn't having a baby with someone else fall into that category? Not if he told Louise, included her. He almost laughs. Yeah, right, 'Eh, Louise, I've something to tell you . . .' Not that he's going to do anything anyway. He's just thinking. Working it through.

'I'm curious,' he says eventually. '*Hypothetically* how would a couple go about this?'

'Easy,' she says, perking up. 'I've checked it all out. You just provide me with a,' she pauses, 'donation. And off I go.'

'To a clinic?'

She waves away that concept with her hand. 'Home insemination kit.'

He tries not to imagine what *that* looks like or where she

got it, if she already has. 'Wouldn't a clinic be better?'

'Maybe, but in this wonderful country of ours, the only option for artificial insemination is using a sperm bank. No facility if you know the donor. Medical Council guidelines or some shit.'

The words 'Medical Council guidelines' ring alarm bells. As a doctor, he can't go against them. Then again, he wouldn't be carrying out the procedure. Not that he's doing this. But the questions are piling up. 'How many donations would it take, hypothetically?'

'Up to eight – one a month, until we hit the jackpot.'

Sounds like Las Vegas.

When he has finally exhausted every question, he says, 'Liz, I don't see myself going for this . . .'

'I'm not asking you to make a decision now. Just think about it. Please, Rory, give it some thought. That's all I ask. Think about what *you'd* do if time was running out and you knew you might never have a child.'

He doesn't have to think.

When he picks up Jason, straight after, he barely hears a word Orla says to him and now, in the car, on the way to the barber, Jason has to repeat his question three times before Rory manages to concentrate long enough to digest it. Has he ever done the splits?

No. No, he hasn't.

'I done the splits once and nearly broke me crown jewels,' Jason volunteers.

'Crown jewels?'

'Willy.'

Rory laughs. They walk into the barbers, a no-frills place where Rory has witnessed the slow, imperceptible to others, retreat of his hairline, something that worried him once. It is a short wait before being asked to take their seats, side by side, in front of the mirrors and have their hair sprayed wet. Rory looks at Jason through the mirror. The boy is sitting upright, a black cape wrapped around his neck, admiring himself. Rory looks back at his own reflection. Father material?

He'd like to think so. He should tell Louise. But he knows what her reaction would be. Theoretically, though, this is the perfect solution to his problem. He could stay with the woman he loves *and* become a father. Well, not *perfect*, but a lot closer than what's available to him at the moment. The barber says something. He has no idea what but nods anyway. What if he told Louise and she agreed that he should go ahead? Would she mean it? Or would she change her mind, too late? Rory tries to think ahead. What if he and Louise stayed together and never had children, but he had one with Liz – he'd be a parent and Louise would have missed out. Or what if they had a family together – there would always be That Other Child.

Jason is saying something.

Rory turns to him. 'Holy shit,' he says. 'Where's his hair?'

The barber, who looks more like a retired boxer, is unruffled. 'You asked for a zero blade.'

'I did not.'

'OK. *He* asked. I checked with you. You said go ahead.'

'I did not.'

'OK, then, you nodded.'

'Cool, isn't it?' Jason is turning his practically bald head from side to side.

'Jesus. What'll I tell his foster mother?'

The barber thinks for a moment, then smiles, 'Lice?'

'I haven't got lice,' says Jason indignantly.

'Not any more you don't.'

Rory gets out of his chair feeling weary. He pulls up the hood on Jason's favourite grey top, telling him it's cold outside. Jason puts his hands in his pockets, head down and slopes out as though trying to recreate a look he has seen somewhere before. And suddenly, Rory flashes back. To the attack. Then forward to the future. Jason's future. All addicts start off as innocent kids.

'I've changed my mind,' he says to the boy. 'It's not that cold. You can take the hood down.'

'Weirdo,' Jason says.

How can he let him go back to that? And in just one day.

15

Rory and Louise are driving to Orla's for Jason's mini send-off party.

'I can't believe how quickly the time has passed,' Louise says. 'I can't believe he's going back already.'

'Yeah.'

'I'll miss our Saturday lunches with him.'

Rory looks at her, surprised.

'He reminds me of myself, when I was a kid,' she explains.

'How?'

'Oh, the tough act.' He imagines her as a spunky kid that he instantly likes. 'His adult take on the world. The motherly concern he shows for the one person who should be mothering him.'

Rory puts a hand on her thigh. She never talks about her childhood. But suddenly he understands how tough it must have been.

'The way he has blossomed when shown genuine affection. You should be proud of what you've done for him, Rory.'

He *is* proud, though he'd never admit it. 'I've only done what Tom did for me.' All those years ago.

The introductions are short. The only people at the party outside of themselves and Jason, are Orla, Jenna, Orla's friend, Sal, and Naomi. After months of imagining Jason's mother, he is surprised by the reality. How young she looks.

Not much more than a child herself. A faded child with haunted eyes, tired, bleached out hair and bad teeth. She looks uncomfortable, out of place, as though this is something she has to get through, before she can take her son home. Rory has to remind himself that this is the person who put her son in danger in countless ways yet refuses to allow him to play rugby on the basis that it is dangerous. What, she's had a sudden rush of conscience now that she's clean and is overcompensating on caution? More a case of not wanting to put herself out, Rory guesses. Either way, he is amazed at how Jason accepted her ruling without question, as if afraid to upset the unsteady equilibrium that has begun to settle on their lives.

'I'm just going to talk to Naomi,' Louise says.

Before Rory can ask, 'Why in the world would you do that?' she is gone.

He sees Naomi step back when Louise approaches, but whatever Louise says seems to set her at ease.

He turns. Looks around. Jenna is talking to Sal. Jason is busy giving Lieutenant Dan more doggie treats than is generally allowed. A smell of baking comes from the kitchen. This is where Rory finds Orla taking cocktail sausages from the oven.

'How can you do this?' he asks.

'What?'

'Celebrate.'

'He's going home. It's supposed to be a victory.'

Rory considers the high-risk environment he's returning to. 'Some victory.'

'OK, then. It's called putting on a brave face.'

Rory starts lancing the sausages with the cocktail sticks she has handed him. 'What are you going to do now?'

'Miss him. Try not to. I've a course coming up. Introduction to psychology, a one-week residential course in Cambridge.'

'Cambridge?' What Rory wouldn't give to escape for a week – from the deep disappointment he feels that Louise doesn't want a family with him, from Liz's proposition that has been haunting him all week, and from the terminal diagnoses he once made without blinking but can no longer face since delivering Tadgh O'Driscoll's death sentence. 'It'd be good to get away.'

'Yeah, and it's a great course. Really good guy running it. James Bingley. You must have heard of him.' Rory hasn't. He's not into psychology. 'I've read all his books. Didn't think I'd make the course, but with Jenna at boarding school and staying with her father at the weekend, and Jason back with Naomi, I can do it. Must be fate.' Rory doesn't believe in fate. 'He does a whole module on taking control of your life. Something I could do with right now.'

Something Rory could do with too. But he's dubious. 'Do you really think a one week course could achieve that?'

'People swear by him. I've a programme here somewhere,' she says, opening a drawer. She hands it to him. 'Been reading nothing else for the past week.'

He skims it, semi-interested – until he sees that there is a module called 'getting beyond fear'. He thinks of his fear of breaking bad news, of making the wrong decision with Liz, of losing Louise if he pushes too hard for a family. 'And this guy has all the answers?' He is cynical.

'No. But he gives you the skills to help you find them for yourself. Or so they say.'

'It's probably full at this stage,' he says, talking himself out of it.

'The course?' She sounds surprised. 'I don't know. I could check. D'you want to go?'

'I don't know. Probably not.' People sitting around contemplating their navels.

'Let me check.'

'Nah. Forget it. It's probably full.'

'I'll check.'

Rory takes the plate of sausages out to the sitting room and places them on the coffee table. He sits for a moment, glancing over at Naomi. She looks so frail. How will she do it – give her child everything he needs, stay off drugs, protect him from that life? Love him? Rory's eyes follow Jason, who is heading for the kitchen. If she loved him, truly loved him, she'd understand how much he wants, *needs*, to play rugby. Too dangerous! Doesn't she think that overdosing in front of him is too dangerous, or shooting up, or leaving contaminated needles lying around? And what is Louise talking to her about anyway?

He gets up suddenly and goes after Jason, finding him at the kitchen table building up a store of crisps and asking Orla if he can take them with him. For a moment, it looks to Rory as if her heart is going to break, but she forces a smile and tells him she'll pack a bag of goodies. Rory knows it's going to be a big one.

'Hey, buddy,' he says to the boy. 'I got you . . .' (he can't seem to say 'a going away present') '. . . something small.' He picks up a large box covered in bright red wrapping paper that he has hidden in the kitchen. Inside is the only present he truly longed for as a child, a proper train set. Though his was a middle-class family, very little was spent on birthdays – on principle – his father's principle of children not turning out 'soft', and learning that they have to

125

work in life for what they want. Rory had got used to it and learned to accept that that's just the way it was. But Christmas was different. Someone else was in charge of presents. A jolly man with a white beard. Christmas was when Rory allowed himself hope. Every year he had asked in vain for a train set. When finally, 'Happy Hobo', arrived, he stopped believing. This was no train set. This was something altogether different, a standalone engine, no controls, no carriages. You pushed down on the chimney to make it go. Now, in front of him, he watches Jason's face light up as he sees, emerging from the wrapping, an electric, red-engined, six-carriage train set. Tracks. Bridges. Controls. Jason is speechless – for a change. He jumps up and hugs Rory.

'Hey, look,' Rory says, to distract himself from the emotion he feels. 'A Simpson's cake.'

Orla has just removed it from the fridge and is decorating it with candles.

'Wow,' says Jason. 'And it's not even my birthday.'

'Want to help me light them?' Orla asks.

'How come there's nine?'

'One for every month you were here.' Her voice breaks and she turns away.

'Hey,' Rory says to Jason, 'let's stick this one on Homer's ass.'

The boy laughs. 'Sicko.'

They carry the cake inside. Everyone gathers. But the gesture falls flat. There are no songs for goodbye. So Jason blows out the candles in silence. Everyone cheers. Rory watches as the boy's eyes find his mother as if to say, 'Did you see that? I got them all in one go.' Rory watches her reaction. When she smiles, he feels relief. Maybe she does love him. Maybe it was the drugs. Maybe she'll stay off. He hopes for this, yet all he sees before him is a nervous young woman surrounded by strangers, just wanting to get home with her son to the life she knows. He almost feels sorry for her. With his slice of cake, he sits beside Jenna on the couch.

'Hey,' he says.

She is looking at Jason. 'Who's he going to play chess with now?' she asks.

'You taught him? I never knew.'

'He's a real smart kid.' She pauses. 'I thought he was a pain in the ass in the beginning. Always hogging the telly.' She smiles. 'But if I'd a kid brother, I'd want one just like him. He's a tough little softie.'

Tough little softie. Rory looks at her and sees that Jason is not alone in that. He puts an arm around her shoulders and gives her a little squeeze.

When it's time for Jason to go, most of the 'party' leaves with him, Orla and Jenna driving him and his mother home, the boot full. Rory and Louise stand at their car, waving goodbye.

Driving back, Louise asks Rory if he'll keep in touch.

'I'd like to. I've said I would. But what if he gets back to his old life and just wants to get on with it? I don't want to be sticking my nose in where it's not wanted.'

She is quiet for a moment, thinking it through. 'I'd be very surprised if that happened. You mean a lot to him. If you disappeared off the scene now, he'd think you'd stopped caring what happens to him.'

'I'm not going to disappear. But I don't want to interfere. Once a week is a lot. Maybe I should cut back to once a fortnight or once a month.'

'Play it by ear. See how it goes.'

'Yeah.' He thinks for a moment. 'If it *does* peter out,

eventually, I'd like to think I've passed something on to him – a love of movies, rugby – something.'

'I imagine you already have.'

His frustration erupts. 'What good will it do if she never brings him anywhere?'

'She is going to try, Rory.'

'And you believe that?'

'Yes. I do.'

'Why were you even talking to her?'

'Because I know how tough it is for her. And I wanted to help.'

He snorts.

'I know her life, Rory. It was my mother's.'

'Your mother wasn't a junkie.' There is disgust in his voice.

And now anger in hers. 'I'm sorry, but which do you think is worse, an addiction to drugs or alcohol, because from where I'm sitting, I don't see that there's a hell of a difference. Not for the kid.'

He says nothing, appreciating how hard it was for Louise, but thinking that alcoholics don't expose their kids to AIDS and hepatitis.

'She's not the enemy, Rory. Helping her is helping Jason. I was trying to encourage her, make sure she's accessing all the support that's available to her. Believe it or not, I was trying to help Jason.'

'I was thinking of going on a psychology course,' he says to Louise, in bed, a few evenings later. There has been a cancellation. And that has decided him to go. 'It's in Cambridge.'

'You, psychology?'

'Yeah, why not?'

'I didn't think you were into that kind of thing.'

'I'm not. Usually. I just thought it might help at work.' He's told her of the problems he's been having breaking bad news. And she seemed to appreciate that he was being more open with her.

'It's still worrying you, isn't it?' she says.

'A bit.'

'And you think this course might help?'

He tells her what Orla said about Bingley.

'Hang on. You're going with *Orla*?'

'Is that OK?'

She just looks at him.

'I don't have to go if you don't want me to.'

She pinches her lower lip between her thumb and index finger. It is a moment before she lets it go. 'If you want to go, you should go.'

'Maybe I should leave it.'

She is quiet.

'I'll leave it,' he says again.

She runs a hand through her hair. 'Look, Rory. Do you genuinely think this course could sort the problem out?'

'I don't know, but I'd like to give it a try.'

'Then go. Sort it out.'

'You could come,' he says, enthusiastically, the idea suddenly occurring to him. 'Take a week off. Stay with me at the hotel. The course is only nine to five. You could see Cambridge. And we could hang out as soon as I'm finished. I could even skive off a bit. It'd do you good to get a break.' Then again, how is he going to make all these decisions if she's there with him?

She seems to be considering it. Then says, 'Nah, you go ahead. I can't leave the shop that long. Not yet. No, you go.'

'You sure?'

She nods. Then a thought occurs to her. 'Will you be able to get time off?'

'I'm due quite a bit, though I mightn't even have to use it up. This is all about patient communication. And there's a big PR push on in the hospital at the moment, thanks to some really bad press on the Joe Duffy show. They're big into courses like this.'

The hotel in Cambridge where the course is being held turns out to be a basic three-star overlooking the Cam, which looks more like a canal than a river. The lobby is busy with people checking in. Orla and Rory join the queue. In front of them is a woman of about fifty, with tangerine hair, tight-fitting clothes in various shades of purple and an enormous black shoulder bag covered with silver studs. When she gets to the desk and the receptionist hands her the keys of a 'double room', she insists that she had booked a suite. Her accent is American but diluted. Rory wonders if she will be on the course. He also wonders if he has made a mistake. Does he really want to be trapped with a group of strangers in a faded hotel for an entire week? What kind of people go on psychology courses anyway?

Finally, check-in. There doesn't seem to be anybody to help with luggage. Normally, Rory would be pleased. Problem is, the lift is out of order. And Rory's groin is killing him, thanks to an injury sustained on the pitch one evening after a phone call from Liz checking to see if he'd made a decision. He clenches his teeth as he carries both his and Orla's luggage up the timber stairs. Lights click on by sensor as they make their way up. By the time he gets to the second floor, he feels he has given himself a hernia. At least they are on the same corridor. Four doors apart.

Rory uses the free hour before registration to lie down. He pops two Ponstan and thinks about ringing Louise. Instead, he turns on his side and closes his eyes. He doesn't want distractions, just a clear head to make the decisions he has to make. He sets the alarm on his mobile in case he falls asleep.

It goes off leaving him five minutes to spare. He washes his face and grabs his key. Passing Orla's door, he can't decide whether or not to knock. This is her course. He doesn't want to crowd her. He probably shouldn't even have come. Still, he knows she'd think it odd if he went ahead without her. He knocks. And she's at the door in seconds.

'Good timing,' she says, closing the door behind her, not before he catches a quick glimpse of her room. Everything neat and put away, not still dumped at the door, as in his room.

'Are you limping?' she asks as they go down the stairs.

'Groin injury,' he says.

'I'll have a look at it later,' she says, matter-of-factly, as though talking to a kid.

He looks appalled.

She bursts out laughing. 'Joking,' she says.

They reach the registration desk, sign in and take possession of their course folders. Rory slips his name badge in his pocket, while Orla clips hers on. They scan the room. Queuing for coffee are: a thin guy with long grey hair in a pony tail, the woman who booked a suite, and an attractive, dark-haired woman in her thirties holding her folder close to her chest. Orla smiles at her as they join the queue. The two women start an 'I'm-from-Ireland', 'I'm-from-Wales' conversation that Rory avoids, concentrating on pouring coffee. It tastes stewed but he needs the caffeine so he adds as much milk as he can tolerate, then excuses himself and finds a quiet spot where he opens his course folder, checking the programme. He's here for a reason. And it's not to make friends. He sees that much of the timetable is taken up with practical sessions. What the hell are they? And what will he be expected to do?

They're called in to the conference room. About twenty tables and chairs are arranged in a semicircle. At the top of the room stands a flip chart and screen. At the rear, a woman controls the audiovisual equipment. Rory watches Orla take a seat next to the dark-haired woman. He selects one about six up from them and tries to get comfortable on what feels like garden furniture, all bamboo and floral cushions. Slouching with his legs wide open seems to be the least painful position.

A tubby man, sporting frameless glasses, stands at the top of the room. He is wearing a short-sleeved shirt though they're only just into April. A row of pens lines his chest pocket, like military honours. He introduces himself as James Bingley. When he calls out his qualifications, the woman with the dark hair, and one or two others, start taking notes with the pens provided. Rory wants to go home.

Bingley, walking into the semicircle, explains that the practical sessions will involve participants pairing up and discovering more about who they are.

'To understand others, we must first understand ourselves.'

Oh oh, Rory thinks.

Before they start, Bingley asks participants to introduce themselves to the room. One by one, they share the most basic of details. The mix is eclectic – teachers (including the dark-haired woman), social workers (the man with the ponytail), one actress (the woman who booked a suite). There is even a novelist, some guy Rory has never heard of. Still, he doesn't read much fiction, just the odd crime novel that Louise might rave about. This guy doesn't seem pompous, which is a start.

Rory is paired with the novelist, Paul Morel. They have been allocated a supervisor, Tom Denham, a stocky man in his fifties with a shock of grey hair. Their first exercise is 'simple'; to take turns asking each other about themselves. They will do this in the privacy of Denham's room, a suite. Nothing fancy, similar to Rory's, only with a sitting area.

Morel volunteers to go first.

Rory starts his questioning with something neutral – work. If he avoids getting personal, maybe Morel will reciprocate when his time comes. Unfortunately, it turns out that asking a writer about his work is akin to asking him about his life, or at least that is the case with this writer, who readily volunteers intimate details of a neglected childhood. Easy for him, Rory thinks, he probably reveals it all to the media every time one of his books is published.

The tables are turned. And the lies begin.

'Yeah, no, my childhood was grand,' Rory says.

'Perfect?' Morel sounds dubious.

'Happy, you know.'

'Never wanted for anything?'

Rory thinks of Happy Hobo, rugby matches without his father, the lack of one word of encouragement. 'No. Not really.'

'Wow. And your parents, you loved them both equally?'

Rory hesitates. He knows that if he states a preference, Morel will focus on the opposite party. 'Pretty much.'

'And why are you here, on the course?'

'To try to be a better doctor, to communicate better with patients, that sort of thing.'

'Aren't you communicating properly with them as it is?'

He asked for that. He was beginning to sound like a fucking saint. 'Well, doctors aren't the best communicators in the world, are they?'

It was rhetorical. But Morel eyes him meaningfully and says, 'No, I don't suppose they are.'

The last person Rory wants to eat dinner with is Morel. But that is what he has to do. Everyone has been asked to dine in their pairs. The idea is to relationship-build. Rory is furious. Bad enough having your life dissected for an afternoon, without having to sit opposite your interrogator for another two hours.

'At least there's wine,' Morel says, when they sit down.

Rory reaches for it, glancing over at Orla who is sharing a table with the woman with dark hair. His sister-in-law laughs. Why hadn't he got paired with her? At least they could have had a bit of fun.

'That was tough going, this afternoon,' Morel complains.

Rory stays quiet. The author hadn't seemed bothered at the time.

'Invasive,' Morel says.

'I thought you were OK with it.' His tone is challenging.

'You must be joking. I came here to learn about human behaviour, not to discuss my private life. If I'd wanted to be analysed, I'd have gone to a psychiatrist.'

That's more like it.

'Of course, you realize, I made it all up,' Morel continues.

Rory is both appalled and amused. 'You bastard! You concocted a life, then put me on the rack.'

'You didn't *have* to be honest.'

'I wasn't.'

'I know.'

They laugh. They're on the same side after all.

'I think we should object,' Rory says.

'They'd have *great* fun analysing that.'

Morel has a point. 'I guess they're not going to change the course now.'

'No.'

'So, we're stuck with each other.'

'Looks like it.'

They smile and raise their glasses. 'Cheers.'

Morel turns out to be a pretty good mimic. He has Bingley down pat. He also shares Rory's passion for rugby, movies and sport generally. When he asks him detailed medical questions, Rory has a problem answering them as they are forensically based. In fact, Morel seems to know more about forensics than he does. Years of researching crime novels, he explains. Must be a great life, Rory thinks. By coffee, the wine is gone and they move to the bar.

That's when Morel asks, 'So, tell me, why are you *really* here?'

Rory hedges. Then decides, fuck it. Morel might be just the man to talk to – a perfect stranger, who has been around, knows a thing or two about life, women. There is something about him Rory admires, not that he can pin it down to any one thing. And of course there's the added bonus that Rory will never see him again.

'Some story,' Morel says, after Rory has told him about Louise and Liz. 'So, tell me, do you *always* date such decisive women?'

'Decisive?'

'They mightn't want the same thing, but they do know what they want.'

Rory does a quick review of his relationship history. And detects a pattern. 'What would *you* do – if you were in my shoes?' he asks.

'Make a decision.'

'Very funny. Which one?'

'The way I see it, it's easy. Give them both a wide berth.'

'Even Louise?'

'Where's the future in the relationship if you both want different things?'

Morel doesn't understand. 'I love her.'

'You're considering having a baby with someone else.'

'Maybe "considering" is too strong. Mulling over. I really don't think I'll do it, not in the end.'

'So you're happy never to have kids.'

'I didn't say that. But I'm not going to finish with Louise just because she doesn't produce kids for me.'

'Why not?'

'What kind of person would that make me?'

'A smart one. She knows what she wants. What you want doesn't seem to concern her.'

'Not every woman wants a child,' he says, in Louise's defence.

'So get one that does.'

Rory catches sight of Orla, who appears to be on her way over to join them.

'Listen,' he says to Morel. 'Confidential, OK?' He looks in Orla's direction to drive home his point.

Morel follows his eyes. He seems surprised. 'Yeah, OK, sure.'

Orla joins them. Rory asks, 'Where's your partner?'

'Wanted an early night.'

'Who d'you get?' Morel asks.

'Gloria.'

'Gloria?'

'Dark hair. Takes a lot of notes,' Rory says.

'Oh, her.'

'She's OK,' Orla says.

'How did your session go?' Morel asks with a knowing look.

'I need a drink,' she says.

They laugh. 'Join the club.'

'Heineken?' Rory asks.

'Heineken,' she confirms.

'How do you two know each other?' Morel asks.

Orla explains while Rory gets the drinks.

Reaching for them, he says, 'So basically, it's her fault I'm here.'

To Morel, she says, 'I hope you went easy on him.'

'What and miss all the fun?'

Orla is serious. 'It was awful, though, wasn't it? Who'd have thought that such simple, basic questions could be so threatening? I couldn't stop crying.'

Rory puts an arm around her. 'You don't have to tell the truth, you know.'

She looks surprised. 'What would I get out of it if I lied?'

16

The following morning, Rory is still in bed with no plans to change that any time soon when the phone rings on the bedside locker, its red light flashing. He wonders who it could be. Louise would call his mobile.

'Is everything all right?' It's Tom, his supervisor. 'I didn't see you at breakfast.'

'Oh, right, sorry, slept in. I'm on my way.' What kind of course is this? Are they watching everyone or what?

Getting out of bed, Rory reminds himself not to mix wine and beer again. The Ponstan he takes has to work its way up and down – head and groin. And while he might be 'on his way', he's in no rush. He arrives to find the meeting room empty. He checks his timetable. 'Warm up', it says, whatever that means. The audiovisual person, Sally, he thinks, comes in to set up. She directs him to a room in the basement where he finds the class looking flushed and ridiculous. They are raising and lowering floppy arms and walking in a slow circle. He is reminded of a flock of tired seagulls with no sense of direction. For once, he's glad of his groin injury. He makes his excuses to the co-ordinator, and takes a seat by the wall. He suspects that he's already been pegged a troublemaker; drinking till late, sleeping in and opting out of team activities.

The seagulls have landed. Next exercise: staying in the circle, pass an imaginary tennis ball from person to person, gradually speeding up, then changing direction. Rory and Orla exchange glances. She grins and crosses her eyes at him. It's weird watching her as part of a group. She looks fun. Cheeky. Cool. If he didn't already know her, he'd have gravitated to her naturally. He admires the way she is embracing this, despite its craziness, despite the tough time she had yesterday. He should really get more involved.

Next session and Bingley is standing in the path of the projector, unaware that words are being superimposed on him. Breathless, he is talking of Freud – or at least he was, ten minutes ago, when Rory was listening. While everyone around him is taking notes, some constantly, others selectively, Rory is doodling, filling his page with cubes and pyramids. He should say no to Liz. Definitely. But what about Louise? He doesn't want to lose her. Then again, he wants kids. With Liz's offer, everyone could have what they want. Only he can't bring himself to tell Louise. He's going round in circles here. Why can't he date women as indecisive as he is? He'd be able to talk them round – when he finally made up his own mind about what he wanted. The irony is, he has ended up with decisive women because of his own indecisiveness – always letting them make the first move. And the last, he realizes now, finally facing up to the habit he has of making life so difficult for them they're forced to end it. He runs a deep and fast line through the page and turns it. He zones back in on Bingley, who has great patches of perspiration under his armpits. Rory is tempted to take him aside and suggest Botox.

After another ten minutes, Rory's concentration slips again. His eyes wander around the room. Morel is gazing at Orla, who is concentrating on Bingley. The guy with the grey hair (Adam?) is alternately rubbing and scraping the top of his head. Fungal infection, Rory guesses, before looking away. Samantha, the actress, seems to be eyeing Rory up. Or is she? He is not waiting to find out. He drops his eyes to his jotter and doodles with sudden purpose.

On his sixth cloud, he begins to zone out. Bingley's voice comes and goes. Rory's thoughts drift back to decisive women. Easy to encourage your partner to set up in business when all the risks are hers. He flings his pen down, stands suddenly and leaves the room, failing to notice the glare Bingley gives him.

He walks outside and over to the river where he sits on the weathered lock, relieved to feel the breeze on his face. He watches a nearby barge, its paint faded and chipped, its tired curtains pulled shut, the only sign of life a thin trail of smoke rising from a rusted metal chimney and a part-wolfhound mongrel stretched out on deck enjoying sheltered sunshine. Rory feels like joining him. Must be a kindred spirit living here, Rory thinks, someone who, like him, has opted for a free and easy life. Only there is romance to this: taking your home on a slow trip up a river, your dog at your side. The door of the barge opens and a hippie with Rastafarian hair and bare feet steps out. He drags on boots and lifts an old racing bike that has been propped up against the window ledge on to the towpath. Slowly he cycles off. The dog briefly raises his head and goes back to sleep.

'I was wondering what happened to you.' It's Orla, leaning against the lock beside him. 'What are you doing out here?'

'Do *you* think I'm indecisive?'

She laughs, surprised. 'I don't know. Do you?'

'Don't know.' It would be the perfect quip, if he were joking.

'Would it be so bad if you were?' she asks.

'It wouldn't help.'

She slides her hands into her pockets and looks down at her feet, crossed casually one over the other. After a few moments, she speaks. 'I think you're pretty decisive for someone who grew up being told he was useless, that he shouldn't try because he'd fail. You can't expect to sail through decision-making with the same ease as someone who grew up being told they were great.'

Rory may have a problem with his father, but he still feels he should defend him. He is family. 'He wasn't all bad.'

She raises an eyebrow.

'He didn't want us to get cocky.'

'I might believe you if I hadn't been subjected to him myself. First time I met him, I thought he hated me. I thought I'd done something wrong. Took a long, long time and a lot of family get-togethers to see it wasn't me; it was him. He's a bully. He enjoys upsetting people. And I get so *angry* when I think of him being like that with his own kids, who were too young and then too close to him to appreciate that it was his problem, not theirs. There you all were, trying to love him, look up to him. And he cut you down at every turn.'

'All fathers were like that back then. It was their generation. We've turned out OK.'

'Owen, Mr Union Head, making a career out of his hate for authority figures. Siofra, opting for a safe civil service job because she didn't have the confidence to follow her dream of being a musician. At least you believed in yourself enough to go to college.'

Much of what Orla has said is so uncomfortably true that Rory is glad to prove her wrong on this. 'I didn't go to college because I *believed* in myself. I went to spite him, to do the very thing he didn't want me to do – medicine.'

She looks surprised. 'Why didn't he want you to do medicine?'

'Because that would have made me like him. A doctor.

He couldn't have the person he hated turn out like him, could he?'

'He doesn't *hate* you, Rory.'

'So why did he try to turn me off his noble profession?'

'Maybe he'd have tried to turn you off anything you tried.'

'You know what pisses me off? How *hard* I tried to please him, to make him notice. If I played better, maybe he'd turn up at a match. If I studied harder, maybe, for once, he'd say "well done". You know when I gave up? When I got the highest marks in the country in the Leaving Cert. and he still didn't open his mouth.'

'So the only reason you did medicine was to spite him?' Orla sounds dubious as if there were other, more honourable, *subconscious* reasons.

He's going to put her right about that. 'No. Not just that. I wanted him to fork out for a nice long stint at uni, to make him pay for being so tightfisted all my life. Seven years felt about right.' He eyeballs her. 'So what do you think of me now?'

She slips her arm into his and leans on him. 'I think you're great.'

She thought that of Owen too. So much for her judgement.

After a silence, she asks, 'Do you like being a doctor?'

He's annoyed by the question. 'You know I do.'

'So you've your father to thank for something after all.'

He is suddenly furious. 'You've it all sorted.'

'If I had, do you think I'd be here?'

He stands, letting her arm slip from his, and walks towards the hotel.

She follows, saying nothing until he has stopped to hold

the door open for her. 'If you want to be decisive, listen to your gut.'

His reply is an upward movement of his chin. He has spent so many years mistrusting it, he's not sure he can hear it any more.

Rory has mentioned his 'girlfriend Louise' a lot in the last half-hour. Even if he didn't have a girlfriend, he'd have invented one. Samantha seems to have had too much to drink and has come over all touchy-feely. At the third mention of Louise, though, she dances off towards the bar, then in behind it. The barman looks nervous, as though trying to figure out if he should ask a paying customer to leave or if he should humour her. He opts for the latter while simultaneously trying to keep his distance and get on with his job. It's late and there are not many left in the bar – Rory, Orla, Morel and Gloria and a young couple sitting up at the counter, a teacher and a social worker from the course. Their bodies lean in towards each other, the attraction between them obvious. Orla can't take her eyes off them. Wistfully, she says, 'They probably don't even notice how much they touch.'

Samantha is salsa dancing closer to the barman. When she reaches him, she pulls him to her. He is shorter than her and his face ends up in her chest.

'Death by bosoms,' Gloria deadpans.

This, from someone so seemingly conscientious, causes an eruption of laughter.

Rory is first to recover. 'Maybe someone should rescue him.'

Orla calls to Samantha as if there is something she wants to tell her. Rory is surprised when the actress responds, dancing out from behind the bar and over to them in four-inch wedges. He wonders if she has South American blood in her. She can really move.

'Yes?'

Orla hesitates, unprepared. 'Eh, I was just wondering where you got your top. It's really lovely.'

Samantha looks down and sees cleavage. She squints at Orla. 'Are you *mocking* me?'

'No. God, no.' Orla is blushing.

'I might have had a few drinks, but I'm no fool.'

'Of course you're not. We're *all* having a few drinks.' Orla looks mortified.

'Do me a favour,' Samantha says, totally sober. 'Next time you've nothing to say,' she pauses, 'don't say it.' She turns, chin in the air and dances back to the bar.

Orla drops her face into her hands and groans. 'I wasn't laughing at her. I mean, I did, at the bosom thing – I couldn't help it. Oh, God. Someone take me outside and shoot me.'

'I volunteer,' Morel jokes, then gets serious. 'Don't worry about it. Here, let me get you another drink. My round.'

Rory was beginning to wonder if the Englishman knew the meaning of the word. As for Gloria, she hasn't exactly been blazing a trail to the bar either.

When the drinks arrive, Gloria reaches enthusiastically for her fresh Cinzano. 'So,' she says to Morel, a man she normally seems to have difficulty making direct eye contact with, 'why is a *novelist* on a course like this?'

Is she flirting or just in awe? Rory wonders.

Either way, Morel is totally at ease with the question. 'To learn more about human behaviour. I thought it would help with characterization, motivations, that sort of thing.'

At the words 'characterization' and 'motivations', Rory

feels like asking for a sick bag. Gloria looks like she might swoon.

'But in actual fact,' the author continues, 'I'm learning more about human behaviour right here.' He eyes the love-birds at the bar, then Samantha, who is helping the barman pull a pint. It all seems innocent now, which makes Rory wonder if he just misinterpreted. 'What old Sweaty Pits says about actions speaking louder than words is only partly true,' Morel continues. 'You can tell a lot from words, maybe not always in the way they're meant. Take the way people talk to me about my books . . .'

Do we have to? Rory thinks.

'No matter what they say, I always know what they're thinking.'

Orla and Gloria lean towards him.

'If they say their *friend* loved it, they didn't themselves. If they say they *enjoyed* it, they thought it was OK. If they "really enjoyed" it, they thought it good but flawed.'

'So how do you know if they really did like it?' interrupts Orla.

'Oh. They say they *loved* it. Or else just keep talking about things that happened in it.'

Rory gets up and stretches. 'I think I'll call it a night.'

Back in his room, he calls Louise, surprised she hasn't been in touch.

'How's the course going?' she asks.

'OK.'

'Good.'

Good? He'd expected something like 'only OK?' and some concerned probing. 'I miss you,' he says.

'You too.'

'What are you up to?' he asks.

'Nothing much. The usual.'

'How's work?'

'Fine.'

She seems so far away. 'You'd hate it here.'

Her 'why?' sounds like it's being asked because it's expected of her.

He struggles to make a connection. 'You'd have to carry a hot-water bottle around, the hotel's so damp.' She'd done that in the first apartment they'd rented together, a draughty first floor of a Georgian building that has since been sold, creating another Dublin multi-millionaire ex-landlord.

'What are the people like?' she asks.

He thinks of Samantha, Morel and Gloria. 'OK.'

'How's Orla?'

'Orla!' He laughs. 'Unbelievable. You wouldn't recognize her. Last to bed. Drinking like a fish. Mixing with everyone. But still turning up for every lecture, really getting involved. The only place I can keep up with her is at the bar.'

Louise is quiet and it occurs to him that he's done it again – become animated when talking about his sister-in-law. 'Love you,' he says.

'I better go,' she says, her voice higher.

'Don't,' he says, but she has hung up.

17

Next morning Rory comes back from a toilet break to see that they've broken for coffee. Morel is pouring a cup for Orla. There's something protective in the way he hands it to her. She smiles at him. They look cosy together, a unit. Morel's body language subtly says, 'Do not disturb'. So Rory does exactly that. Orla seems happy to see him. Morel, he feels, pretends to be. Rory peers at his sister-in-law. Doesn't she see that Morel is into her?

During the next lecture, Rory watches Morel, whose eyes keep drifting to Orla. She's too busy taking notes to notice. When Bingley finally decides to halt for lunch, and everyone starts to file from the room, Morel makes his way over to her. Instantly she brightens and they fall into easy conversation. At the buffet, Morel stays by Orla's side. She's not exactly shooing him away. She seems animated but there's an innocence to it, as if she's simply happy, as if she sees him as a friend. She'd want to watch out, Rory thinks, Morel is interested – and married. He wonders about that – the author wears a ring but doesn't talk about his family, except in sessions, when he can't exactly avoid it. Other people talk openly about their families. Why doesn't he? Isn't he happy with his?

Orla selects an empty table. Morel positions himself next to her. Rory has had enough. He scans for an available seat with its back to them. There is a last one free beside Samantha, not ideal, but better than watching Morel drool into his lunch.

Samantha is talking about star signs.

Rory examines his pasta. Salmon in dickey-bows.

'So, what are you?' she asks Rory.

He looks up. 'Sorry?'

'What sign?'

'Eh. Virgo.'

'Oh, like me. And your Chinese sign?'

'Haven't a clue.'

'What year were you born?'

He tells her, noticing while he does that her eyebrows are pencilled in.

'Then you're a pig.'

He laughs. 'That's not very nice.'

'Pigs,' she tells him, 'are sociable and popular.'

'That would be me, all right,' he smirks.

'They hate conflict and rarely argue.'

'Is that right?' He'd prefer to be a lion.

'Pigs like to have a cause,' she continues. 'And will often rally others to it.' Now, that, he thinks is wrong. His whole problem is that he has a cause and he can't get Louise behind it at all. He listens politely but eats fast, skips dessert and is out at the lock, which, short of peeing on it, he has now claimed as his territory. He leans back against it, closes his eyes and holds his face to the sun. It's got to be at least five degrees warmer here than at home. He thinks of home, and Louise, pulls his mobile from his pocket and switches it on. Messages, yes. But none from Louise. He calls her.

'Hey,' he says, cheerfully.

'Hi.'

'How are you?'

'Busy.'

'OK. Won't keep you, then. Just called to tell you that

Orla has . . .' He is about to say a secret admirer when she cuts across him.

'I'm really busy here, Rory. I have to go. I'll call you later, OK?' The line goes dead.

He closes his phone, thinks for a second, then opens it again and texts Louise the news. But before he sends it, he deletes it. Maybe she doesn't want to hear about Orla at all. He puts his phone back in his pocket, tilts his face to the sun again, closing his eyes. He stays like this until it is time to go back in, at which point he gets up and walks in the opposite direction, along the river, towards Cambridge centre. Morel and he are supposed to pair off again this afternoon. Morel, he knows, will have no problem talking to the wall.

The day is bright and optimistic, on the verge of hot. On a whim, Rory hires a punt from one of the numerous college students selling guided tours or simple unaccompanied boat rides. He opts for the latter. With difficulty, he manoeuvres the punt out onto the lazy river with the long pole provided. Each side has traffic going in the opposite direction. He tries to get in line, but his lack of experience as a Cambridge gondolier shows and he drifts into the path of oncoming traffic. He almost loses his pole. Finally, he develops a rhythm and sense of direction and relaxes enough to enjoy the pleasure of doing something purely physical, no analysis, no difficult questions. Just survival. The river is busy, mostly with tourists. There is much for the photographers among them to capture – the imposing university buildings whose grounds they are gliding through, Canada geese grazing on the grassy banks, and the many bridges they have to manoeuvre their way under. A young American takes loud pleasure in careering out of control and into Rory, her laughter drowning that of her party. Rory smiles and untangles himself, while an older couple in a nearby boat, tutt-tutt at the disturbance.

He recovers in an Internet café with a giant mug of coffee and a newspaper. He comes across an article on sperm donation. Some teenagers in the States are trying to trace their sperm-donor fathers. Rory wonders why they'd do that. If a man donates sperm, that's all it was to him. Sperm. He doesn't think of it as a child. He won't want it coming back to haunt him. The world, he thinks, is just getting stranger and stranger. He closes the newspaper.

Activating the Dell in front of him, Rory sets about easing the computer game withdrawal symptoms he has been plunged into since leaving home. He should have remembered to bring his PSP. After a few bouts of stick wrestling and an old-fashioned game of space invaders, he is beginning to feel better. He goes into YouTube to watch rugby highlights and leaves the Internet café feeling more relaxed than he has all week. The rest of the afternoon is spent wandering around the shops, selecting presents for Louise: a book on small businesses and marketing, a hot-water bottle, though it's heading for summer, the latest yoga gear, a holder for her incense sticks. And a giant bar of soap guaranteed to lodge at her breasts when she tries 'playing' with it in the bath.

When she doesn't ring that night, he does.

'You sound like you've a cold,' he says.

'A bit tired. That's all.' She sounds it.

'Were you in bed?'

'Yeah.'

'Sorry. Will I call back in the morning?'

'If you want.'

There's enthusiasm. 'Love you.'

Silence.

He's not going to say it again. If she doesn't want to, fine. 'Good night,' he says.

'Night.'

The following morning, Rory disconnects his phone from the charger. He's about to ring Louise, as promised. But stops. He's tired of being the one to make all the calls, only to be fobbed off. If she doesn't want to talk to him, fine. If she insists on thinking the worst of him, let her. She's just going to have to start trusting him. He shouldn't feel guilty about his friendship with his sister-in-law. He shouldn't have to watch every little thing he says to Louise about her. He goes down for breakfast in a foul mood.

Orla and Morel are leaving the restaurant as he arrives, Orla laughing at something the writer has said. Rory just about acknowledges them. Breakfast is stewed coffee and cold toast. He arrives late for the lecture, and couldn't care less. When it emerges, as Bingley drones on, that Orla has started to return Morel's glances, and even initiate a few of her own, Rory feels like standing up and saying, 'Would you both just cop on.' Then he reminds himself it's none of his business.

After lunch, when everyone is getting ready to pair off, Orla and Morel are missing. Also gone is Adam of the itchy hair. Bingley expresses his disappointment at the fall off in attendance, looking primarily at Rory, as though he's to blame for setting a bad example. Rory is close to suggesting he hold the course in a hotel surrounded by a desert in future. What does he expect? Of all people, surely a psychologist knows he's dealing with human beings.

So utterly pissed off is he that he doesn't care when he is paired with Samantha, normally Adam's partner.

'Why don't you go first,' he says, not in the mood for talking.

He half-expects her to argue, 'No, you.' If she does, he will walk.

She pulls her chair closer and with no meandering says, 'I'm here to learn how to cope with cancer.'

Whoa! he thinks. Back up. This woman does *not* have cancer. She's too . . . he's not sure . . . flamboyant, jolly? Must be a relative. Or maybe she's playing the part of a cancer sufferer in some production somewhere . . .

'I was diagnosed nine months ago.'

Shit.

'Colon. I've been operated on, had the chemo.'

He glances automatically at her hair. She has a bright pink scarf wrapped around it.

She touches it and smiles in fake seductiveness. 'I'm not a natural redhead.'

He doesn't know what to say. 'I'm sorry.'

'Don't be.'

'I mean . . .'

She waves away his awkwardness. 'So, what are *you* here for?' she asks, as though they're prison inmates.

He pauses a moment, wondering if he should say it. It's like a bad joke. 'I've a problem breaking bad news to patients.'

Her whole body shakes as she laughs. 'A match made in heaven.'

He manages a smile.

'So,' she says. 'What *is* your problem with breaking bad news?'

He shrugs. 'I just can't do it.'

'Why not?'

He explains, summarizing with, 'Survivor's guilt, I guess. I got off, they didn't.'

'Ah!'

They're quiet.

'When *you* were told,' Rory says, 'the doctor, did he . . . she . . . do an OK job? I mean, what I'm trying to say is, *is* there a right way of doing it?'

She frowns, looks down, as though trying to remember. 'I don't know. It's such a shock. You're not really concentrating on the person who is telling you; you're just trying to take it in. Your life has stalled. You're just so stunned.'

Rory knows that feeling.

'I'm trying to remember,' Samantha continues. 'My doctor. He was straight. The English usually are, I find.' She smiles, as though they share something by being outsiders. 'But that was good. If he'd tried to comfort me with platitudes I might have hit him. I remember him being very patient, waiting while the truth sank in. Then answering every question, though they came in no logical order and I'm sure I repeated myself.'

Rory is nodding, taking it all in.

'You know what?' Samantha says. 'He *was* good.'

'He wasn't nervous, telling you?'

'He didn't *seem* to be. If he had, I guess I'd have been even more terrified, imagining he was hiding something.'

Rory nods. It makes sense. Still, he's not sure that knowing the downside of being nervous will make him any less so.

'Can I talk about acting?'

He's bemused. 'Sure.'

'On stage, if all you think about is yourself and how well you're performing, how you appear, what you're doing, you're going to be self-conscious, you're going to *die* – excuse the pun.' Rory notices how well she speaks, her voice and enunciation so clear. He imagines her on stage, her voice projecting effortlessly. 'But,' she continues, 'if you think of your *audience* and giving them what *they* need, the result will be different. Better.' Her voice returns to normal. 'If I were you, I'd focus on the patient, on what they need to know, what they might want to ask, but don't know how. It's not your fault that they have what they have but it is your *job* to make it easier for them.'

He summarizes, mainly for himself. 'Concentrate on the patient, what they need to know, how to make it easier for them . . .' If nothing else, it's a start, somewhere to work from.

'You should read Elizabeth Kubler Ross,' she says.

'*On Death and Dying*? I've read it. I know the principles.'

'Read it again. After what you've been through, it might mean more now. Her books have got me this far. She's my saviour.'

'How *are* you?' he asks.

She laughs. 'Well, you've probably gathered, along with everyone else, that I could drink less . . . When you're my age and alone in a country that isn't your own and something like this happens, it hits you hard. You don't have anyone. Your friends have their own lives, their families. You think about death and the fact that you have no one to pass anything on to. I'm not talking money, I'm talking wisdom, the little things you learn along the way . . . mostly when it's too late . . .' She smiles.

This makes so much sense to him.

'I may get through this,' she continues, 'I may not. It's the not knowing that's hard.'

'I know.'

'You do. I can hear it in your voice. And you should use

that. Just like I use how I feel on stage.' When their session is finished, Rory's preconceptions of Samantha have been blown out of the water. Feeling a real fondness towards her, he does something very unusual for him, he hugs a woman other than Louise.

'Let's go AWOL,' he says, remembering a restaurant he passed the previous day.

Next morning, walking out into the corridor, Rory sees Orla's door open. He is about to call out but something stops him. She is glancing back into the room, talking to someone. He hears Morel's voice and ducks back into his. He has seen this so many times, at so many medical conferences, whirlwind attractions, passionate affairs, regardless of personal situations. He has never been tempted. Life is complicated enough. But Orla! Orla's an angel. Isn't she?

In the conference room, Morel moves places to sit beside her. They're behaving like the young lovers perched at the bar every night. It's like a light has been switched on in Orla, adding colour to her skin, life to her eyes, lightness to her movements. She seems younger. Happier.

When they break for coffee, Rory doesn't hang around. In the bar, Gerry produces a perfect cappuccino and Rory wonders why he never thought of doing this before. He drinks in silence, enjoying the barman's easy presence as he goes about his business, drying glasses. No talk. No psychobabble, no analysis. Just perfect, perfect silence. Until Rory's peace is disturbed by a 'Hey!'

He turns.

Orla. Damn.

He forces a smile.

'Have you been avoiding me?' Her voice is jokey.

'Coffee's better here.' He nods to his cup.

She sits up beside him.

'Cappuccino?' he asks.

'Thanks.'

He orders it.

'You don't approve, do you?' she asks, quietly.

'Of what?'

'You know what.'

'It's none of my business.'

'I can't explain it, Rory.'

'I'm not asking you to.'

They're quiet. Her cappuccino arrives. She talks into it. 'I never thought I'd feel like this again, being so attracted to someone. I never thought *anyone* would be attracted to me. It's mad, I know, but I feel young again. Alive. I want to be with him all the time, hear what he has to say, tell him things.'

It reminds Rory of Owen's reasons for leaving his marriage. He wonders if humans really are cut out to stay faithful to one partner all their lives. Or if Owen was right — the marriage really was 'dead in the water'.

'He has a wife and kids but I don't feel guilty. And I don't know why.'

Rory can't help her there.

'This course has been so intense. In so many ways. But it's been good for me, Rory. For the first time in a long, long time, I'm doing what *I* want. I'm having fun, staying up late, drinking too much, and I don't care. I've got to know people I'd never have otherwise met, I've allowed myself to let go, be attracted to people I get on with, people who make me laugh.'

He'd noticed.

'I've started to remember who I am, or at least who I was before I became a wife, mother, ex-wife, before I became defined by other people.'

He thinks he prefers the Orla who was defined by other people. She was safer.

'You're not saying much.'

'I'm glad for you, Orla. Honestly. But you don't need my approval.'

'I'm not looking for it,' she says, her tone changing. 'I just wanted to tell you. I wanted you to understand.'

'Be careful, that's all. I've seen guys like . . .'

'I can look after myself.'

Morel comes into the bar.

Orla's face lights up.

'They're starting up again,' Morel says.

Orla hops up and goes to him.

Rory watches them leave, wondering if they'd agreed she would come and talk to him, like a child that needed to be placated.

That afternoon, in their pairs, unsupervised, Morel is all buddy-buddy. He asks Rory what he thinks of the tutor who does the warm-up sessions.

Rory is non-committal. 'Big feet.'

Morel looks over at her. 'Jesus, you're right. They're enormous.' Then as an afterthought, 'of course, you know what that means?'

Rory knows what it's supposed to mean – for men.

'Big flaps,' Morel says.

It takes Rory a second. Then he laughs – at the sheer schoolboy humour.

'I'll tell Orla,' he warns, jokingly.

Morel laughs.

Rory waits for him to stop, then looks straight at him. 'Don't mess her around, OK?'

'I've no intention of messing her around.'

Rory knows that whether or not Morel means to, he already is.

18

In the bar that evening, Samantha and Rory are talking about the things they'd like to do before they die. It is not a morbid exchange, just practical, the conversational equivalent of going through a to-do list. When they come to the subject of children, the tone changes.

'It's too late for me now,' Samantha says, regret creeping into her voice.

Up at the bar, Orla laughs at something Morel has said. Samantha and Rory automatically look up.

'What about fostering?' he says. 'Orla had this great kid, fantastic little fellow, natural rugby player. He was learning chess.' Rory, who didn't get a chance to see Jason before leaving for Cambridge, wonders how he is doing. 'A survivor,' he says, for himself.

'You said, she "had" him. Where did he go?'

'Back to his mother.' Rory is surprised by the emotion he feels.

'That would be my problem,' she says, 'giving a child back. I'm not sure I could.'

'It *is* hard. But not all have to go back. Some need permanent homes. I think you just sign up for long-term fostering. Orla didn't mind either way.'

'I wouldn't be suitable though, would I?'

Rory curses his stupidity. How could he have brought up fostering given Samantha's prognosis? Why didn't he *think* before opening his mouth?

He is about to apologize when she says, 'I'm a bit long in the tooth.'

'No. No. I wouldn't think so. The rules are nowhere near as strict as they are for adoption. Orla's separated and she'd no problem.'

'It's something I've never considered,' she says, sounding like she might yet. 'It would give me something to aim for, look forward to.' She reaches out and squeezes his hand. 'Thank you, Rory. You've given me something to keep me going – through this.'

If he'd thought about her illness before he'd spoken, he never would have.

Rory wakes the next day, knowing what to do about Liz. It is a gut feeling and before he starts to question it, he picks up the phone. He stands, having heard somewhere that it makes you sound more authoritative.

'Sorry for taking so long to get back,' he says.

'It's OK.'

He senses her eagerness. Is deliberately firm when he says, 'I've made my decision.'

Silence at the other end.

'I'm sorry, Liz.'

'What does that mean?' She sounds impatient. 'If it's a no, say it's a no.'

He pauses, knowing what he's doing to her, and regretting it. 'It's a no. I'm sorry. I've given it a lot of thought. I can't do it.'

'Why not?' There is desperation in her voice.

It's important to him to get this right. 'Because it takes two people to make a baby –'

'*What?*' she interrupts before he can finish. 'Don't you

think I know that? Don't you think that's why I *asked* you? What are you *talking* about?'

He takes a deep breath. 'You asked me to be a sperm donor. But if you get pregnant, I become a child donor.'

'That *is* the point.'

'I'm not going to *donate* any child I'm lucky enough to have. If I'm going to be a father, I want to be a father, twenty-four/seven.'

'You could do that. I've said that to you.'

'I'm in a relationship, Liz.'

'So end it.'

'*What?*' he laughs.

'We could start over.' He should have suspected this all along.

'Liz. I'm not doing this.'

There is a long silence. Then, 'You always were a coward.'

'Goodbye, Liz. I hope you get what you want.'

The line goes dead.

Rory sits heavily onto the bed and drops back, extending his arms out on either side. 'Thank *God* that's over,' he says aloud. Lying flat on his back, looking up at the ceiling, he smiles. He has done it, trusted his gut, made a decision and seen it through. It feels good.

There is no such thing as accidents; everything happens for a reason. One of Bingley's hobbyhorses. One Rory had scoffed at. But now, after five consecutive days of being asked 'why?', of being pushed up against a wall and faced with the realities of his life, he is beginning to see possibilities that never occurred to him before. Maybe he put off settling down for so long because he is afraid of becoming his father. Maybe Louise doesn't want to become her mother. Maybe she's afraid that if she becomes pregnant, Rory will leave, just like her father left. And maybe even Rory's father has a reason for being the way he is. Rory remembers one of the many stories Tom told him as a kid, a story that had somehow become buried under the silt of life's memories. When Rory's father was a boy, he went swimming in a local river he had been warned was dangerous. He got into trouble. A teenager jumped in to rescue him, and drowned. What if Rory's father never got over that? What if he truly believed that the safest thing for his children was not to take risks, not to have adventures, not to be impetuous? Could religion be a lifelong attempt at forgiveness? Or maybe Rory is over-analysing. He is punch-drunk on questions and interpretation. Only the night before, Samantha had confronted him with a scenario he is now beginning to consider potentially valid – which is worrying.

'Maybe you wanted to be jabbed by that syringe.'

'That's ridiculous! Why would I want to risk my life?'

'To change it.'

'Come on!'

'Why didn't you throw him the bag?'

'I didn't think. I trusted that he'd take it.'

'You *trusted* him?'

'It was what he wanted. I was giving it to him.'

'It *has* changed your life, though, hasn't it?'

'But I didn't know it needed to be changed.'

'Maybe subconsciously . . .'

It would take a massive leap of faith to believe that he risked his life in order to change it. He's not sure he's ready for that.

Two days before the course is due to end, Rory decides it's time to go home. He's got what he came for. Knows what he wants. He has made another decision. And needs to talk to Louise.

'I can't believe you're going,' Orla says. 'Wasn't the course helpful at all?'

'It's because it *was* so helpful that I can go. I've learnt what I came to learn.'

'Which is?'

'Oh. Lots of stuff. Too much to go into.' He smiles. 'Will you survive without me?'

Her expression changes to one of worry. 'You won't say anything, will you, when you get back?'

He winks. 'What happens on the course stays on the course.' He is suddenly optimistic, relieved to have made the decisions he has and eager to get home to see them through. He feels like he does on a run when he turns a corner and the wind is behind him. He has momentum.

'Be careful,' he says.

She smiles. 'Always.'

Louise is at the airport waiting for him, dressed in tracksuit and runners, which is unlike her. She's pale and tired-looking. When they hug, she doesn't squeeze as he does. There is something different about her.

'How's your cold?' he asks, as they walk to the car.

'Cold? Oh, yeah, fine.'

'You look worn out.'

'I'm OK.' Her smile is bigger now, reassuring.

They get to her car. He offers to drive. She tells him she's fine.

Heading towards the city, she is unusually quiet.

'So do you want the scandal?' he asks.

She gives him an expectant look.

'Orla met some guy. Married.'

Her eyes widen. 'Really?'

'I *know*.'

'Who was he?' she asks, returning her eyes to the road.

'Some writer I never heard of. Paul Morel.'

'Paul Morel? He's pretty good. Paul Morel! Wow!'

'He's an OK guy.'

She throws him a look. 'How can he be? He's playing around.'

Rory stifles a sigh. Looks out the window. They drive in silence, until they cross the toll bridge to the south side of the city, when he decides to try again. 'What d'you want to do tonight?' he asks, wanting to stay in but giving her the option.

'I'm kind of tired. I wouldn't mind an early night.'

Which makes Rory think of sex. They've been apart almost a week, and, for him, it's been a week of watching other people getting together. He runs his hand up her thigh.

She seems to tense.

He looks at her. What's wrong now? She knows that Orla is with someone else. What has he done now?

When they get back to the apartment, Louise kisses him on the cheek, tells him she's glad he's home, then in the next breath asks if he'd mind if she lay down. She's not feeling the best.

He's disappointed but also concerned. 'I hope it's not flu. Do you have a temperature, headache?'

'No. I'm just wiped out.'

'Do you feel hot or cold?'

'Cold,' she says, then smiles. 'As usual.'

'Want me to lie down with you?' They could chat.

'No, thanks. I'm OK. I just need sleep.' She kisses him

again and looks guilty. 'I'm sorry. I know you're just home.'

'S'OK. I'll just sit out here and contemplate my navel.' She smiles.

When she's gone, he puts on the kettle, opens his case and takes out the hot-water bottle he bought her. When he brings it to her, filled, she's already in bed. Her reaction to a simple hot-water bottle is bizarre. At first she looks genuinely touched, then her eyes fill.

'I love you,' she says.

'I love you too.' He feels her forehead, baffled as to why such a simple present would get such a reaction. She doesn't have a temperature. Course or no course, he will never understand women.

The next morning, having convinced her not to go to work, he makes breakfast in bed. She seems in better form, not so shattered. He gets in beside her and chats about the course, characters he met, things he learned. He's not dumb enough to share his revelations about her, as if he's some sort of expert analysing her life, her motivations. But he does want her to know that she can trust him, that no matter what, he will never leave her. He's not like her father. And she's not like her mother. They will be OK. It's going to be different for them. He is solid, reliable and can be trusted to make the right decisions about their relationship. To prove this, he will tell her about Liz. What was offered. And turned down.

At first she says nothing, just stares at him. Her first words are spoken very slowly. 'When did this happen?'

Not wanting to admit that it was weeks ago, he hedges. 'Before the course.'

'And you're only telling me now?'

'But I *am* telling you.'

'Why?'

'Why what?'

'Why *are* you telling me?'

'Because I want you to know that you can trust me. Because we've no secrets.'

'It was a secret until now.'

'Only because I wasn't sure how to tell you.'

'The truth usually works for me.'

'Which is why I'm giving it to you now.'

'You were considering it, weren't you? That's why you didn't tell me, because you hadn't decided.'

He should have known she'd react like this. 'I didn't do it – even though you don't want kids and I want to stay with you. I didn't do it. Isn't that what matters? That and the fact that I'm being open with you?'

'You're only being open because you decided not to go ahead. *And* you want me to feel guilty about not wanting a baby. To put me under pressure.'

'My God. I just wanted to show you how important you are to me. I don't want anyone else's baby, only yours.'

'You see. You want me to have a baby. You *are* putting pressure on me.' She reaches for the pack of nicotine gum that is on the bedside locker, can't seem to get the wrapper off fast enough.

'What's so wrong with a baby?' he asks.

'We've been through this.' Then under her breath, 'A million times.'

'I know and you've given me reasons, but not the *real* one.' He softens his voice when he asks, 'What are you afraid of, Lou?'

She kneels up suddenly. 'I'm not afraid of anything. Jesus Christ. You come back from some psychology course and put me under a microscope.'

'I'm just trying to understand you.'

'Am I that bloody complex?'

'Everyone's complex.'

She throws her hands up. 'Oh, for fuck's sake.'

She gets up and leaves the room. He is about to follow her when she returns looking as if there is something important she has to add. 'I'm not abnormal just because I don't want a baby.'

'I'm not saying that.'

'What then?'

He goes to her, takes one of her hands and brings her back to the bed, where they sit down again. 'We're together four years, Lou. We love each other. Why haven't we made any sort of commitment to each other? Why aren't we prepared to risk anything to strengthen our relationship? What's stopping us?'

'You get a needle-stick injury and suddenly you want a family. What about me?'

'I want this for us.'

'Even though I don't?'

'I'm never going to walk out, Louise. If we have a kid, I'm going to stay.'

'What are you talking about?'

'I'm not like your father . . .'

'I don't want to hear this, OK? I don't want to hear it.' She stands abruptly, flinging off her robe. She hurries into yesterday's clothes. 'I'm going out,' she says, before he's figured out what to say. She grabs her keys and is gone.

He stands alone in the bedroom, admonishing himself. Didn't he learn *anything* on that course? He has really messed up this time. Edgy and unsure what to do with himself, he starts to clear up. He fills the dishwasher tray and slams it in. Plates roll out of their positions with a clatter.

'Pissy, shitty machine,' he says to it. And kicks it shut.

Wanting to keep busy, he decides to unpack.

He opens the case. There, on top of his clothes, are the presents he got Louise. He picks up the soap and smells it. Sighs. Hopes she's OK. She wasn't well and he had to go and upset her. What kind of fool is he? He wonders where she has gone. Hopes she's not driving fast, which tends to happen when she's angry. He puts the gifts under her pillow for when she gets back. He hopes it's soon.

He tries her phone. But she has left without it.

He tries the shop, but she hasn't come in.

Hours pass and his anxiety grows.

It's evening when he finally hears her key in the door. He goes straight to her. She looks wretched.

'I'm sorry, Lou. I am *really* sorry. I thought I understood. I tried to ring –'

'I can't do this,' she says. 'I can't do this any more.'

His stomach lurches.

'I love you, but I can't be with you any more.' Her tears come quickly and he knows they're not the first she has shed today.

He starts to panic. He didn't do this. He didn't make it so difficult that she'd leave. She can't leave.

'We both want different things,' she says, as though it's part of a pre-prepared speech she is determined to get through. But her tears give him hope.

He puts his arms around her. 'Shh,' he says.

She pulls away. 'Let me do this.'

'I pushed you too far, I know, I'm sorry, I won't –'

'I'm moving out. I don't need this pressure. I can't handle it.'

'Louise, please. I'm sorry. Forget what I said. I won't bring it up again.'

'You will.' Her voice is suddenly calm. 'And you should. It's what you want. And you should have it. But it's not what I want. We have to draw the line here.'

'No.'

'It's over, Rory. If we don't end this now, you'll only end up resenting me, hating me. It's better this way.'

'You're tired, not feeling well. Sleep on it, Lou. Stay tonight and we'll talk in the morning.' He'll convince her.

'Nothing will have changed.'

She walks to the bedroom. From the high shelf on the wardrobe, she pulls down her case.

'Let's talk about this.'

She starts to throw clothes in. Flinging, not folding. She won't look at him.

'Where will you go?'

Without meeting his eyes, she says, 'Lesley and Mark's — until I find a place of my own.'

His friend is supporting the break-up of his relationship? Rory can't keep still. As she packs, he paces. When did they become Lesley and Mark? They've always been Mark and Lesley. Why the reversal? Has her relationship with Lesley overtaken his with Mark? Maybe Mark doesn't know about this. No, Lesley wouldn't invite Louise to move in without checking. So, Louise must have gone straight to them. He thinks of Mark in comforting mode. And wants to kill him.

19

He helps her with her case. Going down in the lift, he asks himself what he's doing – he doesn't want her to go, but he's helping her leave. She's unwell and he loves her – how can he let her carry the case?

Louise is crying when she tells him she'll be back for the rest of her things. Her body is shaking when she hugs him goodbye. But she is first to let go. And she doesn't look back. Not once.

He can't believe it. It couldn't be over. Just like that. Finished.

As her car moves away, it makes a loud grating noise as she fails to go into gear properly. He sees her tuck her hair behind her ear as she always does when stressed.

What kind of fool is he? He loves her and he's letting her go.

Her car disappears from view.

He stands looking after it. Only when a neighbour asks him if he's OK, does he move. Head down, he walks back inside. But he can't stay in the apartment. Doesn't want to think. He needs distraction. And work is better than most. Officially, he's still on a week's leave, but he's going in. He dresses, his movements determined. His thoughts turn to Louise. He imagines her unpacking at Mark and Lesley's. He yanks his belt a notch tighter. How much time did she spend with them when he was away? Was she complaining about the pressure he was putting her under? He flicks the fat part of his tie over the thin and knots it right up to his neck. Reaching under the bed for his shoes, he pulls out one of hers – high-heeled, maroon – for special occasions. He runs a finger along it. He should stay home in case she comes back, try to talk her round. Could he though? Nothing has changed. As she said, they both want different things. And no matter how hard he tries to convince her that having a family doesn't matter to him, he knows she won't believe him. And maybe she's right, maybe he can't suppress for ever something he so passionately wants without ending up resenting her.

Her sunglasses are on the dashboard of his car. He puts them in the glove compartment. He turns the engine and her Coldplay CD comes on. He deposits it with the sunglasses. He drives on autopilot, failing to notice the rain or the woman at a bus stop he soaks with a puddle.

Walking up the corridor he sees Sinead, the casualty registrar, coming towards him.

'I was just talking to Debbie,' she says. 'The camera crew is on your ward.'

'Bugger,' he says. A reality TV crew is filming the working lives of four interns. Most other staff spend their time avoiding them. This involves tipping each other off.

'Want to get lunch?' she asks.

He wasn't aware of the time. He should eat, he supposes.

They sit opposite each other. She smiles at him, but it doesn't register.

'You don't look like a man who just got the all clear,' she says.

He shakes his head to bring himself back to the present. 'Sorry. Miles away.'

'Wish I was,' she says. 'New Zealand would be nice.'

He raises his chin to acknowledge that.

'You know, after what you've been through, you and Louise should take a holiday.'

His throat tightens. 'Yeah.'

She covers her salad in mayonnaise, then looks up suddenly. 'Hey, did you hear about that bus driver?'

'Bus driver?'

'You haven't heard?' she sounds astonished. 'Drove his bus into a crowd and killed two people.'

'Really? Where? When?'

'O'Connell St. Last night.'

'You're kidding.'

'No. I'm amazed you haven't heard. It's been on the news everywhere. Everyone's talking about it.' She starts to recount the story.

Rory is all ears, until he catches sight of Lesley coming into the canteen, when he lets go of his cup. Tea spills down his shirt, scalding him.

'Jesus!' Holding it out from his chest, he hurries from the canteen making for the locker room. By the time he's reached his locker, his shirt is off. He throws his white coat on the door and flings the shirt in an angry ball to the bottom of the locker. He goes straight to the shower and blasts on cold. He points the nozzle at his chest, just above the burn. Ten minutes, he tells himself, freezing to death. But in a way, it is a relief to feel something other than the shock of Louise leaving. He wants to blame her for this. But can't. He tries to imagine life without her. And can't.

Back at his locker, he fishes his phone out of the pocket of his white coat, knowing at last what he has to say to her. It's simple. He loves her; they'll work something out. That's all. He has the phone in his hand. She is his first quick dial number. He sees her face and remembers. He was pressurizing her. If he rings, he will be doing it again. And that will always be the case, as long as the thing he longs for is the very thing she is running from. The phone follows the crumpled shirt. Leaning against the locker, he does something he hasn't done in years. He cries.

'How exactly do you *close* your head?' the patient he is examining asks.

'I'm sorry?'

'You just asked me to put my eyes back and close my head.'

'I did?'

The patient, a young man with unexplained neurological symptoms, says, 'You did.'

'Oh, right. Sorry. Other way around.'

The man smirks. 'Thought so.'

Smart-ass.

For the rest of the morning, Rory watches what he says. In conversation, though, his mind wanders and he misses large swatches of information, which might be fine, if it wasn't about diagnoses, treatments and consultations. On his way to the coffee shop, he sends a lost visitor in the wrong direction. And doesn't notice when she passes him again going the opposite way, and glares at him. He buys apple juice though he has never liked it. A nurse he knows for years as Sarah, he mistakenly calls Louise. Finally, he gives in. He should be home in case she calls. He should at least try. He rushes back to the apartment, but is too late. She has been and gone, her side of the wardrobe empty bar clothes hangers, which clang together when he accidentally knocks against them, the bathroom cabinet bare apart from his toothbrush, shaving foam and razor, the razor he once worried might have put her at risk. She has left the toothpaste.

None of the other rooms look changed. And it occurs to Rory how little personal impact either of them has made on what has been their home for three years. He tells himself it's because the apartment came fully furnished. But he knows it has more to do with commitment. Or lack of it.

He picks up a cushion and flings it across the room. Why did he have to push it? Why did she have to close her mind to the possibility of what could have been? How could Mark betray him? He can't stay in. Doesn't want to go out. Can't meet Mark. *She could have thought of that.* Barry and his happy family would be too much. He has other mates. But, Christ Almighty, he doesn't want to talk to them. He could ring Orla. She'd be back from the course. And all optimistic and in lust. No, thank you.

Louise still has a key. Could call any time.

What if she doesn't? Will he never see her again?

The possibility of that stuns him.

In casualty, after the attack, he put her down as his next-of-kin.

20

Motor neurone disease is not common, and yet Rory has just diagnosed another case. He's discussing it with the man who got the job he coveted, Dr Graham Traynor, newly appointed consultant neurologist at St Paul's. Traynor is a balding but handsome forty something, who had been practising in Canada and Boston before returning to Dublin with his family to take up this post. Rory doesn't have the energy to envy him.

'Do you want me to tell him?' Rory volunteers.

'Would you?' Traynor looks relieved. 'Dashing to the airport. Conference in Basle.'

'Sure.'

Rory makes his way to the patient's room, going over Samantha's advice in his head. There is no nervousness now, just determination to do the best he can. When he gets to the room, he's glad to find the patient alone. That he is reading a motoring magazine saddens Rory. It will no longer be of relevance to the handsome young man in his thirties once he hears the diagnosis. Rory closes the door, pulls up a chair. He doesn't allow his eyes to slip from the patient's. He speaks slowly, clearly. Repeats whatever he has to, answers questions, some more than once. Most importantly, he stays until he senses that the stunned young man finally wants to be alone. He closes the door behind him, knowing that the next time he passes him on the corridor he will not look away. He will stop. Ask how he is. Listen. He will be there.

*

That he has managed to do this is such a relief to Rory that he wants to share the news with Louise. But it has been a week now. No messages. No texts. Long enough to know that there won't be any. Every day Rory notices little things missing from the apartment that he failed to spot that first day, not just physical things, like lilies too open to sell, but intangible things. Sounds – high-heels clicking on the wooden floor, tuneless singing from the bathroom, a lipstick being pulled from its container with a gentle pop. Fragrances – incense, flowers, her moisture cream last thing at night. Colour, too – the bright pink yoga mat he used to have to step around. Everything is blander, especially his life. The bed seems enormous. And cold. It's harder to fall asleep. He has not told anyone. Orla rang to talk about the course (and no doubt Paul Morel), but Rory rustled up some excuse not to have to meet her.

Louise is gone. But she is everywhere. A jacket draped over a chair in a coffee shop, the way a stranger's hair bounces from behind, a laugh that is almost hers. Simple things bringing with them such an overwhelming stab of loss that Rory is in no doubt that he loves her. Why didn't he bother to remember the name of her favourite flower? Had he assumed she would always be there to remind him?

He needs to toughen up. What did they share apart from a mutual fear of commitment? If they fell apart so easily at the first hurdle, they'd never have survived marriage. It's for the best. He wants to leave something behind, however egotistical that may be. He has been wasting time. Better this way. Start from scratch with a woman who wants what he does. Problem is, can he ever find someone he loves as much as Louise?

*

176

In between missing Louise, Rory has thought a lot about his father and the possibility that occurred to him on the course. If it's true that there's a reason for the way he is, then perhaps it's up to Rory to give him a chance. Maybe the way forward is to try to get him to view Rory as more of an equal, rather than a son. If they could just take the father-son thing out of the equation, maybe things could work out . . .

After five stalled attempts over two days, he allows his parents' phone to ring until it is answered.

'Hello?' His father's one barked word translates as six – 'Whoever you are, you're disturbing me.'

Rory tenses. 'It's Rory.'

'Yeah?' As in: what d'you want?

It would be *so* easy to just hang up. 'I was thinking of calling over.'

'Why?'

Oh, fuck off, Rory thinks. I'm your son. I'm supposed to call over. But he stops. Maybe that's the problem. Rory never does call. Why now? his father is probably wondering. Well, honesty would be a mistake. An olive branch would be dismissed. 'Why not?' is the best alternative he can muster.

'I'm going to Mass. I'll get your mother.'

It's as if Rory has nothing to do with him at all, the way it's always been. As usual, he's left feeling flattened.

'*Rory?*' His mother's one word is entirely different – warm, optimistic, loving.

He relaxes again. 'I was thinking of calling over.'

'*Tonight?*' Translated as: is the house clean, are there any biscuits?

'Or we could go out?' he suggests, suddenly wanting to be anywhere other than the house he grew up in. 'Town's still open.' But then he starts to worry about her stamina. 'We could go to the Merrion Hotel for coffee.'

'Your father . . .'

'Has Mass. I know. Come on. The world's our oyster.'

He can't remember when they last went anywhere together, just the two of them. Probably when he was a kid, and she was the one organizing the trip. He feels guilty for not putting in an effort before now. Unable to drive, June has had to rely on a husband whose idea of an outing is a visit to the supermarket, the church or a funeral. Rory knows that she accepts this life without regret. Still, why has his father, largely absent in favour of his busy medical practice, never encouraged her independence? Why has he never taught her to drive? He publicly criticizes Rory for not handling his responsibilities. Doesn't he feel any towards his wife? Rory knows that neither is he blame-free. He could have lent a hand. But then, he has always left things like that to Siofra – who is better at them.

'I'll pick you up in an hour,' he says, knowing she'll want time to change.

Arriving at his family home, Rory is relieved to see no sign of his father's car, a navy Nissan Micra that had to be ordered especially from the manufacturer given his father's specific requirements – manual controls, wind up windows, key operated locks. Declan Fenton is a man who trusts little, and that includes technology. Rory opens the latch on the wrought-iron gates of the three-bed semi, passes through the space the car normally occupies – no oil patches here. Rings the bell. When there is no reply, he wonders if she hasn't heard. Then he catches her outline through the frosted glass, moving slowly towards the door. It saddens him to see how she has aged. If he had a key, he could have saved her getting up. Why haven't any of them been given keys to the family home? What if there was an emergency?

The door opens and Rory is greeted by the same olive green carpet that has been in the hall all his life and probably longer. He is relieved they are going out, and not sitting looking at each other, in a house stuck in the past.

'This is such a surprise,' she says, happily. 'Are you sure you're not busy?'

'Never too busy for my mum.' He realizes as he says this that, given his track record, it is untrue. 'Thought you might like a change of scene.'

She smiles. 'That'd be very nice.' She gets her coat.

'You're going to miss Siofra when she moves.'

'Hugely. But they need the space . . . I just didn't think they'd find somewhere so quickly.'

'With prices going up like they are, they were right to buy while they still could.'

'When is it all going to end?' she asks, closing and locking the door behind her.

'Does Dad have his key?' Rory checks.

She nods. 'And I've left him a note.' Her smile is mischievous. '"Don't wait up".'

That's what Rory loves about her, that gentle defiance, still there bubbling under the surface after all these years just waiting to be given an opportunity. He has an urge to hug her. But lets it pass. It's been a long time. He holds an arm out to her. She smiles as she slips hers into his.

'Where to, madam?'

'Bermuda looks nice,' she says, quoting from one of Rory's favourite TV ads as a child.

'Simon,' Rory says, to an imaginary pilot. 'Bermuda.'

He steers her to the car.

'So, the Merrion?' he asks, as he turns the engine.

'It'd be nice, but, I was thinking, it's late-night shopping, and, do you know what I'd love?, a quick trip to the new shopping centre.' Siofra, it seems, used to bring her. Not that it is new. It opened two years ago.

It is also where Louise works. And Rory is very much aware of that.

'Why don't we go for a trip on the LUAS instead,' he suggests. The LUAS is Dublin's equally 'new' tram system that she will not have tried.

She considers it. 'I could do with a new pair of shoes.'

What if he bumps into Louise? What if he doesn't? What if he works up enough courage to go into the shop and face her?

When they arrive at the centre, his mum insists on going around on her own. 'I don't want to slow you down,' she says.

'You won't.'

'I'd feel I was.'

He worries that she will be all right, but doesn't want to crowd her. Neither is he in a hurry to look at ladies' shoes. She wants to meet in the coffee shop she and Siofra used to go to. It is across from Louise's shop. He suggests another.

'They don't have Danishes there,' she says.

They arrange to meet in the one she favours in an hour. He buys a newspaper and goes to the other coffee shop to kill time until she is ready. But he can't concentrate – not with Louise so close by. He imagines her in the shop, on the phone to a customer, talking to Lolita, or carefully putting together an arrangement. What would she say if he walked in? What would *he* say? He finishes his coffee quickly and spends the rest of the hour touring the mostly British shops located in the centre. When he arrives at the arranged meeting point, his mother is waiting, looking across at Louise's shop.

He sits down, deliberately blocking her view of it.

She strains her head to the side. 'Is that where Louise works?' she asks, sounding as though Louise is someone famous.

'Eh, yeah,' he says, reaching for a menu. 'So, what did you buy?'

'Well, actually, I came away empty-handed. I saw a lovely pair of shoes but they didn't have my size. They're ordering in a pair for me.' She closes her menu. 'This is my treat.'

'No. I'm getting this.'

'You brought me here.'

'I invited you out and I'm paying.'

'We'll discuss it later,' she says. Again she glances over at the florist shop. 'Is Louise working tonight?'

'Eh, yeah,' he says, frowning at the menu as though it is written in Japanese.

'It'd be rude not to pop in and say hello,' she says.

Now is the time to tell her, get it out in the open. If he does it now, it'll save him having to tell the rest of the family. He imagines Siofra's Spanish Inquisition. What happened? Who broke with whom? Why? Rory's mother has always respected his privacy, probably because he has always guarded it. 'Louise and I split up.'

Her eyes widen and her mouth makes an 'O'. Her voice follows with the same sound. Her worried expression leaves him in no doubt that she still sees him as her child, someone she doesn't want hurt. This thing with his father is going to be harder than he imagined.

'Are you all right?' she asks.

He offers what he hopes is a reassuring smile. 'Yeah. Fine.' And then he does an unusual thing for him – he explains. 'We wanted different things.'

'Ah,' she says, nodding knowingly, putting down her menu. 'Louise wanted to settle down.' She sounds like it was inevitable.

'Actually, no. I did.'

At first she looks surprised, then pleased, as if this is something she had given up on. 'Then you will. You'll find the right woman and you will settle down.'

He is offended by how easily she has moved on. 'I thought you liked Louise.'

'I'm very fond of Louise.'

He pictures them chatting together at various family events and knows it's true. He's glad. Not that it means anything now.

'But if your relationship is over, it doesn't really matter how much I like her, does it?'

And once again, he is reminded of the finality of it.

His father's car is outside when they get back and Rory considers leaving his mother at the door. In great form now, she assumes he's coming in. He hesitates, remembers his mission, then follows. In the sitting room, his father, watching the evening television news, ignores them, apart from telling his wife to 'shush' when she offers him a cup of tea. She rolls her eyes as if to say, 'Isn't he incorrigible?' Rory stays in the room with his father, as is expected in his family – to go out to the kitchen to help would be unmanly. He knows not to interrupt the news with small talk he couldn't think up if he tried, so sits, in silence, watching debris in Iraq. When his mother finally carries in tea and biscuits on a tray, a current affairs programme is on.

'Turn off that old rubbish,' she says, her voice warm, unchallenging, knowing that the TV always goes off when they sit down to eat.

Rory's father gets up and manually switches off the TV, doing so with a grunt, so that everyone knows that he is being put out.

June talks about her trip to the shopping centre.

Her husband actually seems interested. Until she finishes, when he says, 'Those fancy places, all they do is put local traders out of business.'

'Well, I think it's grand and handy,' she says. 'Thanks, Rory, for taking me.'

He winks at her.

'How was Mass?' he asks his father, deciding to stick to a safe subject.

His father peers at him as though checking to see if he's being mocked. 'I hope you're still going,' he says.

Rory considers telling him about the novenas, but his father is strange about religion. There are some things he doesn't go in for at all. Novenas may well be one of them. So Rory says nothing, just nods.

His father slurps his tea, something Rory is *convinced* he does to annoy people. Rory forces himself to take his time finishing his tea. As soon as he has, he stretches before getting up, to let his mother know he is on his way. He stands, putting his cup and saucer on his plate. It *is* acceptable to bring his dishes in to the kitchen and he does.

'Leave them, Rory,' she says, 'I'll do them.'

'It's on my way out.'

She starts to get up.

'Stay where you are,' he says, putting his hand on her shoulder, aware of how unused he is to touching her. 'I'll let myself out.'

'Thanks for this evening,' she says. 'It was great to get out.'

'We'll do it again, sometime.'

'And *I'll* get the coffee.'

21

What the apartment is missing is flowers, Rory thinks. Lilies, too open to sell. He looks up the Golden Pages. His eyes are drawn to Louise's ad, the ad they worked on together. It's good. He'd buy from it. If it wasn't Louise's. He can't believe she hasn't called. Well, he's not going to. He practically begged her not to leave. And she went anyway. Maybe it had nothing to do with babies. Maybe she was just fed up with him. She was so cold and distant when he rang from Cambridge. He'd come home, dying to see her, optimistic, thinking it would all work out. And boom, she'd cut him off. Still, when he tracks his finger down the list of florists, he finds he can't give the business to her competitors. He closes the directory. Visits her website. After all, it is *her* flowers he is used to, not anyone else's. He lingers on the site, his mind travelling back to when they set it up together. He'd forgotten how involved he'd been. And how much fun it was. Adventurous. He remembers back to before the business, when she was working at the florist's in the hospital, and the first time he saw her, passing a bunch of red roses over the counter to a customer. He sees it all in slow motion now. That smile! Those eyes. Her thick, fabulous hair. Enough! He clicks the shopping basket to complete the transaction. Then panics. Who'll deliver them? She has that delivery guy. But, sometimes, when he's busy, she does the odd drop. What if?

When the lilies arrive, he gets what he expected, a double disappointment. Delivery man. Closed lilies. He puts the flowers in the sink and goes in search of the vase. He hopes she hasn't taken it. No, there it is, tucked in behind the breakfast cereals. He remembers the steps. Cut stems at angle. Plunge into cold water. Arrange. Sounds simple. And it is. But no matter what he does, he can't get them to look right; all closed up, tight, alien. He is tempted to prise them open himself, but instead abandons them in favour of *Grand Theft Auto, Vice City*.

Days later, they open. He rolls up his sleeves and has another go. He covers himself in pollen. But that's not what bothers him. What does is that he still can't seem to get the flowers looking right. How hard can it be? If only she were here. His phone vibrates in his pocket and for the briefest moment, he is hopeful. But it isn't Louise. The number is vaguely familiar. Local.

'Rory Fenton?' Though he hasn't heard it in months, he recognizes the voice as Sergeant O'Neill's.

'This is Rory.'

The policeman introduces himself too quickly for this to be just another check-up call.

Rory waits, unsure what it could mean.

'There has been a development. We've nominated someone for your crime.'

'Nominated?'

'We arrested a youth last night for a similar offence. While interviewing him we questioned him about your attack. From his reaction we think he might have been involved.'

Rory didn't expect this, having written off the idea of him ever being found. 'Did he admit to it?'

'No. But we were wondering if you'd come down to the station and have a look at a picture of him.'

'Of course. When?'

'As soon as is convenient.'

'I'll come now.'

'Good. Ask for me.'

At the station, O'Neill shows him into the interview room.

'Won't take long,' the guard says, opening a folder and passing a photo across to Rory.

Rory freezes, realizing too late that he should have prepared himself for the shock of seeing that face again. He lets the photo fall.

O'Neill looks at him expectantly.

'It's him.'

The guard smiles. 'Thought so.' He puts the photo back in the folder. 'So. We have our man.'

Rory's heart rate is returning to normal. 'What happens now?'

'We'd like to organize an identification parade.'

'A line-up?' He is thinking of movies he has seen, like *The Usual Suspects*.

'Yes. Though in Ireland, you're not behind a screen. We need you to walk up to your assailant and point him out. Then take a step back.'

Rory imagines it. Facing him. Looking into his eyes. Pointing him out. He could do it – if he was certain he'd be put away for a long time. But what if he gets off? Or is out in months? What if they meet on the streets of Dun Laoghaire and he has a syringe and isn't too thrilled about having been locked up?

'What if I *don't* do the identification parade?' Rory says carefully.

'He'd probably get off, for your crime at least, and it would be harder for us to get a conviction for the other, seeing as he hasn't offended before yours. The courts are more lenient on first-time offenders.'

Rory thinks of the difference between a first-time offender and someone who has been *caught* for the first time. He becomes aware that his hand is flat against the top of his head. And takes it down. 'I don't want to hold you up. Do I have to decide now?' He wonders how many cowards they see in the average day.

'Think about it overnight. Here, let me give you my card.'

'I have it.'

Rory starts to get up, when, unexpectedly, he wonders what his attacker's name is. He is about to ask but then decides that, on reflection, he's better off not knowing.

'We want people like him off the streets,' O'Neill says, as if to help Rory with his decision.

And though he nods, he is thinking that he doesn't want them back in his life either. He shakes O'Neill's hand and walks out. Into the fresh, clear air.

Rory feels guilty that he is only contacting Orla now that he needs to talk to someone.

'Sorry for taking so long to get back to you,' he says. 'Things were a bit crazy.'

'No problem. So, have you recovered from the course?'

'The course,' he says. It seems worlds away.

She laughs. 'God, I was like a zombie the week after I got back, talking rubbish, missing what people said, spilling tea on myself.'

Weird, Rory thinks. He was the same, though that was to do with missing Louise. 'Have you been in touch with anyone? Morel?'

There is a pause. 'Long story.'

He'd like to hear it. 'You doing anything now? Want to go for a drink?'

'Love to.'

He calls for her, and they walk to her local. She hasn't lost any of the glow she developed in Cambridge. In fact, she is looking better than ever. Still in love, then, Rory assumes. On second thoughts, he doesn't want to talk about love.

'The police have got the guy who attacked me.'

Automatically she puts her hand on his arm. 'Oh, Rory. That's great.'

It's as if he doesn't hear her. 'They want me to walk up to him in an identification parade and point him out.'

Her expression changes to one of concern.

He feels better already. 'I keep thinking – what if he gets off on a joke of a sentence and I bump into him again in Dun Laoghaire?'

'That could happen, couldn't it?'

'Which makes me wonder if I should risk getting involved again.'

'What happens if you don't?'

'He'll probably get off with a fine. A fine he won't be able to pay.'

'Free to attack again.'

'I know.' He thinks of vulnerable people visiting the flats – public health nurses, social workers, Orla. 'You haven't been to see Jason, have you?'

'As it happens, I have.'

'You've gone into the flats alone?'

'During the day. It was fine.'

'You shouldn't call for him alone.'

'They're different flats.'

'With the same risks. His own mother . . .'

'Rory, let's not go there.'

'OK, but next time, I'm coming, all right?' He should have been to see Jason anyway by now. He has been putting it off. Not wanting to get in the way. Not sure what to say to Naomi. Maybe it would be easier with Orla there.

'We'll talk inside,' she says, as they arrive at the pub.

But when they get inside and have settled she has an announcement to make that throws him completely. 'I'm filing for divorce.'

He doesn't know what to say.

'I need to move on,' she explains.

'Just like that?' So different from her attitude only weeks before. Something must have happened. Morel! Is he leaving his wife?

'I've learned a lot,' she says. 'About what's good for me, and what's not. Being tied to Owen is not.'

'Morel must be pleased.'

She looks at him. 'This has nothing to do with Paul.'

He opens his mouth to speak.

'He's married,' she says.

'I know, but . . .' He's about to say, 'that didn't stop you before', but thinks better of it.

'What happened on the course, ended on the course. It was so bizarre, like being in a time warp. I told myself going over there to be open. I didn't mean to men. But I let myself go, acted on instinct. And ended up doing something I'd never normally do. Everything was so intense. I don't regret it. Maybe I even needed it – to remember who I was. But it's over. To carry on would be to turn it into something different, something destructive. Paul has a family. He's never done anything like this before.'

'You think?'

'I know.'

They are silent.

'Has he been in touch?'

'He's emailed a few times. I haven't replied.'

'I'm impressed.'

'*Are* you?'

He doesn't know. He has no idea why he made that remark.

'If he'd got in touch that first week, I'd have folded. I was stupid, missing him *so* much, thinking of him all the time, wanting to tell him the smallest things, Googling him, reading his CV, and trying not to contact him to slag him when I found out he was into wrestling. But I heard nothing from him. And managed not to get in touch. When he did, I was stronger.' She looks down at her drink. Her voice quietens. 'But if I saw him again, I'd crumble.'

'Do you love him?'

'Love,' she says, her voice soft.

They're quiet for a moment.

'It's like an addiction, like craving something that's bad for you. The only solution is to go cold turkey.'

'Couldn't you keep in touch, just stay friends?' He thinks of Louise, and knows he's talking crap.

'No.'

'So that's it then?'

'I don't want to be the Other Woman, hanging around for the scraps from someone's table.' She pauses. 'And I never want to care for anyone the way I cared for Owen.'

So she hasn't got over him, despite how it looked in Cambridge. 'What're you going to do now?' he asks, caring very much.

'Divorce Owen. Get on with my life. Look after *myself*

for a change, do what *I* want to do. I'm going back to college.'

'*You are?*'

She smiles. 'I'm going to become a counsellor. The agony aunt thing is fine. It's an income, and I'll keep it up, but it's not enough. With Jenna at school and Jason gone . . .'

'How *is* Jason?' He feels bad for not being in touch.

'Doing well. They both are. I'm taking him out for the day on Saturday . . .' She hesitates. '. . . If you'd like to come?'

'That'd be great.' His relationship with Jason is one of the few things he hasn't messed up. He wants to keep it that way.

'Then it's a date.' She takes a drink. And for a while there is nothing to say. 'You heard from Samantha?' she asks eventually.

'I emailed her the other day to thank her. Her advice on breaking bad news really helped.'

'Really? That's great.'

'Well, I've managed it once, so I'm hopeful.'

She smiles. Then asks after Samantha.

'She's feeling a bit more energetic. Optimistic.'

'God, remember the night she thought I was taking the piss? I nearly died.'

He thinks back. None of them really knew each other then. 'In some ways, I miss it, the course, the way we were all in it together.'

'Me too. But at least you've Louise. I'd to come home to an empty house.'

His chin juts out. 'We broke up.'

'Oh, God, Rory. I'm sorry.' She puts her drink down.

'I asked her to marry me,' he says, eyes wide, staring at

nothing. 'She turned me down. She doesn't want that life. She doesn't want a family.'

She reaches out and touches his arm. 'I'm so sorry.'

He spends a sleepless night trying to decide what to do about his attacker. He switches from one side of the argument to the other – do the identification parade, don't do it. He had left all this behind him. He doesn't want to go back. He wants this guy put away, of course he does, but enough to risk facing him again and the consequences that might result? Then he thinks of people like Orla going in and out of the flats. And decides.

When he calls to the station for the identification parade, O'Neill comes out to him straight away and asks him to come inside to an interview room. Rory senses that something is up.

'I'm afraid we've had to cancel the identification parade,' O'Neill says once they are seated.

'*Why?*' Now that Rory has decided, he is gung-ho.

'Our suspect won't agree to it. He had, but changed his mind at the last minute.'

'Sorry. I'm confused. Are you saying that he gets a *choice*?'

There is a weariness to the policeman when he nods. 'By law, we can only do an identification parade if the suspect is willing.'

'But what guilty person *would* agree to an identification parade?'

'It's been known to happen.'

'So that's it?'

'Well.' O'Neill takes a deep breath. 'There is another possibility.'

Rory isn't hopeful.

'You could happen to see him somewhere and informally identify him.'

'Where would *I* see him?'

'He collects the dole on Wednesday mornings.'

'Are you saying you want me to go to the dole offices in the hope that I'll see him?' There is the issue of work. There is the issue of looking suspicious loitering around the dole office all morning. And there is the issue of seeing him again, in the flesh.

'We'd wait with you in an unmarked car outside the dole offices. He's desperate for cash so he'll show early. When he does, all you'd have to do is say to me, "That's the fellow who attacked me." That will give us enough to arrest him.'

'There and then?'

'My partner would follow him, you'd head off and we'd arrest him on his way out.'

'And that's the only way?'

'It's our only way of identifying him, yes.'

Rory sighs. 'OK.'

'Good,' the guard says. 'I'll call you Tuesday and we'll go through everything.'

Rory nods. Gets up. Shakes the guard's hand – again. He'll be relieved when he never has to see him again.

22

Rory, Orla, Jenna and Lieutenant Dan arrive at the flats to collect Jason. Rory suggests that the dog stay behind to guard Orla's Volvo Estate. It is two weeks after the date she'd arranged to take Jason out, Naomi having cancelled twice. Rory views this with suspicion. He expects to be greeted by a defensive, jittery, strung-out woman. He doesn't want to think about the state Jason might be in. He says nothing. On the surface, he is calm.

When Naomi answers the door, Rory notices the difference immediately. She is holding herself straighter, hair neatly tied back, the dark line at the centre gone. Her face is not so gaunt, eyes not so empty. By some miracle, she has stayed clean.

He hangs back, lets Orla do the talking. Naomi seems more comfortable on home ground. The gentle suspicion that seemed to hang between the two women has eased, though Rory notices that they are not being invited in.

Jason appears behind Naomi having been 'in the Jacks'. Already he has grown his hair longer. Even his face looks different to Rory. Has he moved on, forgotten them? Does he want them here at all? Orla doesn't seem to have any such reservations, warmly embracing him. When he hugs her back equally tightly, resting his head against her, Rory begins to relax. Jenna, who insisted on the visit being arranged when she was home, raises her hand for a high five. Jason smacks it on target, as if they've been doing it all their lives. He stops. Looks at Rory. Who instantly feels guilty.

'How's it going?' Jason says this in a man's voice. But there is something awkward about him, a new shyness reserved for Rory.

What can he say? There is no excuse good enough. He gives Jason a light punch on the shoulder. 'It's good to see you, Jason.'

The boy smiles and seems to relax. 'Where's Lieutenant Dan?'

'Waiting for you in the car,' Rory says.

The plan is McDonald's followed by a movie. First though, some time with Lieutenant Dan. It's a short drive to the wooded hill that is popular with residents of South Dublin for walking their dogs. Sunlight pierces through luminous green leaves in shafts. The undergrowth is sprinkled with bluebells. Rory, Orla and Jenna stick to the narrow path. Jason has other ideas. In among the trees he charges, Lieutenant Dan in hot and barking pursuit. Jenna follows, then her mum and uncle. Jason finds a knobbly old stick and fights an imaginary enemy. He scampers up on a fallen tree and walks along it, arms out to balance, cheeks rosy, eyes sparkling. And Rory knows he was wrong about him growing up and moving on. He hasn't changed at all.

'What's that woman doing?' Jason asks, pointing through the trees.

They follow his finger.

'Hugging a tree,' Orla says.

'Gawd. Sicko. What's she doing that for?'

'She's getting in tune with nature,' says Jenna, sarcastically.

'Wha'?'

'It makes her feel good,' says Rory. 'Let's try.'

'No *way*,' says Jason.

Orla goes up to a very tall pine and wraps her arms around it. Her fingers barely meet. Rory selects another tree. And tries not to laugh.

'Feel anything?' he asks Orla.

'Yeah, dumb,' says Jason, who has clung to the opposite side of Orla's tree.

'You look it,' says Jenna, who is standing watching them, arms folded. But smiling.

When nothing happens apart from their arms tiring, one by one they let go.

For the rest of the day Rory finds answers to the many questions he has regarding Jason. No, he hasn't got *too* thin. At McDonald's he doesn't stow away food. He is non-stop chat, raving about Munster winning the European Cup in rugby, and declaring that Peter Stringer is the best player in the whole world – even if he isn't a Dub. He is, it appears, happy.

'Have we time for a knock around before I go home?' he asks Rory, as they walk into the cinema.

Rory pulls a doubtful face. After the movie they're meant to bring him straight home. 'Next time,' he says.

Jason's eyes light up. There's going to be a next time.

Waiting for the movie to start, Jenna pulls out her portable chess set. Jason grins. 'Prepare to die.'

On their way back to the flats, Jason and Jenna are chatting in the back of the car.

'Guess wha'?' Jason says. 'Me ma's got a new job.'

Rory looks at him through the rear-view mirror.

'In Louise's flower shop,' he continues.

'*Louise?*' Rory asks.

'Yep.'

Rory glances at Orla, expecting her to share his surprise.

She has developed a sudden interest in what's happening outside the car.

'Since when?' he asks Jason, looking at Orla again.

'I dunno. Two weeks. Something like that, anyways.'

Rory's mind is racing. How did this come about? Naomi and Louise met once. At the party. That's it! The party. Did Naomi use the fact that Louise was pleasant to her to approach her for a job? If so, it is he who put Louise in that position. 'So, your mum asked Louise for a job?'

'No, sure she didn't even want it.'

'So, Louise *offered* her the job?' Rory is baffled.

'Yeah, what's wrong with that?'

'Nothing. Nothing's wrong. I'm just wondering how it happened, that's all.'

'Louise came to see me ma.' He sounds bored. 'She said she was stuck and that Ma'd be *brilliant*. I said she would too. But Mam said she didn't know nothing about flowers. Louise said it was real easy, like, and she'd show her. Mam *still* said no. Then Louise asked her to give it a try for a week, like, and see.'

'And now she works there every day?'

'Yeah, but only when I'm in school.'

'I see.'

'After school Mam learns me about flowers. Louise gives her these books, see, and we do get more in the libree. They're real good. Nice pictures and all. And on the telly we watch all the gardening programmes, Mam and me. We do lotsa stuff since she started working. And she gets up every day. And brushes her hair and she even puts on make-up. She walks me to school an' all. But d'you know the best thing? If she says any curses, even "God", she has to give me twenty cents. I tried a euro but she hasn't got as much money as yous but that's OK 'cos she curses a lot.'

*

'You knew, didn't you?' Rory says to Orla, as soon as Jenna has gone up to her room. They're in the kitchen and Orla is putting on the kettle.

'Louise rang me for Naomi's address.'

'Why didn't you tell me?'

'I thought you were trying to move on from Louise.'

'I am.'

'Well then, I'm not exactly going to bring her up, am I?'

'You could have told me *that*.'

'I thought it would come up sooner or later. Now it has.'

'I don't know how you can be so cool about it.'

'Cool about what?'

'Louise employing a drug addict.'

'A reformed drug addict. Named *Naomi*.'

'Yes, and she seems to be doing well. But hardly reformed. She's only been off drugs weeks. She went back once. What if she does again? What if she's desperate for money and there's Louise's till right in front of her?'

Orla puts down the teapot. 'If everyone thought like that people like Naomi would never get a break.'

'She's an *addict*.' And he knows from experience that they can't be trusted.

'So condemn her,' Orla says, losing patience. 'Don't, whatever you do, give her a second chance. I thought you wanted to be a father, Rory.'

'What's that got to do with anything?'

'What would you do if your kids turned to drugs? Just dismiss them?'

'Of course not.' But he'd make damn sure they never touched the stuff.

'People rise to the responsibility they are given,' Orla says.

199

Rory can't see the guy who stabbed him rising to anything. 'Why take the risk?'

Orla's voice fills with anger. 'People make mistakes, Rory. They get caught up in something that's bigger than them and they can't get out. Louise knows what that's like. No one was there for *her* mother. This is something she can do, *wants* to do.' She pauses. 'And it's working out.'

'Are you *in touch* with her?'

'No. But I am with Naomi. And all you have to do is look at her to see the turnaround.'

He'll give her that.

'She needed someone to have faith in her, Rory, and something to be proud of. She needed to get out of that bloody flat. This job is giving her so much. Fair dues to Louise for putting her money where her mouth is, for taking the gamble.'

That's what he's worried about. It is still a gamble.

23

'You know the shoes I ordered? They've got them in,' Rory's mother says to him over the phone. He is surprised and pleased that she has taken the initiative to call him. He'd forgotten all about the shoes.

'No problem,' he says. 'We'll go get them.' And they organize it.

Like last time, she shops alone and they arrange to meet an hour later. The difference this time is that Rory decides to spend that hour in the coffee shop opposite Louise's. It's late Saturday afternoon and he knows that Naomi won't be working. Still, he finds himself looking out for trouble, unsavoury contacts she might have who could be hanging around. When he doesn't find any he ends up playing a game: watching people going in and guessing what they will emerge with. His hit rate is high, knowing as he does from years with Louise the popularity of lilies.

The door opens now. Out comes a man who is glancing back into the shop, holding the door for the person behind him. Rory doesn't remember seeing him go in. Must have been inside a while. Though his back is to Rory, he looks familiar. The woman coming through the door certainly is. Louise. The fountains between them are making it impossible to make out the details of her face, but Rory knows it's her. The way she moves, her hair, the fact that she's wearing clothes that are too warm for the early-May day. His heart thuds at the sight of her. The man lets the door close and falls into step with her, putting an arm around her shoulder. She leans into him. A blow to Rory. A second blow falls almost instantly – the man is Mark.

They walk slowly away from the shop and the centre. Just before they turn the corner that will take them out of sight, they stop. She says something to him and he embraces her, his hand holding the back of her head. Rory has never seen Mark show such tenderness. He doesn't want to witness any more. Forgetting to pay, he strides from his al fresco table, away from the woman he wanted to share his future with, away from the man he would like to flatten. Back in the shopping centre, he marches past shops without seeing them. They've split up; she can do what she wants. But with Mark? And so quickly? What if it's not quickly? What if she finished with Rory to be with Mark? What if they were already seeing each other? Did something happen when Rory was in Cambridge? How much time did they spend together? Where was Lesley then? And where is she now? Isn't she still going out with Mark?

When Rory finally remembers his mother, it is twenty minutes over time. He rushes back to the café where a waiter hands him his bill and stands beside him until he pays. Rory does so while scanning the place. He doesn't see her. Has she been and gone? Has she wandered off, searching for him? Or is she lost? Did she even make it here? He describes her to the waiter, who doesn't remember seeing her.

He heads for the concourse again, breaking into a sweat. She doesn't get out much. This place is huge. No mobile phone, of course. He starts checking every shop he thinks might appeal to her. Imagines what it must be like to lose a child. Tells himself to calm down. If she were lost, she'd ask for directions. She's a grown woman. Marks and Spencer?

To his great relief he sees her: she's closely examining the stitching on a leather handbag, holding it up to her nose, then turning it to the light, oblivious to the world, just enjoying her freedom, away with the fairies, as she'd say herself. Despite everything, he smiles as he approaches. This time he does hug her.

Driving her home he is quiet, remembering the scene outside the flower shop. His mother chats while he tries to reassure himself that they never kissed, that maybe there's an explanation. But he knows Mark. He knows the explanation.

He has to stop thinking about her. He has to get over her. Switch off.

His father is at the front door, in conversation with a woman whose back is to them. As they approach, it seems to be more of a rant. He is telling her that she is wasting her time collecting for the wrong charity. There are better causes than the Irish Kidney Association. She is trying, as politely as she can, to disengage and make a polite exit. From her appearance, Rory gathers that this woman has had a kidney transplant. To her that charity must be the most important in the world. Rory remembers something Orla said about his father taking pleasure in upsetting people. He is a bully. And he will never change. It occurs to Rory that, growing up, he put all his energy into the wrong parent – in trying to please his father, he neglected his mother. And, subsequently, in avoiding his father, he has also avoided his mum.

Rory bins Louise's sunglasses and Coldplay CD. The vase she left behind goes too, and whatever bits and pieces she forgot in her rush to get away. He has never actually removed songs from his iPod before and doing so turns out to be trickier than he'd imagined. But he works it out and deletes all those tracks he downloaded for Louise. And any that remind him of her. Which turns out to be most. His music library is now bare, an over-thinned forest. He will quickly tire of what's left. He needs pre-Louise music. And a reminder of what that was. He checks iTunes. And it all starts flooding back, music from his single life. The Cure, The Christians, Fine Young Cannibals, Pet Shop Boys, tracks that remind him of how free he felt before he made the mistake of falling in love.

He rings Johnny, a mate from uni. 'You heading out?'

'Is the pope Catholic?'

'Mark going?'

'Mark? I haven't seen him in ages. Out of the scene completely.'

Other things to keep him busy, Rory thinks bitterly.

'Want me to give him a buzz?' Johnny asks.

'No. No. Don't. I was just wondering. Count me in for tonight.'

'And Louise?'

'No. Not Louise.'

They meet in a pub in Blackrock village, one Rory hasn't been to in a long time, a posers' paradise, brown leather chairs, plenty of space, cream walls, people smartened up for a night out, women dressed for the wrong climate. Johnny introduces Rory to his mates, two guys he's never met before. Though Irish, they could be Australian, dressed as they are for a day on Bondi – surfer T-shirts, three-quarter-length combats. Flip-flops. All they're missing are coloured strips on their noses. And boards. Johnny, as always, looks younger than his thirty-six years. Rory now understands why. He puts in the effort. His hair is in organized disorder, teased into shape by some product marketed at men. Rory imagines a whole pre-night-out routine involving shower, shave, aftershave and facial cream. Rory just changed his shirt. His hair has no particular style. Just short. Being in a four-year relationship has done nothing for his marketability. He does not look like a man who is 'out there'. He's going to have to work on that. For the moment, a beer will do.

One beer follows another. The pace of the rounds is faster than he's used to. Soon he is buzzing. The conversation, not that he gives a fuck about the conversation, is every so often interspersed with hottie-spotting. It works like this: someone spots a 'hottie' and signals her location using the twenty-four hour clock. Uniform headturning follows. If the Gods are smiling and she is part of a group of hotties, Johnny is dispatched to 'open up' a conversation. His hit rate is impressive.

By closing time, they are doing their bit for Irish-Polish relations. Rory is involved in a conversation with a blonde whose name might be Ulrika. She's doing the talking. He's doing a good impression of listening. Her English isn't great. He's a bit pissed. And he couldn't care less about Irish food versus Polish. It's all a bit too much like work. But she has an amazing mouth, if she could just stop moving it for a while. Finally, he stops it himself by landing his on it, pulling her close, taking her hand and leaving without a word to his mates. Outside in the cool night air, he becomes aware of just how hammered he is. He puts an arm around her and hails a taxi. One stops immediately. In the back, he finds that mouth again. And more.

He should have gone to her place. It doesn't feel right having her here in the apartment. Oh, fuck it, he'll turn off the lights. He takes her hand and leads her to the bedroom in the pale orange glow of the streetlights outside. Once she is in bed, he closes the door. Complete darkness. Better.

He strips quickly and after a bit of comic groping, finds her. He is glad of her soft nakedness, her hair, breasts, mouth. He is glad not to be alone, and relieved that someone is attracted to him. He hopes he can do this. Maybe then he can forget.

There are no glitches in his performance and that's a relief. Lying on his back afterwards, he smiles in the dark, beginning to think that maybe this was easier than he'd imagined. Her feet brush against his. Warm feet. Not the ice-cold blocks he is used to. There is a stranger in his bed, a stranger who is interested in the difference between Polish and Irish food. What is he doing? He doesn't want this. But what can he do, ask her to leave? And so he lies there listening to the whistling sound she makes when she breathes, telling himself that there's got to be a better way of getting over someone.

He wakes to the sound of the doorbell and a dog barking. He lifts his head. It feels like it is about to explode. He eases it back onto the pillow. His tongue is stuck to the top of his mouth and his stomach feels like it's fermenting. Someone moves beside him and he turns his head – slowly. Blue eyes. Poland, he thinks. He smiles awkwardly and nods hello as though meeting her for the first time. Then alarm bells go off – if that dog doesn't stop barking, he'll be evicted. He checks under the quilt with his hand and is relieved to confirm that, yes, he did put his boxers back on after that brush with her feet. He hops from the bed, grabbing his denims and T-shirt and dressing in transit. He is almost at the door when he turns and runs back to the room. He makes a 'don't shoot' gesture with his hands. 'Stay here,' he says. 'Stay here.'

He closes the door behind him.

The bell rings again and this time he runs. Tripping over

a red shoe, he flings it aside. Orla is turning to go when he opens up. Lieutenant Dan dashes in.

Rory stands, smiling, his hand up against the doorframe, casually blocking Orla's way should she decide to follow.

She raises an eyebrow. 'We're on our way to the pier. Don't suppose you want to come?' She smiles as though she knows he's hiding something.

'Eh, no. Thanks, anyway.'

'No probs,' she says, turning. 'Oh. Here, got you this.' She hands him a bag containing a book.

He takes it. 'Great, thanks.'

'Aren't you going to look at it?'

'Eh, yeah.' He reads the title. *Go Ask Alice*. Cover is bleak enough. 'Great, yeah, thanks a mill.'

She's still there.

He feels under pressure to check the back. Some sort of diary. A teenager who got involved in drugs. Not his kind of thing at all.

'True story,' she says. 'Though there's been some controversy about that.'

'Great.' He puts it back in the bag. 'So!'

'So,' she smiles, 'good night, eh?'

He follows her eyes to the other red shoe, lying on its side.

She calls the dog. And, luckily, the bastard goes to her. She winks at Rory. 'See you later, lover boy.'

After she's gone, he throws the book on the couch and walks out on to the balcony, his head back. He watches them cross the road, Orla leaning down, holding the dog's collar. They run across, then up the steps of the pedestrian bridge crossing the DART line. He turns and goes back inside. What's he supposed to do now, cook her breakfast?

*

Later, he calls over to Orla. To explain. He brings flowers – bought at Louise's most detested competitor, Tesco. While she puts them in water, he, in the minimum of words required, explains the situation he found himself in.

'I wasn't getting rid of you,' he says when he has finished.

'Yes, you were.' She smiles.

'OK, well, maybe I was. I'd just woken up. I hadn't figured out what to do about her. All I knew was I wasn't going to complicate things by introducing her to my friends.'

'Your friend. I'm flattered,' she jokes, putting her hand to her chest. 'So, who was she?'

'A mistake.' He rubs an eyebrow.

'Not the kind you normally make.'

'No.' He tells her about Louise and Mark. 'Why Mark? Of all people?' he asks. 'Louise is *paranoid* about men walking out on women. And who does she end up with? The one man who changes girlfriends faster than razor blades. I just don't get it.' He stops. 'Or maybe I do. Maybe it's simple. I propose. She bolts. Into the arms of the nearest playboy. Doesn't take a genius. She's running from commitment.' He looks at the lilies. 'She couldn't *love* him, could she?'

Orla says nothing.

'She's going to get hurt,' he says, adding, when he sees the surprised expression on his sister-in-law's face, 'not that I give a shit.'

They're silent.

'There is another possibility,' Orla says eventually.

He looks at her. Finally, some answers.

'I don't know whether this is the case or not but they *say* that we're attracted to replicas of our parents so we can get a chance at making the relationship work second time round. Louise could be attracted to Mark *because* he's like her father, giving her the opportunity to break the cycle of abandonment.'

'But that's ridiculous. She's stacking the odds against herself from the beginning.'

'Yeah.'

'Then why do it?'

'It's subconscious.'

'So, hang on, wait a minute. Are you saying that Louise was only interested in *me* as long as I was like her father, that our relationship had nothing to do with falling in love with a person for who they are, that all relationships are down to what happened when we were kids?' He can't believe that.

'It's just a theory.'

'It's rubbish. I don't believe it.' He can't accept that their four years together could be based on nothing other than his lack of commitment. 'Well, then,' and Rory thinks he has Orla here, 'why did she leave me when she got what she wanted? I changed, became committed.'

'Yes, but she wasn't the one to change you.'

Once again, she has all the answers. And Rory resents her for it. Like a child who lashes out when hurt, he says, 'I don't think you should go into counselling.'

He doesn't want reminders. At work he avoids Mark, steering clear of the canteen, buying what he needs from the tiny coffee shop and eating outdoors in the cold, overcast Irish 'summer'. Where possible, he avoids public areas like the main concourse. Where impossible, he doesn't linger – the locker room, corridors. He has another reason for bypassing the concourse; it houses the florist that Louise used to run before setting up in business. To wipe a person from your mind, best to avoid anything that triggers a memory.

He looks out for Lesley, though. Seeing her might answer some of his questions. Does she know? Is it over between her and Mark? Or is he seeing Louise behind her back? He tells himself he doesn't care. But still watches out for her. An unfamiliar speech therapist arrives on the ward to see a stroke patient, making him suspect that Lesley has returned to England. He wouldn't blame her. He'd do the same.

The only positive outcome of his misery is that when Wednesday comes and he has to identify his attacker at the dole office, he is too down to worry. Sergeant O'Neill was right. The guy arrives first thing. Rory confirms it's him. And leaves. O'Neill later phones to thank him. He'll keep him informed, he says.

Rory thanks him in return, but can't seem to lift his mood to match the guard's.

Reading in bed at night is an effective way to avoid thinking, Rory finds. He has just finished *One Flew Over The Cuckoo's Nest*, and without a book, he is edgy. He remembers the one that Orla left, stuck down the back of the couch, and throws back the duvet. Catching his reflection in the mirror, he notes how middle-aged he looks in pyjamas, a new addition to his wardrobe. He is cold without Louise. Has even started to wear socks.

He retrieves the book, sits on the couch, turns it over in his hands. The subject matter is, of course, the problem. It is short though. And written by a teenager, so it can't be rocket science. He flicks through it. Lots of white space where one diary entry ends and another begins. It'll do for tonight. He'll buy another novel tomorrow.

The heroine, Alice, seems a normal kid, a bit insecure, but so what? She moves house. Goes to stay with her grandparents. Yeah, yeah. Oops, at a party, new 'friends' spike her

Coke. The feeling of confidence it gives her is alien, and a relief, but once she discovers what has happened she is guilty and afraid. She has been warned about drugs. It won't happen again.

Her new friends seem to really care though. They want to include her, share their drugs with her. Alice is no longer a social outcast. For the first time in a long time, she feels happy. But guilty. She should stop, she knows. She wants to tell her parents, but they're back home. She asks to return, but her grandfather is ill and Alice has been such a help. When she does return home, she tries to stop but makes a new friend who is also on drugs. She slips deeper and deeper. She and her friend run away. Their lives darken. She wants to escape, get home, get clean. Rory, unable at two in the morning to put the book down, is hoping that she will.

She does.

But other druggies, former friends, put pressure on her to get using again. It is extreme, threatening. Her family is doing its best, but she is afraid and embarrassed to tell them everything. She meets a good guy and he helps her. She is still consumed by the bad things she has done and that were done to her. Guilt erodes her strength. As Rory nears the end of the book, he is reading about a battle; on the one side, her family and the boy, on the other, her guilt, addiction and enemies. But it is beginning to look hopeful and that the battle might be won. The diary ends positively. Rory is relieved. Then he reads the epilogue: three weeks after her last entry she overdosed. And died. At fifteen.

Rory is gutted. A life full of potential, wasted. This was no 'drug addict' but a fifteen-year-old, insecure girl who became a user, then a pusher, who was still a fifteen-year-old insecure kid trying to do the right thing, clean her slate and start over. Maybe it's not true, Rory hopes, all of a sudden.

Maybe it didn't happen. Didn't Orla say something about a controversy? Doesn't matter, he decides. This story is being replayed over and over around the world every day. He is in no doubt about that. He thinks of Naomi and hopes that she hasn't had to go through any of that, the sexual degradation, the violence, the pressure. He has refused to see her side, allowing his own experience to cloud the fact that she is a person involved in a struggle, trying to do right by her son, when the easiest thing would be to give in. He claims to want to help Jason, but what has he done to help Naomi, the most important person in Jason's world? Nothing except distrust her. She is struggling in a potentially fatal tug of war and it's about time he started pulling on the same side as Louise.

24

The following Saturday, Rory is alone when he calls for Jason. No Orla to act as a buffer. No dog in the car.

Naomi answers. 'Oh, God. He's gone to the shop. He should be back by now. I thought you were him at the door.'

'No worries,' Rory says. 'I'm in no hurry.' He thinks she will ask him in.

But she doesn't.

They stand facing each other. Equally awkward.

He smiles to break the tension, puts his hands in his pockets. 'So, how are things?' he asks, as if he really does care.

This seems to surprise her. She blushes. 'Good,' she says. 'Good. Thanks.' She steps out, peers over the balcony. 'Where is he?'

He wants to reassure her, tell her he's on her side, that he didn't understand before, but does now, as much as anyone who hasn't been through it can. But the words don't come.

'Here he is,' she says, sounding relieved.

Rory is relieved himself. He hears the sound of running feet on the steps, then sees the top of Jason's head. It makes the boy seem vulnerable. Suddenly, Rory worries that he's too young to be going to the shop on his own, especially in this neighbourhood. He checks himself. He has to start trusting Naomi. She knows her son. And she knows the neighbourhood.

Jason hands her a pack of cigarettes and change and turns quickly to be with Rory.

'Bye, Ma,' comes as an afterthought.

'See you later,' she says, a smile in her voice.

As they walk down the steps, Jason asks, 'Which would you like for a pet – an electric snail or five hundred sticky lizards?'

'Hmm. Difficult choice. I think I'd go for the electric snail.'

'But you'd only get one of them.'

'I know but I'd really look after him.'

Two weeks pass since Rory saw Louise with Mark. In that time, he has avoided Mark's calls, letting them go to voicemail. He has ignored his texts. He wonders how long it's going to take for him to get the message.

One evening, though, Mark rings the landline and catches him in.

'Hey, stranger,' he says. 'What's up? Where've you been?'

'Busy.'

'What have you been up to?'

'Not much.'

Mark laughs at the contradiction.

Fuck off, Rory thinks.

'So, want the good news or the bad?' asks Mark.

Rory presumes he'll get both and care about neither.

Mark does a drum roll. 'Mark Keohe is finally getting hitched.'

Rory wonders if this is some kind of joke.

'I've finally met the right woman, and this time I'm not letting her get away.'

Four years and she couldn't marry Rory. Weeks and she's marrying Mark.

'Would you do me the honour of being best man?'

What is he doing, trying to rub Rory's nose in it?

'Go fuck yourself,' he says, slamming down the receiver. He stands, looking at the phone. How could he do that, ask him to be best man at the wedding of the woman he still loves? However quickly Louise has moved on, Rory can't imagine her agreeing to that. But the biggest shock is that she is gone. Really gone. Alone in the apartment they once shared, he clears the fridge of its remaining beers and falls asleep in his clothes.

At work the following day, bleary eyed and numb, he is waiting in the corridor for a petite Indian nurse to finish with a patient. He is checking the chart and thinking about the tests he should run. He is also thinking of applying for a neurology post in England. He doesn't see Lesley coming until she is on top of him.

'What's your problem?' she says.

He looks up, surprised. 'Lesley.'

'Don't you Lesley me.'

He takes a step back. 'I thought you were in England.'

'Do I *look* like I'm in England?'

He glances around, hoping not to see an audience. 'Let's talk outside,' he says, dropping the chart quickly into the room, then taking off along the corridor, Lesley keeping pace. The day room is free. He holds the door open for her. She goes inside. He follows, his arms automatically folding in defence.

Lesley doesn't waste time. 'Did you have to be so heartless? If you didn't want to be best man, you should have just said. An explanation would have been nice. But you didn't have to tell him to go *fuck* himself.' A passing visitor peers in through the glass door. Rory shields his face with a hand. Lesley doesn't notice.

'What has he ever done to you? All right, I admit, Louise stayed with us for a while. That was my idea. Mark wasn't at all keen. But I talked him into it. So, if you have to get all shirty with someone, get shirty with me. Just don't throw his offer back in his face. He might not look it, but he has a sensitive side. He does get hurt.'

Rory is busy playing catch-up. So Mark and *Lesley* are getting married. Does that mean he's having an affair with Louise? Or was it a once-off thing? Should he tell Lesley? And why does he feel like laughing?

'Well, aren't you going to say something?' Her hands are on her hips.

And suddenly he thinks that she's great – straight, spunky, standing up for 'sensitive' Mark, defending him. If he knew, he'd die of embarrassment. Lucky bastard, though, to have someone care so much about him.

'I'm sorry,' he says. 'I thought . . . well, it doesn't matter what I thought. I was wrong. I'll call Mark, OK? Tonight.'

'OK,' she says, firmly.

'And, eh, congratulations.' He feels he should ask: 'When's the wedding?'

She smiles. 'Six weeks. We don't want to wait. We want to start a family.'

That evening he rings Mark. It's awkward.

'Sorry about last night.' He hesitates, not wanting to get into explanations. 'I'd something on my mind.'

'What, narcotics?'

Rory laughs. But hasn't forgotten what he saw. He wants to sort it out. 'Can I buy you a drink?'

'As long as you've nothing on your mind.'

They meet in a bar in Dun Laoghaire. And after some

initial jokey banter Rory gets to the point. 'I saw you with Louise.' He watches Mark carefully.

'What?' He seems confused.

'Outside the flower shop, a few weeks back. Looking very cosy. Too cosy.' He doesn't take his eyes off Mark, who appears to be trying to remember.

'That must have been . . . it was the day . . .' Mark stops, as if to check himself. 'She was upset.'

'What?'

'I was comforting her.' Mark scratches his head. 'Hang on. Is *that* why you hung up on me, you thought there was something going on between myself and *Louise*? Jesus, Rory.'

'What was it then?'

'Something happened. I came to take her home.'

'Why you?'

'Lesley asked me to. She'd a private client who'd just arrived when Louise rang. I brought her back to our place and looked after her till Lesley got home.'

'You were *looking after* her long before you got home.'

'What?'

'You were all over her.'

Mark is impatient now. 'What? Jesus, I might have hugged her. She was upset.'

Rory doesn't believe him, can't let himself. 'About what?'

'Like I said, something happened.'

'What?'

'I can't tell you. You'll have to ask Louise.'

'Come on, Mark. Louise and I aren't exactly in contact.'

'Maybe you should be.'

'Yeah?' Rory says, sarcastically.

'She still loves you, Rory.'

For a moment, that thought lifts him. But he shuts it down. 'Love isn't the issue.'

'You need to talk to her.'

'There's nothing to talk about.'

'You'll have to trust me when I say there is.'

'What is it?'

'You'll have to talk to Louise.'

'Come on, man. If you want me to talk to her, tell me what it is.'

'I can't.'

Mark will not be budged. No matter what Rory says, he can find out no more. Mark moves the conversation on to the wedding and Lesley, his first real love at the age of thirty-seven. Rory envies him. Hard to believe that Mark, of all people, is settling down, starting a family. He is even talking about moving to Birmingham. All it took, he guesses, was the right woman.

They leave the pub after last orders, the groom and best man.

Lying in bed, unable to concentrate on his latest book, *The Bonfire of the Vanities,* Rory tries to adjust to reality revised. Louise and Mark were never together. Louise was upset. At what, though? Something to do with the shop? Naomi? If so, why didn't Mark just tell him? Why the big secret? It hurts that it was to Lesley and Mark that she turned. She should have known he'd have been there for her. If she really does love him, as Mark says, if there really is some reason they should talk, where is she? He's not difficult to find. If something has changed, it's up to her to say so.

'I think you're making a mistake,' Orla says. 'It's too early, too soon after Louise.'

'Louise has moved on. Time I did.'

'Not necessarily.'

'Look. The reason we split up was because I wanted a family. The least I can do is go out and get one.'

'Fine. But do you have to rush?'

'I'm not rushing. I'm just being proactive.'

He's decided to be like Liz, take control of his life. In fact, he has even *considered* Liz. At least they both want the same thing. He could just pick up the phone. Not after their last conversation, though, where she turned on him when she didn't get her way. No. Letsbefriends.com should have what he's after: a woman that he has no history with, who wants what he wants. And let there not be any confusion about that. He wants commitment, a family. If what Orla says about everyone marrying his or her parents is true, then love is an illusion best kept out of the equation. He's done love. He's not in a hurry to do it again.

There is one problem. He has no experience of women who want commitment. He has always avoided them. What do they want in a man? Sincerity? Honesty? Stability?

He asks Orla over.

'What made you fall for Owen?' he asks. They're sitting side by side on his couch, checking out the Letsbefriends. com website.

She smiles, remembering. 'The way he carried his one.'

'*What?*'

'Oh. He'd brought me to a restaurant and was working out the tip. When he was adding up, he carried his one.'

Rory laughs. 'You're kidding.'

'No,' she says, laughing too. 'That was it. The moment.' Her face becomes sober. And sad.

'God,' he says, looking down at the laptop, 'how're you supposed to visualize anyone from these descriptions?

What's wrong with photos? It's like when newsreaders describe a person as being five foot eleven with dark hair and blue eyes. Could be anyone.'

'And of course they all lie,' she says.

He looks at her, relieved to see that she has recovered. 'Really?'

'Sal has been Internet dating for over a year now and you wouldn't *believe* the amount of guys who've lied about their age. It's practically standard. When she reads an entry now she automatically adds five years.'

Two things shock him, the lying and the amount of time Sal has been looking. 'Maybe only the men lie,' he suggests.

'The women are worse. They lie about their age *and* size.'

'How are you supposed to choose if everyone's lying?'

'Check the other stuff.'

'Like what? GSH – what kind of person with a Good Sense of Humour describes themselves with three letters?'

'The TV programmes they watch.'

'Let's just pick all the Sopranos fans then.'

'Maybe we should just do your entry first?'

He grimaces.

'Oh, come on. It'll be fun.'

They eye the blank questionnaire.

'Maybe we should examine the competition,' Rory suggests. 'See what they say about themselves.'

'Then go one better,' Orla says optimistically.

'Or at least try.'

They check out some of the male entries and begin to get a feel for ones that work.

'Let's not bother giving your dimensions. They mean nothing,' Orla says. 'We should just say who you look like.'

'Who *do* I look like?' He sees his first problem – he doesn't look like anyone.

'George Clooney.'

He laughs. 'I do in my arse.'

'You absolutely do.'

'Yeah, right. Can you imagine some poor woman thinking she's meeting a George Clooney lookalike and then coming face to face with me? I am *so far* from George Clooney.'

'Not to me.' She says it seriously.

He looks at her.

She looks at him.

A beat.

His heart is pumping.

Jesus Christ. They're going to kiss.

This is Orla. What the hell are they doing? But their mouths are together, his hands cupping her face. He is hungry for her. She lies back. And he goes with her. Kissing deeply, his hands explore her body, one moving to her ass, pressing her to him. He tells himself he doesn't want this, he wants commitment, family . . . he wants to fuck her brains out. And it looks like she wants the same, on top of him now, however that happened, straddling him, unbuttoning her shirt, eyes locked to his. Unable to wait, he pulls her down to him, has to touch her, kiss her, have her. Her moans urge him on. And on. They are moving together in a fast, urgent rhythm when he remembers the condom. It's too late. Nothing can stop him now. He doesn't care. And she doesn't seem to. They should. They really should. But he can't. Not now. God, not now.

They're lying side by side, on their backs, facing the ceiling, chests rising and falling in unison. He is afraid to move. And suspects she is the same. Where do they go from here, lying half-naked, wholly-embarrassed on his black leather couch? She turns to look at him and he is glad to see eyes filled with amusement rather than dreamy undying love.

'What was *that* about?' she asks.

Relieved, he laughs. 'I don't know.'

Moments pass.

'Who'd have guessed Internet dating could have such speedy results?' she says.

He laughs again. She has always been able to make him laugh.

'God.' Her voice is serious now. 'What would they think if they could see us now? Owen, Jenna, your parents.'

'Jesus.' He visualizes his brother. 'Owen would swing for me.'

'He couldn't care less,' she says, sitting up, putting her feet on the floor, and reaching for her clothes.

Rory, stuck on the inside, manages to reach his sweater, which he slips over his groin. 'I wouldn't be so sure.'

From where she is sitting with her back to him, she turns, curious.

'He asked me to stay away from you,' Rory explains.

'What? When?'

Rory sits up, making sure the sweater stays in place. 'Way back. When I was helping you find a house.'

'He told you to *stay away* from me? What did he think you were doing?'

'I don't know, interfering with his family, something like that.'

'His *family*?' She looks incredulous.

'That's what he said.'

'Unbelievable.' Violently, she forces her arms into her

sleeves. 'Oh, we're his family when it suits him, when he can use it to stop me getting on with my life.' She stands suddenly, either unconscious or uncaring that her lower half is still naked. Rory feels a repetition stirring and turns away while she finishes dressing. Doesn't take long. She is furious. 'You think you know a person,' she says, seeming to have forgotten completely what has just happened between them. Rory takes advantage of the moment to grab his boxers and denims. Once dressed, he begins to feel a little less awkward. Still, he moves away from the couch.

'Want a coffee?' he asks, to clear the air, move back to safer territory.

'Got anything stronger?'

'Beer?'

'That'll do.'

They sit at the kitchen table. Owen's presence lingers.

'At least you're divorcing him,' Rory tries.

She avoids his eyes.

He tries unsuccessfully to meet them. 'You didn't tell him, did you?'

Her silence answers for her.

'Why not?' He doesn't understand. What about getting on with her life?

Finally, she looks at him. 'Jenna and I have been getting on so well since I got back from the course. At first, it was because I was such a zombie; I couldn't get into a flap about anything. She failed an exam and I didn't care. I told her not to worry; there were more important things in life. We haven't been getting on like this in two years. She's finished up for the summer and we've been spending so much time together. She needs it. I do too. I don't want to ruin it by telling her I'm divorcing her father. Let him make the first move.'

And Rory sees that, however temporarily, she is sacrificing her freedom for her daughter. When will she be able to break free? Rory wonders. When will she be able to get on with her own life?

25

Rory hasn't called Orla. Neither has he heard from her. Though it has only been a week, he misses her company, hadn't appreciated how much they talked, supported each other, how up she made him feel. Will they ever be able to go back to the closeness they had? He wonders what she's doing, and what her silence means.

Late Friday night, when his doorbell rings, he doesn't delay.

It's Owen, looking wretched. He pushes past Rory.

'Come in,' Rory mutters, with quiet sarcasm.

Owen turns, swaying slightly. 'Who is he?' he asks, words slurring.

Rory closes the door. He is tired. Disappointed it's not Orla. 'Who is who?'

'This bloke she's supposed to be in love with.'

In love? His mind is racing, but he tries to play it cool. 'I presume you mean Orla?'

'You know who I mean.'

'Who says she's in love?'

'She does.'

Another surprise. *She must mean Morel.* 'How should I know who he is?'

'You went on that course together. She must have met someone.' It's as if Owen can't imagine her meeting anyone normally.

'Just because you met what's-her-name on a course, doesn't mean . . .' He stops, realizing suddenly how ridiculous this all is. 'Hang on a minute, why should you care?'

'Because,' Owen's body sags, 'I miss her.' He sinks onto the couch.

Rory tries not to think about what happened between them. If he does, Owen might sense something.

'Any chance of a drink?' he asks.

Wordlessly, Rory heads to the fridge. Pulls out two beers. Not bothering with glasses, he hands a can to Owen, who snaps it open and takes a long drink. Rory sits on the armchair opposite, his own can untouched, looking at his brother.

'I've made the biggest mistake of my life,' Owen says, his voice heavy with emotion. 'I love her.'

'No, you don't. You can't – not after the way you've treated her.'

'I do.' His voice softens. 'The only reason I don't want to see her happy is because I don't want her happy without me,' an admission, Rory feels, that would never have been made without booze, and by the looks of Owen, a lot of booze. 'I'd go back tomorrow if she'd have me.'

'And what's-her-name, does *she* know you're here, talking like this?'

Owen's eyes are wide and vacant. 'I don't love her. I thought I did. Orla was never like this when she was pregnant.'

'Kate's *pregnant*?' Rory doesn't get it. Why leave one family only to start another? He remembers Owen's you-don't-know-what-marriage-is-like speech.

'You're telling *me* she's pregnant. And acting like a princess. Treating me as if I owe her something, as if I'm there to serve her. She sees the world only from her point of view.' Rory knows someone like that, and he's not too far away. 'If it weren't for the baby, I'd leave.'

But there is a baby. 'When is it due?'

'December.'

'Maybe you should go home,' Rory says.

'To Orla?' he asks, suddenly hopeful.

'No, Owen.'

'I don't want to go back.' He sounds like a child.

Rory stands. 'I'm making coffee.' He heads for the kitchen. Does Orla know about this baby? Does Jenna?

When he returns with two mugs, Owen's face is enthusiastic. 'If I left Kate, became single again, and really *tried* with Orla, do you think she'd have me?'

'Owen. Your girlfriend's pregnant. You've a baby on the way.'

'Yeah and it's ruined everything. Jenna thinks I'm trying to replace her. She won't believe me that it was an accident. She doesn't want to see me, Rory. She doesn't want to see her own dad.'

Rory's mind plays catch-up. It was an accident. He has told Jenna. So Orla presumably knows. Maybe that's why she hasn't been in touch. Maybe it has nothing to do with what happened between them, rather the latest bombshell that has been dropped on her life and that of her daughter. She's probably trying to cope with the fallout.

'This is not my fault,' Owen says. 'The baby wasn't planned.'

'Maybe not by *you*.'

Rory expected this suggestion to surprise Owen.

He doesn't blink.

Rory stares at him. Maybe now he finally sees that walking out on a marriage isn't the simple, clean act he thought it would be, and that his all-encompassing need for passion is having ramifications that have him trapped, like a train stuck on the wrong tracks, moving away from everything he loves.

*

Owen finally crashes out on the couch. Rory finds a sleeping bag and throws it over his shabby, snoring frame. He starts to pick up the empty beer cans and coffee mugs, thinking that Owen isn't the only one to have messed up. What happened between himself and Orla was a mistake he never should have let happen. It's too complicated. Her life is still intertwined with his brother's. Rory needs to keep things simple, focused. He lost Louise because he wanted a family. If he doesn't find one, losing her will have been pointless.

In the privacy of his bedroom, he pulls out his laptop. He opens the home page of Letsbefriends.com. One very simple action will bring him to the list of female 'members'. But for some reason, he can't do it. He clicks the tiny 'x' at the top right of the screen, then shuts down the computer. He reads his novel until he falls asleep.

In the morning, he finds Owen a different man, controlled and determined. He has showered, borrowed a razor and somehow managed to lose the scruffy down-at-heel look. He is going home, back to Kate.

Rory offers to take his mum to visit Siofra in her new home. He's decided that with his sister living so far away now, he'll see to it that June still manages to get out and about a bit. And what better outing than a visit to the daughter and grandchildren she misses so much. Time Rory caught up with the kids anyway. Thankfully, his own father isn't interested in coming.

They pull up outside a big, modern house on an estate just outside Kildare. The garden is dug up. The place has a bare, barren look about it.

'I should have brought a plant,' his mother worries.

'I think it's you they want to see.'

And that's the truth. When Siofra gets Rory on his own, she thanks him.

'It's so good to see her. I rarely get to call, what with rushing out of Dublin as soon as I finish work so I can have *some* time with the kids, then trying to settle in here at the weekends. The commute's a killer. I'm shattered most of the time.'

'She understands.'

'I know, but she misses the kids. Grandparents should see their grandchildren.'

'Look, you needed the space.'

'I'm beginning to think that maybe we didn't need it so much.'

Their mum has heard none of this conversation, busy as she is with Daisy and Alex. And yet before they leave, she expresses regret that she never learned to drive. 'Imagine how handy it would be for everyone if I could get down here under my own steam.'

On their way back to Dublin, Rory's mother is marvelling at how quickly her grandchildren are growing, when he drives into the grounds of a five-star hotel.

'Where're we going?' she asks.

He pulls up in the car park. 'I think it's about time you learned to drive.'

'You've come in here to teach me to drive?' She sounds incredulous.

'It's as quiet a spot as you'll get.'

She laughs. 'Rory. I'm sixty-five years old.'

'Like I said, about time.'

Her hand lands lightly on her chest. 'I couldn't. I'd be terrified.'

He opens the door. 'Let's swap places. Just see how it

feels to be behind the wheel. We won't go anywhere.'

She looks doubtfully at him, but there is curiosity in her eyes.

Sitting across from her, he watches as she leans forward and grips the wheel. He imagines her tearing up a motorway in this position.

She peers down at the pedals. 'Which is which?'

He shows her.

She has an imaginary drive, accelerating, braking, but forgetting to change gears.

He explains how. 'Here, switch on the engine,' he says, 'or it won't work.' When he sees her face, he adds, 'Don't worry, we're not driving, just changing gears. The car won't move.'

She turns the key a notch too far and the engine makes a loud grating sound. She switches it off quickly and eyes him, guilty. 'I haven't banjaxed it, have I?'

'It's fine. Everyone does that. Try again.'

She hesitates in front of the wheel, as though saying a silent prayer. But she does try again. Soon she is saying, 'This is fun,' and, 'I've always wanted to drive, you know.'

'Why don't we take it up the road a bit?'

'No. No. This is fine, lovely.'

'But the car park's empty. There's no one on the road. You'll never get an opportunity like this again.'

'I couldn't.'

'Imagine Dad's face if he heard you'd driven.'

She turns to him, a smile crossing her face. It reminds Rory of the mini rebellions they shared when he was a kid. And so she tries, checking her rear-view mirror every few seconds as though it will keep her safe. She indicates, though the only traffic is a tiny wagtail going about its business. She tries to pull off but the car jumps and cuts out. 'Mother of God,' she says.

'It's fine. Try again, just let the clutch off more slowly.'

They manage to drive two hundred metres up the deserted road through the plush golf course. They've cut out about eight times. She is elated that she has driven at all.

'Don't tell your father,' she says, then smiles. 'Not until I get better.'

'Atta girl,' he says, and gets out of the car to help her from the driver's seat.

26

Rory holds off for two weeks. But it doesn't feel right. And one day, finally, he has to pick up the phone.

'Hey,' he says, nervously, waiting for Orla's response.

'Hey, yourself! It's good to hear from you.'

The warmth of her reaction encourages him. 'I've been meaning to ring. How are you?'

'Fine. You?'

'Is it too late to take Lieutenant Dan out for some fresh air?' he asks.

'Lieutenant Dan would love some fresh air.'

It is a beautiful, balmy evening down at the pier. The clouds are like lily pads of melting ice cream in a clear blue sky. The sea is glassy calm. Not a hint of a breeze. Hard to believe it's Ireland. Lieutenant Dan runs ahead barking at seagulls, knowing he won't get them before they fly off, but trying anyway. They walk in silence. Sunlight glistens off the white hulls of moored yachts. Nothing stirs.

'I heard the news about Owen,' he says, eventually. 'Is everything OK?'

'No.' She half-laughs. Then sighs. 'You know, it wouldn't have been so bad if he'd *told* Jenna.'

'He didn't?'

'Of course he didn't. That would have been the decent thing to do. She read it on Kate's blog.'

'Kate has a blog?'

'Egomaniac that she is.'

'Why would she put that up on her blog?'

'I don't know. She mustn't have thought anyone reads it. Or maybe she didn't think Jenna would find out she had one.'

'God almighty. Is she dumb or something? Jenna spends a huge amount of time on the Net.'

'I don't want to believe she did it on purpose.'

'Jesus.' She could have – if Owen was afraid to tell Jenna, and Kate wanted her and Orla to know. But surely no one is that Machiavellian. 'How's Jenna?'

'Devastated. It's like she's finally admitted to herself that her father has his own agenda and she's not on it. She is *so* hurt.'

'And you? Are you OK?'

'I'm all right. Though I could kill him. He thinks his actions have no effect on anyone. Or maybe he just doesn't care.' She looks away and the anger seems to drain from her. 'I can't believe how much he has changed. There was a time I'd have forgiven him, taken him back.' She looks lost. Alone. Rory has an urge to put his arm around her but after what happened between them, that simple gesture might be confused.

'Sorry for not getting in touch,' he says. 'It was awkward.'

'I know.' She looks down at her flip-flopped feet. 'What got into us?'

He is stuck. Doesn't want to be the one to say it was a mistake – just in case, on the off chance, it wasn't for her. 'You were always better at analysis,' he says.

She looks out over the pier wall towards the city, at a horizon dominated by construction cranes. When she turns back, she is half-smiling. 'Wonder what Bingley would make of it.'

He thinks of Bingley and his 'nothing happens by

accident' theory. Could that be what she means? It was no accident? Or is he reading too much into it? Ever since the course, he's begun to see too many possibilities in simple statements or actions. Life was much easier without insight.

'I was missing Paul,' she blurts out. 'That's why. For me.'

He looks at her. So it *is* Morel that she loves. Relief floods him. He feels like laughing at himself, that she might even *consider* loving him! He'll have to do something about his ego. Still, what's so great about Morel?

'I'm sorry, Rory. When I finally worked out what got into me, it seemed awful, like I was using you, which I wasn't. It just happened, but I couldn't face you.'

He pretends to be appalled. 'So you *used* my body?'

She laughs, relieved. 'Didn't hear you complaining.'

'No.'

'So why, you?'

He shoves his hands into his pockets, looks down. 'I don't know. Lonely, I guess.' Suddenly, he looks up again, 'Not that you're not lovely, you are . . .'

'Shut up.' She links his arm and nudges him with her shoulder.

They walk in easy, companionable, relieved silence. Both heads turn together to watch a dinghy being towed, sails down, into the harbour by a motorboat. A father and son in lifejackets sit staring blankly ahead, disappointed that the wind died and they couldn't make it in under their own steam. The name of the boat is *Tsunami* and Rory is thinking it's about time they changed that.

'How did you know that Kate was pregnant?' she asks, as though it's just occurred to her.

'Owen told me.'

'You were *talking* to him?'

'It wasn't my idea. He barged in one night, drunk, wanting me to tell him who you were in love with. I said I didn't know.' He pauses. 'I wondered why you'd told him.'

'I'm a fool. That's why.' She sighs. 'He called to collect Jenna, had the nerve to say I was looking well. I was so angry with him, going off having another family, upsetting Jenna; I just wanted him to think for once that we were better off without him. I just reacted, blurted it out. Now I'm dreading that he'll say something to Jenna to make out that he's not so bad, he's not the only one.'

'He won't say anything. He's sorry.'

'What do you mean, he's sorry?'

'He told me that leaving you was the biggest mistake of his life.'

'Yeah, right.'

'He said he'd go back to you tomorrow if you'd have him.'

A brief flicker of hope crosses her face. Then it's gone. Replaced by anger. 'What makes him think I'd *have* him back?'

'He doesn't. But he said that if it wasn't for the baby, he'd leave Kate, be on his own and try to win you back.'

She looks at him, eyes so wide and sad, he knows he has said too much.

'Fool,' she says of Owen, but there are tears in her eyes.

'I'm sorry. I shouldn't have said anything.'

'No, no,' she says, her voice high. 'I'm glad you did. It's just that if it's true, it means that everything we've been through has been a waste. We should still be together, happy, not washed up and wrecked like we are, all of us.'

They've stopped walking. Orla's head is lowered, her

shoulders shaking. He puts his arms around her and holds her to him. He thinks about Mark and Louise and wonders again about what might have upset her then.

Later, back at the apartment, having smuggled Lieutenant Dan in, the conversation has moved away from Owen. On to Louise.

'Maybe you should talk to her,' Orla suggests. 'See what happened.'

He thinks of Mark and Lesley. 'She has other people now.'

'But maybe it's you she really wants.'

'She knows where I am,' he says, and hears the hardness in his own voice.

After an hour or so, Rory checks his watch. Eight-thirty.

'D'you need to be somewhere?' she asks.

'Nah, I'm meant to be meeting some friends in Dalkey, but I think I'll leave it.'

'If you've arranged to go, then you should.'

'You could come,' he suggests out of politeness, knowing that a) she'd hate it and b) she'd cramp Johnny's style.

'No. I should be home. Jenna's going out with friends.'

'So?' He doesn't understand. Doesn't that give Orla free reign?

'I like to be home when she's out. You know, in case of emergencies.'

He wonders if she is being overprotective, then decides he hasn't a clue. One thing is clear though, the free spirit she rediscovered on the course is beginning to fade, eclipsed by the roles she has to play. For the first time, he understands what happened with Morel, the freedom that affair offered. What he finds harder to comprehend is why in all the cases he knows, it is men who have left their marriages despite the fact that most of the compromising is done by women. He thinks of Louise and what she used to say about men. Maybe there was something in that, after all.

Rory invests a bit of energy in his appearance this time, showering, shaving and throwing on a white linen shirt he bought that day – a birthday present to himself. When he arrives at the pub Johnny and gang are already there, sitting outside in the beer garden basking in the evening sun. Aftershave floats on the balmy air. As does the hum of conversation and laughter. A lot of the faces are rosy and shiny, a combination of sun and booze. Rory pulls up a chair. After a round of 'heys' and 'how're you doings' the conversation quickly resumes. Johnny is having a go at Mark, calling him MarkandLesley.

'He's turned into a real waste of space, not even hitched and already she won't let him out.'

Rory, remembering what it was like being in a relationship, guesses it's more a case of Mark choosing to be with Lesley over Johnny.

'Ginormous ass at three o'clock,' says Pete.

All heads turn.

'Jesus,' says Johnny, appreciatively. Then it's straight back to the conversation. 'So where's Louise these days?'

Rory tries to sound casual when he says, 'Not around my ankle.'

'What, you broke up?' Johnny looks stunned. But then his face changes, as though he has discovered the reason. 'It was that Polish broad, wasn't it?'

'No. As a matter of fact it wasn't "that Polish broad". We're apart weeks.'

'Fuck me. I thought you guys were together for ever.'

'Yeah, well you were wrong.'

'I'm sorry, man,' Johnny says.

Rory makes a point of trying to attract the bar boy's attention. '*I'm* not.'

Johnny nods with his whole upper body. 'Cool. One more drinking buddy.' Classic Johnny, Rory thinks, viewing his break-up as an unexpected bonus. Johnny's group of single mates is becoming an endangered species. All around him, people are pairing off, getting hitched. Weddings in Italy, Greece, you name it. A regular moan of his is whatever happened to the good old-fashioned Irish wedding where you got smashed and tried to move in on one of the bridesmaids?

Rory manages to finally order. Being Irish, he makes it a full round.

'Hotties at twelve o'clock,' Johnny says, suddenly.

The 'hotties' he is referring to are three girls walking past on the path outside. To Rory they look too young, their hair long and straight, heavy make-up and legs that seem to go on for ever, the tops of which are disappearing under those tiny puffy skirts that used to be in when he was a teenager. Siofra had an orange one. He glances at Johnny. A bit young, mate, he feels like saying. He looks back at the three. And nearly chokes on his beer. The emerging ringleader is Jenna, his sixteen-year-old niece, the same Jenna that he used to bounce on his knee and who is now making eye contact with his mid-thirties friend. Rory looks at Johnny, who is holding Jenna's gaze. Rory reacts by standing suddenly. He assumes that when she sees him, she'll stop, not wanting to risk her mother finding out she was flirting with grown men in pubs.

She does see him, but her reaction is not what he expected. Without taking her eyes from his, she says something quickly to her friends, and, in perfect synchronicity, they start walking towards him.

Crap. What now?

He stays standing – to look authoritative. But slips his hands into his pockets – to seem casual about it. 'Jenna,' he says, when she reaches him.

'Rory,' she counters with a frighteningly sophisticated smile. 'Don't get up for me.' She eyes Johnny as if sharing a joke.

'How's your mother?' he asks, his tone pointed.

It's as if she hasn't heard. 'Who's your friend?' she drawls.

Johnny takes the cue and introduces himself and his mates. She introduces hers. Grown women, all, it seems. Johnny starts scanning for chairs. Rory is ready to punch him.

'They're not staying,' he says, glaring at Jenna.

Johnny looks from Rory to Jenna.

'Actually we are,' Jenna says cheerfully, throwing Rory with her audacity.

He thinks of Orla, at home, innocently unaware of proceedings. 'No. You're not.'

She just smiles, slowly sticks her butt out and lowers it seductively onto the nearest lap, like a professional porn star. She holds Rory's gaze as if daring him to do something about it. The owner of the lap, Simon, seems part pleased, part unsure. The other girls settle in, one on Pete's lap, another on a chair Johnny has gallantly produced. Rory is stunned at how quickly this has slipped from his control. What's she up to? Is she really flirting or does she think that by sitting with older guys she'll get served? In which case she's teenage drinking. As for her blatant sexuality . . . Doesn't she know he'll tell Orla? Maybe that's what she wants – to cause hassle. But she and Orla have been getting on so well. Why upset that? Maybe it's Owen she wants to bug. The bar boy is coming over. Does she really think that her uncle is going to just stand by and let her be served? She can forget it. He knows he was no angel on the underage drinking front, but this is different. Jenna doesn't want to end up on her ear. Not dressed like that. Not behaving like that. And not with guys like this.

'Jenna, I need to talk to you inside.'

She is looking at the bar boy, about to give her order.

'*Now.*'

She sees his face and knows he won't let it happen. Reluctantly she gets up.

They go inside. He glares at her.

'*What?*' she asks, as if he's the most uptight person in the entire world.

'D'you want me to embarrass you in front of your friends? Because I will. If I have to. You're sixteen.'

'So?'

'So it's against the law for you to drink.'

'Coke?'

'What exactly are you doing, Jenna?'

'Having fun. What does it look like?'

'You were sitting on the lap of a man old enough to be your father.' Just about.

'No law against that.' Arms folded. Jaw deliberately out of alignment. 'You finished?'

'You give me no choice but to ring Orla.'

She says nothing, just raises an eyebrow as if to say 'You child'.

He takes out his phone, starts punching numbers into it.

'All right. I'm going. I'm going. Jesus. I was just having a bit of fun.'

'Well, maybe next time you want a bit of fun, you should pull out your chessboard.'

She looks at him with real hatred. 'Fuck you.' She marches out ahead of him. Her friends are sipping beer. Hers is waiting on the table.

Rory glares at Johnny. Moron!

'Come on,' Jenna tells her friends. 'We're outta here.'

'Hey, let's just finish these,' the chubbier of the two girls is saying.

Jenna walks on without looking back. Reluctantly, they get up, one taking a final sad gulp of beer, the other slowly reaching over, and taking Johnny's face in her hands and kissing him on the mouth. Her 'bye' is laced with sex and regret. Rory, who has inadvertently caught a flash of cerise thong is close to collapse. He sinks into his chair.

Finally, they're out of view.

'What is *your* problem?' Johnny demands. All eyes round on Rory. Everyone wants an answer.

Rory focuses only on Johnny. 'D'you make a habit of picking up sixteen-year-olds?' His voice is ice.

Johnny laughs. '*They* were *not* sixteen.'

Pete adds, 'They'd ID.'

'Don't you think it's interesting they were asked for it?'

Johnny shrugs.

'She's my niece for fuck sake.'

Johnny pales. 'Why didn't you say?'

'Next time you see hotties, make sure they're out of nappies.' He is too angry and shocked by what has happened to stay. He wasn't cut out for Hottie Patrol. Johnny needs to wise up. Doesn't he know how quickly girls grow up now? Rory starts to walk home. Though it's more of a march. Down by Bullock Harbour, he sees the flat shiny head of the resident seal who has a very easy life, eating fish and generally larking about.

He should tell Owen about this. After all, it's his fault – him and his second family. But then Owen would probably blame Orla for not managing Jenna better. Rory thinks of the fake ID. Why else would she have it, only to get her hands on booze. He senses trouble. Has to tell Orla. But then, why does she have to be the one to clean up every mess created by Owen leaving? Maybe Jenna was only teasing Rory, pulling that stunt just to annoy him. No. There's more to it. The kid is looking for trouble. And Orla needs to know.

27

In Dun Laoghaire, he takes a taxi to Orla's, stopping on the way for a bottle of white wine. He wants to do this carefully, break the news slowly. Jenna is a good kid, angry, and maybe now a little out of control, but ultimately a good kid. He knows what it's like, underage drinking. It's something you slip into. Having a parent freak out about it might not be the best thing.

Orla is surprised to see him. 'What happened to your friends?'

'They were bugging me,' he says, then smiles.

She opens the door to let him in.

Glasses of wine in hand, they sit out on the patio, catching the last fighting rays of a dying orange sun.

'So, how's Jenna doing these days?' he asks, as casually as he can.

'Ah, all right. This thing with Owen has really upset her. She lets on she doesn't care. But I know she's devastated. She was the only child. It used to be just the three of us. So tight. She adored him, Rory. It makes this all the more tough on her.'

He wonders how to bring the conversation round to the incident in the pub. 'Who does she hang out with these days, kids from her school?'

Orla looks mildly surprised by the question, but then gets absorbed by the answer. 'That's *another* problem. I couldn't tell you who they are. I used to know all her friends. But since she started at that boarding school they've all changed.

I don't know any of them. I should. It's so important. But she won't ask any of them over no matter how many times I suggest it. I'm hoping that because it's a good school . . .' Her voice trails off. And then, as though to reassure herself, she says, 'She's good at picking friends. In her old school they were all lovely girls.'

He nods. Taps his middle finger on his thigh. 'She go out a lot?'

'Why d'you ask?'

'Just curious.'

'You know teenagers, out and about most evenings, now that they've summer holidays. God, it was so much easier when she was younger, always with us, under the same roof. But you have to give them responsibility, allow them to grow up. She's never back late. She has her mobile and always answers it. I always know where she is.' After a moment, she asks, 'Why all the questions about Jenna?'

'I saw her in Dalkey this evening.'

Orla looks confused. '*Dalkey*?'

'Yeah, with some friends.'

She is squinting. 'Are you sure it was Jenna?'

He has an urge to laugh. 'Yeah. I'm sure.'

'What was she doing?'

He pauses, deliberating. 'Walking down the street.'

'She was supposed to be in Dundrum. I'd never let her go as far as Dalkey. She knows that. Who was she with?' Anger gives way to concern.

'Two girls her own age. They seemed fine. No one was bothering them.'

'I'm going to call her. She knows she's not allowed to go that far. She's taking advantage . . .' Orla stands.

'Wait. Before you ring her, let me tell you everything.'

She sits down, worry all over her face.

He tells her.

And she's out of her chair heading for the kitchen. 'I'll kill her. I'll *kill* her.'

From inside, Orla's voice carries. Her words to her daughter are clipped, staccato, as though trying to contain a lot of emotion. Finally, she returns outside. 'She's on her way,' she says, but doesn't sit back down. Instead, she walks about, biting her knuckles. She becomes aware of Rory watching her, and sits. Then gets up again. 'I'm ringing her,' she says, 'I'm going to collect her.'

Orla makes another call and comes out carrying the car keys. 'You coming?'

'Just drop me off on the way. Otherwise it might be awkward for her.' He follows Orla into the kitchen.

'I want it to be awkward. And I need you to back me up.'

'You know what happened. I've told you everything. If I'm there it'll seem like we're ganging up on her.'

'Well, maybe that's exactly what she needs. I'm a walkover. Discussing everything, talking calmly about teenage drinking, and thinking her attitude so mature, believing her, not worrying, and all the time she's been going around with fake ID. Maybe I *need* to explode.' She looks at him.

He doesn't know what to say.

'Oh, God.' She puts her hands to her face, her fingers covering her cheeks. 'I don't know what to do,' she says, doubt and worry drowning outrage. 'I don't know what to do. I'm on my own. If only Owen was here.'

Owen is probably the problem, Rory thinks.

Her sigh is so deep it could affect the tides. 'We'd better go.'

'Orla?'

She stops, from where she is about to set the alarm.

'Maybe Owen needs to be involved in this.'

'*No.*'

'It's his responsibility too.'

She shakes her head.

'What if this is *about* Owen?'

She looks at him for a long moment. 'Didn't you know? Everything is about Owen.'

Orla does drop him off. And he spends the rest of the evening worrying about how it's going. When he doesn't hear from her, he worries more. Next morning, he delays as long as patience will allow him before finally calling her mobile.

'Can you talk?'

'Yeah, just a sec.' He hears her unlock the back door. 'OK,' she says, finally. He gathers she is down the garden, out of earshot.

'Well?'

'Well, I tried to be reasonable.'

'And?'

'Didn't work.'

He waits.

'I tried to stay calm. At first, it was going OK. She looked guilty, remorseful even. But as soon as we got home and I tried to make her see that she was wrong to have broken my trust and taken advantage of how easy I am on her, she blew up. She said that I can't stop her doing what she wants. And that the only reason I don't want *her* to have fun is because *I'm* not having any.'

'Jesus. That's harsh.'

'No. *That's* mild. She said that if I loved her I'd have tried to get Owen back, and now it's too late. She said I've more time for Jason than her. She said so many things one after the other and with such,' she pauses, '*hatred*, that all I can think is that however well I thought we were getting on, I was wrong.'

'It was drink talking. She doesn't mean all that.'

'This is my *daughter*, my little girl. My *angel*. Who used to love me. Unconditionally.'

Jesus, he thinks. *Is this parenting?*

'And you're right. She had been drinking.'

It was the blatant sexuality that worried him most . . . well, that combined with drink. Orla needs help with this, but he doesn't know how to say it. He hesitates. 'D'you think she should see someone?' As soon as he's said it, he regrets it as too drastic.

'*I* do.' He'd forgotten for a moment he was talking to Orla. 'Try telling *her.*'

'Maybe Owen could get her to.'

'Are you kidding? She won't take his calls. But still she wants him back. He's the one who is messing her up. And don't get me wrong – I don't think I'll have any more influence. Just because she's directing a lot of her resentment at him, doesn't mean she feels any less towards me. I learned that last night.'

'Is there anyone she'll listen to?'

She sighs. 'I don't know. Sometimes I think I don't know her any more.'

Rory tries to be hopeful. 'Maybe it was a once off.'

'No.' There's a pause. 'I found cans in her room a few weeks back. When I asked her about it, she said they weren't hers, she was keeping them for a friend. It was staring me in the face, but I wanted to believe her. I took the cans, went into a long explanation as to why drink doesn't solve anything, hoped that would be the end of it. Some agony aunt I am – advising the nation about their problems, when

I can't even face my own.' She pauses. 'Fake ID. That takes effort.'

He can't argue with that.

'I've taken it off her. Grounded her for a week. But I know I can't stop her. If she wants to drink, she'll find a way.'

'What are you going to do?'

'I don't know,' she says slowly. 'I. Don't. Know. She gets too much money. Owen – *again*.'

'Then you'll have to talk to him.'

'She probably won't take it from him now. But it's not just the money. She has to decide not to drink.'

'How is she now?'

'Hasn't come down. And who knows what she'll be like when she does. An angel or a devil, whatever suits. Should I have gone mad, screamed at her, shouted, ranted, *frightened* her into stopping?'

'I don't know, Orla. This is out of my league. There must be someone who can help, someone you could go to for advice.'

Silence for a moment. 'There are one or two good teen psychologists I know from writing the column. Maybe I'll talk to them.'

'I wish you'd tell Owen.'

'Why, so he can blame me for messing up?'

Rory calls for Jason, who is ready this time. Still, Rory lingers.

'How's the job going?' he asks Naomi.

She produces a wide smile, a rare and heartwarming thing, he discovers. 'The job's great. *Great*.'

'Good,' he says. 'Good.'

'You coming?' Jason asks.

'Eh, yeah.' He wants to offer to help Naomi in some way, but can't think of how without sounding charitable or condescending. 'OK, well, see you later then,' he says.

Jason is heading for the steps.

Before Rory turns away from her, Naomi speaks quietly, so her son can't hear. 'Thanks for not forgetting him.'

It catches Rory by surprise. 'I'd never do that.'

'I know that now.'

And it occurs to Rory that while he was busy thinking the worst of Naomi, so was she about him.

They've been in Cabinteely Park over an hour now. Jason has raced to the top of a climbing frame that resembles a giant spider's web of ropes. Rory, worried that he'll fall, has had to look away. Afterwards, they knock a ball around.

Walking back to the car, Jason throws the ball up in the air.

Rory asks, 'So, how's your mum?'

Jason catches the ball and holds it. 'Fine.'

'Job going OK?'

'Yeah, can we get a drink?'

'Sure. D'you ever call in to the flower shop?'

'Sometimes.'

'What's it like?'

Jason throws him a look. 'You know what it's like.'

'Yeah, I know, but I was just wondering what *you* thought of it.'

'I like it, 'specially when Louise gives me jobs. There's this flower, right, called the Amaryllis and it grows real fast and I got a measuring tape an' all and a watering can and I even got a chart to write down how fast it's growing. It's cool. We keep it in the shop.'

We. He imagines the three of them together. Happy. And

249

he wonders: for someone who never wanted a family, Louise seems to have adopted this one. He imagines her with Jason, measuring the plant with him, touching his hair, smiling. And then he makes himself stop.

'How is she, Louise?'

'Louise is *cool*. Don't know why you dumped her.'

Rory's about to say he didn't when he imagines the interrogation that would follow. 'Is she happy?'

He shrugs. 'Suppose so.'

'And everything's all right with her, yeah?'

'I dunno. I'm just a kid.'

'Sorry.'

'Want me to ask her if she's happy?'

'*No!* No. Don't do that. She's fine. She's absolutely fine.'

28

Rory is not a born orator, of this he has never been more aware. Already he has spent days on his best man's speech. And it doesn't show. He is wasting yet another evening in front of the computer, worrying not only about making a fool of himself in public but in front of Louise, who will no doubt be there. Bad enough that he has to face her, but to have to perform in front of her too seems worse than bad luck. There doesn't seem any way around it. When the phone rings, it takes a moment for him to hear it. His worries suddenly disappear. Replaced by another. His father is in A&E. Suspected stroke. Brought in by ambulance. Not looking good. Come immediately.

He is in the car, on his way, imagining his father unconscious, his mother, who is with him, stunned, terrified and surrounded by casualties, noise and bright lights. What were they doing when it happened? Was she with him? Does Siofra know? He calls her. And her line is busy. Maybe the hospital is on to her now. He tries Owen. His phone is off. And the answering machine at his girlfriend's apartment is on. He leaves a message on both.

Pulling into the staff car park he dials Siofra's number again, and she answers.

'Were the hospital on to you?' he asks.

'The hospital? No. Why? Is everything OK?'

Best to be straight. 'Dad's had a stroke.'

'Oh, God.'

'He's in A&E.'

'Where? Paul's?' It's his parents' local hospital.

'Yeah, Mum's with him. I'm just here now.'

'Is it bad?'

'I don't know. But I think you'd better come.'

'Oh, God, Rory.'

He thinks about her speeding up from Kildare. 'Take your time, OK?'

'Is Owen there?'

'No. Can't track him down.'

'Now why doesn't that surprise me?'

Rory's mother is sitting alone on a hard plastic chair. She looks small and frail. When she sees Rory her eyes become hopeful, as if he'll have a solution. He crouches down, takes her hands in his and before he can stop himself tells her it will be OK. Because he wants it to be – for her. She has lived most of her life with her husband, depended on him, and loved him. Rory wants to talk to the doctors, but they're working on his father, so he sits with his mum and wonders if he might have prevented this. If only he'd screened him . . . but then his father, a doctor himself, would have been indignant at the suggestion.

Restless, he goes outside to call Owen again.

This time, he gets through.

'Is he OK?' Owen asks, as if he wants to be told, 'Yes, he's fine, this isn't another life crisis you have to deal with.'

Rory has to disappoint. 'I don't know. It's not good.'

'What do you mean, you don't know? You're at the hospital, aren't you?'

'I haven't spoken to anyone yet.'

'Haven't you seen him? You're the neurologist, for Christ's sake.'

'Just get here, OK?' Rory says and kills the line.

*

He is sitting edgily beside his mother when Siofra arrives, rushing in, looking around for them. Rory's first thought: she lives in Kildare, and she's still here before Owen. But he's glad that she's first. He stands and she spots him. Her eyes move automatically to their mum and she hurries over and puts her arms around her. She asks all the right questions, questions that never occurred to Rory, including the offer of a cup of tea.

She's better at this, he thinks.

Rory has seen hundreds of stroke victims, but he is still unprepared for the sight that greets him behind the curtain. His eyes smart and he has to swallow. The man who dominated his life for so long is lying on his side, breathing deeply, his flaccid cheek moving in and out with every breath, his skin drained of colour, his eyes closed. It is too hard to witness. And Rory can't stay. On the other side of the curtain, he sees that Owen has arrived and is talking to Sinead, the casualty registrar, his face serious, back straight, arms folded. He looks like a man taking charge. Rory has an instant urge to floor him. Owen sees him and nods curtly. Sinead excuses herself. Owen approaches his brother and starts to relate what he has just learnt. It's as though he has made the diagnosis himself.

'It's all right,' Rory says. 'I know.'

Owen keeps talking.

'You better go in to him,' Rory interrupts rather than punch him, then walks away, leaving Owen with no choice but to go to his father.

Their father is finally admitted to Rory's ward. He rallies. Weakens. Rallies again. Hope, no hope, hope, confusion. This cycle lasts for days and Rory's exhausted family look to him for answers. Less than six per cent of his father's brain is functioning. There is no hope. If Rory doesn't let them know, they'll have to hear it from a stranger. Telling his mother is the hardest thing he has ever had to do. For days, he stays with her at the family home, driving her to and from the hospital, making sure she eats, sleeps, takes the tranquillizers prescribed for her, ensuring that she is not alone. Siofra asked her to stay with them, but it is too far from the hospital. In any case, Rory's mother wants to be at home.

She has just gone to lie down, when Rory gets a call from an upbeat Sergeant O'Neill. 'Thought you'd want to know. Your assailant has pleaded guilty to both crimes.'

'Oh.' Rory closes his eyes in an attempt to concentrate. 'Good,' he says, not really knowing the implication of this, and finding it hard to generate the enthusiasm to care.

'He's been jailed for a year.'

'Oh. Right. Good.'

There is a silence on the line. Rory senses that something else needs to be said. Finally, it comes to him. 'And thank you so much for your efforts.'

'Just doing our job,' O'Neill says, but there is pride in his voice.

One afternoon, a fog blows in from the sea. It rolls in fast, like billowing smoke carried on the wind, enveloping the stony façade of the hospital and dropping the temperature instantly. Entering with his mother, Rory feels its chill with a shiver and knows instinctively that his father is dead. His mother looks up at him, fear in her eyes and he puts an arm around her to let her know that he's here for her.

There will be no best man's speech. Not from Rory, at least. The funeral falls on the day of Mark and Lesley's wedding.

That morning, Rory, Siofra and Owen gather at the family home. Owen plays the role of chief organizer, but it is Siofra who gets their mother ready for church. In the bathroom, Rory, supposedly washing his hands, is gazing into the turquoise sink that has been here all his life. Here he washed away the results of his first meagre shave and earth from numerous rugby pitches. The taps stand to attention, like soldiers on opposite sides, tiny blue and red caps identifying their allegiances. He stares into the water, clouded now by soap, trying to remember moments of closeness with his father. Owen calls his name. They're ready to go. It brings him back to when he was a kid, delaying until the last minute to leave for church. It could be his father calling him. He could be alive. They could start over. And get it right.

There is no black limousine. His old man would have hated that. Instead, Owen drives in his car, reversing out onto a road that Rory is more familiar with than any other, the road he grew up on. He glances at his mother, sitting up front. She looks straight ahead, unmoving.

Nobody talks. There is nothing to say.

Arriving deliberately early, Rory is disappointed to see that people have already gathered. Faces he doesn't know and faces he recognizes from various stages of his life, relatives he hasn't seen in years, neighbours, everyone older, some by decades. He looks for faces that mean something to him and is relieved to find Orla's. Jenna's too. When was that kid last happy? No sign of Tony or the children. Rory imagines them still on the road. No sign of Louise. Not that he had expected her to turn up.

He catches sight of Mark and Lesley walking through the church gates. That they should be here on the morning of their wedding touches him. He tells his family he will be back in a moment and makes his way over to them.

'Thanks so much for coming,' he says, holding out his hand to Mark.

Mark uses it to pull Rory into a hug. He bangs him on the back. 'I'm sorry, man.'

'Yeah,' Rory says, not sure how else to answer. He pulls back. 'Look, I know it's your big day so don't feel you have to go to the graveyard or anything. You must've a load to do. I'll see you when you get back from the honeymoon, OK?'

Mark looks at Lesley, then back at Rory. 'We're only going to have a few days, Roars. A job's come through in Birmingham. We've only just heard.'

'That quick? Wow.' He is taken aback. 'Congratulations.' He smiles. 'It's all happening for you.' He glances behind him. Siofra, linking her mother's arm, is starting to guide her into the church. 'Listen, I gotta go. Good luck today. And, you know, for ever, I guess.'

'I'll give you a call when we're back,' Mark says.

Rory nods, then runs to catch up with his family.

Going inside is like entering a time warp. This is the church of his childhood. Over there, the confessional box where he made his First Confession. And there, where the first girl he ever fancied used to sit with her family. Never once, in all his time in this church, did Rory imagine a day he would return to bury his father.

They file into the front pew, Siofra on one side of his mother, Owen on the other, leaving Rory closest to the coffin, the last place he wants to be. He's relieved when Alex comes running up to sit with 'Nana'. She seems to wake from her daze, smiling at her grandson and sitting him up on her lap. She plants a kiss on the top of his head and holds him close.

In front of Rory, the cloth on the altar proclaims Alleluia. Is that appropriate, he wonders. Is this a celebration? Perhaps so. His father prayed enough to go straight up – if that's what actually happens. There's a book open on the altar. The bible, Rory supposes. There's a chalice. One, two, three, four, five, six gold candlesticks. Six lit candles. A golden cupboard the name of which escapes Rory. All these things remind Rory of his father. Whose first love had been the church. Rory wonders why he hadn't become a priest. A priest openly declares his love of God. But he doesn't have to declare love to anyone else. Did his father ever tell his mother he loved her? He certainly never made any such declarations to Rory. And now he is gone. Is it easier, Rory wonders, to lose a parent you were close to? At least you'd have something to cling to, memories of good times you had together. Less regrets.

It is a straightforward, simple Mass, uncomplicated by tributes of any kind – the way his old man would have wanted it. There's singing. Some prayers in Irish. And out of the blue, a memory comes to Rory: he is small – six, maybe seven – and in the bath. He is putting his head back so the shampoo doesn't run into his eyes. His father, rinsing his hair, says 'good boy'. Rory is thrilled at that. He's done something good and his father has noticed. The memory warms him. If only he could think of more. Build a mental scrapbook of them. Rewrite his past. Pretend.

Outside, wellwishers separate Rory from the rest of his family, some shaking his hand, some hugging him, all talking of his father in saintly tones. One man holds Rory's elbow while he shakes his hand, another bangs his shoulder.

'He was a good man,' says a woman he's never met before, who is wearing soft, yellow and white shoes that look comfortable and silly.

'A good doctor,' proclaims a man with a trouser leg tucked into his sock.

'I'm sorry, Rory,' says another stranger. He wonders how she knows his name. When she walks away, he notices that the stitching at the back of her jacket is undone and the lining is gaping.

Then through the crowd, Louise is there, coming to him, holding his eyes with hers. Everything around him quietens. He wonders if it's really happening, afraid to move in case it's an illusion.

When she reaches him she just smiles, eyes sad. She has been crying. Which confuses him. She didn't really know his father – Rory had made sure of that. Her face is so sweet to him, so familiar, and yet, there is something different about it too. Something softer, gentler. He continues to doubt the reality of what he is seeing. Until she speaks.

'Hey.'

'Hey.'

She smiles again and for a moment they're quiet. Just looking at each other.

Her voice is hoarse when she finally speaks. 'I just want you to know that I'm here for you, Rory. If you need me.'

She is so close he could reach out and touch her. He knows that all he has to do is say – I need you – and she'll be back in his life, in some context at least. He opens his mouth to speak, but remembers how she didn't need him and pride hardens his heart.

'Why would I need you?' he asks, looking at her as if she is the woman in yellow shoes, as if he doesn't know her.

She holds her ground, doesn't falter. 'Because,' she says, chin high, 'I know what it's like to lose a parent who was impossible to love. I know what it's like when they've gone and you know you'll never get a chance to make it right between you. I know what that's like, Rory. That's why.' She smiles, her eyes filling. Then she turns. And before he can stop her, she is walking quickly away. He wants to go after her, tell her that of course he needs her. More than that. He loves her. But he doesn't move, immobilized by wounded pride.

There is food for the people who have travelled and anyone who wants to come back to the house. Siofra has organized caterers. It is the biggest gathering his parents have ever had. His father is probably glad he's not there. His house is full. Rory stands at the kitchen sink, his back to the crowd, staring out the window. Grass is growing over the slabs that were once a path. The box hedges they used to jump over as kids, pretending to be horses, need to be cut back. A green chaffinch alights on one of the leylandii the new neighbours have planted, blocking his parents' light. Another memory surfaces, this time of birdwatching. His father had taken him. Just him. He had seemed happy then, his dad, not saying much, just telling Rory which birds were which and how to identify them by their markings, flight and calls. Rory was in heaven. Until he had dropped the binoculars on his bare foot and broken a toe, putting an end to birdwatching for ever. As soon as the toe healed, Rory had asked to go again, but his father said he was too busy. So Rory did it alone. Whenever he was out and saw a new bird, he'd check the book when he got home. He knew them all. Tried to tell his father about them. But it didn't make a difference. He never took Rory birdwatching again. Rory never knew why.

Rory drifts into the sitting room. It's crowded and noisy and people want to talk about his father. They are not his memories. He wanders out to the front room, which hasn't been opened to people. He takes off his jacket, tie. Sits in his father's chair, back to the door, looking at framed photos from his childhood. There aren't many. He remembers trips to the beach in the Ford Cortina, he, Owen and Siofra standing up in the back when his father was about to go over a bump, everyone in good form, so long as no one did anything to upset the boss. And sometimes Rory did – to break the tension, get it over with.

Rory looks at the photos. Parents. Children. He still feels like a child when in the company of a parent. And, he guesses, that's a reality. As long as your parents are alive, you're still their child. Then they're gone. And there's no one above you. No safety net. You have to grow up, have a family of your own, keep the cycle going. He hears the door open at the other side of the room. He knows that he is hidden from view. If he keeps still maybe whoever it is will go away. The door closes.

'How dare you?' whispers a voice.

Silence.

'This is your grandfather's funeral and you use it to get your hands on alcohol? I don't believe you, Jenna. How many have you had?'

'None. You took care of that.'

'This is half gone.'

'Well, a half then. *Obviously.*'

Should Rory clear his throat, let them know he's here?

'You're grounded,' Orla says.

'God, Mum, where's your imagination?' Jenna sounds simultaneously bored and condescending. 'Couldn't you've come up with something more creative? A public flogging maybe?'

He's definitely not budging now.

'I've had enough, Jenna.'

'So have I. Enough of you treating me like a baby. I'm sixteen years old.'

'Too young to be drinking.'

'Too old to be told what to do by her *mummy*.'

'Enough. I want you to stay here and think about what you've done ...'

'What's this, Time Out?'

'Call it what you like. If you want me to stop treating you like a child, stop acting like one.'

Rory hears the door close, then one word muttered in anger – 'bitch'. Nothing for a second, then he hears her coming further into the room. He panics. What will he do? He can't let her know he heard all that. He closes his eyes, tilts his head to one side and breathes slowly and deeply. He hears her sit in one of the chairs opposite and for a moment, nothing else. Then her sassy voice. 'I know you're awake.'

He doesn't budge.

'You heard all that, didn't you?'

He opens one eye, then another, pulls a face. 'I'd my ears blocked.'

'Sure.' But she smiles.

He makes to get up. 'Want me to leave you in peace?'

'God, no. Someone should keep an eye on me – I've had a lot of alcohol.'

He laughs.

'Were *your* parents like that?' she asks.

He puts his hands up. 'Look. I don't want to get involved.'

'You drank, though, didn't you, when you were a teenager? I bet you did.'

'We all make mistakes.'

'I knew it. I knew you did.'

The last thing he wants to do is glorify it. 'It's not something I'm proud of, Jenna. If it wasn't for rugby it might have got out of control.'

'What are you talking about? Rugby heads are real drinkers.'

'Some are. But I took the game seriously, the training, the whole lot. I wanted to play for Ireland.' He laughs, realizing how ridiculous that sounds now. He didn't have the talent. His drive to make his father notice him only took him so far.

'When you *did* drink, what were your parents like?'

'They didn't know.'

'You were lucky,' she says.

He's tempted to stand up for Orla, but knows that if he does he'll lose any influence he might have on his niece. 'My luck was finding rugby.'

Jenna looks towards the door. 'It was just a drink. She needn't have lost it. My grandfather's dead. My father's *girlfriend* turns up looking like she's got twins in there. Jesus. *You* can see why I needed a drink.'

As a doctor, he doesn't like the sound of a sixteen-year-old *needing* a drink. He says nothing.

'*She* can't see anything. I don't think she was *ever* young.'

Any response would be in defence of Orla. So he gives none.

'She's an agony aunt, but she knows *nothing* about agony.'

He wants to say that she's had her fair share. But he also wants to say something that has occurred to him too late. 'Parents die, Jenna, all of a sudden they die. And they're gone. And it's too late to make things right.'

For a moment, she says nothing. Then, 'Didn't you get on with Granddad?'

'We weren't close. Ever.'

'Did Dad get on with him?'

'I think Siofra got on with him best,' Rory says, avoiding

a direct no. 'I think it's easier for daughters to get on with their fathers.'

'Unless their fathers are complete plonkers and don't give a shit about them.'

'He gives a shit, Jenna.'

'How do *you* know?'

'He told me.'

'When?' Not believing.

'He called over one night, very upset about the way things have turned out between you.'

'Sure.'

'The baby was an accident.'

'That wouldn't have happened if he'd kept his dick to himself.'

Rory is suddenly embarrassed by the reference to sex.

'He does love you.'

She seems to have brightened a bit but says, 'Funny way of showing it.'

'He might have made a few mistakes.'

'A few?'

'But at least he loves you, has time for you. At least you've a relationship.'

'Not any more.'

'Well, maybe –'

She stands suddenly. 'I gotta go – get some more beer,' she jokes.

He smiles at that.

'Rory?'

'Yeah?'

'You're actually OK.'

'What, for an uncle?' He smiles.

'For someone who ratted on me to my mom.'

He thinks of that night. 'Those guys are no good.'

'So why were you with them?'

'No good from a woman's point of view. They're not exactly looking for love.'

'Neither was I.'

He doesn't want to ask what she was looking for. And he's not going to suggest sticking to boys her own age, though that's exactly what he'd like to do.

'Anyway. Thanks for listening.'

'Sure.'

29

Owen has called a 'family meeting'. Interesting phraseology, Rory thinks, given that their mother's not invited. Brothers and sister only. In Rory's apartment. Owen, acting like some kind of master of ceremonies simply because he's the eldest, tempts Rory to ask for a written agenda. What stops him is the belief that his brother ultimately has their mother's best interests at heart. The fact that she has been excluded implies that this is about her, about what they are going to do to support her now, or specifically what Owen is going to suggest Rory and Siofra do. Delegation has always been his strong point.

As soon as they've settled, Owen stands and clears his throat.

Rory is so close to asking if he should take minutes.

'I called this meeting,' Owen begins, 'because we need to discuss the way we've been excluded from the will.'

Rory and Siofra exchange glances. Excluded? They never expected to be *included*. Everything went to their mother, the way it should have. The will was no surprise to them.

'There's nothing to discuss,' Siofra says.

'We're entitled to our share,' Owen insists.

'I don't believe this,' Siofra says, looking at Rory, as though for back up.

'He left us *nothing*.'

Rory is calm. 'What d'you want to do Owen, *contest the will*?' Even he wouldn't go that far.

'In a word, yes.'

Siofra stares at him. 'You'd do that to Mum?'

'This isn't about Mum. It's about what we're entitled to.'

'Bullshit,' she says. 'Of course it's about Mum. She's going through enough without worrying about you grabbing from her. And I like the way you say "we". Don't expect *us* to have anything to do with this.' She looks at Rory.

It's as if they're kids again, each claiming that a silent Rory is on their side, speaking for him, making assumptions.

'It's all right for you,' Owen says to Siofra, 'you're not trying to support two families.'

'No, I wasn't dumb enough to walk out on a perfectly good one.' She glares at him.

'If this is a lecture, Siofra, you can just fuck off.'

'You got one point six million for your house. Isn't that enough for you?'

'Not after it's been split in two and the mortgage paid off. You try buying a family home and supporting two families in this country with what's left over.'

'Some of us are prepared to move to the sticks.'

'OK, OK,' Rory says. 'Calm down.' They're reverting to their childhood roles, Rory trying to be peacemaker between his brother and sister.

And as usual, Siofra ignores him. 'And, anyway, it's not two families you're responsible for, Owen, it's three. Mum looked after us all our lives, now it's our turn.'

'Maybe she doesn't want looking after,' Owen suggests.

'You always did take the easy way out.' Siofra.

'Stop,' Rory says. 'Will you just stop.'

'All right for you,' Owen says turning on Rory. 'At least he left *you* something.'

'A stethoscope,' Siofra says, dismissing it.

But to Rory it's more than a stethoscope. It's a gesture, as if, after all these years, his father has finally given his blessing – it's all right that he did medicine. The gesture lifted Rory, but saddened him too. Why couldn't it have been made when his father was alive, when there was still time?

'He left me nothing,' Owen continues, 'not so much as a pair of shoes. Might as well have said, "You're not my son."'

Rory's voice is low. 'It was just his way of making peace with me.'

'So why didn't he make peace with *me*?'

And it occurs to Rory that maybe that's what this is all about. Not money. But love. After a lifetime pretending otherwise, maybe Owen really *did* care what his father thought of him?

'Oh, get over yourself,' Siofra is saying. 'I didn't get a bloody stethoscope. Do you see me complaining? Whatever his reason for not leaving us anything, it has nothing to do with Mum. So don't take it out on her.'

'He was a bastard,' Owen says.

'Stop.' Rory gets up and walks from the room. Behind him he hears Siofra's voice being raised again and his brother's after that. Maybe it meant nothing. Maybe it *was* just a stethoscope. Maybe his father was just being practical. Why would he have changed after all those years?

When he's up to facing them again, it's half an hour later.

Siofra is alone. When she looks up, he sees that she's been crying. 'How did he turn out like that?' she asks.

He sits down. 'He's under a lot of pressure.'

'Pressure, my ass. You always make excuses for him. He knows Mum would do anything for him. All he has to do is ask. And yet he talks about contesting the will. Entitlements. He makes me sick.'

'He won't do it. He's upset about the stethoscope, not the money.'

'Can he contest the will alone?'

'I don't know. I presume so.'

'We have to stop him.'

'I really don't think he'll do it.'

'You don't know Kate.'

'No. And I don't want to,' Rory says, understanding, at last, why the meeting wasn't held at Owen's.

Rory's mother says she's fine, but there's no food in the fridge. She says she's grand but there's no *Irish Times* on the kitchen table. And she has forgotten to offer him tea. She sits in the chair and pretends.

The house is cold. Rory turns on the heat. The place still feels miserable.

'Come on. We're going out,' he says.

'I don't feel up to it.'

'We've a regular date and we're keeping it.' He's glad now that he can say this, because it doesn't seem like pity.

Her smile is weak, but there.

At the shopping centre, he doesn't leave her side, and she doesn't argue. In Marks and Spencer they fill a small basket with food. Siofra has been making up dinners for her, freezing them in batches, to be defrosted daily. Rory works at supplementing that with food that is easy and healthy – soup, smoothies, bread, cheese, ham and yoghurt.

His mother picks up a jar of pickled onions. Then puts it back, remembering that the person who usually eats them is no longer there.

'What am I going to do without him?'

*

The house is warm when they return. Rory unpacks the food. When he checks the freezer, he sees all the dinners lined up, untouched. Clearly, he has to call more often, every evening to start with, until he's sure that she is warm, eating, talking, coping.

He develops a routine, calling in after work, defrosting a meal and eating with her. For almost a week, they say little, Rory taking his lead from her. Then one evening, out of the blue, she starts to speak.

'How did this happen, Rory? He was fine. *Fine.*' She sounds both baffled and distressed. 'Were there signs, things I should have noticed, warnings I didn't heed?' She closes her eyes. 'I keep thinking back, trying to remember. But I can't. I can't remember anything out of the ordinary.' She looks at Rory, needing answers, reassurance.

And Rory is relieved. Relieved that she is finally talking. Because now, at least, he knows what to say, what she needs to hear. 'Mum, there's nothing you could have done. If there were signs, Dad would have picked up on them himself. He was a good doctor. He'd have taken care of himself.' It's a shock to find himself talking of his father in the past tense.

'I can't believe he's gone,' she says, eyes wide. 'One minute he was there, wondering if we should get the gutters cleaned, the next he was gone. *Gone.* I keep turning to tell him things and he's not there.'

They lived together almost fifty years, Rory thinks. His absence must be like losing a limb. 'Would you like me to move in for a while?'

She looks at him, hopeful, but then shuts that down. 'No.' Her voice is firm. 'No, Rory. I need to learn to fend for myself.'

That's when he really starts to worry. His father did everything for the two of them. Made the decisions. Drove.

Handled the finances. How will she cope? How will she even get her shopping done? She can't drive. As well as losing her husband, these are very practical issues she has to worry about now. It's ironic, he thinks, how one of her roles as a parent was to teach her kids independence. Now, at sixty-five, it's her turn to learn. And their turn to teach her.

At work, stroke patients remind Rory of his father. He finds himself spending an unnecessary amount of time with them. In the majority of cases, there isn't much more he can do. And that frustrates him. Maybe he should get involved in research, clinical trials . . .

He has swapped his stethoscope in favour of his father's tattered one. He likes the feel of it round his neck. Considers it lucky. A nurse borrows it, once, shortly before he goes off duty. He's pulling up outside his mother's house when he remembers it. He turns the car around and doesn't relax until he has it back. He tells himself he should be more careful with it. Wonders if he shouldn't use it every day. But then, something tells him his father wanted him to.

30

Late in July, Orla calls Rory one evening, sounding shaky. She asks him to come over. Jenna has been giving trouble, kicked out of summer camp because of disruption and mitching. It has taken its toll on Orla, who has been looking increasingly tired and pale. Rory, worried that she's not coping, has once again suggested getting Owen involved. But she won't have it. Rory can't understand this. He'll find out eventually. Wouldn't it be easier if she were the one to tell him? Rory puts down the phone, thinking that whatever's happened now, the situation has suddenly become a lot worse.

Orla shows him into the sitting room, closes the door and sits on the edge of the couch.

'What is it?' he asks, concerned, and taking the seat opposite.

'I'm in trouble, Rory.'

He could tell that by looking at her. 'What happened? What has she done this time?'

'Nothing.' Her head drops. When she lifts it again, she says, 'It's not Jenna. It's me.' She pauses, then looks right into his eyes. 'I'm pregnant.'

'*Pregnant?*' A picture of her naked and on top of him flashes into his mind. But then he visualizes Morel walking from her bedroom. And hopes . . .

'I'm eight weeks gone,' she says, her eyes full of meaning.

Morel is out of the picture. Rory's mouth is suddenly dry. He doesn't suppose it's a mistake?

'I've tried three separate tests, all positive.'

He thought he was here to talk about Jenna.

'I can't believe . . .' Orla says, 'our *one* time . . . It's just so typical. Murphy's Bloody Law. It was created for me. They should rename it.'

This is not how Rory imagined it would be, hearing he was going to be a father. It was meant to be anticipated, planned, looked forward to. Not a mistake. 'When is it due?' he finally manages.

She covers her face with her hands. 'I can't think about that.'

Good. Because he's not sure he can either.

'What am I going to do?' Her eyes look wild. He's never seen her so distressed.

He gets up and goes to her. 'You mean, what are *we* going to do. We're in this together, Orla.'

It's as if she doesn't hear him. 'What do I tell Jenna? Who do I say the father is? You know what she's like about Owen having a second family.'

Rory hadn't thought of that.

'Both her parents will have new families now, who'll have time for her? That's the way she'll see it.'

'I'm sure if we talked to her, explained . . .' He's not sure of anything. He just wants to stop her worrying.

'How? How can I explain? What can I say? She's my daughter, your niece. She's sixteen.'

'There has to be a solution,' he says, unable to think of one. 'There's always a solution . . . we'll find one.'

She looks at him as if he's out of touch with reality.

Back at the apartment, Rory tries to absorb the news. He tells himself that this is what he wanted, a baby. He just has to get used to the circumstances. Some circumstances, though. He and his brother's ex-wife. That's going to upset a lot of people, all of them family. A problem for him, but an even bigger one for Orla. What will she do about Jenna? What *can* she do? He's going to be more than a little uncomfortable himself, looking his niece in the eye. Not to mention Owen. He sighs, gets up and relieves the fridge of a beer. Out on the balcony, he cracks it open and takes a long drink.

'That's right,' he can hear his father say, 'solve everything with a drink.' His father. He would be disgusted with Rory. Or maybe relieved. He always did say that Rory would mess up. Now he has. He thinks of his mum. What will she make of this? If nothing else, it'll give her another focus. And that can't be bad. Rory wonders if she might even be happy at the thought of another grandchild, a new life to look forward to – once she gets over the shock.

Rory works out the dates. February.

He rechecks.

His child is due to be born in the same month as his father. One life ending, another starting. It really hits him then, in a positive way. He's going to be a dad. No need to strive towards it any more. It is happening. He can get on with life, get over Louise, concentrate on the baby. And Orla. He'll help in whatever way he can. What does she need from him? Why didn't he ask? Should they consider getting married? Would that help? He's not in love with Orla, but marriage might be best for the child and that is a priority. He wants to do this right. But maybe Orla wouldn't want to marry him. She'd have to divorce Owen. Which would upset Jenna. But this whole thing will upset Jenna. There's no way around that. There is so much to think about.

Orla shouldn't give up on her dream of becoming a counsellor. But then, who'd look after the baby?

They need to sit down, talk this through.

One thing, though, he's going to make clear from the start: they're in this together. She is not alone.

The following day, Owen contacts Rory, wanting to meet for lunch. Rory's first reaction is one of panic. *Does he know?* He tells himself to calm down. If Owen knew, he wouldn't be on the phone suggesting lunch; he'd be over here punching his lights out. This must be about their father's will. Why, then, isn't Siofra included? Is Owen trying to get him on his side? If so, he's wasting his time.

Rory tells him he's working. But Owen will not be put off. He'll drop by the hospital, he says. They can eat at the canteen.

They meet at the hospital entrance. Owen, in a dark grey suit, looks all business.

'I don't have long,' Rory says, already starting to walk towards the canteen.

'Neither do I,' says his brother, keeping pace.

An uneasy silence falls between them. Until Owen's phone rings. And he takes the call. Which pisses Rory off. Couldn't he have just turned it off? He expects Rory to drop everything, but it's business as usual for him.

'What do you mean, is she with me? Of course she's not with me.' Owen has stopped dead in the middle of the corridor. 'Are you telling me you don't know where she is?'

Rory knows instinctively that he's talking to Orla about Jenna. He watches as, hand at the back of his neck, Owen starts to pace back and forth while listening to what must be a long explanation. Concerned, Rory wants to grab the phone. But he gets a grip, and tries to make do with waiting on every word his brother utters.

'Where have you checked?' Owen asks. There is a pause while he listens. 'What about Mum's?' Another pause. 'Your parents?' Brief silence. 'What about her old friends?' His voice is very quiet when he says, 'Have you called the police?' Another long pause. Then loudly, 'Why're you only calling me now?' His eyes meet Rory's. There's panic in them. 'OK, OK,' he says into the phone. 'Let's not waste any more time talking. What do you want me to do? Where can I look? Jesus, Orla, where can she be?' After a few seconds, he hangs up.

'Jenna's missing,' he says to Rory, unnecessarily. 'Her bed wasn't slept in last night.'

'But it's lunchtime,' Rory says, without thinking.

'Jenna doesn't get up till noon. Orla went in to see if she wanted a sandwich and she wasn't there. She's tried everywhere. No one's seen her. Her mobile is going straight to voicemail.'

'Where the hell is she?' Rory worries aloud, remembering the way she was in the pub and thinking the worst.

'I don't know. No one tells me anything. Did *you* know she's been drinking?'

Rory doesn't answer.

'Why the hell didn't anyone tell me before now?'

Rory wants to call Orla, but not with Owen there. 'What can I do?'

'Is there anywhere you can think of where she might be?'

Rory hesitates before saying, 'I could check the hospitals.'

Owen looks like he's been kicked in the crotch.

'Let me ring round,' Rory says. 'Why don't you go to Orla, see if you can work together and think of all the places she might be.'

'Maybe *I* should ring the hospitals.'
'I know a few people. Let me try.'

Rory starts to contact all the South Dublin A&E departments. On his third call, he thinks he may have found her. A young girl fitting her description was admitted at seven in the morning, unconscious. No ID. A nurse has contacted the guards, who are checking their missing person's records. Rory assumes Jenna's not on them yet. For confidentiality reasons the doctor can say no more until Rory can identify her as family. Wasting no time, he drives straight to the hospital where he is directed to the appropriate ward.

It *is* Jenna. Still unconscious, and connected to a drip, she's lying on her side, in a hospital gown, all evidence of spunky teenager gone. She looks young, pale and incredibly vulnerable. One of the female doctors tells Rory that she was found unconscious in the garden of a private house in Dundrum, an empty bottle of vodka by her side. Rory wonders what she was doing in someone else's garden. All sorts of things cross his mind. Did someone bring her there? A man? Date rape. He asks the doctor if there were any injuries? She seems to understand and confirms that there is no evidence of any. Rory asks for the address where she was found, thinking that they won't have it. But they do. It is the only information they had on her, the only trace of who she could be. The address is on her chart. It is her old family home.

He calls Orla, who is at first relieved, then immediately concerned. Why's she in hospital? Why unconscious? What's wrong with her? Will she wake up? Where exactly is she?

She and Owen arrive together within half an hour. Rory senses the tension between them. They go straight to the bedside as if competing to show who loves their daughter most. Orla starts to cry. She puts her hand gently on Jenna's cheek. 'My baby.'

She turns to Rory. 'What did they say?'

Though he told her it was alcohol poisoning on the phone, he is careful not to mention it in front of Owen. 'They're hopeful. The next twenty-four hours are crucial.' He pulls up a chair for her.

'Where did she get the booze, that's what I'd like to know,' Owen demands. 'I'll sue that bloody school.'

Orla turns her back to him, smooths her daughter's hair over and over. 'I'm here, sweetie. I'm here.'

'A bit late now,' Owen mutters.

Both Orla and Rory look at him in shock.

'Why didn't you tell me there was a problem?' he says to Orla. 'Why didn't you tell me she was drinking? I'm her father.'

Orla turns back to Jenna, silently crying.

And Rory wants to protect her. Calmly, he asks Owen, 'I suppose it didn't occur to you that this might have *something* to do with you leaving home and starting another family.'

'That's it, blame me. Everything is my fault. Maybe if someone had told me –'

Orla swivels round, fire in her eyes. 'Why tell you when it's clear you don't give a shit.'

'I don't need this.' He gets up to leave.

'Don't you dare go,' she says. 'You're going to stay here at your daughter's side until she wakes up. And you're going to be here for her from now on.'

'She doesn't want me around. She's made that very clear.'

'How convenient. Your only child tells you she doesn't want to see you, and you think you're free to swan off with nothing on your conscience. Well, let me tell you, actions speak louder than words, Owen,' Orla says, looking down at their daughter. 'And what Jenna's actions are telling me, loud and clear, is that she needs you in her life, no matter what she might tell you. And when I say in her life, I don't mean forking out for boarding school and buying her affection. I mean, listening to her, working hard to let her know you still love her, making time for just you and her. Jenna is your daughter. And, though I wish to God it weren't true, she loves you and needs you. And if it kills me, I'll make damn sure she gets you.'

Rory hands Owen a chair.

He takes it and sits down. Sheepishly, he pulls his mobile from his pocket and switches it off.

Two hours later, back at St Paul's and snowed under with work that has stacked up in his absence, Rory gets an emotional call from Orla to say that Jenna has come round. Owen is still there. And for the first time, they are talking, all three of them, together.

It's a week since Jenna was hospitalized and though now discharged, she's still recuperating and may be about to start counselling. Whenever Rory calls Orla to discuss the baby, she's preoccupied with her teenage daughter and he feels it would be wrong to bring it up. He wonders how long it will take for things to settle. There's so much they need to discuss. First off, he wants to tell her how happy he is about the pregnancy. He knows *that* didn't come across. He's with her all the way. She should be convinced of that. They can do this. Of course they can. If she's up to it, maybe they could go over a few medical issues. Obstetricians and their waiting lists. Folic acid . . .

In the week that's passed, Rory has thought a lot about this. He wants to be involved as much as possible – in the pregnancy, the actual birth – if Orla wants him there. Which he hopes she will. One evening, surfing the Net, he Googled pregnancy on a whim and found a website that tracks the changes taking place in mother and baby over the nine months. At nine weeks, a baby is three centimetres long. Its face is developing, mouth and nose clearly visible, arms and legs growing rapidly. That all of this has already happened amazes Rory, who is sorry now he never took more interest in obstetrics.

Sometimes, late at night, his mind starts to race. He imagines the kind of child this baby could become: the spunky kind that push their own buggies, that run rather than walk and that are always difficult to get down from trees. When

Rory pictures his son – and it is always a boy he sees – he is dark, like him, and wears a pale blue T-shirt and safari shorts. It's way too early to think like this and totally premature to consider names, but Rory likes James, a one-syllable, no-bullshit man's name.

Rory wonders if Orla has recovered from the shock – if she's even had time to think, with all that's been happening with Jenna. He should give her at least another week before broaching the subject.

As it turns out, he doesn't have to. The following Saturday, Orla calls, wanting to come over to talk about 'things'.

He is relieved. Until he sees her. She looks pale, tired and thin. He goes to her automatically. 'Are you OK? Here, sit down. Will I make some tea?'

Orla stays standing, looking into his eyes long enough for him to know that something's wrong.

'What? What is it?'

'Rory, I'm not keeping the baby.'

He's not sure he heard right. What did she say?

'I can't. I can't do it to Jenna. You know how delicate she is. You know how she reacted when she heard Owen was having a baby with someone else.'

'What do you mean you're not keeping the baby?' He says it slowly.

'I'm not having it.'

'You're not *having* it?' That means only one thing. She couldn't . . .

'I'm forty-one. Alone. I can't start again. My God.' Her hands come to her face. 'I can't go through with it. I can't. Surely you can understand that.' She is close to tears.

He doesn't know what to say. All he knows is he wants this baby. 'You won't *be* alone. You'll have me. I'll be here.'

'Having a presence, maybe, but it's *my* life that would change. It's *always* the woman's life —'

He doesn't hesitate. 'We could get married.'

Her eyes fix on his. 'What?'

'You wouldn't be alone. We'd do it together. Fifty-fifty.'

A beat. Then, 'I can't marry you.'

'Why not?'

'We don't love each other.'

'We do.'

'As friends. As brother and sister-in-law.'

'So? You said yourself, what's love anyway? You said you never wanted to love anyone like you loved Owen. This is the best way to start a family. No illusions. Nothing to lose.'

'Rory, I don't want to start another family.'

'Then give it to me. Let me bring it up. I'll love it. Teach it things. Be a good father to it. Jesus, Orla, you can't not have it.'

It is moments before she answers, moments where he allows himself hope.

'I can't be pregnant. Not now. Jenna —'

'Orla, please.'

'I can't have it. I can't.'

'This is more than "not having it". This is killing a baby. Our baby.'

She closes her eyes. 'It's a foetus.'

'That will become a baby.'

She shakes her head.

'Orla, this is not you. You love children. You take in other people's, for God's sake. You can't do this.' His voice changes. 'I won't let you.' It's his baby as much as hers.

She is defiant. 'You can't stop me.'

'I can.' Wildly, he tries to work out how. 'I'll tell Jenna.' He is desperate.

281

She looks at him in horror. 'You wouldn't.'

'I would.' A beat. 'If it meant saving our baby.'

'Rory, stop. Please. Let's be rational, think this through.'

'There's nothing rational about what you're suggesting.'

'It's the *only* rational solution. D'you think I haven't thought this through? D'you think that I'd even be *considering* this if there were any other way? This is the very last thing I want to do. But I don't have a choice. I can't be pregnant. I can't do it to Jenna. She could have killed herself, Rory. If they hadn't found her . . .' She covers her mouth and all the emotion of the past week spills over in her tears. 'If I went through with this and anything happened to Jenna, I couldn't live with myself. She's been through enough. I'm her mother. I have to protect her.'

'You're also a mother to this baby.'

'It's not a baby.'

'Please, Orla. Just give it a chance. Give it to me. I'll love it. I swear to God.' Again he changes tack. 'You wouldn't be able to live with yourself. I know you. You wouldn't.'

She covers her ears. 'Stop. Stop it. You don't understand what it's like to have a child; you'd do anything to protect them; you'd give your own life.'

'But this *is* my child. And I want to protect it. Please, Orla. There has to be a way. *Another* way.'

'I shouldn't have told you.'

'I've a right to know.'

'I should have just done it,' she says, as though to herself.

'*Could* you have?' He can't imagine it. Not Orla.

She puts a hand on either side of her forehead. 'I have to go,' she says. 'I have to think. Let me think, please, *God*, let me think.'

Does he have a choice?

*

He stands looking at the closed door, wanting to go after her, but afraid he might make things worse. She's said she's going to think. And that's something. Thinking, not acting. He hopes he's got through to her. He meant what he said about it being a mistake for her. Orla. Earth mother. Foster mother. Godmother. Abortion? That she's even considered it stuns him. He should have been more positive when she'd told him she was pregnant, more excited, supportive, *before* Jenna went off the rails. She mightn't have felt so alone. But he's told her he is there for her now. He's made that clear.

He walks to the window, turns, walks to the door. What's he supposed to do, wait unemotionally while she decides whether their baby lives or dies? He's the father. Doesn't he have a say? He's always been pro-choice. Where is his?

He has to get out, get some air, run. He is in his jogging gear in minutes and gone. Running. Racing. But not as fast as his mind. It's her body, he tells himself. Yes, but it's his child too. She has no choice, she says. Neither, it seems, does he. He speeds up, pumping his muscles harder, pushing them to their limit. If only she hadn't told him. He wouldn't feel the responsibility he does towards this baby. Neither would he feel a conflicting responsibility to Orla, who is in this mess because of him.

Over the next few days, he thinks of nothing else. He knows he has to give her space. Time. But what if she decides to go ahead? What will he do then? It'll be too late. Shouldn't he try to influence her now? But what can he do, send her a picture of a nine-week-old baby, so she can see? Maybe he could, if this wasn't Orla, probably his closest friend now after the year they've been through. Maybe he could if he didn't understand her situation, the risks involved in her going ahead with the pregnancy. If only she was a stranger, a one-night stand he didn't care about. That would be easier.

So he fights the urge to contact her – until one week later when he can bear the tension no longer. He doesn't want to pressurize her, but he has to know. He emails, rather than putting her on the spot.

He doesn't hear back.

32

Since they spoke at the funeral, Jenna has called Rory four or five times to 'talk'. Somehow she has decided that he is 'the only one who understands'. At first that had him baffled. He recalled their (uncomfortable for him) chat in his mother's front room when he'd said little, offered no advice, just let her talk. In retrospect maybe that's what she needed, someone to mouth off to who kept his views to himself. Rory wasn't thrilled when she continued to call him, especially without her mother knowing, but felt that maybe he was providing a service of sorts, letting her offload, keeping her out of trouble. All that changed when she drank herself unconscious. Since then he has found her calls terrifying, as if he's in some way responsible for her. Now, given the latest development, he knows he should avoid her altogether, considering the power she has over his child's future without even realizing it. And yet here he is listening to her latest rant. He wants to tell her to grow up and quit driving her mother distracted.

'They want me to go to some dump for alcoholics for six weeks. I'm not an alcoholic.'

'I know. I know you're not. But it might do you good.'

'How could it if I'm not an alcoholic?'

Rory is all too aware that anything that would help Jenna's stability will increase the chances of his baby surviving. Which makes him feel guilty about offering the advice that Jenna needs to hear. 'Because you do have a drink problem.'

'You just said I didn't.'

'I said you weren't an alcoholic. But you did end up with alcohol poisoning.'

'There was a reason for that.'

'There should never be a reason for that.'

She is silent. Then her voice is accusing. 'I thought you understood.'

'I do. But until you admit you've a problem it's only going to get worse.'

'Has she been talking to you? Has she told you to say that?'

'I presume you mean your mother?' He snaps. Then checks himself. Tries to control his anger. It's not Jenna's fault. She doesn't know.

'This was a mistake,' she says.

'Look, Jenna. I'm just being honest here. I could tell you what you wanted to hear, be your "friend", but what friend would I be if I thought you should do this and I didn't say it?'

Silence.

'Nobody can make you go. But you can *decide* to. You can decide to sort this out. To stop letting drink control you.'

'Thanks for the lecture.'

He says nothing. What did he expect, an admission of guilt?

'If I go, and I'm not saying I will, it'd be on my terms. *I'd* decide.'

'Absolutely.'

There is a long pause. 'I'll have to think about it.'

He wants to ask how Orla is, *where* Orla is, but can't. It would look like he was on her side. And that could ruin all he has achieved here. When she hangs up, he feels more positive. Could this be the beginning of a solution?

*

It's ten days since Orla's visit and still no word. He expected, at least, an email, if only to say 'still thinking'. Doesn't she appreciate what this is like for him? Doesn't she *care*? Well, he's had enough of being patient. He has to do something. With Jenna away in rehab, he has an opportunity, a real chance to convince Orla to delay her decision. Jenna's future is brighter now. And she is stronger than Orla thinks. He is going over there. After work, today.

He grabs the post on his way out, to be opened in traffic on the way.

Stopped at lights, he tears open the first envelope, the one that isn't a bill. It's a letter. And it isn't long.

Rory

It's over. I'm sorry. I know what you wanted and I'm sorry. I had no choice. I had to think of Jenna. I had to think of her future, and mine. I know you said you'd be there and I know you believed you would. But the burden would have been mine. I couldn't take the change that this would have meant to my life. I'm sorry. Please don't contact me. It's over now. I have to put this behind me, get on with my life. There is nothing you could have done.
Orla.

He freezes. She didn't. She couldn't have. Not like this. Not without telling him. Not Orla. He doesn't see the lights turn green, doesn't hear the drivers behind him making their impatience known. He doesn't hear anything except roaring in his ears. He has crumpled the letter into a ball and flung it at the windscreen. Now he is trying to reach it where it has fallen on the other side of the car. There's a knock on the window. He looks up. A guy is signalling at him to roll it down. He does.

'What the fuck are you up to?'

'Sorry?'

'The lights are green, man.'

'Sorry, sorry.'

'Just go, OK?'

Rory takes off, turns immediately left, into the hospital grounds where he throws the car up on a high kerb. He reaches for the note and flattens it out on his thigh. He reads it again, trying to take it in. His running, climbing, busy son. Gone. Dead. He should have stopped her. He should have tried harder. He should have done *something*. He was wrong about Orla. Wrong. 'Please don't contact me.' The last thing he wants to do is contact her. He could quite easily kill her. He gets out of the car, slamming the door. He looks towards the hospital, then turns and walks in the opposite direction. He is glad when the heavens open and the rain that falls is torrential. He deserves every discomfort, every humiliation. He let his son die. He looks up at the clouds and says aloud, 'Bring it on.'

He doesn't know where he is going. Just walks. The rain stops. And later, starts again. He takes no shelter. Just trudges on. He finds himself in a church. At first it feels right, quiet, peaceful, a place of repentance. But then he's haunted by flashbacks. First, his father's coffin being lowered slowly into the ground, the sound of the earth being shovelled in. Second, his attacker, bearing down on him, syringe in hand. In need of air, he stumbles outside. He sits on the steps staring at his surroundings, taking an imprint of them to block out his demons.

And then he is walking again, and crying. When he finds himself back at his car, it has been clamped. He sits inside. Teeth chattering, knees shaking. He is soaked through. But he just sits, staring into the middle distance, doing nothing to get the clamp removed. When they come to tow him, he opens the window and produces a credit card. They explain that it's too late; they have to tow him now – he could have avoided that if he'd called to have the clamp removed. He doesn't argue, just gets out. They take one look at him, soaked and haunted, and ask for the credit card back.

'Just this once,' one of them says.

Rory doesn't thank them. He doesn't care.

He drives home. Climbs into a hot shower and slowly peels off his clothes. He stays under until the water goes cold, then dries himself roughly and dresses. Overtaken by exhaustion, he lies on the bed. In less than a minute he is asleep.

He wakes to the bleep of a text message. It's from the hospital. A third. Groggily, he reads all three. Then rings the ward with an excuse, an apology and some instructions. He'll be in early in the morning, he promises.

He hauls himself off the bed, splashes water on his face. Drinks coffee to revive himself. He has a nagging feeling that there's somewhere he's meant to be, dealing with a commitment he'd mildly dreaded, which is why he remembers it at all. What was it? He checks the calendar on his phone. His mother's financial affairs, something Owen had wanted to handle, but something Siofra didn't trust him to. She'd volunteered Rory who hadn't really wanted to get involved in that side of things. The only reason he agreed was to keep the peace and because he knew his mother needed help. Now, he considers cancelling. But the thought of sorting through bills, accounts and statements is preferable to being alone in the apartment with only one thing to think about.

'Sorry I'm late,' he says, when she answers the door.

'I'm not going anywhere.' She pastes on a smile.

Which reminds him to do the same.

'Better get started,' he says, as soon as they're inside. If they start to talk, he's afraid of what he might say.

She shows him to his father's lock-up desk, traditionally forbidden territory and consequently a source of intrigue. He sits a moment, closing his eyes and inhaling its familiar smell as he remembers his father, hunched over it. Rory's eyes smart and when his mother offers him tea, he opens the desk to avoid having to look at her.

How neat everything is. Bundles of official looking papers held together with elastic bands. Lodgement slips, filed receipts, cheque stubs and cash withdrawal slips. Statements in their navy plastic folder. Sellotape, stapler, envelopes, notepaper, all neatly arranged. A place for everything. He starts to go through the accounts. They are as basic as they could be. No credit cards. No overdraft. No paper trails. No missing statements. Everything balancing, tying up. Rory regrets that it's not more complex. He had hoped that maybe there might be a side to his father he hadn't seen, a careless side that made mistakes.

The tea arrives in his World's Best Rugby Player mug, another silent rebellion against the man who believed that people should drink from cups. He smiles at his mother. She always did understand.

She sits in a nearby armchair, pretending to read an old newspaper. The silence between them is companionable. Finally, Rory finishes up. She expresses surprise at how little time it took.

He shrugs. 'It was all in order.'

She looks proud. 'He always made sure of that.'

'Yeah.'

She gets up and goes to him. As he tidies everything away, she peers over his shoulder. 'Do you think I could handle it now?' she asks.

'There's no need to worry about that yet.'

'Rory. He's gone. I have to learn to cope without him. You all have your lives. I want to be able to stand on my own two feet.'

He nods.

'So let's start.'

'Now?'

'Unless you're too tired.'

'No. It's fine. OK, let's do it now.'

He goes to the kitchen and gets her a chair, which he settles down beside him. It's no job. His mother picks it up very quickly. Nothing has to be gone over twice. He always believed she was brighter than his father gave her credit for, just never got the chance to show it. She quit her job in the bank when she married, as was the custom of the time.

'Sure, there's no mystery to that,' she says, which makes Rory suspect that his father probably had her believe there was.

'I'll buy you a calculator.'

'Rory, I worked in a bank. If there's one thing I can do it's add and subtract.' The achievement of grasping it all seems to have given her confidence, cheered her up.

He closes the desk and they get up. He returns her chair to the kitchen, planning to leave. He could do with a drink. Could have done with one hours ago. He pops his head in the door to say goodbye.

She is holding a photo of him as a baby. 'I remember when you were born,' she says, smiling.

Curious, he comes in.

She looks up from the photo. 'Your father was terrified of anything happening to you. He wouldn't hold you. He wouldn't let the others hold you, either.'

'Was he like that with all of us?'

She nods. Remembering.

He's disappointed. He'd thought for one brief moment that maybe he was special.

'He always worried about you. I don't think he could help it.'

Rory remembers the drowning. Is that what she's trying to say? That he was nervous, afraid for them and that's what drove him?

'He was hard on you, but that doesn't mean he didn't love you. He didn't want you growing up soft. It was the way he was brought up.'

Something doesn't sit right about that and Rory knows what it is. 'But Tom had the same parents and he wasn't like that.'

'No. Tom was more easygoing, that's true. But Tom didn't have children. At the end of the day, you weren't his responsibility. You could have fun together and he could hand you back. I know your father worried too much and I'm not saying his ways were right, but he believed them to be. And he did love you. He just wasn't brought up to express it.'

After a lifetime of believing he wasn't loved by him, this is difficult for Rory to accept.

'I was thinking of giving you all a little something when everything's sorted with the will. There's not a whole lot but . . .'

'Mum. We're fine.' He thinks of Owen. What has he said to her?

'Sure, what would I do with the money?' she asks. 'You don't have an apartment. Siofra's mortgage is crippling. Owen's trying to buy a house and has two families to support.'

'That's called life, Mum. We're fine. Everyone's fine. And, anyway, the money Dad left isn't enough to make a difference, so you might as well make the most of it. Do something you've never done. Go on a holiday, treat yourself.' Start living your own life, he thinks but doesn't say.

'I could sell the house.'

He's suspicious. 'Where did you come up with that idea?'

'Siofra asked me to live with them.'

'Do you want to?'

'No.'

'Then why would you sell the house?'

'If I moved into a bungalow that would give me a little nest egg, wouldn't it?'

'Why do you want a nest egg?'

'To share amongst you. I'm sick of seeing the three of you struggling. You're all I've left. I want to do this.'

And he wants her to take advantage of the fact that for the first time since she married she's free to do whatever she wants. 'No one's struggling. And anyway, a bungalow will cost as much as the house. It's crazy out there.'

Her face falls.

'If you want to move to a bungalow for yourself, because it's easier, then by all means, I'll help you find one. But if you're doing it because you think you'll have money left over, you won't.'

She is twisting the string of, probably costume, pearls on her neck.

'Mum, please. For once in your life, will you look after yourself? This is your neighbourhood. This is where you know, where the shop is, the church, your friends. If you're happy here, then stay.'

She mulls it over. 'Well, then, I'll just give you all a little something from the will,' she says.

And although Rory shakes his head, it occurs to him that

this might be the solution. There's no way Owen would contest the will after this gesture. 'Why don't you give a bit extra to Owen? He could probably do with it most.' That would definitely shut him up, Rory thinks, realizing that he will have to explain it to Siofra.

'I love you all equally,' his mother says, 'and I will share it equally.'

'You'll be OK, Mum,' he tries to reassure her.

'Of course I will.' Her slight irritation comforts him.

Back in the car, he sees the crumpled letter and everything comes stampeding back. The shock. The sense of betrayal. A letter! Didn't he deserve at least to be told in person? He'll never forgive her. In the space of weeks, he has lost a father and a son before he could have a meaningful relationship with either.

That night, his dreams are of dismembered dolls. They moan and call out as if for help. And for the first time in his life he gets up in the middle of the night to get drunk.

33

Rory was mistaken about Johnny. His mate's approach to life is entirely sensible: live a no-strings life, have a bloody good time and a very short memory. Rory used to think Johnny sad when in reality it was *he* who was sad, a nice guy, a fool. No one listens to nice guys. Nice guys get walked on. Well, enough Mr Nice Guy. Rory hooks up with Johnny and the gang with a vengeance, out, three, four times a week, recovering in between. He drinks fastest, laughs loudest, leaves first with the best-looking woman in tow. Rory becomes the alpha male, everyone, including Johnny, deferring to him. Not that he gives a shit.

He's never had so much female attention. It's all very simple. Don't give a fuck. And they do. The more irreverent you are, the more they like it. He feels no remorse slipping from beds in the middle of the night. Takes pleasure in leaving phone numbers behind in waste paper baskets. The only thing he cares about is using a condom. He's not making that mistake twice. On the radio, he hears a woman criticize men like him. Did it ever occur to her that women are the reason men like him exist?

Whenever he sees a baby, he turns away. A boy holding a father's hand churns his stomach. So he avoids families. Barry and Dee. Siofra and Tony. Owen, who is going to be a father. Rory even avoids Jason. Especially Jason, who reminds him, more than anyone, of how his son might have turned out. He doesn't care whether or not people believe the excuses he gives for having to bow out time and again. Let them make their own assumptions.

Work is the only place he can truly block everything out. Work and the pub. He doesn't want to talk about it. What's the point? Nothing anyone can say will make him feel better. He doesn't want to feel better. So he works hard and plays harder. And tries to forget.

Time passes. Jenna calls him from the residential programme. If he'd known it was her, he'd never have picked up. He stands, phone in one hand, can of beer in the other. He'd been getting ready to go out.

'I did need to be here,' she says. 'You were right. I did have a problem.'

He doesn't care.

'I hated it at first. I was so angry. But I've met wonderful people.'

Her voice is irritating him. Would she ever just piss off?

'People who're so bright and had *so much* going for them, but who ruined it with drink.'

He takes a giant slug of beer.

'People who've missed years of their lives. Older people. Important people.'

Now he knows what it must have been like for Louise when he came back from the course. Was *he* this high on life?

'I understand about Dad. And that it's OK to be angry with him, to stop blaming myself and Mum. Blame him instead.'

Does this mean you're going to stop being so egocentric? he wants to ask.

'You're not saying much,' she says.

'I'm listening.'

'Oh, right.' She pauses. 'I'm really happy, Rory.' He

wonders how happy she'd be if she knew that she'd caused an abortion. 'When I go back to school, it'll be to my old school, not that stuck up one where the only way to survive is to become a bitch.'

There's a pause.

'Good,' he says, to fill it.

'How's Mum?' she asks.

Oh, like *now* she gives a fuck? 'I don't know. I haven't seen her for a while.'

'I miss her.' Jenna's voice wobbles. 'She's such a good person. Sometimes I forget that, you know?'

Oh, please.

'You're very quiet,' she says.

'Just thinking about work. I've to go back in. Bit of an emergency.'

'Oh, God, sorry. You should have said.'

'It's OK.' He feels guilty now. She's just a messed-up kid. It's not her fault. 'You take care of yourself, OK?' he says.

'I am.'

'Good.' And despite everything that's happened, he means it.

Before he can leave the apartment, the phone rings again. He allows it to go to the answering machine, but when he hears Naomi's voice, he is so surprised, he thinks that something must be wrong. She has never called him before, never would. He picks up.

'Oh, I thought no one was there,' she says.

'Shower.'

'Oh.' A brief silence, then, 'Jason's going to be nine on Saturday. I'm having a party for him. He'd really like if you could come.'

He feels guilty, knowing they must be wondering what's

happened to him. He wants to say, yes. But the thought of being surrounded by a roomful of boys seems too much.

'I'm not sure I'll be free.' That sounds as if he doesn't care. Which is not true. 'When is it?' he asks, to give the impression that he's going to try to make it.

'Tomorrow week. Jase's never had a party before.' She hesitates. 'My fault.' Another brief silence follows. But when she speaks again, her voice is upbeat. 'He's real excited. He'd love if you could come.' Shyly, she adds, 'We both would. We haven't seen you for a while.'

And now he's really guilty. 'Saturday, next week?' he asks, stalling for time.

'Yeah.'

He remembers what it was like to have birthdays pass without celebration. 'Let me just check.' He appreciates the effort it took for her to ring. 'You know what? I think I *am* free Saturday. What time?'

'Two. At the flat. There'll be football outside. And chips and stuff.'

Something inside him softens. She is trying so hard. For her boy. 'I'll be there.'

It's the first time he has stepped inside Naomi's front door. The place is spotless. Brightly coloured balloons are tied in bunches and a Happy Birthday banner stretches across one wall. Rory swallows and blocks the thoughts that have already started to come. He concentrates on all the effort that Naomi has put in. Rice Krispie buns with Smarties on top, cocktail sausages, popcorn. It reminds him of friends' parties when he was a kid, not that he got invited to many, because he could never ask them back. Despite the decorations and party atmosphere though, Naomi hasn't been able to completely hide the grimness of the flat, the stained Formica surfaces, the worn kitchen appliances and the linoleum floor ripped in places. He looks at her, busy rushing around. What he feels is admiration. It would have been so easy to slip back, and give in.

'Rory! I haven't seen you in *ages*,' Jason shouts when he sees him. He hurries over. 'Where were you?'

Rory's taken aback. 'I was *really* busy at work, Jason, I'm sorry. But it's great to see you. How're you doing? Happy Birthday.' He hands him the gift he carefully selected and wrapped.

'Cool,' Jason says, ripping the bright red paper off to reveal a portable DVD player and five of Jason's favourite movies. 'Oh my God. Thanks a *million*, Rory. I better put them in my room.'

The tiny flat starts to fill with kids. Presents pile up. The noise level builds. Boys, many with zero blades, all with attitude, seem bursting with energy. Jason looks ecstatic. Rory has to distract himself. The bathroom is small and clean, though in need of re-tiling, re-grouting, in fact, replacing. He is tempted to help, but doesn't want to interfere.

He walks back into the sitting room – in time to see Louise entering from the hall. He stops, stunned. It is hard. Seeing her, thinking what might have been. She looks radiant, her hair fuller and wavier. She is talking to Naomi, but her eyes are scanning the room. For whom? Jason? He backs away, towards the kitchen, wanting to disappear from sight, when their eyes meet. And he stops. Did she know he'd be here? If so, why hadn't she stayed away? He would have, if only he'd thought . . . A kid with an earring bumps into her. She steps back, her hand moving automatically to guard her tummy. Rory looks down. And for a moment, everything else fades. He wouldn't have noticed. But now he does. He looks up at her, eyes questioning. Hers confirm it. Emotion is rising in him, swamping him, overwhelming him. He starts to walk. Towards her. But now past her. And out. He takes a deep breath. Grips the black railing on the balcony. Behind him, boisterous kids burst from the flat, heading for the yard below. He doesn't notice.

She arrives beside him, her hand next to his on the railing. 'I'm sorry. I didn't know how to tell you.'

He looks at her incredulously. 'So you thought you'd just *surprise* me?'

'Maybe that was a mistake.'

His eyes cut away from her. 'Is it mine?'

When she doesn't answer, he looks back. Sees that he has hurt her.

'Do you really think there's been anyone else?' she asks.

He stares out over the yard. So this is why she was 'upset'. This is why she needed comfort from his friend. She discovered she was pregnant with his child. 'I'm surprised you haven't got rid of it,' he says, voice cold. 'Must have been a real pain, finding out you were pregnant after you'd left me because I wanted a family.'

'I knew I was pregnant when I left.'

His head swings in her direction. For the first time, he doesn't think before speaking. 'But you knew how much I wanted a baby.'

'Yes.' She presses her lips together. Then adds, 'But I didn't.'

It feels like a weight has landed on his heart. 'So you left to abort our baby. Nice one.' His second unwanted child.

Her hands move defensively to her tummy. Then she seems to gather herself. 'No, Rory. I left because I loved you. I couldn't give you what you wanted, a family. And I didn't want you to miss out on that.'

'So you *were* going to have an abortion.'

'*At first*.' She looks down to where she has placed her hands, as if she already loves what's inside. 'But I couldn't go through with it. I went to Manchester. I was in theatre, had the gown on.'

He thinks about Orla. 'I don't want to know.'

'But lying there, looking at the white walls, hearing the sounds of medical equipment being prepared . . .'

'Stop.'

'All I could think about were the people I knew who had been unwanted – Jason, Naomi, me, people who've had it tough, but who've made it somehow. I finally admitted the truth to myself. This baby was not unwanted; it was wanted very much. All those reasons I gave you, gave myself, for not wanting children were fake. You were right. I *was* afraid. Afraid I'd lose control. That my life would fall apart like my mother's did. I'd done everything to avoid that. Been so careful. Built my own business. Worked so hard. And I thought I could go through with it. But this was our baby, part of you and me. And suddenly I wanted it so much. I wanted to know it, touch it, smell it, see it smile, see what it would become. So I left, walked out, caught the first flight home. I pretended I was OK, went to work, tried to forget what I'd nearly done. Then it all hit me, how close I'd got, but also what was ahead. I was going to be a mother, on my own, with the business. What if I couldn't cope? What if I turned into my mother?'

'Why didn't you call me?'

'I wanted to. But I couldn't. I'd left you. I wasn't going to go running back just because I'd decided to keep the baby.'

'And do you think that's fair, for you to make all the decisions – get rid of it, not get rid of it, not tell me until it suits you?'

'No. I don't think it's fair. That's why I'm here.'

Bitterness engulfs him. Doesn't the father have *any* role? 'Not for child support then?'

She stands up straight, lets go of the railing. 'I want nothing from you, except for you to know.'

'Well, now I do.' He looks straight ahead. Whatever hoop she is holding up for him, he is not jumping through it.

'I didn't expect such bitterness.'

'Sorry to be such a disappointment.'

She says nothing for a moment, then, 'You've changed.'

His jaw moves out of alignment. 'You're right. I have.'

'Well, good for you,' she says, and starts to walk away.

He watches her coldly as she reaches the top of the steps. Which is when he sees Orla, coming up. Her eyes are level with Louise's bump, when her face pales. She grips the railing. The two women greet each other flatly, neither stopping. Then Orla sees Rory. And seems to crumple. But straightens herself, face determined. Then she turns and hurries back down the stairs.

'Coward,' he says quietly to her back.

34

Later that afternoon, still reeling from the shock of Louise's announcement, Rory arrives at his mother's house to take her to an urgent chiropodist's appointment. He lets himself in with his new key. She is carefully strapping on open-toed sandals.

'Just ready,' she says, looking up at him with a smile. Her face changes when she sees his and she stops what she's doing. 'Are you all right?'

'Yeah. Fine. I'll get your coat.' He disappears.

She says nothing until they're in the car. 'You're very pale, Rory.'

'Just tired. Work's been busy.'

The woman who never interferes says, 'You should take a few days off. You've been through a lot in the past few months.'

Which brings it all back. The attack, the break-up with Louise, his father's death, the baby's, and now another pregnancy. His chest constricts, his breathing rapid and shallow. A cold sweat breaks and he feels he's going to pass out. He pulls in at a petrol station and cuts the engine. He can't do it. He can't keep everything together any longer. Something's going to give. 'How do you do it; how do you keep going?' he asks, unaware that he has spoken aloud.

His mother doesn't look up from where she's getting her purse from her bag to pay for petrol she thinks is being purchased. 'You mean since your father died?'

He stares at her. 'What?'

She looks up, confused. 'You asked me how I keep going. I thought you meant since Dad died.'

'No. No, I didn't.'

Even more confused now. 'You mean generally?'

Oh, God. 'No.' He hadn't meant to speak.

'I'm sorry, Rory. What do you mean? How did I keep going when he *was* alive?'

'Yes.' Since she's asked. 'How did you put up with it, him making all the decisions, you having no control.' The way Rory has no control.

She fiddles with the clasp on her handbag. 'In my day, when you got married, it was for ever. That's the way it was.'

'Are you saying it was *easy*?' he snorts.

'No, Rory. It wasn't easy.'

'But you got through.' Sarcastic now.

'All right, if you want me to be honest, it was hard. Very hard. There were times I felt I couldn't go on, times I wanted to run away, go back to being the person I was before I married, free again, young. *But.* All I had to do was look at you, my three beautiful children, to know that I was never going to do that. Being your mother was the most important thing in my life. And the best.' Her voice changes, regret creeping in. 'I know things weren't easy for you. I know you missed out on a lot. There were things I wanted *so much* for you to have. That train set. I tried so hard to convince him. Your face that Christmas. It broke my heart. You have no idea.'

'So we kept you there.'

'It was where I wanted to be. With my children, before anything else.' Her voice fills with strength. 'And for all his gruffness, I did love him. You probably don't understand that.' She looks down. 'I don't always understand it myself.

He was hard on you and there were times I hated him for it. But we were a family. And we muddled through.'

'So that's what we're supposed to do, muddle through regardless?'

'I don't know, Rory. All I know is that if I'd run away, I wouldn't have what I do now. I wouldn't have you, my son, here, driving me to have my poor toe rooted at.' She smiles. 'I wouldn't have Siofra, Owen, or any of my precious grandchildren. I have so much. Because I muddled through.' She pauses. 'Mind you, I would like *you* to be happier. What's wrong, Rory?'

'Nothing.' He wouldn't know where to start.

He doesn't tell Johnny he won't be turning up. He just doesn't show. It might be Saturday night, but after the day he's had the last thing he needs is Hottie Patrol. What's he getting from all this anyway? Temporary oblivion. Not solutions, that's for sure. The pressure keeps building, despite the booze, despite the women. He's had enough.

Hands wrapped around a mug of coffee, he sits out on the balcony, looking towards the glow of the city by night. He inhales deeply. He mightn't own this apartment, but he loves it; the view, the salty air, the simple pleasure of living by the sea. He will always be able to afford to rent this place or somewhere like it. He has a good job that pays well. Whatever about the cost of buying property, rents are still affordable. And markets fluctuate. His time will come. In one way, at least, he has a little more control over his life than he'd thought.

The lighthouse at the end of the pier flashes green. A plane flies overhead, its white, green and red lights winking. Growing up, the view from Rory's room was the road outside and the line of houses opposite. His home was landlocked.

Like his mother. At least, that's how he saw it. He needs to revise that now. She'd a lot more control over her life than he'd given her credit for. She could have left, and *chose* not to. She was where she wanted to be – with her family. It wasn't ideal, but life rarely is and she made the most of it. Her secret was simple. She knew what was important and made sacrifices to keep it.

What is important to him?

He frowns while he contemplates this.

A lot of things actually.

His health. Which he's lucky to have, considering the attack.

His job. Ditto.

His personal life. Scratch that. It's a mess.

He could make it better, though. He could be more like his mother, decide what he wants and let nothing get in his way.

He puts down the mug and stands. Arms folded, he looks out towards the horizon. Inside the phone rings. He doesn't turn. He is not going in.

In the morning, he wakes early. He'd planned on going into the hospital, as he has been doing a lot lately. But decides against it. Work isn't the solution either. He needs to sort out what is. He gazes out at the pier and decides to walk it.

Hands in the pockets of his black khaki chinos, he climbs the pedestrian bridge that crosses the DART line. The buzz of summer sailing courses is over now and the harbour is quieter. He still loves it. Loves the way it's never the same; how every day, every hour, it's different. He chooses the lower level of the pier and walks close to its edge. Below him, a canoeist paddles a red canoe. He wears a yellow helmet. Rory wonders at the point of it. Aren't they for going through rapids? Maybe he wants to keep his ears warm or be seen in case of emergency. Maybe he just likes yellow. Or the helmet. Rory likes his style. Out alone. Doing his own thing. Enjoying the water. Enjoying life. He's right to make the most of it. It can be over so soon, so suddenly. He thinks of his father, his son, Tadgh O'Driscoll. And he thinks of how close he came himself. A breeze stirs the surface of the otherwise calm sea and it looks like a thousand tiny silver fish just below the surface. It reminds Rory of new life. Of Louise and the baby. Their baby.

He thinks back. To the shock discovery. And how he'd lashed out. Angry that he'd been, as usual, left out. But there is something he has ignored, and that is that the woman he loves is pregnant with his child. Still pregnant. Despite her fears. She wants their baby. And was telling him that, in the only way she could. He was being offered everything he'd wished for, and, like a fool, he had swatted it away. Not only that, but in doing so, he had been deliberately hurtful, deliberately cold.

Will she ever forgive him?

He stops walking. Whips out his phone. Dials her number.

'Louise?'

A beat. Followed by a wary, 'Hi.'

'I'm sorry.' He waits for her to say something, but she doesn't. 'I'm sorry I reacted so badly. It was such a shock.' Again, nothing. 'Can we talk? Please.'

He hears her take a deep breath. Then she says, 'OK.'

It's Thursday before she can meet him and he wonders if she's playing it cool. He wouldn't blame her if she was. They've arranged to meet in the café opposite her shop. He thinks it a good sign that she's there before him. But changes his mind when he sees her face. Closed.

He orders a coffee from a passing waiter and takes a seat opposite her.

'Thanks for seeing me,' he says.

'It's OK.' She tucks her hair behind her ears. And it reminds him of the day she left.

He scratches his forehead. 'Sorry, you know, for ... the other day. I shouldn't have reacted like that.'

'I shouldn't have landed it on you.'

'I needed to know.'

For a moment, neither speaks. Then Rory does so suddenly. 'I'm going to honour my responsibilities to the baby, Louise.'

'I was the one who left, Rory. You don't have responsibilities.'

Is that a fob off? 'I'm the father. Of course I've responsibilities. I want to be there for it.' His voice softens, 'Whether you want me to or not.'

She holds his eyes with hers. 'I want you to.' He almost deflates with relief. But then she ruins it by adding, 'Children need their fathers.'

He'd hoped she might need him too. 'When is it due?' he asks, to hide his disappointment.

'November.'

'I'll take time off.'

'You don't have to.'

'I *want* to.'

'I don't want you to feel you owe me anything.'

'I don't,' he snaps. He doesn't owe her; he loves her. 'But I owe the baby,' is what he says.

'Oh.' She sounds disappointed. But nods as if she understands.

He feels at sea, out of sync with the one person he was always in time with. He wants to fix it. Maybe if they started over. He stands. 'Want another smoothie?'

'No. Thanks.' She hasn't touched the one she has.

He leaves the table to order a coffee, but in reality to gather himself. He gets to the counter and asks for a latte. The waiter says he'll bring it to him. Rory says he'll wait.

Too soon, he returns to Louise.

They smile uneasily at each other.

He fiddles with a sachet of sugar. Maybe they should try to forget the past, just plan for the future. But to do that, he needs to know how things stand. 'Is it a secret, the pregnancy?'

She looks surprised. 'No.'

'You mean you've been *telling* people?' Before him?

'No. I haven't,' she says, sounding frustrated. 'I just haven't been hiding it.'

A group of teenage girls alight at the table beside them, setting their mobiles in front of them like doctors-on-call. Bleeping heralds the arrival of a text. A handset is picked up. Four heads merge. A burst of laughter.

Rory is barely aware of them. There's so much he needs to know. 'When did you find out you were pregnant?'

'When you were in Cambridge.'

Cambridge! He rewinds his mind. Remembers how quiet she was, how offhand on the phone. He'd thought she was jealous of Orla. He feels a fool.

'You told Mark and Lesley, didn't you, when I was away?'

'I told Lesley. I had to talk to someone.'

Not him, though. Hurt by that and a vision of her sobbing into Lesley's lap, regretting their child, he says, 'And was she *very* comforting?' He doesn't wait for an answer. 'I don't understand how you even *got* pregnant. You were always so careful.' He doesn't mean that positively.

She looks at him as if to say, 'Do I even know you?'

And suddenly, he's afraid she'll up and leave. 'I'm sorry. I just want to know how it happened.' His voice softens. 'Tell me how it happened, Lou.'

For a moment, she says nothing, then takes a deep breath. 'It was the night you got the test results. I wasn't back on the pill long enough. I was only short a day. I thought it'd be OK. You were so happy. *We* were so happy. I couldn't not.'

It was on his recommendation that she'd taken a break from the pill while they weren't having sex. He was thinking about her health. He remembers the night, the meal, the hotel. At least the baby was conceived when they were both happy and in love – before he'd asked her to marry him, before he'd suggested a family. It's as if the baby had its own agenda, a mind of its own. He smiles at that.

'What?' she asks, for a brief moment, hopeful.

He shakes his head. It's stupid. 'Nothing.' He stirs his untouched, almost cold coffee and drinks from it. 'Who are you seeing?'

'What do you mean?'

'Obstetrician.'

'Oh. Iris Black.'

He doesn't know the name. 'Is she good?'

'Seems to be. I wanted a woman.'

'Are you on folic acid?'

'Yes.'

'Iron?'

'No. My levels are OK.'

'How're you feeling?'

'Fine. Doctor.' She widens her eyes, teasing, the way she used to.

It seems forced to him. Fake. And he doesn't respond. 'Have you had a scan?'

She looks hurt. In silence, she opens her bag and produces an envelope. From it she takes a black and white grainy picture. He's not prepared for this. But it's already in his hands. He looks down. Smiles at the magic of it. *Foetus in foetal position*, is the title he gives it, as though it's a work of art. He touches it with a finger, already feeling love for it. His voice, grainy like the photo, asks, 'How many weeks?'

'It was taken at twelve. But I'm twenty-two now.' Her voice is more business-like. Her shell has been replaced.

And he wonders if he should have pretended, let on they were still natural with each other, and not feeling around cautiously like they had lost all sense of each other.

Over the next few days, Rory develops an overwhelming urge to protect this baby, to make sure nothing happens to it. He checks out Iris Black. A fine obstetrician by all accounts. Still, he wants to be on top of everything. He borrows books from the medical library. Starts to read up. Rings Louise to tell her he'll come to antenatal classes.

'I don't think the fathers' ones are till near the end,' she says.

'I'll come anyway.'

One of the first things he investigates is at what age a baby is capable of survival outside its mother's body. Twenty-eight weeks. He won't relax until then. In fact, he won't truly relax until it is born full-term and declared one hundred per cent healthy. But twenty-eight weeks is the first hurdle. At twenty-two, the baby is almost thirty centimetres long and weighs about four hundred grammes – almost half a pack of sugar, Rory thinks. It's learning about its body and surroundings through touch, frequently stroking its face.

Its fingernails are fully grown. All this blows Rory away. Still, he's not making the same mistakes twice. He's not going to imagine it as a child, boy or girl. He's not going to name it. He's not going to plan its life. And he is telling no one.

On his parents' wedding anniversary, Rory decides to take his mother out.

'I don't feel much like socializing,' she says, when he invites her to dinner.

'Well, then I won't tell you my news,' he teases, deciding on the spur of the moment that it's time she had something to look forward to.

'What news?' Already her spirits have lifted.

'Now *that* would be telling.'

'Is it relationship news?'

'Ah, ah. Dinner first, news second.'

'All right, all right. You win.'

'I'm still waiting for the news,' she says, over dessert.

He smiles at her.

'*Well?*'

'You're going to be a grandmother.'

Her face lights up. She clasps her hands together.

'Louise is pregnant.'

'*Louise?* Are you and Louise back together? Oh, Rory, I'd hoped —'

'No, Mum. We're not.'

'Oh.' She seems to be working through the implications of that.

He knows that she'd have liked her grandchild to be born into a loving relationship. He is sorry he can't give her that. He is sorry he can't give *himself* that.

'But Louise isn't going out with anyone else?' she asks.

'No.'

'So there's hope?'

He doesn't want to let her down. 'Mum. Things have changed between us. A lot has happened –'

'But a baby could bring you back together.'

'Look, Mum, I'm going to be totally involved. I'm going to be a good father. I'll be there for the baby. But please don't expect anything else.'

She nods.

'I'll bring it over to visit. We'll go out together, the three of us.'

'It will be great,' she says.

'I'm not telling anyone else. Not for the moment. Just in case, you know, anything goes wrong.'

'How many weeks is the baby?'

'Twenty-two.'

'Twenty-two? My goodness. I think you should be safe enough.'

'Well, just in case.'

'I won't tell a soul. Well, maybe a soul, but not a body.' She pauses. 'He would have been happy for you, Rory.'

Rory fakes a smile, to keep her happy.

'I'm trying to work out when it's due,' she says.

'November.'

She smiles. 'You'll make a great dad.'

If he ever gets there.

35

Rory takes time off to go with Louise to her next antenatal check-up. In the plush waiting room, shared by a number of consultants, there are about ten women. Only one man. There was another, but he left with his partner, their visit over. Rory watches the remaining couple carefully. Instinct tells him this is their first. It's their enthusiasm. The way they look so united, as if embarking on some great adventure together. Which, he supposes, they are. Judging by the energetic toddlers running, climbing and playing with toys owned by the hospital, many of the other women are veterans. And they're taking this in their stride. No big deal. No need for partners to miss work.

The doctor's door opens and she calls a name. The first-timers look at each other, but only she gets up. Rory wonders why he's not going in. Same thing happened with the other couple. What's the point in coming if you don't go in? Haven't they any questions? Don't they want to be part of the process? Rory imagines what happens in the consultation room. Blood pressure, weight, palpating the abdomen, urine sample (already collected). Nothing to shy away from. Unless of course there's some reason for an internal examination. He thinks of Louise. On second thoughts . . .

When her name is called, Louise stands. She looks at Rory, expecting him to come, as he'd said he would. He stays sitting, just smiles up at her.

'See you when you get out,' he says. As the door closes behind her, Rory thinks of internal examinations, and is glad she picked a female obstetrician. He looks around the room, feeling redundant.

Louise reappears in under ten minutes. Her doctor calls the next patient. As they walk along the corridor, Rory is anxious to know how it went.

'Everything OK?'

'Yeah, fine.'

'Blood pressure?'

'Yep.'

'Urine?'

'Yes, Rory.'

He decides to skip weight. They get to the door of the hospital. For Rory, it's all over too quickly. He hasn't learnt anything. He wonders if he should suggest coffee.

Louise says, 'I'd better get back to work.'

'Yeah. Me too.'

'OK. Well, thanks for coming.' She starts to walk away.

Suddenly he is gripped by worry, the same kind of worry his father must have felt for his children. What if she trips? Gets hit by a car? He doesn't even like the idea of her driving. He catches up with her. 'So, you'll give me a shout when the next antenatal class is due?'

'Yeah. I'll text.'

'OK.' He stands back while she gets into her car. He wonders if he should remind her of the safety belt. But then she puts it on. And he relaxes a bit. Watching her drive away, he tells himself to loosen up. The last thing he needs is to turn into his father.

Two weeks and a lot of research later, Rory has grown very familiar with words like trimester, primigravida and lanugo. He thinks it right that pregnancy has its own vocabulary, words that have no use in everyday language. The more he becomes familiar with pregnancy, the more in awe of it he becomes, how by a certain time certain things happen in every pregnancy, how nature gives a baby a deadline – nine months and everything has to be developed by then, ready. He wonders why he never gave obstetrics a second thought when choosing his specialty. But he knows. He had considered it unchallenging, a production factory rather than life-or-death. Boring.

He was a different man then.

At the next antenatal class, he sits with Louise, surrounded by pregnant women. A plump, over-animated midwife in a tight blue uniform is talking about pain relief options. Rory is up to speed on all of that now and his mind takes a detour to an ad on the mother and baby watch website, very American and completely mad. A 'belly cast'. You can have a cast made of the entire front of the mother's pregnant body. There's a picture of one on the site – the cast, not the body. Rory must be losing it, because to him, it's as good as any sculpture. Beautiful, in fact. Even if they were still together, they'd never have gone for anything like that though. They're too sensible, too Irish. Though the Irish are changing. He imagines a lot of couples opting for belly casts. Something new. Something no one else has. Hard enough, given the booming economy. He imagines a cast of Louise. Imagines her naked. Imagines the soap on its journey down her body. He stops thinking. Is aware of her beside him, so calm, so easy with the whole thing. When he's with her, this calm transmits to him and he worries less about the baby. It seems a contradiction that this is the same person who left him because she didn't want to be a mother.

'Well, that was a waste of time,' she says, when they're outside, other women spilling out around them.

'I thought you'd want to know about pain relief.'

'I know all I need to – there's such a thing as an epidural.'

She always was decisive. 'What's the next one on?' he asks.

'Breast feeding.'

He imagines himself amongst all those women and feels his enthusiasm drain away.

'You coming?' she asks, teasingly, sensing his discomfort.

'I might give that one a skip.'

Her face is serious. 'I'd like your support.'

'Oh, right.'

'I'm *messing*. I was thinking of giving that one a skip myself.'

She's not going to breastfeed?

'I'm going to be working, Rory.'

'So soon?'

'I run my own business.'

He's familiar with all the benefits of breastfeeding now. He'd like the baby to get the best. But then, it *is* Louise's body. An argument that reminds him of Orla. It was her body. Yes, but his child too. Why couldn't it have been easier, more straightforward? Why did the rights of mother, baby and father have to be so at odds? He wonders how Orla is doing now. Has it been straightforward for her? Has she moved on with her life as planned? He remembers her face on seeing Louise and knows the answer to that. 'Have you thought about childcare?' he asks Louise to stop this train of thought.

'If I can afford it, I was thinking of a childminder.'

What other option is there, a crèche? He'd like to argue for that, just so he can have some input, but he likes the idea of the baby having one-to-one care. 'I'll help financially.'

She starts to object, but checks herself. 'Thanks.'

'Should we start looking now?' he asks.

'I've put my name down with a few agencies. But they won't be able to send anyone for interviews until closer to the time.' Suddenly, she stops walking and her hand alights on the gentle curve of her belly. 'The baby's moving,' she says, smiling. 'Do you want to feel it?'

He does, of course he does, but putting his palm against her tummy seems too intimate. He looks at her hands, pressed against the bump and imagines what it might feel like. He is so curious that, without realizing it, his hand automatically travels towards her. Gently, she takes it and guides it to where the movement is taking place.

'Oh my God, I feel it. It's so *weird*.'

She laughs at his face. 'I know.'

'God.'

All becomes still again and he takes his hand away.

'Wow.'

That evening Jenna calls him. He braces himself for a monologue on how she's doing now that she's home from her residential programme.

But he doesn't get that.

'I'm worried about Mum,' she says. 'There's something wrong. She's depressed or something. Like a zombie, ignoring the phone, ignoring everything. She wasn't even this bad when Dad left. She won't tell me what's wrong. I don't know what to do. I didn't know who else to call.'

'What about her friend?' He tries to remember her name. 'Sal.'

'She's away.'

He's not going to suggest Owen. 'What about her doctor?'

'Aren't *you* going to help?' She sounds amazed. 'You always help.'

'I'm not sure what I could do.'

'Come over, talk to her . . . She always listens to you.'

'Not always.'

'Rory, please. I can't handle this. I'm sixteen.'

So *now* sixteen is young?

'She's drinking.' Jenna's voice cracks. 'All that booze around. Mum depressed. Trying to settle back into my old school. I'm afraid.' She breaks off. He hears her sob.

Shit. 'OK.' *Piss.* 'I'll come over. But I don't think it's going to make a difference.'

'Oh, God, thanks Rory. It will. I know it will. Can you come now?'

'Now?'

'Please?'

He looks down at the steak he's just fried. 'All right,' he says, closing his eyes. 'I'm on my way.'

Orla is huddled in a corner of the couch, hugging a cushion and staring into space. An almost empty bottle of wine is on the floor beside her. The room's a mess. Rory moves a heap of clothes off the chair opposite, and sits. Jenna lingers at the door. For a few minutes, Rory sits in silence, looking mostly at his hands. Eventually, he turns to Jenna and asks her to give them a moment. She shrugs, reaches for the doorknob and pulls the door shut. When he has heard her go upstairs, he finally speaks.

'Orla.'

Her eyes turn to his. But her face remains blank.

He is not going to pity her. 'Jenna's worried about you.'

She raises her chin. 'I'm fine.'

'I can see that,' he says, eyeing the bottle of wine.

'I've nothing to say to you. Except that I'm fine.'

'Fine,' he says. He folds his arms.

They sit in deadlocked silence. Minutes pass. When he finally speaks, it is to move it forward, get the hell out. 'You've a responsibility to Jenna. Think of what she's been through. This is not fair on her. She's only sixteen, Orla. And she's struggling as it is. She needs you to be well.'

When she looks at him, he sees a sadness that seems to come from deep inside. 'I had a responsibility to that baby.'

A bit late for that now, he thinks, jaw set.

'I keep thinking of him,' she says.

Him? Rory can't help himself. 'Was it a boy? Did they tell you?'

'No. But I knew.'

'James,' he says.

Her eyes focus in on him. And tears well over. 'I hear him. I hear him cry. I see him in my dreams, dead.' Tears are flooding her face. 'If I could bring him back. If I could swap places –'

He feels his heart soften. He knew her better than she knew herself. Now she, like him, is haunted.

'You were right. We could have managed it. Somehow. But I didn't believe that. It was all too complicated.' She puts her hands to her temples. Then she takes them down, and looks at him as though willing him to understand. 'I thought it was a solution. I thought I'd be able to carry on.'

He swallows.

'I didn't think of it as a baby. I didn't think of it as a unique little person with *so much* potential. Until it was too late. Until it was gone.'

He doesn't want to hear any more. Can't. 'You need to talk to someone.'

'What's that going to do? Bring him back?'

This is Orla, agony aunt, future counsellor. 'OK. You're going to have to stop this. You did this for a reason, remember? And it has worked out. Jenna is great now. She's stopped drinking. She has a chance. A really good chance. Do you want to blow it for her? Because you're putting too much pressure on her, Orla. You can't drink around her. She'll start drinking again. And then you'll have failed. Lost everything.'

She looks at him.

'You did it for a reason,' he says again.

'You'll never be able to forgive me, will you?'

He looks at her in all her wretchedness and understands her pain as his. Worse than his. 'I'm trying,' he lies, because no one should feel this pain.

'Then you'll fail,' she says. 'If I were you, I'd never forgive me.' She looks right into his eyes. 'How you must *hate* me.'

And at that moment, he feels his hatred burn out. She has so much hatred for herself that he doesn't owe it to the baby any more. 'I don't hate you. Please call someone. You know people. Call someone good.'

'Are you?'

'What?'

'Seeing someone?'

'No.'

'I could give you a name.'

And he feels like laughing.

36

A few days later, Rory calls Jenna, not Orla.

'How are things?' he asks.

'Better.'

He hesitates. 'How's she doing?'

'Not drinking. That was the scariest thing, Mum drinking.'

He hopes it might act as aversion therapy. 'Has she been to see someone?'

'Yeah. Some counsellor.'

'Good.'

'What happened, Rory? What upset her? I can't figure it out. Did Dad do something? Did he say something? Is it because he's going to have a new family? Or is it me, the way I've been, the drinking?'

'It's not you.'

He sounds so sure that she asks, 'Then what is it?'

He hesitates. 'I don't know.'

Silence.

'How's school? You settling back in?' he asks.

'Kind of. They think I'm a snob for going off to boarding school. But I'm breaking them down.'

He laughs.

'They're OK though. We're the same.'

'Are you all right for everything?'

'Yeah. Mum did a big shop yesterday.'

Rory takes that as a positive sign.

'Have you seen your dad?'

'Are you mad? D'you really think I want to be over there watching her bump get bigger? Anyway, Mum needs me.'

'Would you like me to bring you to see your gran?'

'OK.' Her voice sounds upbeat for the first time. 'Is she OK?'

'She's OK. Seeing you will cheer her up.'

Louise is twenty-five weeks pregnant now. It's a week before her next antenatal visit and Rory, anxious to know how the pregnancy is progressing, has no excuse to see her. So he makes one up, buying a Dorling Kindersley guide to pregnancy. It looks good. Seems to have everything in it. Would be handy to have. He wonders if he'll get a chance to feel the baby move again.

He calls in to her in the flower shop, Thursday evening, after work. She is alone. And surprised to see him. She puts down the bucket of flowers she was filling with fresh water. Dries her hands.

'Got you this,' he says, handing her the book.

'Oh. Thanks.' She flicks through it.

A customer comes in to the shop. She puts the book down and Rory stands aside while she serves him.

'Your ankles are swollen,' Rory says, when the man has left.

'Thanks for pointing that out,' she says, picking the book back up.

'You should put your feet up.'

'Where do you suggest? On the counter?' She nods towards the high stool behind it. 'One way of frightening off the customers.'

'Maybe you should hire someone to do your evenings.' He knows Naomi can't cover because of Jason.

'Or I could just hide my legs.'

'Might be good to rest, though, in the evenings.'

'I'll see.' Her voice has an edge to it that implies, 'Enough advice thanks.'

But he doesn't hear it. 'Let me see your hands.'

She rolls her eyes. 'You're determined to humiliate me.' She holds out swollen fingers.

'I'd like to check your blood pressure.'

'Rory, this is a florist's, not a doctor's surgery. I've been on my feet all day. No wonder everything's swollen.'

'Still, let me take your blood pressure.'

'No.'

'Humour me.'

'I'm pregnant. Not sick.'

'Does the swelling go down when you rest?'

'Yes,' she says quickly. 'Now, leave me alone.'

'Let me check it anyway.'

'All right. Check it. If it makes you happy.' She sounds like she's given up.

'I have to go get a sphyg. I'll just pop over to Barry's.'

'*Pop* over?' They both know it'll take an hour, there and back.

'I'm doing nothing else.' He's picking up his keys.

Her voice softens. 'Rory, you wouldn't do me a big favour? You wouldn't get me a tub of toffee Häagen-Daz while you're out?'

He smiles. 'Sure.'

When he returns, it's with two tubs of ice cream, Barry's sphygmomanometer and a urine testing kit stuffed into his pocket.

He takes Louise's blood pressure.

'What's it usually?' he asks, when he removes the cuff.

'I don't know. Fine.'

'She doesn't tell you the reading?'

'Why? It wouldn't mean anything to me.'

'It's up a little bit more than the norm.'

'You're putting it up.' But then she looks at him. 'How up?'

'Not a lot, but it'd help if I knew your baseline. I need you to give me a sample of urine.'

'*Rory.*'

He hands her a little glass jar he got from Barry. 'Pee.'

She snatches it. Disappears into the back. When she reappears, she hands it to him in silence. He tests it, checking the dipstick against the colour-coded label on the side of a dark brown jar.

'Traces of protein,' he says, looking up.

'What does that mean?' She is beginning to sound concerned.

'Does the swelling *really* go down when you rest?'

She flushes. 'Not always. What is it?'

'Is your weight going up?'

'It's supposed to be.'

'I know, but fast?'

'I haven't weighed myself. But at the last check-up they said the weight was fine.'

'That was three weeks ago. Have you been getting head-aches?'

'Yeah. But I always get headaches. What's wrong? You're worrying me now.'

'I think we should go to the hospital.'

Her eyes widen.

'Just to check you out. I'm not an obstetrician, but I think you might have pre-eclampsia, high blood pressure in preg-nancy.'

'But you said it wasn't high.'

'Well, it's not. But it is up. And I don't have a baseline to compare with. I think we'd be better off checking it out.'

'You want me to close the shop?'

'You've what, an hour left? I'll wait and bring you to the hospital when it's up.'

She looks worried. 'No. If there's a problem, we'll go. I'll close early.'

They arrive at the outpatient area, which is open for out-of-hour emergencies. There's a couple in front of them. The woman is very young and thin. She doesn't look pregnant. She's crying. Her partner has his arm around her.

'You know,' Rory says to Louise, 'this isn't an emergency. We're just being careful, OK?'

'OK.' But she looks nervous.

Their turn comes and a midwife shows them in. She takes 'a history', asking Louise when her last menstrual period was and the estimated date of delivery.

'It's all in my chart,' Louise says, impatient.

'Your chart is on its way,' the nurse says, unruffled. She asks about foetal movements. How many in the last twelve hours?

Louise sounds hassled. 'I don't know. I was working. Busy. I didn't count them. Was I supposed to? I mean the baby did kick. I'm sure it was the usual number of times. Nothing seemed wrong.' She puts her hands on the bump. 'Nothing seemed wrong.'

'I'm sure all's well. Let's listen to the baby,' she says calmly, as though to reassure Louise. She helps her up onto a bench and applies a simple listening device to her abdomen. When she looks up, she smiles. 'Baby's heart is fine.'

Louise lets out a sigh of relief. As does Rory.

The nurse checks Louise's blood pressure and compares it to the baseline readings in the chart that has just arrived. Rory would kill for a peek.

'Is it OK?' Louise asks.

'Well, it's up a bit.'

'How much?' Rory asks.

The nurse looks at him and seems to gather he knows what he is talking about. 'Well, it's normally on the low side, ninety-five over seventy, around that. At the moment it's one-fifty over ninety-eight.'

For Louise's benefit, Rory nods as if to say 'nothing to worry about'. Inside he doesn't feel so blasé.

The midwife checks Louise's weight and, in answer to a question from Rory, admits that it is up fifteen pounds in three weeks.

'That's bad, isn't it?' Louise asks, sounding panicky.

'It's a bit more than we'd like at this point. You're retaining some fluid. I'm just going to check your sample,' she says, picking up the tiny jar of urine Louise gave her when she came in. 'Then I'll call the house doctor to have a look at you.' Her smile is reassuring.

'How is the protein?' Rory asks.

The nurse looks at him, squinting. 'Do you've a medical background?'

'I'm a neurology reg.'

She nods slowly and Rory knows that from this moment on he and Louise will be treated differently. The unwritten rule will be applied: doctor involved, don't mess up.

'Plus one for protein,' she says. Then to Louise, 'I'm just going to hook you up to this for a little while. It gives us a reading of the baby's heart. Everything's fine,' she reassures. 'The doctor will just want to see a reading.'

When the house doctor arrives, the nurse briefs him in a side room.

When he emerges, he introduces himself and explains that he is going to run some blood tests. He lists off to Rory what they are. Then turns to Louise.

'Do you know what pre-eclampsia is?'

Louise glances at Rory then back at the doctor. 'High blood pressure in pregnancy.'

'Exactly. And has anyone in your family had pre-eclampsia?'

'I don't know. There was only my mother. And she'd never talk about anything like that.'

'Not to worry. Well, you are showing signs of pre-eclampsia.'

Louise looks at Rory again.

'We're going to admit you for the moment for observation and bed-rest. We want to keep an eye on your blood pressure and the baby. I'm going to organize an ultrasound of your abdomen now, just to make sure that everything's one hundred per cent.'

While the nurse and doctor are busy getting things ready, Louise whispers to Rory, 'I thought you were just fussing.'

'I was.'

'But what if you hadn't checked my blood pressure?'

'They'd have picked it up on your next visit.'

'Next week. What if it was too late?'

'We're here now. You're in good hands. You're safe. The baby's safe.'

'What about the shop?' she asks. 'Who'll open up tomorrow?'

'Naomi?' How things have changed, he thinks – there was a time when he wouldn't have trusted Naomi with anything.

'She doesn't have a key. I should have given her a key. Shown how much I trust her.'

'Why don't I call her? Maybe she can come here early and pick up the key?'

'She has to get Jason to school.'

'All right then, after. I think it'll be all right if for once the shop opens late.'

She nods. 'OK.' Then looks as if something has just occurred to her. 'How long will I be in here? I can't be here any longer than tomorrow. There's the ordering . . .'

'Louise. Let's think about that tomorrow, OK? For now, let's just concentrate on getting your blood pressure down.'

Louise is admitted, arriving in the ward by wheelchair, despite her telling them she'd prefer to walk. Now, two nurses wheel a bed containing another patient out of the single room that is across from the nurses' station to make way for her.

'I don't mind sharing,' she says, embarrassed.

The nurse smiles. 'We're doing this for the other patients as much as for you. We'll be in and out a lot during the night, checking your blood pressure. Better for everyone if you're in a room on your own. I'll just give you this gown. When you've changed into it, hop into bed.'

A fresh bed is moved into the room. Louise is wheeled in beside it.

'I'll give you a moment,' the nurse says. 'And I'll be straight in to you.'

While Louise is changing, Rory waits outside. When he sees the house doctor stride onto the ward, he stops him. 'Everything's OK, right? Everything's under control? The baby's only twenty-five weeks.'

'The blood pressure is still rising. I'm going to start a mag sulphate drip to prevent convulsions and apresoline to keep the BP down.'

'What is it now?'

The doctor hesitates. 'One eighty over one ten.'

'Jesus. You have to get it down.'

'That's the plan.' The doctor pushes past him, into the nurses' station. Seconds later, he strides out, carrying an IV tray and accompanied by a nurse who is pushing a drip. They disappear into Louise's room. Outside, Rory is beginning to panic. A blood pressure that high is dangerous to mother and baby. If they don't get it down, they'll have to do an emergency section. The baby's lungs aren't fully developed. It might not survive. As soon as the doctor emerges, Rory is behind him. 'There's a steroid you can give, isn't there, for the baby's lungs, to help develop surfactant.'

'There is.'

'How soon can you give it?'

'We're going to give it now.'

'Has her consultant been informed?'

'Yes. We've been speaking over the phone. And we're keeping her posted. She'll come in if the BP goes up any further.'

When Rory goes back into the room, he senses that an effort is being made to keep the atmosphere calm. A nurse is saying to Louise, 'We'll leave this attached to your arm so as not to disturb you.' It's the cuff of a sphygmomanometer. Louise is hooked up to a drip and attached to a foetal heart monitor. 'I'll leave you in peace now,' the nurse says and goes.

'You don't have to stay,' Louise says to Rory. 'I'll be fine now. Thanks for everything.'

He doesn't want to leave until he's sure the BP is down. He checks his watch. 'I'm all right for another while.'

The doctor is back. He explains to Louise why he's giving her a steroid injection.

'What have the baby's lungs to do with my blood pressure?' she asks, confused.

'Well, in *some* cases of pre-eclampsia, if the blood pressure gets too high we *sometimes* have to perform a Caesarean section.'

She looks shocked. 'I can't have a Caesarean section *now*. The baby.' She looks desperately at Rory. 'I can't. I won't.'

Rory's surprised and heartened by the force of her reaction. She wants this baby as much as he does.

'We haven't come anywhere near that,' the doctor says, in a voice that seems designed to induce calm. 'This is just a precaution. Neither you nor baby is in danger at the moment.'

'But we could be, is that what you're saying?'

Rory doesn't think the doctor is handling this very well.

'You're on medication now and resting. We're monitoring you very carefully. We'll get that blood pressure down.'

'And if you don't?'

The doctor looks her straight in the eye. 'If you or the baby is in danger, we will have to operate.'

By eleven o'clock Louise's blood pressure has stopped climbing.

'You should go,' she says to Rory. 'I'll be fine.' Her voice is drowsy, her eyelids droopy. She yawns. 'This stuff is making me so tired.'

'Sleep,' Rory says. 'I'll just wait here another half hour.'

She seems relieved to close her eyes.

He sits watching her, and the nurses coming and going.

He hopes they can get the blood pressure down. And keep it there. This baby needs time.

By one a.m. Louise is deeply asleep and her blood pressure has finally started to edge down ever so slowly. Rory feels he can go.

As soon as he gets home though, he calls the hospital and is relieved to hear that her BP is still heading in the right direction. He sets his alarm for six-thirty.

When he wakes he rings again. Louise's BP has fallen continually throughout the night. It is still above normal, but not dangerously. Rory gets ready for work. On his way he makes a detour to Naomi's flat, where he drops off the keys to the shop, an idea that occurred to him during the night while watching Louise sleep.

Naomi is concerned about Louise, but not about opening up on her own. She has learnt the ropes, she says, and is glad to be able to do this for Louise. Rory gets to work early, knowing he may have to leave later. The time is close to eleven, and he assumes that Louise's doctors will have seen her by now. He calls her ward and is relieved to discover that they're keeping her in. She can rest while they keep an eye on her blood pressure and the baby. He asks a nurse to tell her that he'll drop by at lunchtime.

'I can't believe they're keeping me in,' Louise says to him when he arrives. 'They say my blood pressure's fine.'

'It was very high. They have to be careful. Make sure it stays down. Certainly for a few days. They're doing the right thing.'

'But the shop.'

'I got the keys to Naomi early this morning. She opened on time, and seems happy on her own.'

'But what about the afternoon?'

'I'll collect Jason from school and bring him to the shop.

332

Naomi said he can do his homework there and then help her. He likes it there. It's peaceful.'

'Are you sure you can take time off? You're already missing work by being here.'

'It's fine. I'll make up the time.'

'Thanks, Rory.' She smiles at him.

'Do you need me to get stuff?'

'It's OK.' She mentions the name of a friend.

He wants to be the one to do it. Wants to have a role. 'I'll get it. Just tell me what you need.'

She makes a list for him. 'I feel so useless,' she says.

'I don't see why. The baby needs you to take it easy. And that's what you're doing. You're anything but useless.'

That evening, when he calls back with Louise's things, he finds Naomi visiting – this after running the shop single-handedly for the day. While Jason puts the flowers they brought into water, Naomi is updating her boss on the day's business, looking as if she's thriving on the responsibility. When Louise thanks her and tells her how much she appreciates it, Naomi's own gratitude is clear.

'I'm just glad of the chance to do something for you.'

Rory feels guilty that he ever doubted her. She is a strong woman, just needed an opportunity to show it. Rory puts the stuff down, silently salutes the two women, then winks at Jason. He's pleased that the boy is here. He can explain about the party. What must he have thought when he found Rory gone?

'Want to go get a Coke?' he asks Jason.

And just like that, it's back to the way it was. Rory puts his hand on Jason's shoulder as they walk from the room to find a coffee shop.

*

The following day, Louise has been weaned off the medication. She is to be monitored for twenty-four hours to see how she manages without it. All being well, she'll be discharged with careful follow-up monitoring. Her blood pressure is being checked every two hours now. Last time Rory rang, it was fine. He strolls onto the ward in good spirits. Everything's looking up. The danger has passed. Halfway up the corridor, he sees a nurse hurrying from the nurses' station into Louise's room. She is carrying a drip. Her face is drawn. Instinctively, Rory quickens his step.

The door to her room is closed. Waiting outside, he spots a doctor in the nurses' station, who is just hanging up on a call. Rory approaches him. He asks about Louise. And learns that her blood pressure has shot back up. Medication has been restarted and her consultant is on her way.

'How high is it?' Rory asks.

'One-ninety over one-twelve.'

'How could you let it get so high?' Rory is furious.

'We were checking it two-hourly. It was creeping up a bit, but not significantly until the last check when it seems to have spiked.'

'Can I see her?'

'Of course. As soon as the nurse is finished.'

When the nurse comes out, he knocks and goes in.

Louise is extremely pale and visibly shaking.

Rory hurries to her side. 'Are you OK?' he asks, really concerned.

'I feel terrible.' He takes her hand in his. It's cold. 'Like something awful's going to happen. Like I'm going to lose the baby.' He rubs the back of her hand.

'My head's pounding. I'm freezing.'

'I'll get you another blanket.'

'The nurse has just gone for one. My feet have never been so cold.'

He sits on the chair that's beside the bed. Takes off his socks, lifts the blankets and puts them on for her. 'They're not smelly,' he jokes, to cut the tension. He rubs her feet to heat them up. 'There.'

'Oh, God, Rory, I think I'm going to throw up.'

She does, all over herself and the bed.

'I'll get a nurse.'

He waits outside while they settle her again.

'How's the BP?' he asks when they emerge.

'Up a bit.'

'How much?'

'Two-ten over one-twenty.'

'Does she need another steroid injection for the baby?'

'Dr Greene is just about to give it.'

Rory stays outside while the doctor gives Louise the jab. He has just returned to the room when the consultant arrives in a breeze. She reassures Louise, sitting on the side of the bed holding her hand. Louise looks a little less worried. She also looks puffy around the face, which is not good. The consultant takes her blood pressure, checks the baby monitor, then uses her stethoscope on Louise's tummy. She smiles at Louise, then looks in the chart.

'Have you checked the platelets again?' she asks Dr Greene.

'Yes, the results should be back any moment.'

'Ring the lab. I need them now.'

She smiles at Louise again.

'My head feels like it's going to blow off,' Louise says.

'We'll get you something, straight away.' She nods to the nurse who disappears. Then she asks Louise about the headache.

'Do you have any pain in your abdomen?'

'No, my back.'

'Your back.'

Dr Greene returns with the lab results.

'OK,' the consultant says to Louise. 'We're going to bring you straight to theatre. You have a condition called H.E.L.L.P. Your body is turning on itself, attacking certain blood cells and raising your liver enzymes. We need to get the baby out.'

Louise's eyes fill with panic. 'But it's too soon. The baby . . .'

'If we don't do an emergency Caesarean section now, it's not just the baby we'll be worried about.'

Rory can't believe it. Hours ago everything was fine.

'Oh, God,' Louise says, 'I think I'm going to pass out,' and subsequently does.

'Baby's heart is dipping,' says the consultant. 'We need to get her to theatre, now. Is she typed and cross-matched?'

Rory follows the jargon without thinking. They're preparing units of blood to be on stand-by in case Louise bleeds. Her platelets, the blood cells she needs for clotting, are incredibly low, which puts her at risk of bleeding. They need blood ready, just in case.

Rory is allowed to scrub up and sit at Louise's head, but out of the way of the anaesthetist. Screens block his view of what is happening further down. He wants to stand, but is afraid he'll be asked to leave. Everyone is working at lightning speed. He hears the word 'catheter'; sees the paediatric team arrive and prepare an incubator, a heater, a ventilator for the baby. He prays they will be needed.

'No foetal heart beat,' someone says, urgency in their

voice, and he wants to get down there, get the baby out himself.

And then the baby is out and over to the paediatrician immediately. Silence. Rory strains to see. But can't. The baby is surrounded. All he sees are their backs in green theatre gowns. He hears a cry. It is weak. But it's a cry. And he feels like crying himself, with relief. Someone who has been blocking his view moves. Rory sees that the baby has been ventilated and put in the incubator, or the other way around, he's not sure how it happens. But it has happened. Already. So fast. Someone blocks his view again. And then he is being called over.

'It's a girl,' a voice says. He doesn't look up to see who is speaking. Can't take his eyes off their little girl. Their tiny, tiny girl. No bigger than his hand. As delicate as an eyelash. And he now experiences for the first time the proud and simultaneously vulnerable feeling of being a father.

'We're bringing her to the Neonatal Intensive Care Unit now,' the paediatrician says.

Still dazed, Rory looks up, his actions delayed.

'You can come see her later.'

He is just taking that in when they wheel her away in the incubator. That's when it occurs to him: he never spoke to her; he never said 'hello'.

'We have a bleed,' someone says behind him, urgency in her voice.

Rory looks back to Louise. Everyone is huddled around. Panic rises in him.

'Where is it coming from?'

'Check the liver.'

'Sponge.'

'I see it. A laceration.'

'Breathing's too shallow. I'm ventilating her,' a voice from the top of the table. The anaesthetist.

'BP falling.'

A theatre nurse, rushing from the operating table to fetch something behind Rory, becomes aware of him. Her eyes widen behind her mask. 'I think it's time for you to go see your daughter,' she says, never stopping from her task.

'We need to transfuse her. Are those units ready?'

The theatre nurse, having delivered whatever it was she was asked to, comes to Rory, takes him by the arm and begins to escort him outside.

'BP eighty over sixty.'

Only too aware of what a sudden severe drop in blood pressure can do, Rory feels his legs weaken. He wants to stay. He wants to help. He looks back, while still being walked towards the doors.

The last words he hears are, 'We can't operate now. We need to stabilize her. Pack the liver and close her. Get those units. Turn up that IV.'

37

He stands outside the theatre. Overcome. For minutes he doesn't move. When he does it's to remove his mask so he can get air. He looks back at the doors shut firmly behind him. And his vision becomes blurred by tears. He hadn't *really* worried about Louise, all along it was the baby. And now she's in there fighting for her life. What if he loses her? He can't bear that thought. So he blocks it and begins to walk. She'll be all right, he tells himself. She'll be all right. They know what they're doing.

It doesn't take long to find the Neonatal Intensive Care Unit. It's close to the theatre, for obvious reasons. So many instructions on the doors. He can't read any of them. He rings the bell outside and leans against the wall. After a few moments, a nurse comes out. When he explains who he is, he's told that the doctors are 'working on' his daughter. He'll have to wait. She shows him to a room and tells him she'll come for him as soon as the team is finished.

He doesn't want to think. He reaches for a magazine, stares at the cover but sees the operating theatre. Hears the voices. Then hears his own: they don't know what they're doing. A bleeding liver is a surgical emergency, requiring a surgeon not an obstetrician. What experience does she have of stopping the flow of blood from the body's most vascular organ? When the liver bleeds, it bleeds. Can it even be stopped in a person whose platelets are as low as Louise's?

At first, he does not hear the nurse calling his name. Then

he does. He gets up, his face expectant. Does she have news of his daughter?

The nurse smiles, holds out her hand. 'I'm Emer Devine. I'm looking after your baby. Would you like to see her now? You'll have to wash your hands and put on a gown. Come with me. I'll show you where everything is.'

'Is she all right?'

'She's doing well. But will need a lot of care. She's very premature.'

He removes the theatre gown he had forgotten he was wearing, puts on another, washes his hands. The nurse warns him that he might find it a bit upsetting as the baby is attached to a lot of tubes and machines. He barely hears her as they walk through the unit. In a daze, he looks at the other babies and their parents. It is quieter here than in the operating theatre, but by no means peaceful. It has its own subtler tension. An alarm goes off on a monitor beside a baby and a nurse reaches to turn it off. The baby's mum does not look startled. It's as if this happens all the time and nothing surprises her any more.

And now he is here, beside his own child, so small and fragile. Hooked up to wires, tubes, lines and monitors, unmoving except for her chest, which rises and falls in response to the ventilator. The sticky pads applied to her chest are the size of cents. Rory tries to ignore the circus around her and focus on the miniature person, lying on her side, naked except for a little white cap and the tiniest nappy he has ever seen. Her legs, bent at the knee, are no bigger than his index finger. He is stunned at the perfection.

'Isn't she beautiful?' the nurse, whose name he has forgotten, says. And already she is back to work, checking a monitor and taking notes.

'Will she be OK?' His voice is hoarse.

She stops what she is doing. 'We will do everything we can to make sure . . .'

'She's only twenty-five weeks.'

'We have had babies make it who were twenty-four.'

He looks hopeful. 'Really?'

She nods. 'It is possible. All I can guarantee you, though, is that we will do our very best.'

He knows the risks – brain damage, lung damage. 'She is almost twenty-six.'

The nurse gives him a that's-the-spirit smile. 'How's your wife doing?'

It is like a hammer to his chest. He looks down at the baby. Can't speak.

She seems to understand and follows his eyes. 'She's sedated because she's on the ventilator.'

'Oh,' he says, though he knows all this. He looks at the tiny fists, the tiny, tiny feet and the little pink name bands that say that she's theirs.

He is sitting in a chair, beside his daughter, trying to keep sleep at bay when he sees Louise's obstetrician heading in his direction, her face deadly serious. Suddenly awake, he stands.

'How is she?'

'I'm sorry we had to ask you to leave . . .'

'How is she?'

'We did our best, but I'm afraid we've had to transfer her to St Paul's Hospital to the liver surgeons there.'

'Are they operating?'

'I'm afraid Louise is not well enough at the moment. She's in ICU. We managed to stem the bleeding, but she has lost a lot of blood. Her blood pressure dropped considerably. She had no urinary output when she was leaving.'

'Her kidneys . . .'

'We have to look at possible renal damage. The renal team at St Paul's is being consulted.'

At least it's St Paul's. One of the guys on the renal team is a mate. Rory's not so familiar with the surgical team, but he probably knows them by sight.

'Could I go over there now?'

'Maybe you should ring the ICU. Check with them first.'

He nods.

'She is still unconscious. She's still on a ventilator.'

Leaving the NICU, the nurse who introduced herself as Emer follows him out.

'I just wanted to check. Would you like the baby baptized?'

He stares at her. Baptized? She just said that twenty-four-week-old babies can survive. This baby's not going to die. She's not going to need baptism. But how can he be sure? What if his baby is not one of the lucky ones? And what if there is a heaven? Would denying baptism mean denying entry? Surely no God would allow that? If so, where the hell is James?

'Yes. Yes, go ahead. Please.'

She smiles. 'OK. We'll see you soon.' She turns to go.

He starts to take off his gown. 'But then,' he calls after her, 'should I be there?'

'No. No, it's fine. You go on.'

He nods.

He drives through the night, eyes stinging, lids heavy, trying not to think of what is waiting for him or what he left behind. When he reaches ICU, he has the same problem. He's not allowed in. The doctors are working on Louise.

'Are you a relative?' a nurse asks.

'I'm her next of kin,' he says to avoid detail.

'I'll let the doctors know you're here. One of them will be out to you as soon as they can. Take a seat.'

There's a line of them against the corridor wall.

Rory has waited thirty minutes and is nodding off when someone taps his shoulder. He looks up. Thank God for a familiar face. Niall O'Neill and he went to college together. Niall sits beside him.

'How is she?'

Niall's face is grim. 'She's had a major bleed, Rory. She's in severe shock. The ventilator's doing ninety per cent of her breathing. There'll be organ damage. Kidneys. Maybe liver. We're trying to stabilize her so the surgeons can go in and fix that laceration. The next forty-eight hours are critical. I'm sorry.'

'Can I see her?'

'For about a minute. We're still working on her.'

He follows Niall into ICU. But the patient he is walking towards is not Louise. It couldn't be. Only the name above her head says it is. She is unrecognizable, face and arms bloated from retained fluid, closed eyelids looking blistered. Her skin is deathly pale in contrast to the bruises that line her arms from where they took blood. In seconds, he logs the various machines and monitors she is hooked up to, the empty catheter, the blood transfusion. Nurses and doctors are busy taking samples, checking monitors, administering medication. Keeping out of their way, he goes to the head of the bed. He has one minute. But wants to say so much. He kisses her forehead. Into her ear he says, 'We've a little girl. She's so beautiful, Lou. You have to wake up and see her. She's so like you.' He closes his eyes and stops for a moment. 'She needs you, Lou. She needs you to be here. *I* need you.' He should have said it before. He should have said it at his father's funeral. He should have swallowed his pride and had her back in his life on whatever terms.

Niall's hand is on his shoulder.

He doesn't want to leave.

'Rory.'

'OK.' And he drags himself away.

Two hours after he has crashed exhausted onto his bed, his alarm goes off. It takes him a moment to remember that his reality is worse than his nightmare. He showers himself awake and calls the hospital. He is taking a week's leave of absence. He thinks about calling his mother to let her know what's happened, but it's early. The phone ringing at this time would worry her. He considers calling Siofra, who will be up, getting ready for her crack-of-dawn commute. No. His mother should hear first. From him. He grabs his keys.

When he reaches the ICU, relatives of other patients are sitting in a line on the corridor outside. A procedure is in progress, he is told. No one is allowed in. Rory knows by the way they look at him that Louise is the beneficiary of the 'procedure'. He worries what it might be. Worries that her condition might have worsened. When the door to the ICU finally opens, Niall comes out, looking almost as drained as Rory.

Rory stands up, ready to go in.

'Not yet,' Niall says. 'The renal team is putting Louise on dialysis.'

Rory looks at him.

'Her kidneys have shut down,' Niall says.

Rory sinks back down on the seat.

'Let's go for coffee,' his friend says.

'That bad, eh?'

'Rory, I'm not going to lie to you. It's not just the kidneys. Her liver function tests are dismal. It looks as if she's going into liver failure as well.'

'She can't be.'

'She's heading for multi-organ failure, Rory.'

Which means her chances of survival are minimal. Rory is desperate. He stands. 'I have to see her.' To tell her how much he loves her. That he's sorry. He has to talk to her. He didn't get a chance with his father. He's not going to let it happen again.

'Not now,' Niall says. 'Look, I'll be out to you as soon as I can.'

Rory's eyes follow him until he disappears. Then starts to blame himself. This is his fault. He wanted a baby. And made Louise pregnant. There's no such thing as accidents. Throat burning, eyes smarting, he paces the corridor, gripping the back of his neck. What can he do? How can he help? His distress is palpable and even the relatives sitting in a quiet line burdened with their own worries give him empathetic glances. A chaplain walks quietly into the ICU. Then a nurse comes out to Rory to ask if he thinks that Louise would like the Last Rites. No, he wants to shout, because she's not dying. She doesn't need Last Rites because she's going to make it. But that is not what he says. He simply tells the nurse to go ahead. For the same reason he told them to baptize his daughter. There might be a heaven.

The nurse comes out to him again, asking about other family members. They should be informed, she says. He knows that this woman is just doing her job, but to him she is like a circling bird of prey.

'There are no relatives,' he manages. 'Just me.'

She looks surprised, says, 'OK', and walks back inside.

He thinks about that, how there are no relatives. Louise's mother isolated herself by drinking, isolating her daughter along with her. Rory knows of no relatives other than Louise's father, who never came back. She has friends, lots of friends. He should let them know. And he will – as soon as he can trust himself to string a sentence together. What will he even say? Not that she is dying. He will never admit that. Then, he stops pacing, walks outside and opens his phone. The person that he calls is Naomi.

'She'll be all right,' Naomi says, with powerful confidence.

She doesn't understand the danger. Rory tries to explain.

'She will be all right,' Naomi insists. 'And I'll keep the shop going.'

'Don't worry about that. It doesn't matter now.'

'I'm opening up today. And I'll keep opening up until Louise is back on her feet. Because she *will* be back on her feet.'

Rory doesn't know why he suddenly feels a whole lot better. But he does.

If he can't be with Louise, he can be with their daughter. He makes a high-speed trip across the city. In the NICU he recognizes a few faces from his last visit. Other parents. All in the same boat. They exchange polite smiles. This time he knows where he is going. This time the shock of seeing his baby isn't as enormous. Voice almost inaudible, he talks to her for the first time.

'Hello. Hello, Thumbelina. I'm your dad. Yes, I'm your dad. How're you doing? Are you nice and warm in there? Are you sunbathing?' He should tell her about Louise.

'Your mum would be here, beside me, but she's not well. She's fighting, like you, to get better. And when that happens, I'm going to make everything OK again. Are you listening? Can you hear me? We'll have fun together. We'll play rugby. We'll go to the movies. We'll even do girly stuff if you want.'

'Would you like to touch her?' a voice says behind him.

'Has Emer gone off duty?' He was familiar with Emer.

She nods. 'I'm Grace.' And smiles.

'Hi.'

'Would you like to touch her?'

'She's so tiny,' he says, afraid he will hurt her.

'It would be good for her.'

He looks hopeful.

He runs his finger along her arm with a featherlight touch.

'I've taken some photos,' Grace says, 'so you can bring them to Mum.'

He swallows. But takes them, thanking her.

'How is she doing?'

His face speaks for him.

'Oh,' she says.

'Yeah.' His voice is hoarse. Suddenly he needs to be with Louise.

This time he gets five minutes with her. He tries to ignore the machines. Wishes he could take her in his arms. He lingers over the kiss he places on her forehead. Still, it is shorter than he'd like.

'Hey, gorgeous,' he says gently into her ear. 'It's your secret admirer.' He sticks the baby's picture to the bed. 'This is our little girl. She's so beautiful. So tiny. You should see her feet, Lou. I don't know what to call her in case you won't like it.

When you get better, we'll pick something together.' Because she will get better.

He doesn't want to know that if not for dialysis, her kidneys would not be functioning. Nor does he want to know the results of her appalling liver function tests. Or that the ventilator is doing all the work. What he wants to do is download all her favourite songs back onto his iPod and bring it to her. He knows that she can hear. The unconscious often do. He can get through to her. He can make her want to fight.

At midday, he calls his mother. When he tells her he has some news, his tone leaves no doubt but that it's not good. 'Louise had the baby.'

There's a second's silence as the implications register. 'Oh, Lord. It's too early. The baby . . . is it . . . all right?' Alive.

'It's a girl, Mum. And she's on life support.'

'Will she . . . be OK?' Her anxiety and helplessness are audible.

'I don't know . . . It's too early to tell.'

'Oh, please, God.' She is silent for a moment, and he guesses that she is in prayer. 'And Louise, how is Louise?'

He could tell her about the liver, the kidneys, the fact that her system is shutting down, but instead, he tells the truth, finally admitting it to himself. 'She is dying.' Downloading all the songs in the world won't change that.

'Oh, God, Rory.'

He clears tears with the heel of his hand.

'What can I do?' she asks.

'I don't know.'

'Should I visit?'

'No. No visitors. Anyway, she's unconscious.'

When his mother finally speaks, she sounds more

confident. 'Well, you can't be in two places at once. Someone should sit with the baby. I will. And I'll tell the others. We'll take turns. Isn't that what they say? Babies know when you're there, and it helps, doesn't it? That's what we'll do. We'll sit with the baby.'

'How will you get there?'

'Don't you worry about that.'

38

The following day, when Rory walks into the ICU, Louise's bed is gone. He looks frantically at the nurse, who comes over to him.

'They've taken her to theatre,' she explains.

'Theatre?'

'We tried to get in touch with you, but your phone was going to voicemail. You've signed a consent form for any procedures that may be necessary.'

'What procedure is she having?'

'Repair of the laceration in her liver.'

He panics. Her situation must have changed. 'Did she have another bleed?'

'No, no. Her surgeon felt her condition had improved as much as it was going to so they should go ahead.'

'How long is she gone?'

The nurse checks her watch. 'Almost an hour.'

Rory takes a deep breath, tries to decide what to do next. He can wait here and go out of his mind or he can go see the baby.

A surprise greets him at the end of his drive. Sitting outside the NICU is Orla. Head down, she is blowing her nose.

'Orla?'

She looks up and he sees that she is crying.

He panics. 'Is everything all right? The baby?'

She shakes her head, eyes wide. 'No. No. The baby's fine. The baby's wonderful. Your mum is in with her.'

'Then why?' And suddenly he understands. He sits beside her. 'Are you all right?'

She nods. 'Your mum asked me to give her a lift. Siofra brought her yesterday afternoon, but Alex is sick today and Owen was in some important meeting. I should have stayed outside. I should have known it would be too much. But I wanted to see her. I want her to make it so much. I wanted to tell her that. But I wasn't prepared . . . She's so small. I just kept thinking –' She starts crying again.

And he puts an arm around her.

'I'm so sorry, Rory.'

'It's OK,' he says. 'It's OK.' And it is. There was a time he thought he'd never forgive her. But he does. He just does. He was too hard on Louise and now it's too late. And he was too hard on Orla. But she is here, conscious, able to understand, and he can forgive. They can have a relationship. Maybe they can even help each other.

A nurse lets him in to the NICU. He washes his hands and gowns up.

His mother is bending over the baby singing softly. 'I'm a bear called Jeremy.'

This makes him smile. 'Hello,' he says.

She jumps.

'I'm sorry, but there can be only one person at a time,' the nurse says, behind them.

'I'm going now, anyway,' says his mum.

'I'll walk you out,' he says.

When they get to the gowning area, she speaks. 'She is the most beautiful creation I have ever seen.' She rubs his arm. Then starts to undo her gown. 'Poor Orla. She was very upset.'

'Maybe best not to ask her again. If Siofra can't bring you, ring me. Or Owen.'

'Wish I'd taken more of those driving lessons.' She smiles, but it fades quickly. 'How's Louise?'

'In theatre. They're trying to repair her liver.'

'Please God,' she says, and closes her eyes as though making a wish. 'I've been praying like mad.'

'Hope you asked for a miracle.'

'Two.'

He sighs. 'I better go in.'

She puts a hand on his arm, to stop him. 'Rory, I've been praying to your father. If he has anything to do with it, that baby in there will grow up to be the biggest, strongest, fastest child in Ireland. And her mother will witness it all.'

He hugs her. And is in no rush to let go.

Two days after the surgery, one of those miracles seems to have occurred. Louise's liver function tests have returned to normal. The surgeon expresses amazement. Three more days and Louise is producing urine, not much, but some. Rory, afraid to allow himself hope, asks his mother to keep praying. He even prays himself. The doctors begin to reduce the amount of work the ventilator is doing to see how Louise's lungs cope. Then one magical day, when Rory kisses her forehead, she opens her eyes and tries to sit up. Alarms go off and a nurse rushes to settle her back down. A doctor gives her sedation. She cannot be awake and on a ventilator. But that is not a worry to Rory. Louise is no longer unconscious. Her sleep is medically induced. Maybe now he can afford to hope. The doctors talk about removing the ventilator altogether. And ten days following the surgery, they do. Louise no longer needs sedation. When it wears off, she opens her eyes. Rory is there, holding her hand, waiting. She is so weak that the only things she seems to be able to move are her eyes. And mouth. Her first words are, 'The baby?'

Rory squeezes her hand then stands up and pulls the photo from the bed. He holds it up to her face so she can see. 'Isn't she beautiful?'

But her face is filled with worry. 'Is she OK?'

'She's perfect. Tiny and perfect.'

'We had a girl,' she says, and looks into his eyes.

'She's almost two weeks old and every day she's getting stronger.'

With what seems like great effort, Louise turns her head. 'I've been asleep for *two weeks*?'

He nods. 'You had us worried.'

She closes her eyes. It seems all she is able for. But then she opens them again. 'Have you given her a name?'

'Thumbelina.'

She smiles. 'I like it.' Then she closes her eyes.

Days later, Louise is moved out of ICU to the renal ward. All she talks about is seeing the baby, but she is still on dialysis, under the care of three different teams, and still very weak. Rory witnesses a fighting determination to get well, get out of hospital and hold her baby. Louise has always been determined, but this is like nothing he has ever seen before. She pushes herself to eat, get out of the bed, walk with the help of the nurses, do every exercise the physiotherapist gives her and more. Sometimes the nurses tell her to slow down. But she will not.

'She seems so far away. Over there, all alone,' she says of the baby.

'She's not alone. She has Mum, Siofra, Jenna. And me. She is loved. She's not alone.'

'I know. But I'm her mother and she's never even seen me. She's three weeks old and she doesn't know what it's like for her own mother to hold her, to tell her she loves her, comfort her when she cries, feed her. I want to tell her I was sick, that's why I didn't come.'

'I've told her for you.'

'She needs to hear it from me.' The genuine distress in her voice saves him from feeling hurt. 'She heard my heart every day, for weeks and weeks. Then it stopped.'

'Thank God it didn't,' Rory says, automatically.

When she looks at him, he holds her eyes, wanting her to know what that would have done to him.

Louise is weaned off dialysis and put on close observation. She hassles the doctors until they let her out for a few hours to see the baby. This they do only on the assurance that Rory, a doctor, will be with her.

'I can't believe we're out,' she says to him in the car. 'I can't believe I'm finally getting to see her.' Her excitement makes him love her even more.

'Last time I went through these doors,' she says, when they arrive at the maternity hospital, 'I'd no idea what was coming.'

Rory offers her his arm. Still very weak, she leans on him, but refuses a wheelchair. As they go up in the lift, she grows quiet. He feels her tense.

'What if she doesn't know who I am? What if she doesn't like me? What if I make her cry?'

'You're her mother. She loves you already.'

He helps Louise with her gown. And they go to their baby. When Louise sees her, she starts to cry. When she speaks, her voice is high. 'Hello, hello, sweetheart. Mummy's here.'

354

One of the nurses pulls up a comfortable chair. 'You might like to sit down,' she says.

Louise looks at the nurse as though seeing her for the first time. 'Thank you. Thank you for looking after my baby. I can't thank you enough.'

'She's doing so well. She's really come on in three weeks.' The nurse starts to explain what all the equipment is for, but Louise appears not to hear, gazing at her little girl as though she is the only person in the room. When the nurse stops talking, Louise starts – to the baby.

'I'm so sorry I wasn't here. But I am now. And I'll never leave you again. I'll be the best mum. You'll see.' Eventually she turns to Rory. 'Her little arms! They're so *thin*.'

'We'll feed her spinach.'

'She's a miracle.'

They're beautiful together, Rory thinks, mother and child, staring into each other's eyes. He is in awe.

The doctors start to talk to Louise about discharge. And home support. She's still very weak and will require a lot of medical care. Her dressings need to be changed, her blood pressure monitored. She needs ongoing physiotherapy, occupational therapy. When they discover that she lives alone, they want to discharge her to a convalescent home.

'I want to get out,' she says to Rory. 'But not to a home. I have to be able to see the baby.'

'Then come home with me. Let me look after you.' He doesn't want to let her go, afraid he'll never get her back. He has his excuse ready: he's a doctor. He can keep an eye on her. They'll let her out if she stays with him. But in the end, that's not what he says.

'I love you. And I don't want us to be apart again – ever.'

She's about to speak, but a nurse comes in to ask if she wants any painkillers.

'No. No thanks, I'm fine.'

The nurse leaves, and Louise turns to Rory.

He clears his throat. 'I love you, Lou. I never stopped, even when I tried to. Don't ask me to live without you. Not again. When I thought I'd lost you –' His voice cracks and he stops.

She gets up and goes to him. Sits on his lap and puts her arms around him. 'You haven't lost me,' she whispers.

Epilogue

June parks her husband's car outside the church and hurries inside. Naomi pulls up in a ten-year-old, slightly battered silver Honda and Jason hops out in shirt and tie. He looks towards the church, just as a priest with long wavy hair and Jesus sandals is walking in a side door.

'Come on, Ma, we'll be late.'

'Coming,' she says, silently cursing the traffic that delayed them.

Inside the church, sitting in the front row, Rory looks up as the priest enters and is reassured that he and Louise made the right decision. This is the kind of person they want celebrating their daughter's christening – a relaxed, easy-going, *positive* man. Rory thinks back to Daisy's christening and his father's presence behind him. Everything is going to be different for Grace.

Rory turns to look at his family, as he often does, as though reassuring himself that they're still there and haven't disappeared. Louise looks up from the baby and smiles. He leans to kiss her, doesn't care who is watching. This is his little family, the two most important people in his world.

Louise passes Grace to him. She is asleep, their angel, her tiny fingers curled into fists. He can't believe the overwhelming love he feels for her, with her little pixie face and tiny pointed chin. She is their miracle child, whose struggle for life has made her all the more precious. Ten long weeks in hospital. Endless ups and downs. It is four months since she was allowed home and, to Rory, she seems so big and strong, though she is the smallest baby being christened.

They will never have another. He'd never let Louise risk it, even if she wanted to. He knows how lucky he is to have her here beside him. And is in no doubt about just how much he loves her. He even manages to share this with her on those scary occasions he remembers how close he came to losing her.

Jason sits in beside him now, asking him to 'shove over'. Rory smiles at him. He must be the youngest godfather on record.

'Rugby finished late,' Jason explains.

'That excuse always works with me,' Rory whispers. He wonders where the other godparent is, but reminds himself of how late he was when it was his turn. He's not worried. Orla will be here.

A baby cries and Rory turns. Owen, father for the first time to a boy, is searching for a soother. In one swift movement, Kate shoves one in. And Owen's shoulders relax. Rory looks at him and realizes that all it took for him to settle down was for the baby to be born. His brother has started over and seems to have accepted that there is no going back.

Behind Owen a woman with short, grey hair, cut into a funky style smiles at Rory. He still can't get used to the new Samantha, the Samantha who no longer needs hairpieces or drink to feel comfortable. In Dublin for a play in which she has a leading role, she has been told she is in remission.

And here is Orla, now, hurrying up the centre of the church with Jenna.

'I am *so* sorry,' she says, as soon as she is seated, 'the *traffic.*'

'Didn't you know,' Rory says, 'only the best godparents are late.'

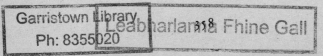